GW00499439

AT THE HEART OF AFRICA

AT THE HEART OF AFRICA

DAVID MARITZ

REACH
PUBLISHERS

Copyright © 2024 David Maritz

First edition 2024

No part of this book may be reproduced or transmitted in any form or by any means, electronic or mechanical, including photocopying, recording or any information storage or retrieval system without permission from the copyright holder.

This is a work of fiction. Any resemblance of the active characters in the story to actual individuals is incidental and unintended.

The book uses the US English spelling convention.

David Maritz

Contact at:
www.davidmaritz.com

1

November 6

The road between the towns of Kasempa and Mumbwa, with its surface pockmarked by ruts and potholes like the wrinkles of neglect
and the blemishes of aged acne, staggers from here to there, but not much
else. Its dusty progress sometimes leans behind a low hill, or teeters around
a marshy patch. It may even stumble unexpectedly sideways to avoid a
freshly fallen tree, pushed over by an elephant, or a recently formed rip
cut into its mud by the wheels of overloaded trucks. The road reminded
Gideon of an aged alcoholic. Like a few of his red-faced friends, it survived due to decades of experience gained from the dictates of a hard and
unsteady life in that remote part of Africa.

"Goddamned trucks!" Gideon cursed as his Toyota Land Cruiser jolted
through an especially deep dip, his muscle memory guiding the vehicle
gingerly between the flaws made by the road's basic construction and the
toll of its abuse. His reflexes enabled the vehicle to progress slowly through
the thick bush tucked to the lee side of a shallow escarpment, marking
the gradual climb up out of the Kafue River Valley, whose wide embrace
spreads its arms north-east to south-west across the heart of Central Africa.

At the top of the escarpment, pulling up before a pivot barrier across the
road, Gideon again exclaimed loudly, "You little bastard!"

The nip of a tsetse fly is painful, especially that of a young one. He glanced up after slapping his calf, following another futile attempt to kill the offending insect.

A uniformed guard slowly rose from a wooden chair. He'd been leaning back on its rear legs in the shade of an austere brick guardhouse set back from the side of the road. It marked the edge of the Kafue National Park, the second-largest park in Africa.

Looking beyond the barrier, Gideon could see how the road crested before dipping down under the tree boughs that dappled the road beyond with the spindly patterns of their shadows. The post was well placed, shaded by a copse of tall elegant mafuti trees. Glancing over his shoulder to check that his equipment hadn't bounced off the vehicle bed on the ride, Gideon saw how those trees joined others—spreading down the slope behind him, lifting their unbroken leafy canopies like a song on the wind, drifting back until its melody spilled over the edge of the horizon.

Watching the guard lazily pick up a big ledger book, Gideon again slapped at the fly buzzing against the dusty side window. Still smarting from its nip, he muttered, "You little bugger. When I catch you, I'll pull off your wings and make you walk."

As the guard, officious in his neat but faded olive-green uniform, unhurriedly walked across the few meters of compacted dirt separating the guard house from the vehicle, Gideon rolled down the window.

Leaning back in the seat he nodded his greeting "*Muli bwanji?*"

"*Bwino, bwanji?*" the guard responded. His flat, smooth, high cheeks echoed the slenderness of his young physique, giving him an elegant, almost effeminate affect. Despite an indolent air as he approached the vehicle, there was an unexpected politeness in his demeanor as he handed the big ledger through the window for Gideon to sign. It expressed itself in the tone of his thick accent, and the way his native Kaunde morphed his

David Maritz

Rs into Ls. His polite deference was welcome. He was the authority figure here—and in Africa, authority matters, no matter how trivial it may seem. From experience, Gideon knew that if treated with disrespect, it could kick down harshly, and expect to be bowed to unreasonably.

"Where do you come from?"

The guard's question was rhetorical. This was a ritual, performed thousands of times daily all over Central Africa, where echoes of its colonial past are still being scribbled in the lines and columns of big ledger books.

"From Kafue River Lodge," Gideon replied politely as he provided details: name, origin, destination, vehicle registration, number of passengers. It was the ritual of pointlessly filling out the information demanded only by the headers of the lines and columns on the thick, blotter-like paper of these big black books.

Closing its grubby, worn cover, Gideon handed the heavy book back to the guard, wondering what they did with these things once they were filled with countless scribbles. The ritual was more than the mere recording of each vehicle passing along this remote road. It suggested to the populous that an effective and watchful law and order prevailed. Like the uncomfortable bumps and jolts of the road, the 'authority', using old colonial laws, is the sometimes-capricious entity in the shabby administrative centers at both its distant ends.

It was this framework which made the inferred threat of the note in Gideon's pocket so unusual, with its challenge to authority. Waiting for the guard to take the big book back to the guardhouse, Gideon felt a pang of regret as he considered the generational gap between himself and the younger man. The guard would not have known the colonial past. Even Gideon was almost too young to remember those British officials who brought those big black books to Africa, and then who'd hastily abandoned their roles as Imperial Bwanas, after a glorious but brief appearance on the stage of empire. They'd returned from whence they'd come, leaving behind descendants who were born and raised on the continent—who were considered neither a true part of the new Africa, nor of the old Europe. By necessity, these vagabonds were condemned to spend their lives with a mental suitcase always ready in case they were told to move on.

Now, himself a relic of that old Africa, Gideon waited for the young representative of the new to lift the barrier pole. At least this was at the limit of tsetse territory: from here on he could drive with the windows open. There would no longer be the need to choose between the sauna-like heat in the cab due to non-functioning air-conditioning, or the relative comfort of the sub-tropical air wafting away his sweat, even as it afforded unfettered opportunity to tormenting flies.

As Gideon watched, the guard set the ledger down on his chair, then returned and stretched out with the timeless pace of Africa to lift the barrier, allowing the vehicle to pass. Craning his neck out the window to peer up, Gideon checked that the pivot pole would clear the Cruiser's roof. With his left hand, he moved the gear shift from neutral to first. He was about to lift his foot from the clutch when suddenly a loud whistle came from the other side of the cab.

"*Eeweh!*" someone shouted. "Hey, you!"

A second guard appeared from behind the building. Older and plumper than his colleague, he was more affable about the weight of his authority, which had settled around his midriff. With a dramatic pause, and a serious tone, but still with a broad smile on his friendly face, the guard shouted his message.

"On the radio. They say to tell you. Back at your camp!" he hesitated. "Someone has been caught by a crocodile!"

David Maritz

2

November 6

A crocodile attack!

"Sheeesh!" Gideon had heard of them often enough, but this was a personal first for him.

It wasn't unexpected. He had watched the safari lodge staff habitually use the same place to pump water. He had even mentioned it to Bright, the lodge manager.

"Sometime or other, one of those buggers will be grabbed by a croc," he had warned. "They need to keep changing where they go down to the river, or put up a barrier further out so those sneaky bastards don't get close. I'll bet there's a croc watching them, learning their habits."

Bright had gestured in unconcerned dismissal. "The river is clear enough," he said. "I've told the guys to check the water before they get too close to the edge."

Gideon was about to reengage the gear to continue his journey when he checked himself. "Did they say if the croc got the guy, or did he get away?" Gideon called across to the guard.

The guard made a face and raised his hands. "I don't know. It was a woman on the radio, and she said the message was for you."

It was now the end of the tourist season. No guests were at the lodge. With many of the staff on leave, and with Bright away on errands in the faraway city of Lusaka, Gideon wondered if the medical proficiency of those left at the lodge would be adequate if the attack were serious.

After all nothing can easily escape the teeth and powerful jaws of a crocodile without suffering plenty of damage. Obviously whoever had been attacked had survived, otherwise it would be the police they were calling on the radio to report a death.

Was that why they had notified the gate guard to turn him around before he got too far away, because they thought only he could help?

Holding the barrier aloft, the young guard stood patiently waiting. He watched as Gideon stared seemingly sightlessly ahead, elbows resting on the steering wheel, his head in his hands.

"Are you okay?" the guard asked.

"Crap!" Gideon exclaimed loudly. Then looking at the guard he replied, "Yes, but my goddamned plans have been messed up."

In remote and traditional Africa, calamity always lurks, like an unwanted visitor at the edge of a crowd. Out here, everyone has watched as the unwelcome serpent of destiny inexorably catches the unwary in its coils. Leaning his head out the window, Gideon called across to the portly guard.

"Will you radio your headquarters in Mumbwa? Tell them that Gideon cannot make the meeting with Ernest." Then he muttered, "Shit!" in annoyance. The meeting with the local park warden had to do with the note in his pocket. That would now have to wait. Motioning to the young guard to lower the boom and thanking the other, he turned his vehicle around and, with a sense of grudging resignation, retraced his path.

* * *

Gideon's years in the military had given him extensive training in field first aid, with ample opportunity to put it into practice on countless operations. His military background was also what had gotten him his job out here. For two years he had been providing additional training to the park game scouts. During this time, he had been allowed to quasi-camp close to the lodge for safety and logistic support. Naturally, having had connections with some of the staff for that long, friendships had formed, especially with Bright, the lodge manager.

With Bright gone, Gideon felt compelled to go back and see if he could be of help. His preoccupation with how best to thwart this form of African reality pushed the Cruiser's speeds beyond its dangerous sliding limits. A lifetime of driving on rough roads had taught him exactly how far he could go in this dance with the dirt. Too slow and the vibrations of the rutted corrugations were intolerable; too fast, and syncopated shudders would bounce heavy-duty tires in unison, loosening their grip on the gravel.

Speeding along the dirt, winding between the trees and occasional patches of burn-blacked winter grass, Gideon considered how lucky it was that the summer rains hadn't yet started. In another month, when the wet season began in earnest, progress along the road would be difficult. Its neglect and abuse would make it challenging, as the oppressive heat of late November mixed with moisture brushed in from the east. The hot humid air would rear up until it climaxed in ecstatic roars of thunder, with flashes of lightning birthing sheets of rain, bringing mud and misery to the road.

Gideon was unsure why the news of a croc attack filled him with such a sense of foreboding. He had seen enough adversity in the past. Nearly two decades ago, the war in Angola to the west had scribbled tens of thousands of victims on its tally sheet, its brutality unnoticed by the rest of the world—but not by those who'd been there. Certainly not by him and his fellow soldiers. At least here his vehicle no longer ran the risk of triggering the thumping flash of a landmine.

Glancing to the side, he watched a herd of impala skittishly trot away from his approach. Beyond them, deeper in the woodland, a few baboons from a local troop, with their young shrieking and scampering about, stopped their foraging to watch him drive by. Despite his distracted thoughts, he marveled at the bushland flowing past. It was resplendent with the emerald green of freshly budding trees all lifting their leafy canopies aloft above long, slender trunks as elegantly as any gathering of Ascot ladies raise their parasols.

He had lost track of time when he saw the big steel anchor pillars holding the ferry pontoon's cables across the Kafue River. He slowed the Cruiser so it no longer drifted dangerously away from the road's rutted crest. Luckily, the pontoon with its crew was beached on this side of the river. It would be a quick crossing.

Reaching the other side and disembarking from the pontoon, Gideon considered how he had made good time. With a bit of fast driving and risk taking, only two hours had passed since leaving the gated checkpoint. He nosed his old scratched and dented Cruiser off the ruts of the main road, and shifted into low gear to negotiate some of the serious bumps of the hand-cut dirt strips leading the last few kilometers to the lodge.

"Okay," he muttered to himself. "Let's see what's going on back here."

Getting closer, the twin strip paths left the press of trees and opened into the wide grassy spread of what would become a water-logged clearing once the rains arrived. This sort of natural feature was called a *dambo* in the local language. Beyond this lay a narrow cuff of thick riverine foliage shading the lodge complex.

A strange, high-pitched trill hovered above the rattle of the vehicle, well before Gideon stopped near the wooded anthill behind the kitchen. Cutting the engine, he sat for a minute, listening to the sound coming over the high thatched fence which surrounded and shielded the lodge's logistics center.

"What the hell is that all about?" he muttered.

It was the tongue trill of a woman's ululation. In Africa it was the sound of celebration, done in unison with others, accompanied by the clapping of hands and the stamping of feet. But here it stood alone. It rose, fell, wavered, then gained strength before subsiding like an echo. Its primitive pitch hinted at ethereal evil, even as it had a sense of selfish relief, suggesting something greater than glee.

Closing the cab door of his vehicle, Gideon stepped through the narrow opening in the thatch fence. The savage, incomprehensible sound came from a woman standing apart from the others in the group gathered there, a head taller, and older than the others. Gideon had seen her often enough in his dealings with the lodge staff, occasionally surreptitiously admiring her figure and looks. However, he had seldom spoken to her directly. She had always been aloof, alluringly distant. Her thick black braids fell long from the back of her head, swaying along her spine, as they now did as she stood in silhouette.

The keening faded. Ancient ritual faded with it, as it had done over the centuries: lurking, watching, and waiting as the new world carelessly reasserted itself.

Walking towards the group, Gideon searched his memory. Getting closer, she turned to look at him with her wide, steady eyes pouring their black ink over him.

Precious. He remembered her name.

Holding her gaze Gideon asked, "Who got caught?"

"Eddie." She answered.

Beneath the ebullient spread of the boughs of the big trees at the river's edge, the sloping cut of the boat launch offered easy access to the river. It was where they pumped the water up into the holding tank standing on the big anthill behind the kitchen. From the drag marks, this was obviously the site of the attack. Eddie had not been moved far. He lay on a blanket at the ramp's eroded crest. The shock on his face was visible from afar. Even the dark ebony skin of the African has a grey pallor in that shocked state. Quickly crossing the distance to them, Gideon moved between three men who stood looking down at Eddie. They stepped back to let him kneel beside the prone man.

Eddie's low moans were barely audible. His expression held the deathly torpor Gideon had seen so many times elsewhere. This too was part of Africa: the acceptance of one's fate. Dire situations had been woven into the fabric of life so often there was seldom enough time to pick apart the tangled knots of cause and effect.

"How did this happen?"

"We were pumping water, Bwana, and the croc grabbed at him. He was getting ready to start the pump's engine."

It was Kings who spoke. A big, muscular man, his voice was deep and the skin between his eyebrows tended to crease into furrows as he talked.

A sense of helpless frustration crept into Gideon's voice. "Why didn't you change where you pump water?" he admonished. "So that the crocs don't learn your pattern."

"Yes, Bwana, but the water is so shallow. We aren't sure how the croc got close. Eddie hadn't even put the hose into the river. It was so fast."

David Maritz

Gideon cut in sharply, "You were careless. That thing waited for hours. It let the weeds drift over it so its shape was broken under the water."

"Bwana, we were careful!"

"It was smarter than all of you," Gideon replied tersely.

A scowl crept over Kings' broad face. Creases of tension appeared at the corners of his lips, which to a casual observer would appear to be the start of a smile. Having dealt with soldiers for years, Gideon knew how far to push a point, and when to ease up. Everyone has a tipping point, even the most disciplined, and Gideon doubted that Kings had much self-control.

Focusing his attention on Kings and directing his question to him, Gideon asked, "So what is the plan?"

Kings shrugged.

"Do you know any first-aid?" Gideon queried them all.

Kings responded with a dismissive toss of his head, while another of the men replied that he had some knowledge.

"Why has nothing been done to help Eddie?"

The man looked at Kings as if waiting for him to reply, but Kings continued scowling until the man also shrugged.

Gideon realized that he had to take the initiative, but carefully if he wanted cooperation. Giving orders seldom elicits willing participation, and if anything this was being discouraged by Kings' big scowling presence.

"How did Eddie get away?"

"Bwana, he was lucky." This time a third thin, wiry man spoke. "He held onto the pump. It had the hose up to the kitchen, so it wasn't easy for the croc to pull him back quickly. He held on until I found a big stick and hit the croc. I hit it many times before it let go."

Kings kept scowling. Gideon couldn't place the source of his sullen hostility. Maybe his mood wasn't personal, but the net of his petulance was catching the others in its mesh. Glancing towards the river, Gideon saw the small box-like engine and the centrifugal pump where it had almost been dragged into the water as Eddie hung on for life. For a moment, as Gideon considered what to do, the world held its breath. Even the birds were silent. There was only the rustle of the leaves as the trees draped their shadows over the corrugated tin roof of the vehicle shed.

The hierarchical protocol of rural African life waited for Gideon to speak, say what to do. He was older than they; here one seldom disrespected age. Even Kings held his silence, as if waiting to see if Gideon could challenge the deference the other two men afforded him.

Turning his attention back to the injured man, Gideon remained on his knees, aware that the silent group of women were also onlookers.

Out here, time and urgency were seldom considered when solving problems. Why bother? Rarely would haste affect fate's outcome. One could not get an ambulance here earlier or get to the hospital quickly. The town of Kasempa was 93 kilometers away, and Mumbwa, 120. With the road's condition, it would take at least four hours to reach the minimal basics of a clinic.

There was a serene expression on Eddie's face. His eyes were half open, clouded with a distant unfocused stare, as if in a trance.

Gideon was keenly aware that everybody was watching, waiting to see what he would do. Without looking up, he reached behind his hip for his bush knife in its sheath. Taking it out, he cut away the legging of

David Maritz

Eddie's long pants to expose the jagged gashes left by the reptile's teeth. The puncture marks of the bite had been further ripped by the beast's violent twisting and shaking as it tried to break Eddie's clutching hold on the pump. It had exerted powerful backward lunges with its thrashing tail in its savage efforts to drag Eddie into aquatic oblivion.

Examining the wounds, Gideon spoke to no one in particular. "Can someone get me the medical box from behind the seat of my vehicle?"

Eddie had lost a lot of blood. This was evident from the broad spread of dark stains on the blankets, blood flowing from a deep gash ripped almost to the bone before it wrapped around the side of the leg and disappeared behind the knee. It was clear that Eddie needed to be transported to a clinic. But being so far away, Gideon realized something had to be done to prevent further bleeding from the jolts of a long, rough ride. As it was, Eddie was on the brink.

Looking over his shoulder, it was with a flicker of surprise that Gideon saw Precious carrying the large water-tight first aid kit. As her tall, athletic figure approached and crossed to where they were at the top of the ramp, she appeared to glide towards them with scant bob in her assertive stride. Watching her approach, his eyes were drawn to the white speckles of the small river snail shells strung on a simple strand around her neck. These, he noted, color-contrasted with the smooth chocolate of her skin. Then, as she set the box down next to him, his curiosity with the shells faded. He became business-like. His focus switched back to Eddie's wounds.

"Help me turn him over," he said to Precious.

Pulling and placing Eddie's knee across his other leg, then holding Eddie's hips while Precious held his shoulders, they rolled him onto his side. Eddie was not responding to commands. Gideon shifted Eddie's head sideways. Then, with a signal to Precious and a gentle push, they rolled him onto his belly. Using the big non-sterile pads from the kit's second drawer Gideon wiped away the debris and matted blood from around the deepest lacerations. A slow, thin ooze of blood reappeared from the longest gash. It was what Gideon feared. Taking a tourniquet from the bottom drawer, he wrapped it above Eddie's knee and pulled it tight. Then, pushing and releasing his fingers into the back of Eddie's calf, Gideon checked that it filled back out, indicating that the tourniquet wasn't too tight.

"Take those gloves and put them on," he ordered Precious.

The three other men looked on with emotionless expressions. Standing further back, the group of women were now murmuring softly amongst themselves.

Addressing no one in particular Gideon looked up at the men. "You will need to ready the lodge's old spare Land Cruiser," he said. "Check its oil and water. If necessary, take out a fresh barrel of diesel. Use the hand pump to transfer 40 liters into its tank. That should easily get you to Mumbwa and back. Also, pull one of the mattresses out of the storeroom and lay it on the Cruiser's back bed. You can lay Eddie on it."

Gideon waited to see if he had broken Kings' restricting hold over the two others. They turned and moved away. Then, with a sullen look on his face, Kings followed them across the open ground to the sheds.

Shifting his attention back to the woman kneeling beside him, Gideon noted that she exuded confident dependability. There was something different about her. What was it? He pointed to a pack of sterile alcohol swabs. "Use those to clean his leg."

The latex gloves were too large for her long, slender hands, but even with the encumbrance of its folds, it was easy to detect the dexterity of her fingers.

"Now take some of that cream," he instructed as he pointed to the antibiotic ointment. "Smear it on his cuts."

David Maritz

While she was doing so, Gideon cut a length of fishing line and threaded it into a suture hook. Using the gloved fingers of one hand, he pinched together a section of ripped flesh and quickly hooked the curved needle through and out. Eddie didn't flinch. He cut and tied the ends of the line. This was performed three more times, which took care of the long, slightly oozing gash. Gideon tore open the covering to three large gauze abdominal pads: Eddie's wounds were so extensive that anything less would not have sufficed. Being pads, they weren't adhesive. They would have to be fastened to secure them over the extent of the ripped flesh. "Press your finger on these," he instructed.

Precious placed a forefinger at the top and bottom of each pad in turn as he tagged them with athletic tape. Once this was done, Gideon asked her to hold and raise Eddie's ankle so that he could use Coban tape to wrap around the leg in a swaddle. The suturing should allow the blood in the deep wound to re-clot he figured. However, his final touch was done with duct tape. It would keep all the wrappings together on the long, rattling journey to the clinic.

While he waited for the men to ready the vehicle, sitting back on his haunches with his arms stretched out with elbows resting on his knees, African style, Gideon lifted his eyes to gaze at the high cirrus clouds etched in the sky above their pitiful drama. He felt the tautness in his body drift away like the fallen leaves spinning in the eddies of the river drifting past. The cycle of life: to eat and be eaten. Eddie had nearly been a straggler in that ancient process of predator and prey, a cycle which seemed to have disappeared from the modern reality which people so foolishly assume they shared no part.

Gideon randomly thought about how, in this huge wilderness region bisected by a single paved east-west road and a few laterally oriented dirt side strips, it was no wonder that misfortune was so impactful. It was a wilderness area the size of Belgium. He considered how here it was not a bankruptcy or stock market collapse which blights life. The red was not in an accountant's tally. Instead, like the burgundy on the blanket, it was often spilled blood which indicated a deficit.

But, in many ways he realized that despite it all, it was how he preferred things, closer to the way it always had been. Cloaked within its harshness, its beauty kept the destructive ugliness of the modern world at arm's length. It was easier here to know what was good, and what was bad. Then, looking at the sudden bustle of the three men, Gideon considered how Kings' sullen hostility was new. In the two years he had been here, not being part of the lodge's direct operations, he had had only superficial interaction with the man. This made his change of attitude perplexing.

Now it was touch-and-go if Eddie could survive the shock of the attack and his blood loss in the aftermath, and the yet-to-be-endured bumps and jolts of the arduous drive to the clinic.

Kings had the old Land Cruiser backed up with the tailgate down when a voice broke the busy silence. It rose above the sound of the flock of trumpeter hornbills braying in the thick tangle of trees on the island opposite the lodge.

"Leave him alone!" The voice's command had a quiet tone of authority, with a raspy roughness like the creak of steps in wet sand.

"Leave him alone!" it repeated. "Stop your meddling! Do not touch him!" A very thin, almost scarecrow-like figure dressed in a camouflage uniform stood leaning against one of the support posts at the far end of the vehicle shed, half hidden by the clutter of equipment. He was slightly stooped, with grey hints of age in his unusually long crown of tight African curls.

Gideon jerked back in shock as a curdling shriek erupted beside him. Precious snapped to her feet with the speed and surety of a striking scorpion. The air was filled with the shrill howling wail of her ululating. Completely confounded, Gideon rocked back on his knees and watched as Precious, her head thrown back to fill the air with her savage cries, advanced step by deliberate step towards the interloping stranger. Halting before him, her demonic sounds faded like the echoes of a wild dream. Then she screamed again.

"*YANGA! YANGA FUMAPAPO!* Go! Get away from here!"

In the profound silence that followed, the mysterious figure turned. With his camouflage uniform blending into the bush, he melted away.

Gideon looked at Kings in dumbfounded shock. "Who the fuck is that?"

Wordlessly, Precious glided back. She nodded to the three men. With each of them holding a corner of Eddie's blanket, they lifted him to lay on the foam rubber mattress on the vehicle's bed. Then Kings moved across to re-enter the cab as the other two climbed onto the back, where they sat alongside Eddie. They drove away.

"What the hell is going on?" Gideon exclaimed incredulously to Precious.

"Bad witch medicine," she whispered. "Bad *muti*, Bwana!"

3

November 6

Northof the Zambezi River, October is known as suicide month.
It is when the vestiges of winter are burned away by the resurgent
vitality of the sun sliding south across the equator. The early summer heat
is unbearable, so hot the only relief is said to be death. Now in early
November that heat had yet to dissipate.

As the sound of the vehicle taking Eddie to the clinic faded into the bush,
Gideon felt his stress and tension subsiding. This came together with a
growing realization of how hungry he was, with a thirst exacerbated by
the warmth of the day. Having left before dawn, he hadn't eaten or had
anything to drink since then.

While packing up the medical box, he asked one of the kitchen staff if she
could make him a sandwich and give him something to drink. Now waiting for the fare, he sat under the high thatched roof of the lodge's large,
open-walled communal area (known as a *chitenge* in the local language)
where lodge guests could relax or be served meals. Retreating from the
sun's glare on the *chitenge's* deck where it cantilevered out over the water,
he moved to the head of a polished mahogany dinner table. Its position in
the shade under the roof's eaves offered respite from the heat.

David Maritz

He contemplated the day's events while sipping a tall glass of soothingly cool orange juice. Fortunately, no guests had been present to witness the morning's struggle to save Eddie. If the events left him unsettled, they would certainly have shaken foreign visitors. With Bright, the manager, away, Gideon was glad to have returned in time to help.

Swatting his hat at a bee persistently buzzing around the rim of his glass, Gideon looked up to see Precious approaching through the gap in the fence from the kitchen. She held a plain white plate with a neatly sectioned sandwich on it. He looked at her curiously, as she had not been the one from whom he had requested the food and drink.

"*Twasanta*," he thanked her, then listened to her footsteps fade as he savoured the salty grits of biltong jerky in the sandwich.

His mind returned to mulling on the morning's events. *Muti* is the stock-in-trade of the *nganga*, the African witch doctor. Gideon wondered what sort of *muti* Precious was referring to. He knew that in rural Africa there was still great respect and even fear of its potions, spells, or curses.

Recently, a devoutly religious scout he was training had disappeared for a week. When the scout finally resurfaced, his explanation was that some romantic rival had paid a *nganga* to cast a curse to impair his performance. It put him to sleep for a week, he said. Gideon smiled as he thought how a story like this was accepted as a plausible explanation. Africa was full of the unusual and unexpected, which was hard to explain to outsiders.

'If anything,' Gideon thought, 'the unexpected is the usual.' The morning's events certainly served as a confirmation.

A soft, polite cough came from behind. Glancing over his shoulder, there it was: the unexpected. She was in the shadows of a low wall leading to the deck, sitting on the concrete floor. She supported herself gracefully with an extended arm. The other lay languidly across her lap. Her long legs were tucked sideways, forming a parallel V in the traditional way a woman shows respect.

She was patiently requesting an audience, as if Gideon were a chief. This display of patient supplication, coming from Precious, halted Gideon's chewing as effectively as a slap in the face. After how she'd held herself aloof, then from the way she came forward with confident self-assurance to help with Eddie that morning, this traditional politeness was not what Gideon expected. He stared wordlessly at her as, once again, she regarded him with the raven of her gaze.

"Okay, what in the world is going on? Come over here and explain things."

"No, Bwana. Not here."

"Precious," Gideon reiterated. "What the hell is going on?"

In the darkness of her eyes, Gideon detected the simmering glow of deep passion.

"Bwana, I need to talk to you, but not now. Wait for me at your camp. I will be there later when I finish. Here there are too many ears."

She rose and disappeared through a gap in the fence. Dumbstruck, Gideon left the other half of his sandwich untouched. This behavior coming from a woman of this culture, flipping from obsequiousness to instructing an older man to do something out here in the bush, an order to an authority figure, was, to put it mildly, unusual.

Even more perplexed than before, Gideon wiped his mouth with the back of his hand, then rose to walk the kilometer to his campsite.

* * *

David Maritz

From the *chitenge*, the path leads across a small gully towards the chalets before edging back towards the river, past the open firepit, and on upstream to the campsite. The firepit is more a platform than a pit. In the evening, logs gathered from the bush provide the fuel. The best, longest burning wood grew in shallow, austere soils, toughening it. It would smolder for hours, long after any guest dinner is served, glowing all night long, until its glow is coaxed back to life to warm the outstretched palms of early-rising lodge clients as the hippos splash back into the river at dawn.

Gideon once again mentally flipped through events: the note in his pocket, the crocodile attack, the appearance of the old man; add to that Precious's strange request, all potentially smeared with witchcraft. He dearly hoped it wasn't. But was something stirring beneath the surface? Was some *nganga* bringing nonsense to ignite old ideas in people's minds?

Passing the fire platform Gideon noticed a still-smoldering log issuing a thin wisp of pale smoke which twisted upwards, rising high to split and scatter into the hot air. It seemed a lifetime ago that he'd heard the shout of "*Eeweh!*" coming from the portly gate guard. Instead of heading along the inland track to his camp, he chose to stroll beneath the hanging branches of the big river trees which formed a curtain between the open grassy dambo and the river.

He had time: no training was scheduled for the day. He wasn't directly connected with the tourism activity at the lodge. Although, like with the medical aid, he did occasionally volunteer his services when a special request came from Bright. Through the scout training program, Gideon was indirectly (but actively) connected with anti-poaching efforts all over the park, especially in the northeast corner where the lodge and his camp were located. Given the vastness of the area, this arrangement allowed him a convenient support base.

It also let him remain in contact with the outside world via the lodge's satellite link. To be polite, he generally kept a low profile when lodge clients were present so as to not spoil their sense of bush isolation and ambiance. A big canvas tent—set up near a small thatched *chitenge*, and standing across from a smaller ablution structure—had been his home for two years.

As he sat waiting for Precious in the evening gloom, sipping a cup of strong coffee, he could make out the outlines of the leafy acacia and leadwood trees of the riverine tangle stretching away downriver. The view from the campsite was one of his favorites. There was something about its simplicity, its lack of clutter that appealed to his sense of aesthetics.

Minimally touched by the hand of man, it was unchanged from how it was over a hundred years ago when Orlando Baragwaneth paddled his dugout canoe past on his way to discover the copper of Katanga. On one side, the thick arbor line defined the river's edge. On the other, copses of big trees appeared to float on abandoned anthills as if laid out by some master gardener. These thickets spread back from the breadth of the *dambo* like freckles merging up into the abundance of thick hair.

The sun's rays were stretched and oblique when Gideon noticed her crossing the open ground beyond his tent. The swaying float of her stride had lost its assertiveness. She glanced back over her shoulder a number of times. When she was near enough to meet his eyes, he offered her a chair. They sat in silence, looking out at the view before Gideon asked.

"So? What's going on?"

She took her time. "It is bad *muti*, Bwana!" Extending a long leg, she kicked at a leaf on the floor. "In the village, they say that there is muti put on us. We knew it would happen."

"Okay," Gideon responded. "Why are you telling me this?"

"Bwana! You know the ways of Africa. You, from what they say, have always lived with us Africans, and you know these matters, how they affect us."

Gideon looked carefully at the enigmatic woman. The long braids which had dangled down her back earlier in the day were now looped around the crown of her head in a single twist, like a coiled cobra. There was nothing frivolous about her demeanor. He sensed she should be taken seriously.

"So, what is the word?"

"Bwana, they say that the poachers have a powerful *nganga* on their side. An *nganga* who gives them *muti*, even makes them invisible."

Unease niggled deep in Gideon's gut.

"Bwana, this *muti*, they say it may be able to curse the people here, to harm them. We didn't know when it would happen, or to whom. Eddie was the unlucky chosen."

"Can't you get some other *muti* against it from an nganga around here?" he asked.

"Bwana, I have done that. But the *ngangas* we have here are nervous. They are unsure of the new potency."

"What did you get?" he asked. Delicately, she fingered the snail shells on the leather strand around her neck.

"The *nganga* gave me these to keep away the bad spirits. He said I was to make loud noises or to sing loudly to warn the spirits away."

This explained her ululating, and why she screamed before chasing the old mystery man away.

"So, Precious, doesn't that mean everything will now be okay?"

"No Bwana, this new *muti*. It was brought here by a special *nganga* from far away. They say he flew here on the back of a hyena."

"From where?"

"From south of the Zambezi, from the Mlimo."

"Mlimo?" Gideon queried, incredulous. "Are you sure?"

"Yes, Bwana. They say it is the same *nganga* who a long time ago gave the muti to Mushala. I have a relative who saw that *nganga* flying at night."

Gideon knew of the fable of Mushala, and he detected a tone of reverence in the way she mentioned his name. Again, he could see the black ink in her eyes, and how the sensuous pout of her lips barely moved as she spoke. Gideon was vaguely familiar with the faraway cult. But up here on the other side of the Zambezi? Why would a *nganga* stretch a tentacle out this far? Still, there was no way that she could have made that up if there wasn't some fire smoldering at the base of her smoke. He sat for a minute looking sightlessly at his toes jutting out at the end of his sandals as his mind flipped back through his memories. It had been decades since he'd visited the hills which were the home of the Mlimo. It was an eerie place, with its sense of the spiritual, its oracle heart hidden among magnificent, massive, inselberg boulders. Legend had it that there, occasionally, in the moonlight of midwinter, the ghost of Cecil Rhodes rose from his grave to link arms with the moon shadows of the men of the Shangani patrol. The myth told of them descending from the fresco of their monument to greet their rival: Chief Lobengula and his Matabele warriors. Forming a circle, they clap and shout their despair in unison, mourning the Africa they, in disparate and futile ways, still hoped for, even as it has been recklessly pulled from their grasp by successive uncaring generations.

Gideon waited for Precious to look up.

"Why are you scared to tell me in front of the others?

"Bwana." Her hands were folded in her lap as she quietly spoke without raising her eyes. "Do you know that Eddie was paying my uncle *lobola*?"

Lobola is the rural practice of buying a wife from her father, mostly in payments of livestock.

"No, I didn't."

"Bwana. He has made half the payment. Another year and he will be able to buy the last few cows to give to my uncle." Seeing the question in his raised eyebrows, she added.

"He pays my uncle because my father is dead. The staff here are from my village. They think I resist the *nganga* because he is going after Eddie, but they worry if I resist too much."

"Why?" Gideon queried.

She crossed and uncrossed the long, lovely length of her legs as she nervously looked around.

"Even the local *ngangas* will expect me to resist, as long as it isn't too much. They don't want me interfering in powerful *muti* that may go wrong for everyone."

"But Precious, I still don't understand why you tell me these things and hide it from the others."

She shook her head, almost as if weary at having to explain the obvious.

"Bwana, did you not see that stranger? Did you not hear him tell you not to meddle?" The gaunt features of the old camo-clad man flashed into Gideon's mind.

"Did you not recognize the crocodile? It came back to claim its sacrifice in disguise. They say if I interfere too much, like you did, that crocodile will come back to take some other appeasement. That is what they are scared of. They will force me to leave, but I am not ready to go.

"Only you, as a *mzungu*, can help me. They haven't perfected their curses on the white man." She fingered the snail shells strung around her neck.

"You must act. That crocodile has been moving for hours. It will be meeting with the hyena when he brings the *nganga* of darkness. They will be talking about you. They will be discussing what to do about your interference."

Gideon's unease increased. Dealing with poachers was one thing: they could be tracked, hunted and trapped. This he could do. Tracking and dealing with mystical witchcraft figures was something else. Precious broke into Gideon's thoughts.

"You interfering with Eddie showed me that you can deal with them. If you are clever and careful you will be able to confront the crocodile."

Staring at each other, Gideon couldn't match the unblinking intensity of her dark gaze. Why did she care so profoundly?

"Go! Go before it is too late," she ordered. "You need to get close and discover his weaknesses. You must stop them, if he has helpers."

With that, she stood. He stared after her as she walked away, her floating swagger rejuvenated. Leaning back in his camp chair, arms folded across his chest, legs spread, Gideon half closed his eyes, making it appear as if the embers of the fire were caught between the bookends of his sandals.

A mosquito hummed close to his ear, but he ignored it. He was too wrapped in his thoughts to slap at it. Slowly, gingerly, he let his mind drift back, searching for those odd instances where the riffs of witchcraft had rippled the surface of his life, remembering the hushed undertones of his parents discussing the murder of one of the *bafana* boys he played with, the son of one of the farm workers.

The police report was that the murder had been for the harvest of body parts to prepare *muti* to give luck in gambling. Surely since then modernity had pushed the ugly side of African witchcraft into a closed chapter of its history?

Maybe not.

Straightening in his chair, Gideon took out the handwritten note from his pocket and read the words scribbled there.

Mzungu - Leave here. Stop your meddling. The spirits do not want you here. You have been warned. If you interfere, you will be punished by the spirits.

It was signed 'Crocodile'.

Cloaked in the darkness of the night, with a chorus of chirping crickets and peeping fruit bats, Gideon leaned back in his chair. He let gravity pull his head back so that his face pointed up at the sky as he emptied his mind of thought. Cupping his hands behind his neck as a brace, he let his soul be filled with wonder at the Milky Way splashing its splendor across the night sky.

4

November 7

The splash of a bull hippo returning to the river from its nocturnal grazing nudged Gideon awake. Like a breeze ruffling the surface of a pond, the sound added texture to the vibrant bird calls already saturating the dawn's tepid air. It was going to be another hot day. Savoring the comfort of his bed, in the cocoon of his tent, he listened to nature's harmony. Gradually his niggling mental ruminations faded as the dawn light crept into the corners of his mind, pushing aside the threads of anxiety which had morphed into uneasy dreams during the night.

"To hell with that old *nganga* prick," he muttered to himself.

Sitting up from his semi-naked sleeping state, he reached for his shirt before slipping his feet into a pair of sandals. Unzipping the flap of the tent he stepped into the ambiguous light of dawn as it filtered through the thick riverside vegetation. Like a grey ghost, an African goshawk flicked its wings and glided through the foliage above his tent, searching for a careless bulbul to feed its youngsters in a nearby nest. He barely managed to get a glimpse of the fine russet barring of the bird's breast as it flipped past above him.

David Maritz

Stepping over from his tent and crouching before last evening's fire, he blew onto its embers beneath the old metal kettle, making it hiss quietly as the fire glowed back to life. A halo on the horizon hinted at the spot where the sun would soon creep up into the sky across the river. He was training a scout team later in the morning. A six-man team was back from a patrol. It would be ready for further instruction before it headed out again. Today would be a 'theory' day.

Gideon briefly let his thoughts meander over the note that was still in his pocket. Did it tie in with yesterday's events? Did it portend greater poaching pressure? If so, what to do about it? A greater policing presence would be the preferred solution. That would mean more manpower. If that wasn't available, would it be okay to patrol the area with smaller teams? Would they be effective if the poachers started working in larger groups?

Why did competitive groups often consist of eleven members? Soccer, cricket, football all had eleven players. An infantry section, an armored company. All eleven. Was it aeons of experience which found eleven to be the efficient cognitive limit to effective cooperation? An idle thought struck him. When next in the city, he would check if some of the more messed up countries in Africa had more than eleven cabinet members. He bet that the same went for companies with more than eleven board members. Anyway, scout teams that size were wishful thinking here, although maybe not for the poaching cartels.

Could a four-man scout team stand up to a large gang? Were poaching gangs here likely to get bigger? Rhinos had long since disappeared; elephants were heading that way. What if the Asian demand increased? The incentive to poach would rise. As it was, other products were being sought by the Asian markets: pangolin scales, lion gallbladders. All a consequence of the rise of the Chinese middle class and its buying power.

Gideon swirled the coffee in his cup before taking a sip. Today it would be crime-scene preservation and evidence collection: how each snare, dead animal, or poaching camp should be considered as part of a crime that needed to be recorded appropriately. Who should be the crime scene manager? How to set up a perimeter if a large poaching camp was to be searched and its evidence documented. How to minimize evidence disturbance by establishing an access path to the perimeter. What to look for. How to place any critical findings in plastic bags, label and note in a log. Nothing complex; only the fundamentals.

If there was time in the afternoon, he would give tips on photography. Law enforcement should get some use from the ubiquitous cell phone cameras to document evidence. It would be a way of giving a boost to the good guys instead of the bad, who used the phones to communicate to avoid the authorities when transporting their spoils. Gideon thought about each member of this particular team. It behooved him to learn the talents of each one. Who was capable of writing a comprehensive report? Who was the best tracker, the best evidence gatherer? Much of the training was basic, but crime scene documentation would go a long way to getting convictions to stick.

The yelping cries of a fish eagle signalled that the day was underway. It was time to go. He swallowed the last sip of coffee. Another hippo's splash was heralded by a chorus of communal, harrumphing grunts. Dousing the fire, Gideon readied to go.

Today, he would ride his bicycle. It wouldn't take long. Line of sight, it was only twelve kilometers to the scout camp near the pontoon; two or three clicks more if you rode along the game-viewing tracks which parallel the river, about an hour and a half. A tad more if he came across something interesting, or he had to wait for a herd of elephants to pass without getting upwind of them.

His ride had been a weekly ritual since the beginning of September, when a chick in a crowned eagle's nest hatched. He liked to keep tabs on the chick. By now it should be big enough to peer at him as he climbed higher up the slope behind the nest and looked down on it.

David Maritz

Setting out from his campsite, he rode past the thatch-roofed chalets of the lodge. The only sign of activity was the clunk of pots being stacked in the kitchen. Crossing the breadth of the open *dambo* on the other side of the lodge, Gideon followed the tree line back down towards the river's edge. Here, before reaching the river, the *dambo's* grassland spread out wide to parallel the river in a wide floodplain. It was where the river would spread out later in the summer when it overflowed its banks. Being alone in the vastness of the bush was exhilarating. Apart from a handful of lodge staff scattered downriver and some game scouts, there was no human interference between him and nature.

He was about to cut north away from the river over the small ridge with the eagle's nest when something caught his eye. It was in a small gully draining the *dambo*. Dismounting, he left his bicycle at the edge of the dirt track, and pushed his way through waist-high grass to get a better view. A big animal lay cooling itself in a pan of water. The lower third of its body was submerged, and its head bowed forward as if drinking.

Facing away, it held still. Too still.

Gideon carefully edged to the side and around to get a better frontal position. By now he could see that it was a zebra. He crept closer, and yet the animal didn't move. Very strange behavior. He was now close enough that the animal should surely hear or sense his presence.

Africa, he knew, was full of the unexpected. Gideon straightened and walked around to the fore. A young stallion zebra lay in calm repose, exuding sleek power. Its wide-open eyes looked down at the glass blue of the sky and its own death reflected in the still mirror of water.

Exhausted, the animal must have felt its head dip, and raised it, dipped, and raised again, until it was too tired to hold it up. Able only to widen its eyes as its nostril sank below the surface for the last time, leaving it staring in helpless terror at its own death. Had it broken a leg and settled in the water to escape a hyena? Was it disease? Or had it got stuck in the mud?

Gideon wasn't going to wade in to investigate. The crocs would be there soon enough. Returning to his bicycle, he was still too fixated with the image of the zebra to check the eagle chick.

He cut to the main road and headed for the scout camp, with the uneasy sense that he had been witness to an omen.

* * *

The scout camp consisted of a small, scruffily thatched *chitenge* standing next to three squat, featureless buildings. Their dilapidated state reflected the budget allocated from the national coffers to the parks. Maintenance was not a priority. When Gideon arrived, a few of the scouts were still eating breakfast. They sat on their haunches, with others on rough wooden chairs around a metal pot containing *n'chima*, their staple cornmeal food. Gideon joined them in slowly reaching out to scoop a turgid lump of dough out of the pot with his fingers, rolling it into a ball in the palm of this hand, before dipping it in a bowl of relish set to the side.

Looking beyond the scouts, Gideon could see a low dyke ridge which cut diagonally across the horizon. Its march was chopped short by a cliff where the Kafue River had rubbed its ancient way through the rock, and where the Lunga River on the other side of the dyke flowed into the Kafue. Upstream from this confluence lay a huge, lush bushland, interspersed with wide-open grass *dambos* which spread northwest to the distant, game-rich Busanga Plains. It was this region that held his concern, linked to the note he had been on his way to show to the local park warden.

All this weird crap happening! he thought. The frozen panic in the zebra's eyes just seemed to compound it.

Finishing their meal, the scouts arranged themselves under the roof of the chitenge. Gideon began the rote of his instruction. As it proceeded, his lecturing had its usual air of informality, but he found it more difficult than usual to adhere to his lesson outline. The note, the *nganga*, Kings, Precious, the zebra. Like a tongue to a chipped tooth, his mind kept flipping back over all the strange goings on. Connected? Circumstantial? Was witchcraft behind it all? Why? If it were so, Precious was correct that, as a mzungu, he was most suited to step into the witchcraft she claimed was afoot. Many of the locals would be unwilling to push their noses into dealings which scared them.

By early afternoon, after some hours of light-hearted but laboriously given instruction to the men who sat in a semi-circle before him, Gideon decided to call it a day. His head and heart weren't into it. He would join them on the next patrol and do some practice, he told the men.

Leaving the scouts, with one of them stirring a late lunch in the three-legged pot, Gideon rode back towards the pontoon crossing, still mulling things over. In the background, he heard the single cylinder chug of the pontoon plying its way across the river. Then came the unmistakable sound of a Land Cruiser starting its engine. He listened as it headed his way, turning down the track leading to the scout base. It was Lodge Manager, Bright. As the vehicle came to a stop, Bright smiled at him warmly.

"I hear you had some drama yesterday," he said without even bothering to extend a greeting.

"So you heard about it."

"Yes, from the gate guards and from the pontoon crew. Such things travel fast on the bush telegraph."

Bright beckoned. "Come on, now that I've found you, climb in and I'll give you a lift back to the lodge.

Gideon loaded his bicycle onto the back of the Cruiser and clambered into the cab, where he gave a short account of events.

"I have something weird to show you," he said to Bright, as he indicated to turn off the road and head down to the spot where the zebra had been.

When they got there, there was nothing.

"Damn!" Gideon said. "The crocs must have pulled it into the deeper water."

"What was it?" Bright asked.

"It was a dead zebra, just lying there staring into the water. It must have died only minutes before I got there, because its eyes were still wide open and bright as if it were staring at itself. It was so strange it freaked me a bit."

"There have been strange goings-on around here for some time," Bright said. "Some of the staff are becoming nervous."

"This is the first I've heard of it," Gideon retorted in surprise. "Is Kings one of those scaring people?"

"No. Why do you ask?"

"Because he acted weirdly yesterday." Gideon scratched his chin. "He was hostile, as if he wanted to prevent anyone from doing anything."

Bright shrugged as his lips tightened into a faint grimace.

"Kings," he said, "is a difficult person. He is moody, and he has a chip on his shoulder." He reached down to scratch an ankle. "Has anyone told you some of the history of this place?" Bright raised his eyebrows, emphasizing the question.

"A bit," Gideon replied. "I know that during the '60s and '70s this area was a logistic and transit base for an insurgent movement fighting down south. This was a no-go area."

"That is correct." Bright shifted in his seat. "But it's the rest of the story which may explain some of Kings' attitude. During that bush war, the animals of the park were the meat pantry for the insurgents. The local poachers who shot and supplied the meat didn't forget their practices. After the war, they simply switched to different markets. Kings was one of those suppliers." Bright rubbed his broad chin.

"He is a man with an attitude. He doesn't like being reprimanded. He tends to think of this whole area as his own, to do with as he pleases. The only reason he is no longer a poacher is that he is not the brightest flame in the fire. He got caught too many times, so he has stopped for a while. But, even so," Bright went on, "he is like a pet jackal: it doesn't take too many howls in the moonlight to get him thinking about raiding the chickens in the coop." Bright pulled a sour face. "I sometimes have trouble getting him to follow orders."

"Interesting." Gideon slapped at a tsetse fly. Bright looked at Gideon.

"By the way, this morning I stopped at the park headquarters. Ernest Banda said to tell you he would be available for a meeting tomorrow, if you can make it."

5

November 9 - 10
Claudia

The Lubungu pontoon crosses a wide stretch of the Kafue River, where the broadness slows and smooths the flow of water. Here the current's sideways tug on the floats is reduced when the old rusted raft plies its way back and forth. Pulleys hold it on course, with the guide cable being like the harness tether of some old worn-out biblical beast still serving an ancient destiny.

The still morning air found Gideon watching the low sun etching long tree-shadows out onto the almost mirror-like surface of the river. At that time of day, when the ferry crew were still rousing in their huts across the river, it often took a lot of shouting and banging on the steel anchor pillars to get a response.

Luckily, the occupant of a small waiting vehicle was already doing some boisterous rousing. His vehicle was a sad little sedan, its scratched surface so dented it obscured precise brand recognition. Gideon couldn't make out if its dull grey color emanated, like the camouflage of a chameleon, from its original enamel hue, or from its thick coat of dust. Bald tires and a crack running the length of the windshield added to its air of fateful resignation.

Some of its passengers, children, stood skipping stones at the water's edge, while two women sat on the bank formed by the cut of the road as it dropped down to the load point. Gideon had a vague sense of unease as he watched the kids tossing the stones across the river. Eddie was still fresh in his mind. The kids had never seen how shockingly quickly, and how far, a crocodile can reach when it erupts from the river's sluggish margins, and this section of the river held some of the biggest crocs he'd ever seen.

While exchanging a few pleasantries, the owner of the dilapidated sedan said he was heading with his wives and their five children to the faraway city of Lusaka, then continuing another four hundred kilometers to the town of Chipatat on the other side of the country.

"A long way to go!" Gideon replied with a hint of sympathy for such a journey cramped in that size car.

But the man shrugged. He didn't expect or need sympathy. This was Africa. Few people from outside could fully understand how limits didn't apply. Expectations of comfort and crowding had different metrics. Anyone who was comfortable sleeping on a straw mat spread on the hard dirt floor of a hut wouldn't be bothered with the discomfort of being crammed into a small car in a way that only students do as a stunt in the West.

As they waited, a dilapidated old Bedford truck pulled up behind them. Its occupants, and there were quite a few, included women dressed in long, billowing black skirts and red jackets with wide white lapels matching their head scarves. Jehovah's Witnesses, Gideon surmised, or maybe not: there should have been some blue somewhere. Gideon couldn't remember. In any case, their colorful garb reflected the tribal predilection for a uniform, even in religion.

As they invariably do, the children joined the others skipping stones over the water. He watched, and an image of the camo-clad man's wrinkled face flickered into his mind, contrasting the women's colorful garb. They would find it more difficult to blend into the bush than that old man with his drab clothing. There was something vaguely prophetic about that, Gideon thought.

He wondered if the mission-molded ideas in the women's heads were as colorful as their clothes. Could those ideas blend into the fabric of Africa, be as durable as the black magic under the camo man's grey curls? In two hundred years, whose ideas would still be skipping across the waters of this river: the old traditional, or the recently imported? Ah, but it was all bullshit. Gideon envied the ability to believe in anything that can anchor oneself in place when the tides of life were running fast. Too bad he didn't have some belief to darken the hue of his already sunburnt soul.

Finally, Gideon noticed the crew slowly walking across from their huts to where the pontoon was beached on the far bank. Then, after they pivoted and gunned the engines to grind the heavy drawbridge into the gravel of the bank below, he cautiously followed the dusty little sedan over the stones and up onto the pontoon's platform. The old Bedford with its colorful burden of belief would have to wait for the next crossing. It was time to move. Ernest would be waiting.

* * *

David Maritz

November 9, Midday

After the climb out of the valley, past the guard post and the prison, and two hours further down the dusty rut-surfaced road, Mumbwa appeared beyond the low northeast ridge. From there, the view looked across a shallow valley towards the town. For Gideon it was always a relief to see the dull reflection of the sun shining haphazardly off the corrugated tin roofs of the town's structures.

Drawing closer, the road succumbed to increased traffic density with gaping, potholed submissiveness, abandoning any pretence of being a convenient way of getting from here to there. This ignominious state deteriorated as it wove between outlying huts, low brick buildings, and a plethora of untidy, improvised roadside stalls. Where the road bumped into the central traffic circle, a ragged asphalt surface offered some respite, running a short distance to the main Lusaka highway.

Here Gideon headed the opposite way, past the mosque's tall steeple which spread its influence over untidy Indian-owned store fronts on each side of the diagonal crossroad. Further along, a few turns down streets lined with tired and poorly maintained colonial houses shaded by big trees brought him to his destination.

The Zambian Wildlife Authority headquarters were housed in what once was the large home of a colonial administrator. The building now reflected a seemingly broad lack of concern for tidiness and aesthetics, but it wasn't aesthetics which brought Gideon here. It was the authority that spread from the place itself.

In his office, Ernest Banda, the regional head warden, could be quite a handful. He didn't care to spend too much time away from headquarters. Although a big, strong man, it was clear that his paunchy belly was beer bolstered. Gideon was lucky to have the man make time on such short notice.

From experience, he knew that the best way to access Ernest's helpful side was to extend a lunch invitation. Thus, sitting in the plastic chairs at a table on the porch of the little Somali-owned store at the junction with the west road, Gideon told Ernest about the crocodile attack. Yes, he had heard about it. Gideon also showed him the note that had been left on the slashed bags of cement. It didn't trigger much of Ernest's interest.

"Yes, they will need to patrol there some more," he said.

After two steak and kidney pies plus another two sodas for the road to go along with his offer of a jerry can of diesel, Gideon broached the subject of the additional scouts and their training. Ernest was well-practiced in dealing with 'favors'. He hedged, hemmed, and hawed around the issue. It was possible that this extra patrolling could be organized. It was best if he made a trip himself to headquarters in Lusaka. He would do this as a special favor, due to their good relationship, but, as a trip would not be part of his regular schedule, his travel may require some extra diesel. He may need, he said, to take officials out for dinner, and lodge for two nights in a hotel bracketing both ends of his going the extra length. What did Gideon think, he asked, of some spending money to cover other unexpected necessities?

It amused Gideon to listen to the pitch. "Hey, *Iweh*," Gideon wanted to say. "I am from a tribe of Africa: the white one! I know Africa as well as you, so don't give me your bullshit." But knowing that authority mattered and must be pandered to, instead he said, "Let me call my boss in Johannesburg to see what they can do."

David Maritz

Having learned he would get further with honey than vinegar, Gideon gave Ernest enough money for two jerry cans of diesel before setting off for Lusaka. At the end of the day, he needed Ernest on his side. As they say, 'Friends come and go. Enemies stay forever.' It would be stupid to carelessly piss the man off.

As a *mzungu*, he would have enough other problems, especially if Precious was correct. Gideon would work his own contacts. Instead of funding a binge on the town for Ernest, why not spend the money on Claudia? He hadn't seen her in six weeks, so she was certainly a motivating reason to head to the big city again. Dodging potholes in the tar, Gideon set off south towards the junction with the main West Road.

* * *

Slowing down to round the traffic circle at the town's center, a familiar vehicle stood at the fuel station next to the spoke which led its daunting way northwest back to the Lubungu pontoon. Standing to one side, talking to a mechanic, was Kings. Swinging on around the circle, Gideon drove across to where Kings stood. Pulling up next to him, Gideon poked his head through the open window and called out a cordial greeting in his own Kaude language.

"*Baji byepi mwane.*"

Kings turned and looked at him, then frowned, the skin between his brows wrinkled in its characteristic way. Ignoring Gideon, he turned back to the mechanic and continued speaking. Gideon waited. Finishing his conversation, Kings then walked, without looking at Gideon, across to his own vehicle.

Annoyed, Gideon got out, and walked over to where Kings had started his engine. Knocking on his window, and when Kings rolled it down, he asked, "How is Eddie?"

"I don't know," Kings replied. "Why don't you go to the clinic and ask them yourself?"

Gideon felt anger trigger his readiness for confrontation.

"I don't know what's up with you, but I know crap when I see it. We both know that you are full of it."

Engaging his gear, Kings glared back. Gone was the politeness of 'bwana'.

"Listen to me, *mzungu*. You are the one who brings your meddling ways here where they are not wanted." Licking his lips he said, "You're the one who had better watch out if you meddle too much."

He drove away, leaving Gideon smoldering at this unprovoked display of hostility. He walked back to his vehicle and sat for a few minutes to regain his composure. As he did, he felt the buzz of his cell phone in his pocket. He had flipped it to silent during his meeting with Ernest. Taking it out, he stared at the text message: a few simple words.

Is it you? I am older now, and younger! - Sophia.

He sat transfixed, staring at the screen. The words reached across over two decades.

'Jesus. Talk about prophetic,' he thought.

Another instance of the unexpected in Africa.

* * *

Gideon loved returning to his single-room digs in Lusaka, tucked behind a big garage across from Claudia's cottage. Waiting for her, he sat, updating his journal on the comfortable cushions of the couch in her abode, a home situated in one of the old dilapidated eastern suburbs of the city. Looking up from his laptop, he marvelled, as always, at how she had beautifully upgraded the old building, creating a cloistered oasis surrounded by tall, red brick walls high enough to hide the scruffiness outside, thereby giving it a hidden anonymity by screening it from the attention of passers-by.

Inside, the high walls afforded the place a courtyard-like atmosphere and a sense of security. The cottage's brick work was fresher than that of the wall and the servants' quarters behind, hinting at a common vintage with that of the old gracious Jacaranda trees whose shade somehow ameliorated the squareness of the structures they covered.

"The thing I most missed about London after coming back here," Claudia had said, "was its little, tucked-away courtyards. So I have made my own, with an African essence."

Instead of English ivy, she had trained bougainvillea to grow along the top of the walls, draping down in flowery hues of red, white, pink, and purple profusion. The creeper's thorny prickles provide a further obstacle to anyone attempting to clamber over the walls.

It was by lucky word of mouth that Gideon had stumbled on this place and become Claudia's tenant. With two grown sons and an ex-husband in the UK, Claudia no longer had dependents. Her relatively undemanding lifestyle meant she didn't need servants. This freed up the small servant apartment, which was Gideon's formal digs.

From the moment they met, her hybrid mixture of culture and self-appeal matched his own kaleidoscopic background. Claudia's father had been a sergeant in the British army, who had stayed after independence to train the new Zambian military; her mother, his Bemba nanny, taking care of his children. He had only acknowledged his part in Claudia's existence after his divorce, but that was sufficient to get her a good education, leading to an accounting career, which she had embraced with a lifetime fervor.

When Gideon arrived back from the bush the day before, Claudia had been away. He had wasted no time. He contacted an acquaintance who had served with the current head of the wildlife authority when they were young rangers. The contact said he would see about setting up an audience when Gideon next visited. Gideon was pleased with himself; this was better than he had hoped for. He could possibly reach higher up the chain of authority than if he'd contracted Ernest's help, not to mention far less expensive.

Now, settled back on the couch, Gideon's usual thrill of anticipation at Claudia's impending return was ruffled by the text he had sporadically glanced at for the last two days. He looked out onto the courtyard through the open double doors. To one side of the door was an assegai tripod holding up a floor lamp. Opposite was a large soapstone sculpture of an old African man clad in a loincloth. The figure and face had a vague resemblance to that of the Crocodile man. Looking at the sculpture's stony stare, Gideon rhetorically asked, "So, old man! What should I do? Answer, or ignore?"

"Heck! Hadn't she knocked him around enough for him to figure it out?" Gideon mused.

Returning to the couch, he rested his feet on the wooden coffee table. Leaning back with his hands linked behind his head, he stared sightlessly across the room.

"Dammit!" he thought. "Why now? This haunting echo!"

How could a single text so effortlessly scrape the scab off an old wound? Gideon wished he could sweep away some of his messy past as easily as the dust from the tiles of this floor, because, for the first time in his life, it was this place, this courtyard, this room, this Claudia who had begun to give him a sense of homecoming. He would be stupid to blow on old embers and risk setting fire to it all.

David Maritz

He placed his phone on the table and the note from his pocket next to it: two disturbing messages. If the one was a twist in the progress of his job, the other was a bend in the buckles of his heart, clipping him to a past and a place from a long time ago.

Is it you? I am older now, and younger! - Sophia

Intuitively he knew he shouldn't pick at the wound. Had time worked its weathering? Now he would probably pass her, unrecognized in the street. Yet, even though he had not heard it for twenty years, he could recall the lilt of her voice as clearly as the crooning of the doves outside. Like that old Africa, she had once been part of his dreams of a future. The timing of her re-emergence seemed as ordained as it was unsettling. He was beginning to wonder if he was mistaken to discredit the bewitching supernatural. Had she remembered that today was his birthday?

The back door opened, startling Gideon from his reverie. Claudia's hour-glass figure, clad in an austere monotone business suit, was silhouetted in the brightness of the outside sunshine. Gideon hadn't heard her car entering the garage, or her walking across the paving to the back door. Holding a leather briefcase in one hand and a grocery bag in the other, and with a wide smile on her happy face, she called out to him.

"Hi, I'm home." And followed up with a blown kiss.

Gideon wasn't accustomed to seeing her so businesslike. Usually she dressed in relaxed, comfortable, eye-catchingly colorful attire. It was a reason she liked working back in Africa, she claimed, "Here people are more individually extravagant, they like to show off more emphatically, and bright clothing is not discouraged in the workplace. Why not?" she often iterated. "Color is good for the soul!"

Claudia was one of those people who never seemed to have a bad day. She was always full of smiles, laughing at something. Gideon guessed if her predilection for color had a part in this, he was all for it. It was part of what made her so attractive to him: her warmth glowing in the calabash of her ebullient body, tempting and tantalizing with its ochre ebony, willing to spoon its joys onto those beside her also feasting on life.

"Wow! You look so businesslike!"

Setting her leather briefcase and keys down on the table, and the grocery bag on the floor, she gave Gideon a hug. "I've come straight from the airport. Occasionally I need to dress this way," she said wryly. "When I dress in a smart professional way, my 'no' answers carry more weight."

Claudia handled the financial and accounting side of some of her boss Mohammed Bahadur's more sensitive activities. Exactly what these were she never overtly explained, but she seemed to be needed whenever an important meeting was scheduled. From what Gideon gathered, she was brilliant at keeping her boss's affairs sailing as close to the wind as possible: knowing what to do, ease the tiller, or tighten the jib when the sails began to luff. One didn't accrue such a reputation, and the reputed wealth as Mohammed, without sailing close to blustery business.

Like a pet dog, Gideon often sniffed out enough to know what business was being served: snippets of phone conversations, rare expressions of frustration. He wondered if it was for his protection that she withheld information. Was this why, despite her extrovert personality, outside the walls of her courtyard she preferred to keep him at a distance, without shows of public intimacy, not even hand holding. Thankfully, behind her walls she was very different. Nevertheless, it had taken over a year before any affection between them had germinated into intimacy, but so far, so good.

"Would you like a cup of tea?" Without waiting for a reply, she poured him a cup.

He took the cup and a biscuit from the plate she presented.

"Where were you this time?" he asked.

"I was up in Mufilira, meeting a few crude types from across the border in the Congo, but hang on. I am going to get out of this straitjacket." She disappeared into her bedroom.

Emerging after changing into a loose t-shirt and a light floral skirt, she sat next to him on the couch. Twisting sideways, leaning back, she laid her head on his lap.

"It was a tough day! I need a little pampering," she smiled up at him.

Gideon stroked her forehead and brushed his hand over the curls of her thick black hair. "Why do you have to answer 'no' in those meetings?"

"Oh, it's nothing much really," she replied. "Sometimes there are men who still live in the last century. They don't realize that today, even here, the rules have changed when it comes to interacting with women." Rolling onto her side, with closed eyes Claudia asked, "Can you give me a massage?"

Obligingly, Gideon moved his strong, workman hands over her back and pressed up onto her shoulders. He kneaded as she continued.

"With those types, a good business suit keeps their inappropriate habits at a distance. It's like wearing a uniform. It sends a signal. Most of them get it. But some need a bit more of a discouraging hint."

"Does this happen often?" he asked. "Your boss is a son of a bitch when it comes to business, but from the little I know of him, he appears to be a well-mannered sort. I wouldn't imagine he would let people treat you badly."

She sighed. "Actually, all men need to be reminded of the rules occasionally. Even you." She looked up at him pointedly. "You should know this better than anyone! Wandering hands are seldom far behind wandering eyes."

"Hey! You haven't too much to complain about," he said grudgingly. "Look how much fun my wanderings have brought to you." Gideon gave her shoulders extra-long, drawn-out strokes.

"Yes, you were lucky! I was in a good mood. I should have worn a police uniform. Then you would have behaved yourself."

Gideon kept massaging, moving his hands lower down her back. "Luck comes to those who look for it," he said.

She smiled. "It's a delicate game. Being strict would stop the monkey-business. However all men are stupid in certain ways, even the clever ones. I get a bonus when certain deals are signed. I don't count on only my expertise at these meetings. If I look good, a hint of carnality, cleavage or whatever, the more likely a deal. They sign to impress and find favor in my eyes. Our guy up there knows that he can trust me to swing the deals."

"Crap," Gideon expressed. "I was born the wrong sex. If I was a woman, I would be making deals all over the place."

"Yes, you would." She reached back to smack his leg playfully. "It's like your coffee: the mix of the bitter and the sweet. Both are needed to make it work. My business suit is the bitter for these guys, and what is inside is the sweet, which is out of bounds, but they respond to the hints." Claudia opened her eyes. "At least the guy on my side of the table is good to work with. We have a lot of fun at the meetings."

"Who is that?" Gideon asked.

"He's related to my boss by marriage, originally from East Africa somewhere."

Gideon stopped to take a sip of his tea, then went on massaging.

"Ahh, that feels so good." Claudia half opened her eyes as he kept kneading her shoulders.

"I have something to show you," he said, picking up the note from the table. "Look at this."

She read it, turned it over to look at its crumpled brown paper, then handed it back.

"So? Who wrote it?"

"I don't know. It was found on some slashed cement sacks at the building site of a new lodge in the park close to where I sometimes do some field training. Someone must think that I'm involved with the new lodge construction, and doesn't like it."

Returning the note to his pocket, he went on massaging, making her purr with pleasure. She rolled onto her belly, to lay across his lap.

"My back needs more attention."

Gideon pulled her t-shirt out from the waist of her skirt, lifting it above the clasp of her bra. Unclipping it, he let its straps drop down to bare her back. With his other hand, he lifted the hem of her skirt to expose the back of her thighs. Then, with long hand strokes, like those of women washing clothing on a riverbank, his hands kneaded up along her spine to the base of her neck, before returning to drift down over the roundness of her rump, and down the back of her thighs. He followed the rhythmic cadence of his rubbing with the drift of his eyes, admiring the bell-shaped breadth of her hips and soft smoothness of her legs.

"So, what is your plan?" Lying face down, her voice was muffled by the cushion of the couch.

"I don't really have a plan." He hesitated. "I'm trying to get a meeting with the head of ZAWA to see if he can authorize more game scouts."

"Is the note tied to the old man at the crocodile attack?"

"I don't know," he said. Sitting up, Claudia leaned against him. "Bright told me that there have been issues for some time." Gideon felt her rest her head on his shoulder.

"As an outsider, I don't want to get wrapped up in some witchcraft bullshit, but if it is connected to poaching, I need to be involved." A peevishness entered Gideon's voice. "You know how difficult dealing with this superstition stuff can be. So why get involved, when some locals deep down don't really accept me or want me here?" Gideon told her about Kings' behavior.

"You used to talk about your platoon sergeant in Angola," Claudia looked at him as she spoke. "Wasn't he from here somewhere?"

"Yes. What about him?"

"Do you still have contact with him? Wasn't he involved in the sort of security thing like you?" she asked. "Why don't you see if he is around? You may be lucky if he's a drifter and is available."

"That's too much of a long shot," Gideon replied dismissively.

"Give it a whirl," she said. "What have you got to lose? I bet he could help you sort this stuff out. The locals would tell him stuff they would never tell you."

Gideon sat with his arm over her shoulder, the tips of his fingers drifting over the fullness of her breast as she leaned against him.

"Yes, but it has been years since we last had contact."

Turning her head to look at him, she said, "Wasn't he raised on a mission out west towards the Angola border? Go see if you can speak to someone out there. Maybe they will know where to find him." Claudia stood, kicking off her shoes. "By the way, it's your birthday, isn't it?" Seeing his curious expression, she continued. "I have a present for you."

"You remembered!" he said in surprise. He hadn't expected that. "What kind of present?"

"You have started unwrapping it. Why don't you unwrap some more and see what's inside?"

She reached for his hand, then led him across the room.

6

November 9

L ying next to her softly breathing form, Gideon toyed with Claudia's suggestion. Why not? What had he to lose? If someone like Mohammed trusted her judgment, so should he. It was a long way to the Angola border and the Mission, but he had time and enough cash to pay for the fuel to get there and back.

He would be dipping deep into the past. Maybe that text reaching across the decades was an omen, a call to finally confront some of the old demons, to find out what had made them dance. Feeling her stir next to him, he leaned across and kissed her lightly on the forehead.

"I'm going to leave early," he whispered. "Do you want a cup of coffee before I go?"

Claudia rolled onto her side as she sleepily gave him a one-armed hug.

"No, I'm still half asleep. Drive carefully and best of luck."

Quietly closing the door, Gideon headed out into the morning's early half-light.

Like its peers, the Great North and East Roads, the West Road starts inconspicuously as a spoke of the traffic circle on Cairo Road at the center of old Lusaka. Its routing has not changed since the layout of the city almost a century ago, but, like with the runt of the litter, the bustling vibrancy of the placenta which feeds it favors its other siblings.

The Great North Road heads up and is burnished by the copper in Katanga, and all the promise of Africa beyond, even reaching as far as the city from which Cairo Road derives its name. The next spoke of that circle spawns the Great East Road, which reaches down to the humid coastal plains and is fed by the growing artery of trade from the ports of Mozambique.

Lacking even the pretence of greatness, it doesn't take long for the West spoke's fizz to falter. The surge of traffic along its arterial begins before dawn as it pours into the choke of industrial area jams, then scatters through the squalor and chaotic informality of the backstreet repair shops, black-market stalls, and informal vendors which line its grubby verges.

It being early morning, Gideon was not overly affected by the crush of traffic. He was leaving the city and going against the flow. The slums pressing in at the road's flanks squander its verve as it wanders westwards. The flow simply stumbles fitfully over the potholes, between capricious road-blocks or speed strips as they exact their retribution for overuse long before reaching its extremity. Like the wilting of a long-etiolated stem, the West Road sags towards the sunsets across the flat wide spaces of the country, until its shrivelled florets lean up against the borders of Angola. There, as if in a last budding act prior to desiccation, its colorless petals spread into the forlorn town of Lukulu.

Once there, if today it is true to describe the settlement close to its western tip as just another chaotic and shabby African town, it was definitely more appropriate six decades ago. It is not much more than a conglomerate of stores and some administrative offices, plus a prison, where the prisoners sit outside, self-guarded, in the shade of one of the few big trees out on the Liuwa plains. After all, where would they escape to, out in the vacuum at the center of this vast, empty area?

Of course, now there was the nearby Mission complex, with not many more buildings than when it was founded decades ago, still so remote that only the hardiness and willingness to accommodate frugality, the very attribute which originally brought the Jesuits to minister to the heathen of these parts, still keeps them here.

Gideon knew that Claudia was correct: he should seek that legacy of physical and mental frugality, with its underpinning of determination and persistence, to aid his tactics. He could figure out the what, where, and when, but he needed Moses to help him with the how: that time-tested relationship between an officer and his sergeant. Would he be able to find it in that godforsaken little town? After all, if the narrative related by Precious had any underpinning traction, the Lord only knew what struggle lay ahead.

* * *

David Maritz

November 9, mid-afternoon

The Mission hadn't changed much. The weathering of the roofs along the long narrow buildings standing at right angles to the river is more obvious; the rusting of the upper corrugated tin sheets more pronounced.

On some buildings, the lower sheets had been replaced. This meant that the blend of the old and the new gave an artistic flavor to the roof line, with streaks of rusted russet leaching down from the higher to stain the shine in the corrugated gullies of those below. Gideon was struck by its symbolism: the old earthy ideas of Africa still seeping down to taint the shiny recent.

The Mission had a new, larger church building, its exterior painted with upper light and more durable, lower colors, where the rain splattered specks of mud onto the walls. Gideon sensed a metaphor in the color contrast. Durable or transient, how tenuous would its ideas be with the rubs of time pressing against this bastion of beliefs?

"What is the problem that brings you here?"

The priest held one arm tucked behind his back, hooked through the elbow of the other and dangling down to sway slowly to the cadence of each of his deliberate steps.

"I am looking for someone," Gideon replied.

From the office, they had strolled to the barn-like building of the church, which looked out over the breadth of the Zambezi River where it curled south out of Angola, loosely cradled in the flatness of the Lozi Plain. On the distant far bank, across the river, the scrawny straggle of civilization was strewn about like the chaff from a village threshing floor.

Inside they halted before the altar, standing in the gloom. The bright outside light was restricted through four narrow windows high in each wall. What remained of this light reflected from small, shimmering pools of sunlight on the floor. At each corner of the cavernous space, banners dangled from the corrugated ripples of the church's tin roof. Gideon thought how they could be mistaken for political propaganda, with their colors emulating revolutionary national flags in this part of Africa.

He admired the ingenuity. Both priest and politician were in the business of winning the hearts and minds of the plebeian poor, so why not use tested techniques? The thin wooden carving of a crucified figure hanging on chains above the altar reminded Gideon of wizened strips of meat hung up to dry into biltong jerky. He couldn't suppress the visual similarity: food for the soul on one hand, for the body on the other.

Standing before the altar, he felt as if he had come to confess his issues and needs. He was cognizant of standing at the front line of a vaguely similar conflict to his. It was a struggle for the fundamental heart of Africa. However that was where the similarity ended. The priests' spiritual cause was only two thousand years old. Gideon's reached further back to ancient Africa, teeming with its unique fauna and flora. Unlike the priest and the witch doctor, Gideon's goal was secular: to save the rest of creation, not only its people.

Father Xavier turned and gestured to follow, pacing measuredly with long, slow strides as they moved out into the bright afternoon sunlight.

David Maritz

"I see that you must spend a lot of your time outdoors. You are even more sun tanned than I remember." Father Xavier continued to walk slowly, looking down after casting a glance at Gideon.

The distant singing of school children came from a classroom opposite them. Small groups of pupils sat on the sand in the shade of the trees. A teacher was with each group, either standing or sitting on a chair. Some groups had an assistant, perhaps trainee teachers. A Mission education is a treasured luxury and in this part of the sub-continent the Jesuits provided some of the best. As they passed between the groups, Xavier sometimes tarried to listen. Occasionally he would swap a few words with the teachers, and with a nod, would acknowledge the greeting given to him as his smile peeped out from under the shroud of an inner joy. It was intriguing. Was it that joy which had provided this old man the fortitude to be a missionary in this remote outpost for five decades? How else could anyone remain here without relief for so long? Leaving the children behind, they continued back to Xavier's office.

Sitting opposite him, Gideon noticed deep wrinkles originating at the corners of the old man's eyes, which then drifted over his high cheekbones. From there, they angled lower, whereupon they seemingly attached to the lobes of his large ears, holding them to his head like the stay lines of a vintage square-rigger.

As he leaned forward to pour the tea into tin mugs on the simple table between them, Father Xavier lifted and squinted his turquoise gaze at Gideon. Avoiding it, Gideon's eyes drifted over the wrinkled hollowness of the priest's cheeks. He saw how other lines reappeared with unusual severity as they wrapped around the corners of the man's wide mouth before fading into a sequestered smile.

"It has been a while!"

Even after fifty years, the lilt of drawn-out vowels in his thick accent clearly indicated the priest's Portuguese origin.

"Yes, Father, it has been a while. We will need the fingers on both our hands to count that far back."

Xavier responded with a broad smile twitching at the corners of his mouth, accenting the pale hue of his papery lips.

"I was never good at math," Gideon said, "so if you want an accurate count, you may need to remove your sandals to help count with your toes."

They chuckled in unison. Stretching a long, bony hand, the old man passed Gideon one of the mugs on the table. With the other, he proffered a small bowl of lumpy sugar. Ignoring the teaspoon in the bowl, using his gnarled fingers, Xavier then dropped a lump into his own mug.

"What have you been doing since you were last here?"

"Well Father, I have done a lot," Gideon cleared his throat. "But I guess if I'm honest with myself, it was mostly reacting to what happened." There was no need to embellish his answer with this priest. "I haven't achieved much. Mostly I just stumbled onto things."

Reaching across the table, Gideon picked up a small ceramic jug. From it he added a dribble of milk to his tea. Then using the spoon in the sugar bowl, he stirred it.

"It's like yesterday, all that turmoil of war happened. When it was over, as you know Father, we came here for a short while, on the way to the rest of our lives. I assume you know who I'm talking about when I say we?"

Xavier answered a soft "Yes" over the top of his mug, cupping it in both hands, lifting it to his lips. "I remember how close you were."

Gideon put down his cup and folded his arms across his chest as he went on talking.

"When we were last here, we were looking for something to do. I was also looking for a place to stay. He at least had a place. So for me not much has changed." The old man nodded.

"He had a wife in a remote village down in the Zambezi Valley. I think he also had children. At some stage he even contemplated getting a second wife: his first wife's sister. It would make raising the children easier, he said. He could afford it with the extra danger pay we were getting. If I remember correctly, he said he would speak to you about it, the morality of it, that is. So you probably know more than I do. All that Old Testament stuff he was talking about." Gideon waited for the old man to speak, but there was only the sound of an occasional sip of tea.

"Yes, he spoke to me about that," the priest finally said without elaborating. Gideon went on.

"Without finding much else to do, we went back to doing the only thing we knew well: to fight, but in different places. He went way up to West Africa, which is where I lost track of him." They sat in silence until Gideon broke the reverie. "We were all affected by the collapse of what we'd fought for," he sighed.

"I sometimes wonder which of us was more affected by being on the losing side. My whiteness made it obvious, and in some ways acceptable, that I was on that side of the struggle, but that was not true for him. Those who are now writing the history take a dimmer view of his involvement than of mine. He was a black man fighting on the white man's side."

The old priest sat staring intently at Gideon.

"We were both basically well-educated. He got his here on the Mission, and I got mine at a private school down south. But neither of us went on to get higher training after the war. When it ended, it wasn't easy to change careers. By then, we had obligations: children to support and, in his case, wives. So why go and get trained in some humdrum morning-to-dusk boring sameness, if we could get good money fighting other people's wars? Although, I have to grant him, he was more responsible than I. Which is why I think he had a harder time. He felt he needed to marry the mothers of his children. Sheesh."

"And you?" the priest asked.

"I have two mothers for my two kids." He paused. "That I know of. I told you I was not as responsible."

Suddenly feeling uncomfortable, Gideon rose to set his mug in a steel sink on the far side of the room which served as the old man's kitchen.

"I guess it's more obligating to get attached to a wife than a child-support payment. So we both chose to keep doing what we were good at. We both became private military contractors to make the payments. Afterwards, I returned to the bush." Gideon shrugged. "It took a long time. Now that I'm back, I don't want to leave. I've realized that it's been my home for most of my life. It's all I have left of that old Africa."

The priest nodded again. "Yes I know. There are others like you out here."

"It was one of the reasons I stayed with the Buffalo soldier unit, 'The Terrible Ones', for so long. Because we always operated in the bush."

Gideon stopped talking. Maybe he was saying more than he should. He always took too long to explain. However, he had a flashback to an impression from decades ago, of a trait of this serene old priest's character. It was his quiet, tranquil, entrancing way of listening.

Where others would be waiting primarily for the break in a speaker's flow to interject, with Xavier there was quality and depth to his listening. It was hypnotic, drawing one on, effortlessly loosening the halter on the self-conscious, enabling the catharsis of telling.

David Maritz

The quietness of his listening let one feel that it wasn't necessary to hold on to the rocks in the stream of life. It was okay to let go and allow the words to flow, and by doing so with him alongside, one would be swept to better places.

Gideon knew of only one other man with that gift. As a fresh, wide-eyed one pip officer, full of blustery theory and inexperience, he wouldn't have become a good leader, let alone survived, without his unflustered sergeant alongside to listen quietly, offer suggestions, and make things happen.

"Father," Gideon said. "I have trouble back where I'm working. I need a good, dependable person who doesn't scare easily." He looked pointedly at the priest. "Do you know where I can find Moses?"

With narrowed eyes, suddenly making him look much older, Xavier asked, "Do you want him to go back to doing what you both did in the past, that work of the devil?"

"No!" Gideon stated emphatically, but he could see that it didn't dispel the faint suspicion on Xavier's face. The old priest shrugged.

"We have also been out of touch for some time. I am not sure he would want to be contacted. The last time we spoke, he had no enthusiasm to go back to chasing other men."

Gideon picked up his floppy bush hat, flapping it at a fly buzzing around his head. He detected the priest's reluctance.

"Father, I am trying to protect the work God did in the first six days of creation." He let that sink in. "As you know," he said, "Moses and I spent a lot of time together. It was only after a while that I discovered he was religious, which was unusual among the men in our unit. He told me he was fighting to stop the forces of evil, that the communists were the Antichrist. He wanted to stop their spread into Africa. I was in it for the excitement and the money. These days, it's pointless fighting communists. They are their own worst enemies. So Moses is not going to fight them, and with my kids grown I don't need the money as much. I want to save the other piece of Africa that God created." The old priest contemplated his words.

"I don't want to harm people, only to save the animals, birds and plants of God's creation. Father, Moses grew up here on the Mission. I would like you to help me find him, and even more importantly, convince him to help me.

"There are things that as an African he will immediately recognize and know how to deal with. Things that those like me, and maybe you, even though I grew up here, amongst the Africans, will never fathom." Gideon cleared the dust in his throat.

"I work for an international non-profit conservancy. I have been hired to reduce the poaching in the Kafue National Park and its surrounding areas by training game scouts. But Father, strange things are happening. Witchcraft is involved. I don't understand why. You and I know the people better than most others. You know that traditional witchcraft always lurks below the surface. Where I am working, these forces are subverting good men. To find out why and what is going on, I will need to track the footprints of the bad people, and the spirits motivating them. But I am too pale in my soul to reach that dark side of Africa. That is why I need Moses' help." The priest sat staring at his hands as he trimmed the nails of one hand with a small pen knife in the other.

"Okay," he said. "I will see what I can do."

7

November 9

"Come." The old man broke the silence. "I have a story to tell."

The big indigenous trees shading the rows of classrooms and offices were the remnants of what once was rich riparian bush, and their random spacing balanced the regimentation of the buildings. The mix of orderly and haphazard gave the Mission its sense of a melded Europe and Africa. The scrub and grass which once filled between the trees was gone, leaving only pale sand. It was the daily sweeping of this soil with hand-held grass switches which added to the African-village feel. The priest led the way to the upstream corner of the Mission. There, looking down on the sluggish brown eddies of the river, the bench they sat on was in one of these swept spots, beneath the spread of a huge fig tree.

An appropriate setting for telling a African story, Gideon gave a mental nod to the priest's sense of drama.

They sat for a while.

At the end of the dry winter, much of Central Africa is set alight to flush small creatures into the jaws of scrawny village dogs. It being early November, there wasn't much more left to burn. The smoke from the fires hazed the sky, yet the sun's perpendicular rays were so bright they imparted a lightness to the grey tint of this wash. The two men sat beneath these nebulous skies, silent, listening. Rising above the background of multiplication tables children rote-chanted in their nearby classrooms, from somewhere far away across the river, came the lilting sounds of a radio playing a haunting 'Tuku' song. Neria, maybe? As the music faded, the sky was filled with the tinkling chatter of European bee-eaters, recently arrived after their migration south from the Levant. For the rest of the summer they would grace the land with their beautiful presence.

Father Xavier sat on his hands, leaning forward. His long, lanky body held his clothes as loosely as a scarecrow keeps its rags. He looked down between his knees at the leather of his sandals, listening to the birds, the children, and the distant bark of a dog. Without raising his head he asked, "How did Moses fit in when you were together in that war?"

A strange question. Gideon hesitated. It was the sort of question he remembered when seeking a job after the war. The sort that invariably showed him the exit, deepening the bitterness, whose vestiges had yet to be worn away by the pestle of time. But as with a tug on a bridle, the drift of Gideon's thoughts were edged back by the priest as the old man straightened to look directly at him.

"We all fitted in," Gideon stated. "Whoever could stay the course. We shared a bond of mission and spirit, judged by worth and merit."

Singing came from a classroom.

Gideon cleared his throat and spat to the side. "We were the first truly multiracial unit in the army. Most of us were volunteers. He fitted in better in the unit than I do in this new Africa. Is that why you ask?"

The priest shrugged. "No, not really." The old man reached down to where a few straggly stems of grass survived the daily sweeping. Plucking one and straightening back up, he rested his elbows on his spread knees

David Maritz

as he delicately picked the strand apart with rough, calloused fingers. At first he spoke softly, then, as he continued, he told his story more emphatically, even angrily. "Moses carries a mark. It is why he loved being with you in Angola—because you were too busy to notice it. That mark could be a blessing, if you want him to help with your sort of troubles… but you have to know Africa well to understand why. In life, there are no second first impressions." A soulfulness effused the old priest's voice, so palpable that Gideon glanced at him to check if anything was amiss. "My first impression was of her face: big sad charcoal eyes and the tight curls of her flame-red hair. It was the face of an albino child, maybe three or four years old. She was over there." The priest pointed at the wide, lumpy surface of the huge tree. Following his gesture, Gideon looked up to see how the tree lifted its branches high above them before they spread out and drooped down to cloister them in a leafy bower. "She was hiding over there, behind the trunk. I asked her: '*Zina yako ndiwe ndani?* What is your name?' Only her head was peering out from behind the tree. 'Dinai,' she said." The old man leaned forward. Using a stub of grass he drew lines in the sand between his feet. "It was in the mid or late fifties." He paused to scratch out the lines in the dirt with the heel of his sandal. "I was young when I first arrived here, full of enthusiasm. I wanted to change the world, bring all of the kingdom of God to this big, flat, empty land. The child had discovered this quiet spot under a dome of branches where she could hide from the world. Its shelter wasn't as thick in those days, but it was adequate. I had surprised her, which was why she was hiding." He lifted his head to look at Gideon, brushing him with the turquoise squint of his stare. "As I said, there are no second first impressions. Her face was one of the most striking I have ever seen. Seldom does one confront such a visage in such an unexpected manner. Even though it was long ago, I can still see that child's eyes, which always seemed to be peering into a special sorrow." He straightened, then leaning back he cocked a knee to lift his leg so that the tip of his sandal now erased the lines.

"What is it about a little girl that will help me get the better of bad men?" Gideon asked.

"I will get to that," the priest said. "But now, let us walk while we talk. I don't like to sit still for too long."

They passed through the Mission gate and headed along a dusty track, which circled upstream from the mission before cutting back and running parallel to the river. A big, black and white pied crow rowed its way through the air over them, eyeing them to see if they would discard scraps to scrounge.

Xavier halted momentarily and with a lick of his lips said, "You need to know about his mother. Moses carries her mark." The priest spoke slowly. "Some say it is her curse." He nodded a greeting to two women walking past with buckets of water balanced on their heads. "Of course, to understand one needs to know about some of the darker side of Africa." A scrawny dog barked at them from where it was tethered next to a shack. "Here, the way of life is still very tribal. Many marriages are arranged, with the bride often purchased with *lobola*, even amongst the faithful."

"Does that not bother you?" Gideon asked. "Arranging marriages, and buying a wife or two?"

"No, the word of God is not like a computer program that needs upgrading to fix bugs. If it was good for Abraham and Isaac it isn't evil in God's eyes; only in the eyes of those who came later and misread God's will."

Gideon raised his eyebrows and hummed softly to hide his reaction.

"Dinai's grandfather, a Lozi man from around here, sold one of his daughters to a man from the Tonga tribe in the Zambezi Valley. This is where the mark that Moses bears began. Her first child, a daughter—Dinai—was born an albino and, one needs to understand the position the albinos hold in African superstitions. Giving its flavor to all of life out here, like the sea its salt, is witchcraft. The spiritual world of Africa is all around us all the time. Their dead don't travel far away to a heaven or hell. They wander the darkness in the lonely places around us. They believe these spirits are sometimes benign, even good. Others are evil, able to take possession of the soul of a living person. When someone has been possessed by a devil, the belief is that the way to get rid of the evil is to banish or kill the possessed. In Dinai's village, children had died. A *nganga* was summoned to sniff out the witch causing the deaths. There were whispers. Dinai's mother, a Lozi, and with an albino daughter, saw the writing on the wall. She took her daughter away before she could be identified as a devil."

The bleakness edged back into Father Xavier's voice.

"I often wonder if it was the constant threat of witch accusations that etched the sadness in the little girl's eyes." Pausing his stride, the old man stooped to the side of the path to pluck another length of grass, which he chewed on pensively between his words. "The little girl I first saw hiding behind that tree trunk had been brought back to live with Lozi relatives in this area. Her mother dared not stay, lest she be possessed by proxy. The rumors of who the child was clung like blackjack burrs. The other children shunned her. Even adults kept their distance. Even her relatives. Which is why she came to be a virtual orphan of the mission. A nun working here took the child under her wing. I am eternally grateful to that nun. She helped me raise the child. Dinai grew into a wonderful girl, but the mark of destiny followed her. It wasn't the stark difference of the color of her skin and hair that made her stand out. It was the echo of her past trailing behind, like a zephyr, whispering that somewhere was a spirit waiting and lurking to take possession of someone's soul, with the special potency of an albino witch."

The priest's tone brightened.

"Dinai attended school here at the Mission. On many an afternoon and on some days on the weekends, the child, and later the girl, met me out under these trees. We talked about religion, politics and history. We played checkers and chess. I spoke Portuguese to her. She learned fast. Her mind was a sponge. She soaked up knowledge and information. At the Mission in those times we only provided classes up to the end of junior school.

She was so talented. It would be a travesty if she didn't finish high school, maybe even get a teaching diploma so that she could return to the Mission as a staff member. She dreamt of attending Fort Hare in South Africa, or Makarere in Uganda. So I arranged with a friend for her to stay with them while she attended Munali Girls High School in Lusaka."

An image of the school flashed into Gideon's mind. He always passed it on the way to Claudia's cottage.

"We wouldn't see her for months. Only during the school holidays would she come back to stay with us. I had begun to hope that she had escaped her curse. The sadness left her eyes. Then, just short of her sixteenth year, she stepped down unexpectedly from a bus. Her pregnancy was obvious."

The men walked in silence until they reached the Mission gate before the old man spoke again.

"It took a long time for her to tell me about the father of her unborn child. He was dark, an African with fine features, she said. The only clear feature she remembered was a burn scar on his chest. It had the big shape of an upside-down map of Africa. She had been raped!"

Xavier unlinked his bony hands from behind his back.

"She gave birth to a son. When the baby was a year old, Dinai announced she had received a message from her mother, the mother who had abandoned her and whom she could barely remember. Dinai was determined to see her mother and show her her baby.

"A month later a stranger appeared at our Mission gate. He had the baby. As you know, here in Africa when a child is born out of wedlock it is raised by the father's family. The stranger said that the baby was being brought back for us to send to the father. We never saw Dinai again. She disappeared. I sent people to search for her, but nobody knew anything. Thus it was that Moses came to stay. I gave him the name of Moses. He had been

David Maritz

abandoned on the banks of an African river, and I didn't push his cradle away. But, for her baby son, the whisper that followed his mother, with its spiritual smoke, continued to fan the same embers in peoples' minds. He inherited her curse."

Gideon had listened without interrupting. Now he said. "But Father, how does this help me with the issues I have back at the Kafue?"

"The Lord works in mysterious ways," the priest said. "I suspect that mark I tried for so long to eradicate could be a blessing for you. If we can find him, Moses will be good for your cause because even the *ngangas* will be scared of him. Somehow they will know that he is the son of a white witch. They will be wary of challenging you. It would be good to have Moses at your side."

8

November 9 - 10

As beetles kept slamming into the overhead light, midnight found their conversation still twisting around subjects untouched for years. In this cultural wilderness, Gideon felt like a wedding guest trapped by an ancient mariner. It wasn't often that the priest had someone with whom to discuss ideas.

"Why do you feel that you haven't much relevance to Africa?" the old man asked. Gideon cleaned thoughtfully under his fingernails with a match stick.

"Father, if you don't mind flowery language, ever since European explorers discovered Africa, northern ideas have slid south like sand in an hourglass."

"Isn't that a good thing?" the priest interrupted heatedly before Gideon could go on. "The idea of this Mission. Look at the good it has brought to this area." Gideon dipped his head in acknowledgment while continuing to scratch under his nails.

"Yes. However, some of those ideas weren't beneficial to Africans: European domination, for example. Moses and I fought for that idea. In the trenches at the time, I didn't think much about the principle. I was drafted, and that was it. I was interested in excitement: money, fun, and getting laid.

For Moses it was different. He had a religious moral aspect to joining in the fight. I only found that out much later.

"It turns out the idea we fought for, and many of our friends died for, got tossed onto the scrap heap of history, and us with it. We lost."

"What about the new replacement ideas?" the priest asked. "They are also northern: socialism, communism." He leant forward, resting his elbows on the table with his hands clasped and his chin supported by his meshed fists. Gideon waved his hand contemptuously.

"Those are crappy ideas made crappier when they got here. Turned into corrupted forms of despotism. The archaeologists say that Africa is the mother of mankind, but as we know she has been pillaged and raped so often by arrogant outsiders that nobody particularly cares. These days it's the turn of the Africans themselves, or the Chinese to do the pillaging, but if anything goes wrong, and they are caught, or someone complains, they still need someone to blame.

"My generation still seems to be a convenient group: easy to identify, easy to blame. " Gideon said wrily. ""After the war I started wondering if Moses and I had been rapists? We weren't outsiders, except for the ideas in our heads." It was the priest's turn to shrug.

"Ironically," Gideon continued, "these days Africa's soul is oozing back up to paint the pale surfaces of the globe with its dark color. Isn't that a good thing?" Gideon asked rhetorically as he went on fidgeting with his nails.

"All those ideas floating across in overcrowded boats, being held for a while on islands in the Mediterranean, or sneaking across the English Channel at night in rubber boats." Gideon dropped the matchstick into an ash tray.

"The war had different effects on us. It deepened Moses's beliefs and shredded mine. You see Father, Moses and I are hybrids in spirit: each raised in two cultures. The inequality of Africa has deepened. The ideas used to kick out the colonialists have been hijacked all over the continent for personal gain. Moral superiority can be trumpeted to rectify racial injustices by stamping on minorities. Unfortunately, that can be fed and believed by the poor for a long time."

"So what kind of minority are you and Moses if you lump yourselves together?" Xavier asked.

"We both fought the same way, but differed in the way we lost. We are spiritual orphans with no assurance of being adopted back. He physically, me spiritually. Nobody really cares. Africa is still full of exclusion." Gideon yawned. "What the heck, the story under my sunburnt skin is just another sordid tale in Africa's long unnoticed history. Which is why I question my relevance. Nobody cares."

"Except me!" the priest said. "Which is why I will pray for you."

* * *

As the tinge of dawn began to fulfil its threat to push away the confetti strewn across the last of the night's indigo, roosters began crowing across the river. Gideon walked towards the Mission office. His thoughts were dismissed by the ping of a text message on his phone.

Two elephant carcasses found; tusks hacked out, it read. A second message followed on its heels:

A scout is missing.

Both came from Dimas, the lead of a scouting team Gideon was training. Outside the office, sounds of activity and the chatter of voices gradually filled the air as the Mission came to life. Sitting at a simple wooden table in the dawn dimness, waiting for the kettle to boil, Gideon couldn't see the old man's eyes, but he could make out the manner of his gaze, peering out from beneath bushy eyebrows, with unblinking attention focused on his face.

"Tell me about your work" the old priest said. "What do you actually do? How did you get the job?"

"Like anyone around fifty," Gideon replied, "I've had a hard time finding work. Black empowerment down south makes it difficult for an older white guy like me. So I'm lucky to have found this job; even luckier that I was given a work permit. Thankfully my military experience worked in my favor, especially when it came to bush policing." Gideon watched Xavier ladle instant coffee and powdered milk into two mugs before pouring in hot water.

"Mainly I got my job because I knew my boss from the past. We give additional training to the park scouts, because the main funders are interested in increases in game numbers." The old priest listened as Gideon went on.

"I love what I do and where I am, but if I lose my job, who knows? Become a sidewalk beggar in some slum city down south." Gideon noticed the mirth sparkle in the priest's eyes.

"That wouldn't be bad," Xavier said. "It could make you appreciate my prayers for you." Gideon laughed back.

"I will need more than prayers. I will become a priest myself, if the Devil gives me time to study." Father Xavier laughed with him.

"But you can understand why I'm concerned about witchcraft. I can't afford to have things get messed up. If my results don't please the funders, my job will be on the line. The chances of getting another gig like this will be slim."

There was a knock on the office door. Xavier stood and walked over to step outside. Gideon sat sipping his coffee as he heard the priest talking to someone. Gideon had almost finished his beverage by the time the old man returned.

"Someone wanted malaria treatment pills," he explained.

"Is this place also a clinic?" Gideon asked.

"In some ways yes," Xavier said. "We get donations of expired drugs from all over the place, mainly Europe. In reality those drugs are still effective for years after the expiry date."

"Well, Father," Gideon said, "It isn't just drugs that are effective in Africa after their expiration date is up: look at you and me." They both laughed.

With that Gideon tossed back the last gulp of coffee. He reached across to shake the priest's hand.

* * *

The return trip from the western edge of the country is a long, arduous affair, full of flat monotony, made more uninteresting by increased settlement having scratched away the vegetation like the hair on a mangy dog. However, for those who are alert, few places in Africa are really monotonous.

Gideon saw beauty in the plumage of the lilac-breasted rollers. He counted how many were perched atop bushes at the side of the road waiting for a passing vehicle to flush a grasshopper which they could fly out and snatch. Spotting a pair of Lanner falcons further on helped to push back the boredom. It would be the chicks of the village chickens that the falcons would be after. Three hours after the last slice of toast with Father Xavier, the road ahead was already breaking up into shivering aqueous ripples, refractions from hot air. It would be a long, hot journey.

David Maritz

Despite avian distractions, Gideon couldn't shake his apprehension. The croc man, the text, now two poached elephants together with the disappearance of a scout, which couldn't be due to an overnight booze binge: that sort of occurrence was too regular to merit mention.

"Goddammit," he thought. "Some trickster Tokoloshe god must have me in his sights." It was enough to make him a believer.

As he drove, he noticed more huts clustered along the roadway than in the past. They stretched into the distance, fed by arteries of dirt tracks spreading out like the varicose veins on the cheeks of a drunkard. The untidy clusters came with their symbionts: a few sporadic cows to supplement the goats, ubiquitous chickens scuffling between the corn stalks clinging to barren soil.

Long gone was the tree canopy whose leaves once provided shade and fallen mulch which had caressed the soil for eons. Instead, like the flat, wizened breasts of an old woman after decades of monotonous childbirth, most of the flush and fertility of life had been sucked out of the land. In the face of it, Gideon wondered why he bothered struggling to preserve what remained.

If Africa was the mother of mankind, in many places she was so worn out she wouldn't even be worth raping. Gideon wondered if a secular soul like himself could make the magic to delay the old hag's menopause, filling it instead with milk and honey. Could saving some of the old Africa be enough for him to sense that he had achieved something worthwhile in life? Perhaps Father Xavier with his crucifix, or Precious with her snail-shell necklace, had insight into spiritual realities hidden from him. Possibly he did need to be prayed for or would it be better to be on a street corner with a cup in his hands? Which would be the bigger failure: becoming a beggar, or a believer? Both would guarantee that he'd have to give up and pass the buck. He wasn't ready for that yet.

After some hours of driving, Gideon stopped for a break and a pee where the West Road crossed the Hook Bridge over the Kafue River. Stepping out onto the bridge Gideon stood beneath the glare of the zenith sun, savoring his thoughts. He then walked to the center of the bridge to look down at the slow eddies of the water. It was relaxing, even hypnotic, to watch the river's roll passing below his feet. Unlike his dried up distant past, the flow of its waters now sustained his soul like milk flowing from the big, ripe breasts of a different, younger Africa. Gideon let space and time work its magic. Closing his eyes he suddenly had a surreal sensation of being suspended in time. Everything had stopped. He could reach out and touch both the past and the future. It was all linked: part of the same left/right, up/down thing, and the present would be where he opened his eyes. Listening to the echo in his soul, with the azure of the huge sky above, the ghosts of his past stood beside him, reaching across space and time. This was Africa, and here the spirits were everywhere, not just in the haunted darkness of the night or a person's imagination. The immensity of the sky above was enhanced by the flatness of the unfettered perspective when viewed from the center of the bridge.

Over the river, there was little to obscure the vista in any direction. It was as if the heat of the sun shining directly above, glaring remorselessly down, had melted away all the lumps in the landscape. Reaching into the distant past with Xavier unconsciously fomenting self-examination, had rekindled a special ghost.

Is that you? I am older now, and younger.

Would she somehow be linked to the future, not just the past? Over the dull jade of the waters, the river flowed towards him, but if he turned around, it flowed away, like time. He squinted to cut down the glare. All he saw was the huge, flat horizon. Like the rip of a tide, it cut across his perception, stretching seemingly forever with its left and right, it's before and behind, and with the ripples of the bush below and the sky above.

David Maritz

How could he not be affected, standing in the middle of this wide womb, attached to that far-away placenta with its hint and hope of a rebirth, even as high above, he detected its morticians. Gideon was reminded that Africa was also about death.

Mere specks in the sky, less than a handful, distributed vertically in a loose, slowly twisting column, gaining altitude in the updraft of a powerful thermal. When he raised his binoculars, the speck at the top had risen three thousand feet above the tree canopy, whereupon it peeled off and drifted north in a flat, shallow glide, with an occasional dipping wing beat: a signal to others that food was nigh.

Vultures!

Following its flight with his binoculars, he picked up the next column. In the direction of his scan, another pillar of circling birds rose, so distant it was barely visible even with ocular magnification.

The birds were on the march. Somewhere far away to the north was a bonanza. They were gliding across the bush using thermal elevators. Gideon methodically scanned the skies in every direction. Off to the east towards Mumbwa was another column: another progressive, avian line heading to where they could join a feasting frenzy. He wondered if it was an elephant carcass they had spotted.

Most of the birds would be whitebacks: the most common. A pair had a nest in a tall tree above the dirt road leading upstream from his campsite. There was a noticeably larger bird in the nearest group: a Lappet-faced vulture who would dominate the feast for a while. The column was too far to pick out any of the smaller, more delicate, hooded variety.

He watched as the nearest pillar moved gradually closer, pushed along by the same breeze as made the tall, dry, elephant grass lining the road nod and sway in unison with its eddies. It was dynamic. The birds at the top peeled off out of the spiral. They were replaced by others, approaching from the opposite side in a well-spaced direct line.

With a sharp left bank of their huge wings, they slotted into position at the bottom of the vortex a few hundred feet above the trees. The vultures circled effortlessly, ignoring gravity as they spread across space and time with impunity. Their niche required them to fly high in the sky, to stay there almost effortlessly, enabling their incredible vision to seek the dead or dying. They needn't get anywhere fast. Their prey couldn't run away.

He let his binoculars hang on the strap around his neck. Space, time and gravity. He knew that no bird in history was disappearing off the face of the earth as fast as vultures. Like him, both wardens and poachers would be watching. Maybe it was this stream of birds which had alerted Dimas. Any poacher who kills an elephant, creating a vulture feast, would know the birds could alert the warden.

Perhaps that poacher, if he had access to poison, would taint the carcass so there would be no future vultures to alert wardens of nefarious feasts. Gideon knew this wasn't the only dark cloud on the horizon for these magnificent birds; their old Africa was also disappearing. Hidden away in backstreet shops or warehouses were the bushmeat and muti markets where totems giving luck to almost any endeavor could be found.

Crocodile heads, pangolin scales, owls' talons, jackals' fur, plus one of the most sought-after: vulture heads, with their power of sight sparking the belief they would enable the possessor to see into the future: a clear benefit for any aspiring politician, business person, or anyone who could afford such a totem. Gideon turned to walk towards his vehicle.

Is that you? I am older now, and younger.

Three decades seemed an eternity, but in the up-down-left-right relativity of his exile from her, it was nearly the same time it had taken for these gracious gravity-defying birds to quietly disappear.

David Maritz

Ghosts? He wondered if any of them had the eyesight of a vulture. Would they let him look into the future?

Sheesh. He was letting the bush get to him. A ghost? Had she been brought back on the wings of an angel, or a vulture?

* * *

Turning off the west road onto the short, tarred stretch that led into and through Mumbwa, Gideon drove past the tall steeple of its mosque, its untidy pavement markets and storefronts. At the other end of the town, after passing the shabby entrance to a hotel, half hidden behind a screen of exotic trees, the road turned sharply as it led to the ZAWA building where he hoped to find Ernest.

He wanted to follow up on the terse text of poached elephants and a missing scout. Luckily Ernest was in his office, and in an accommodating mood. He was willing to make time for Gideon. Nothing wrong with that!

Again at the little Somali store-café at the junction, they sat outside on cheap plastic chairs watching the slow unhurried passages of customers sauntering in and out. The pies were hot and the cola cold, the store sufficiently set back from the highway so the sound of the passing vehicles didn't make it difficult to hear each other.

Ernest confirmed that the first clue to something big being poached was, as Gideon suspected, the convergence of vultures in large numbers. A patrol had been sent to investigate: two elephants were the target, shot in quick succession, close together. From the size of the carcasses, the tusks couldn't have been big. It surprised Ernest that the poachers were going after such low-grade animals. Was it worth their while?

Ernest magnanimously offered to show Gideon one of the victims. The carcass was not far off the road out to the Lubungu pontoon: he could show it to him on Gideon's way back to the lodge. Two jerry cans of diesel would go a long way to help taking him to the site.

Gideon appreciated the inexpensiveness of this man's friendship. He paid the bill and headed to the vehicles to collect the empty jerry cans from Ernest's Cruiser, conveniently brought along. Even from a distance, it was evident that a piece of paper was tucked under the wiper of Gideon's windshield.

You are warned again, it read. *Leave the area. Stop your meddling else you will be punished.*

Like the first, it was signed:

'Crocodile.' This time it was written in bold, decisive letters. Ernest shrugged as he read the message.

"You have stepped on sensitive toes," he said. "Don't worry. We will get them."

Leaving the town behind, Gideon followed Ernest's dilapidated, government Cruiser along the road towards the Lubungu pontoon. After they dipped into the Kafue Valley, through thick thorny bush below the shallow rim of the basin, Ernest turned off the dirt road to follow the track of a vehicle already blazed into a rough trail through the long grass and dense shrubbery layered under tall trees.

Although their progress was slow, it took less than a half hour after leaving the road to reach the site. Gideon had to acknowledge the poachers' audacity in killing an elephant so close to the road. The carcass of the first was in a small clearing. At its center, where the fracas was most intense, it was like an out-of-control soccer riot.

Pecking, pushing, some using open-winged intimidation, the vultures jostled each other. Some were intent on digging their heads deeper into the stench to tear off another beak-full of putrid flesh. The less aggressive stood scattered around the periphery, their swivelling heads scanning the scramble, waiting for an opportunity to hop into the epicenter.

In the midst of this chaos, a hyena stood like a half-hearted referee trying to reestablish order, unconvincingly baring its teeth. Every so often, it lost interest in the boil of birds. It would shove its head through a hole in the thick, grey hide stretched across the dead elephant's ribcage. Crawling deeper into the cavernous chest, leaving only its tugging haunches visible, it would rip free the hidden flesh lodged between the ribs themselves.

The chitters and excited chuckles of the avian crowd was underpinned by the hum of myriad clouds of flies whose wings sounded like swarms of bees. It was doubtful if their maggots would have time to hatch before the scavenging horde finished this banquet. Wandering in and out of the crowd were three more hyenas whose bloated bellies indicated why they were no longer interested in the carcass and the frenzy.

With pricked ears and heads looking out into the bush beyond the scrum, it seemed they were more concerned with a possible appearance of a lion: an unlikely event. Cat tracks were visible in the peripheral sand, not yet trampled into a dustbowl around the carcass. The remaining meat was too tainted for any self-respecting big cat's palate. At the far edge of the surge, a few marabou storks stood like retired schoolmasters, looking disdainfully down their long beaks at the unruly mob. Gideon wondered why they even bothered to show up.

One wretched elephant had been wounded by the poachers. The skin at the back of its head had been hacked open by a bush axe so its spine could be chopped apart, thereby ending its writhing. The poachers either didn't want to waste precious ammunition, or didn't want another shot being noticed. To get at its tusks, the front of its face was hacked off, leaving pitiful eye sockets staring emptily across the blunt mash of flesh where there once was a trunk. The jostle of avian activity only came to an end when their two vehicles were within meters of the shambles.

As the men exited to walk towards the carcass, the rush of wings of birds taking to the air sounded like the approach of a train. Some struggled to get into the air with bloated, meat-laden crops. Ernest and Gideon hurried to the upwind side to minimize the retch-inducing stench clinging to the scene.

They didn't stay long. Ernest said the poachers' tracks departed in a north-easterly direction. Initially on finding the carcass, one of the scouts was sent back to HQ to report the incident, but after a day not having any response from HQ, another scout was sent to follow up on what was happening. There was no sign of the first scout.

Gideon brought up his request for more scouts to be trained and brought on duty. Ernest was nonchalant. If he got the funding it would be easy, he said. Furloughed scouts could be brought back on board.

Rejoining the main road, Gideon left Ernest to return to his headquarters. Pointing the nose of his own vehicle northwest to head across the valley, he looked at the bold, handwritten note on the seat beside him.

Did it have a connection to the poached elephants? He couldn't think where he had trodden so hard to warrant a second warning. Gideon had no faith in Ernest's ability to get the note scribblers.

Maybe it behoved him to start watching his back.

"Fuck it," he muttered. With the same air as pulling a Tarot card, he silently asked an unknown god to find his sergeant.

'Shit,' he thought. 'All this bullshit: gods, ghosts and *ngangas*. Life in the new Africa was as complicated as in the old.'

David Maritz

9

November 14

Gideon woke some hours after midnight. The old boy of the Chamafumbu pride was roaring, filling the monochrome clarity of a full moon with his bellows. His drawn-out rumbles had ruffled the evenness of Gideon's sleep. Somewhere far away upstream, on the opposite side of the river, one of the Mushingashi pride was also sounding off. Over there, two young short-maned males had recently dethroned the old king.

Wrapped in darkness, swaddled within the layers of his sleeping bag like a silkworm in the comfort of its cocoon, the rumbles kept Gideon mentally wide-eyed. There was no fence between the roars and himself. It produced a visceral reaction: evidence of how many countless thousands of years lions were an extant part of human reality.

In the past, the unwary and nocturnally reckless were eaten. Instinctively Gideon knew it best not to draw the attention of a big prowling cat at night. He would tarry until the roars receded before relieving himself. The rumblings were so close he could discern the intake of breath between the big cat's bellows.

As dawn approached, relative quiet returned to his riverside camp. The birds began to rouse and the big leadwood and acacia trees would soon take form. The moon which had earlier been hazed over by frills of fine clouds was more clearly revealed as it brushed the landscape with its last silver light.

A Heuglin's robin who frequented the thickets behind his tent was the first to herald the pending day. After its tentative start, as if to clear its throat, the bird's crescendo rose to climactic perfection. It was for Gideon a sound as emblematic as that of the fish eagle. The beauty of its song symbolised the dense, bushy parts of Africa: the warmer, wetter, enticing parts laden with salve for his soul.

As the serenading of the robin increased in intensity, the distant fading amplitude of Chamafumbu's vocalisations allowed Gideon to overcome his reticence to rouse. Soon he was sitting in the predawn dimness with bare legs extended towards the fire. Its rekindled embers were wedged in the V formed between the sandals as his feet hooked over each other.

Taking time to sip his coffee: French pressed, strong, sweetened with two spoons of sugar and mellowed with a dash of powdered milk. It was perfected by two rusk biscuits to dunk. With elbows on the armrests of his camp chair, he held the mug high, cradled in both hands with the rim of the cup barely touching his lips. He drank with quiet, shallow sips, barely moving his wrists.

It would be a pity to disturb the small herd of puku that had spent the night out in the open grass of the *dambo*. A few of the does, which had scampered into the bush line as he had moved to sit next to the fire, were now cautiously venturing back to graze close by. The wisps of steam rising from his cup faded the outline of the antelope. Then, as the vapor leaned askance, the puku reappeared with sharpened shapes. The steam was nudged by the imperceptible drift of the air; its cool weight pressed slowly between the tree trunks where it crept across the *dambo* before gently spilling into the broad rut of the river.

David Maritz

It was still early. Without guests at the lodge, Sunday had a relaxed routine: things got started later. Gideon considered heading across to the lodge. He wanted to see Bright's reaction to the new threatening note. He could get his opinion over another cup of coffee.

He could also get an update on anything that had happened while he was away, or he could take the boat to head a few clicks upriver to meet with neighbor Alan at his camp. Gideon was curious if Alan was aware of anything unusual in his sector of the game management area adjacent to the national park. He could brief him on developments with their cooperative anti-poaching activities, but that would only be after a meeting with Scout Leader Dimas to get a follow-up report on the elephant poaching. Hopefully, Dimas had put into practice his instruction on crime-scene management. Dimas would be back at the pontoon base sometime later that day.

Or, ignoring it all, Gideon could experience the wonderful escape from the apostasy of modern progress. Every time he ventured from the national park boundaries, he would notice another few steps of civilization creeping closer to his sanctuary: a few more trees cut down, more land cleared, another structure built, a few more electrical poles.

Depressing.

Could he halt some of the abrasions in the skin of Africa? Curb some of mankind's sense of entitlement? Change an uncaring world jaded by the images of dead elephants and rhinos with hacked-off horns?

Here Gideon's tent was pitched in a sanctuary far more magnificent than any man-made cathedral. Here he could commune with any conventional god far more effectively than sitting on some hard wooden pew, listening to some old fart drone on about how God gave mankind the world and its blessings. On a day like this, he could set aside his frustrations at those who poached from the tithing bowl of nature's cathedral. As the dawn light filtered through the leaves, his attention was drawn to the hum of thousands of bush bees gathering nectar from the composite flowers of the tree above his tent: the mating music of flowers, a natural porn show. The bees didn't care.

By midmorning outside the tent it was hot, and hotter inside. He furled up the window flaps to let in a breeze flowing across the dambo as it tickled the leaves gently, making them giggle lightly in response. By late afternoon, Dimas had yet to appear.

Procrastinating, Gideon finally showered and shaved, getting ready to join Bright for a sundowner drink. In the background came the rumble of distant thunder. As a precaution, he unfurled and secured the window covers in case it rained. Walking between his camp and the lodge, spits of rain began to dimple the dust. Despite ominous distant thunder, he judged that a storm wasn't imminent. However to prove him wrong, the heavens rapidly darkened the bushland stage, signalling that a show was about to begin. Halfway down the road, the clouds were coalescing overhead, turning day to dusk.

Crash! The skies split with a flash so intense that it could only have escaped from Zeus's toolbox. A massive, juddering strobe lit the darkness overhead, freezing the candelabra branches of the euphorbia trees like Satan's pitchfork on the retina of his eyes. The deafening clap of thunder which blew away those images arrived a split second later.

Gideon dashed from the road, away from the tree line. It is dangerous to be close to trees with lightning about. His sandals had thick rubber soles, but they would be useless in a close strike. From the center of the open *dambo* he saw the southeast sky flooded with a roiling wave of angry purple, oozing danger.

The setting sun lingered, highlighting wispy front-running clouds painted in shades of light lavender; the purple wall behind flickered with bolts of hell rippling across its surface like the licks of a serpent's tongue. The rumbles of thunder overwhelmed the swish of his feet through the thick grass of the dambo.

Gideon made it to the *chitenge* before the rain arrived. From its deck, cantilevered over the riverbank, he had a great view of the show. Like the roar of traffic from a highway, rain came rushing from across the river. The trees on the opposite bank danced and lashed about like possessed dervishes.

Then, with a panting growl, it arrived: the blasting, flapping, tumbling body of wind and water. Trees everywhere bent against the pillaging pump and thrust of the wind's roar, thrashing their boughs, shuddering off leaves, resisting and succumbing. A crash came from the vehicle sheds: something big was pushed over.

The heavens gushed. Sheets of rain lashed the trees, ran under the thatched roof of the chitenge, and splashed against the furniture. One of the staff came running across from the kitchen. Gideon helped him drag the padded chairs further back under the roof, out of the rain's reach as water poured from the roof, flooding across the lawn. The rain and the wind went on for half an hour until, with a sigh of submission, the storm's force and fury was spent, replaced by the soothing brush of a warm drizzle. The summer wet season had arrived, heralded by the power of a big, bruising African thunderstorm.

Then there it was again: the unexpected: from a gap in the fence, instead of Bright coming to join him for a belated sundowner, it was Precious who ran across the lawn through the soft drizzle. Her wet clothes clung to her figure, showing her femininity as well as indicating that she had come all the way from the staff quarters, not from the kitchen.

This time she showed no air of supplication. She strode up to him. Gideon saw that she had caught the flick of his stare at her taut, dimpled reaction to the rain. Looking at him coldly, she tugged her wet shirt away from her shape, lifting it from the fullness of her chest, signalling her disapproval.

"Bwana, we need to speak again." With an edge to her voice she added, "The Crocodile man was here last night. He talked with some of the staff."

"Can we meet tomorrow morning?" Gideon replied. "Bright will be here in a few minutes."

"No, Bwana. I want to speak to you privately. I will come to your camp this evening."

She turned to walk away, skipping to avoid the puddles which were now flooding the pathway.

* * *

Gideon wasn't sure if his first reaction was a gasp of surprise, or a quiet whistle of wonder. The cut was conventional. Sleeveless frugality together with the austerity of its square neckline freed his eyes to drift over the sumptuous pattern of the fabric. From there, they could revel in the exhilaration of the slide over the fit on her figure as it reached down to a modest termination. It was all about color and pattern. Its subtle simplicity avoided conservatism with a hem a hand above the knees.

"Wow! That is a stunning dress."

The intricate intertwining of the underlying pattern of orange-gold and yellow was overlain with dominating splashes of windowed rectangles and eye-like circles. The starkness of these black and white dashes was ameliorated with an occasional substitution of turquoise grey. The dress could have been picked directly from the wardrobe of Adele Bloch-Bauer after she had modelled for Klimt.

The smooth, ebony slenderness of one arm demurely crossed over her midriff as she cupped the elbow of the other where it in turn dropped like a shadow at her side. Maybe the visual shock of these colors appearing out of the night would have been less impactful had it been a Paris cat-walk highlighting Lagerfeld creations rather than his remote campsite.

"Thank you," she murmured quietly. "I wanted you to see it." Her words were accompanied by a mock curtsy with a toss of her head, hinting at an air of indifference to any compliment.

"Where did you get it?"

"I made it."

Recovering from his surprise, Gideon pulled another camp chair closer to the halo of the fire, indicating for her to be seated.

"Where did you get the fabric?"

"In Lusaka, at Manda Hill."

"Do you go there often?" His question was rhetorical. The women who worked at the lodge didn't earn enough to afford frequent travel to the far away city.

"I don't go enough!" There was bitterness in her voice. He changed the subject.

"So how is Eddie?"

Leaning back in the camp chair, he stretched his legs. He felt self-conscious of his attire. Even though there had been an evening cooling in the aftermath of the downpour, it was still sufficiently comfortable to sit outside in his drab khaki shirt and shorts. Was it the contrast in their clothing, or something else?

Like a pond ruffled by a breeze, he was uneasy.

Gideon reminded himself that she was an employee at the lodge, and much younger than himself. Although he wasn't part of the lodge staff and hence needn't concern himself with maintaining a formal distance, he was still associated closely enough for it to be murky territory if he made assumptions as to her motives in showing up dressed in this way. She had been a butterfly with its wings closed, blending with the bush. Now, in the blink of an eye, she had opened her wings to reveal the brilliance of hidden colors, along with a possibility to fly higher than he'd imagined.

Was she dressed this way for him?

There was also the surprise of the brazenness in how she had earlier ordered him to meet. Maybe there was a crack in his armor; maybe she'd detected it when he let his gaze drift for too long over the wet cling of her uniform. Staring at the flicker of the fire's flames, he felt that almost-forgotten sixth sense one learns to sense when walking onto the killing ground of an ambush.

There's nothing on which to place a validating finger, just a feeling that someone else has the advantage. To survive, sounds need to be listened to more carefully, eyes opened wider, glances cast quicker, footsteps more cautious; there comes a need to move away from the obvious, to hug the margins. But what the heck! What could go wrong, he would follow her lead. The sparkle of her figure was spectacularly augmented by her attire. He ignored the tickles of caution at the back of his mind. As it had done so often before, his ego reasserted itself. Yes, she was younger, but not youthful. Despite his age, the bush life had kept him fit and trim, so why not assume the obvious? Why else would she come to his campsite three hours after sunset when the rest of the lodge had shut down. Why would she endure a distant walk in the darkness? Why else would she dress so sumptuously?

Precious sat without moving, seemingly mesmerised by the flames. The rhythmic, monotonous peep of a fruit bat came from the foliage of the water trees behind them.

David Maritz

He asked again, "How is Eddie? Have you heard from him?" Staring at the flames, she slowly straightened, then crossed her legs, one over the other, her arms folded tightly across her chest.

"They say he will be fine." The gold of her dress reflected the warmth of the flames, its yellow bright in the light from the propane lamp as it hissed quietly on the table beside them. The lamp's light stretched the umbra of her shadow like a faint stain over the pale sand.

He relaxed, enjoying the strangeness of her company. Sophia could wait. Claudia could wait. Moses, Bright, Kings could wait. The whole goddamn world could wait. Caution be damned! Why not walk brazenly into the center of her wide-open whatever?

"Can I offer you something to drink? I have some mango juice, or cola. Do you drink alcohol?" he asked. "I keep some gin and tonic for special guests." Without answering, she rose and stretched, catlike. Picking up the kettle from the table she placed it between the logs of the fire.

"Do you have tea? Tanganda? Rooibos?"

Without waiting for a reply, she turned to face him from the opposite side of the fire, looking down on where he sat with fingers furled on his lap.

"Bwana," she stated firmly. "Look at me! Why do you think I am standing here dressed like this? Do you think it is to entice you?" He stared at her in silence. He had been led into her virtual openness for a reason: the dress was a ruse.

"I wear this to show you that I am different. I see you looking at me. I see how you speak to me. Yes, you are a *mzungu*, but you have spent your life here. Many of your friends are African. You have their attitudes because I am a woman. You take me to be weaker, less capable, inferior." She moved back to the table, placing two tea bags in two mugs.

"I watch you watching me. You know I am looking for something else, yet you still look at me in that way. I see how you ignore the obvious. You don't see that I am different, that I want more than what you can give." She stepped back toward the fire, extending a long shapely leg. With the toe of her sandal, she pushed a log closer to the hiss of the kettle. "Do you think just anyone can produce a dress like this out here?"

When caught in an ambush, if alive after the first shocking seconds, the only way to survive is to surprise the surpriser: to attack back, hoping to win the firefight rather than running away, getting taken down from behind.

She had caught him out in the open mentally. Before he could respond, she sprang another surprise. All he could do was let her pick him off at her convenience.

"I also ask you: are you lazy? Are you scared? Why have you not responded to what I told you? Why have you not acted quickly?

"Bwana, I have told you that the Crocodile has powerful *muti*. He makes it himself. It is attracting attention from distant places. That is why the Hyena is here. He flies when the moon is full. You are a *mzungu* who understands these matters of *muti*. You know where the most powerful *muti* comes from.

"Bwana, you are here to stop the poaching. In the villages we know of poachers who have got rich on the sale of elephant tusks to the Chinese. Our elders tell of those who got even richer selling rhinoceros horn when there were still rhinoceros in the park."

Using a hand towel, she grasped the hot handle of the kettle. Lifting it from the fire, she poured the water into the cups, then added sugar with a teaspoon of milk powder.

"But it is not only the poaching of animals that has to be stopped." Precious spoke slowly, as if explaining to a child.

"Today in Africa there are people with money who want more than bits of tusk and horn. The word in the village is that the Hyena also wants the medicine made from human parts, especially that made from the parts of the *mwaabi*: the albinos." She sat back down on the chair and looked across at him.

"You got in the way of that Crocodile's plans with Eddie, but they say the Crocodile is still hungry. He was back here last night. You need to remember that you have white skin, so be careful that the Crocodile does not mistake your whiteness for that of a *mwaabi*." She leaned back to sip her tea as she allowed her words to gain traction. "Do you think that I want to spend the rest of my life married to Eddie, to be forced to live in the village?" she snorted, contemptuous. "My skills are lost here. This place is just a stepping stone to the big world.

"Now, when I warn you, don't be lazy. If you don't find him, the Crocodile may find you when you least expect it. I need you around, alive and well. I want your help to keep this lodge open so that I can find some way to get myself out of this old part of the world."

Gideon sat staring at her, digesting her words.

"So you see, Bwana, we can help each other, but you will need to show me more respect."

He looked across the fire with newfound admiration.

"Please stop calling me Bwana," he said quietly. "Call me Gideon, or Gidi for short."

10

November 15

Gideon concluded that somewhere deep inside the core of his adult soul there must be a child lurking, peeping out with a sense of wonder. Since that child never aged, it lost track of the gap between its yesterdays and his today, but because only fools and children speak the truth, it took other's youthfulness to make the fool within himself aware of the magnitude of that daily tally.

If all he saw of himself was a few minutes in front of a morning mirror, how could he be blamed for ignoring the progress of his decay? It was that disparity which Precious had used to wipe the fog from the mirror of his mind.

"You are too old for me."

Her truth had touched a sore spot. The weaving woof of a woman threading the warp of his own. She was also right about his old attitudes. Despite his relatively liberal upbringing, he found it hard to readjust a woman's position on the totem pole of life. He bridled at imperatives, especially if given by a woman younger than himself. However he wasn't so foolish as to let his old attitudes blind him to the young reality.

David Maritz

Her imperatives were not from cheekiness: they were from annoyance at his slowness to recognize that under her deliberately passive guise was a new, driven spirit of Africa. She was telling him that circumstances would have them sharing a boat, not a bed. They would have to equally pull on the oars if they were to get where they wanted.

Should he look longer into the mirror, to check if his wrinkled efforts were up to the task? If he was too old for her, maybe he was too old to be out here with its challenges. He loved the bush, but it could never love him back. The old adage surfaced in his mind: Never love anything that doesn't love you back. Neither she nor this bush would ever do that.

Ah, fuck it, he thought. Where's Moses when he's needed?

Walking across the *dambo*, the long tongues of grass sodden from the previous evening's downpour, licked moisture onto his legs. From there, the droplets trickled over his ankles into the tops of his leather shoes. Without socks, he could feel the moist squishiness between his toes.

The mix of water and warmth would soon transform the dry, somber winter hues into the bursting, iridescent vitality of the hot wet rainy season. Feeling the dampness of this long grass caress his bare legs, his preoccupation with the enigma of this determined woman faded as he crossed behind the chalets and continued as far as the office. He was looking for Bright and a cup of coffee.

Approaching the lodge along the road where it led past the administration area, he couldn't see anybody, although there was sounds of activity from the kitchen.

"Hey," a woman's voice called out. Precious craned her head over the sill of the kitchen's high side window. "I want to show you something." Stepping out of the doorway she said, "It's over there, behind you."

With Gideon following in her wake, she led the way to the vehicle shed. At its far end, she pointed to the corner post where the old Crocodile man had been leaning when he first appeared.

"I don't see anything," he said.

She stepped closer to the post, pointing to an object hanging from the stub of a knot in its wood. On a thin strip of leather were threaded some vertebrae and a shrivelled, furry foot.

"A jackal's paw," she said. "A jackal's spirit is watching us."

Gideon stepped across to remove the thong with its bones, then he searched the ground. It didn't take long to find boot prints clearly preserved in the soft sand under the tin roof. Staring at the imprints, a dead man stepped over his soul.

During the war when tracking, they needed to know who the players were and how to recognize them. The boots supplied to the insurgents by the Russians in the war across the Zambezi river had unique X-shaped studs on the soles of their boots. These footprints came from such a boot. They were fresh.

"How did you find the thong?" Gideon asked Precious.

"I didn't. Kings did. He told me about it."

"Kings?" Gideon asked sharply. "What was he doing here to find it?"

"I didn't ask him."

"Anything else to show me?"

David Maritz

"No," she said. "It is your turn to find something to show me. The Crocodile is dragging his tail for you to follow. Let's see if you can. Or would you prefer something easier?" Her sarcasm was obvious.

Little bitch, he thought. They walked back to the kitchen in silence. Gideon continued on without acknowledging her taunt.

"I know you can do it," she said as they parted.

Gideon tried to blow the virtual dust off these X-shaped prints discarded in his memory for so long. Staring at them, his mental skitterings had stumbled over possible explanations, none satisfactory as to why this particular old *nganga* should be so uniquely interested in this location.

This muddle was messing with his mind. For years it had been straightforward, working in his beloved bushland with just enough visits to the city and an accommodating, easy-to-satisfy landlady to keep him from howling at the moon.

Anyway, he thought, at least I can depend on the ritual of coffee. Bright would be sitting out on the deck overlooking the river having his usual morning beverage. Without guests in camp, Gideon could join him.

Getting nowhere with the muddle, his introspective mood took him the long way around. He wanted to think before he met Bright. From the sheds, he moved between the haphazardly parked game-viewing Cruisers, the tractor, various structures, with assorted equipment needed to run a self-sufficient lodge in a remote part of Africa.

From there he circled behind the big anthill with giant trees shading the laundry and kitchen block. He was in no hurry. The coffee could wait. If he let a mental hound cast about a tad more, maybe he would flush a clue from the thickets of his memory.

A swish from a branch high above his head disturbed his ramblings, followed by the chatter of a vervet monkey from the crown of the biggest tree, which was growing in one of the herbaceous islands which flared up between the chalets. The monkey's chit was a 'watch-out' notice to the others. Perhaps one of them recognized Gideon as that nasty guy with the slingshot. The monkeys had moved their nocturnal roosting spot from the trees above his campsite to the kitchen copse. Gideon wished the rest of his problems could be solved as easily with a slingshot. These dash-snatch-and-grab thieves had learned the hard way that his carefully carved slingshot was not just a work of art. He gave the finger to the small primates watching from their lofty perches.

"Little buggers," he muttered to himself. He wished he had brought his slingshot, so he could then take out his frustrations on the hapless primates.

"But that's not reality," he muttered before he called out louder: "*Mwabuka byepi*" (good morning) to Bright, who sat out on the chitenge deck with his legs extended, his ankles resting on the guard rail, with a cup of coffee in hand, watching and listening to the raucous snorts of the pod of hippos in the river.

Crossing to the small table at the back of the *chitenge*, Gideon made himself a strong cup of coffee. Bright turned his head to look at Gideon, returning his greeting before asking, "How was your trip?"

Pulling up a chair next to his, Gideon joined Bright in the morning ritual. As they chatted about Gideon's trip, they both noticed Precious approaching. Stopping a few meters away, she gave a curtsy in African style: one foot slightly to the rear; more a bob than a curtsy. At the same time her hands, held as if praying, were clapped softly and slowly together, signalling a request to speak.

Was this the woman who only the previous evening told Gideon that he had to show her more respect? What an actor she could be! Playing every part as appropriate. Where was she going with this? Bright nodded an acknowledgment.

"What is it?" he asked.

"Dimas has left a message for Bwana Gideon to say that he is at the scout camp." With that she bobbed her head and turned to walk away.

"An unusual woman," Gideon commented as they watched her go. "I don't know her as well as you, but, from our few interactions, she is full of contradictions." Bright rocked back in his wooden chair. He lifted one leg, resting its shank on the knee of the other.

"Gidi, around here people advise to do as she instructs because it is not wise to mess with the spirit of Mushala." He looked seriously at Gideon as his voice lost its flippant tone. "Do you know anything about Adamson Mushala?"

"Of course I do," Gideon retorted with surprise. "Anyone who spends much time here soon gets to hear about Mushala, the rebel Robin Hood purported to have had magical powers, who terrorised whole swathes of the country, acting against officialdom and helping the poor, after being shunned by government in the years following independence.

"When I first came here, I was shown around by Kings. Back then he was friendly to me. As I was cooking one evening, he happened past. I invited him to eat with me. He told me how Mushala was finally killed, betrayed by one of his mistresses. She revealed his hideout to the soldiers, who were given strong *muti*, making them invisible." Bright nodded.

"Yes, but that isn't the end of the story." Looking down at his empty cup, he tossed its dregs over the railing. "The people believe that Mushala's ghost still wields power. It is said that after his death, Mushala's ghost tormented President Kaunda, who'd ordered his killing.

"To play tricks on him, he'd swap the knives and forks to set a place for himself at state dinners, because he was left handed." Bright reached into a pocket, taking out a small knife. Unfolding its blade, he cut a loose thread from the hem of his pants.

"Gidi, do you know anything about Precious's background? I know she talks to you. Did she tell you about herself?"

"No." Gideon retorted.

So much for Precious keeping meetings with him a secret; it was hard to keep secrets in Africa.

"Well," said Bright, "she had a strong-willed mother who didn't care about taking risks, who went against the advice of her parents from her earliest years." Bright dropped his voice. "Precious's mother was a teenager when she ran away from home. She was being pressured to marry a man chosen for her. A large lobola payment was on the table. So she ran away. Her parents and relatives could do nothing about it, because they were scared to get involved. She went away to be with her lover. She was Mushala's favorite mistress, and no one messed with Mushala." Bright paused.

"So you see, Precious is Mushala's daughter. She has everything of the wild independent spirit of her parents. It's all rolled up and mixed into her single personality. Gidi, it is said that she has her father's magical powers, which is why even the local *ngangas* avoid her. They believe she is bad news when messed with." Bright looked at him pointedly.

"I don't know what she is up to, but you may find it best to listen to what she says."

Staring at the river flowing past, Gideon also wondered at the game Precious was playing.

David Maritz

11

November 16

Here the night is never quiet, not even when the moon is at its darkest new phase. Crickets, frogs, hyenas, owls, night-apes... all open their scores to sing in the darkness. Of course, additionally there is the summer flood's powerful murmur, and the river's trickle during the winter's ebb. It is only on rare occasions when there is nothing but the sound of the river that hackles rise to indicate danger.

It had rained earlier. It hadn't been heavy. Each time Gideon woke from a fitful sleep, a grainy rattle sounded on the canvas of his tent as droplets were shaken loose from the leaves of the trees by the thunderhead's parting sighs. It didn't take long after the storm pushed to the southwest for the bush sounds to pick up where they'd left off. First came the peeps of tree frogs, then the creak of crickets, and finally the calls of some of the night birds. The rains heralded the end of the tourist season. Gideon deemed it unlikely there would be further visitors at the campsite. He had moved his tent close to the front of the small *chitenge* for convenient access. He lay motionless on his camp bed, listening to the night sounds, mulling over the reason for Bright avoiding the subject of the Crocodile man when Gideon had casually mentioned it the previous evening.

He felt a tightening of the skin at the back of his neck. His subconscious, awake and alert, was the first to notice something amiss. Outside–it had been quiet for too long. The rustle of the river emphasized the silence.

Abruptly, Gideon's thoughts were disturbed by a surreptitious sound. Something had bumped into one of the heavy mukwa wood dining chairs in the chitenge. There was the scrape of its legs on the concrete floor. With adrenaline surging–triggering a taut, searing alertness; with his mind and muscles poised to burst into fight or flight–he strained to detect nuances of the night's sound. The genes of those who had fought when they should have fled, or vice versa, hadn't trickled down to him. But it didn't matter. Wrapped in his sleeping bag and enclosed within the tent, he could neither fight nor flee.

Barely breathing, it didn't take more than a few seconds for the adrenaline to abate, and with it came the return to rational thought.

Something was moving around on the floor of the chitenge. What could make a chair scrape? It had to be larger than a jackal. What animal would venture under the roof of a structure? Not a baboon. They stole during daylight. In the darkness, they would be sleeping at the tops of the biggest trees, out of reach of prowling leopards. Lions? Chamufumbu had passed by two nights ago. On a few occasions, Gideon had found their tracks circling his tent in the morning. But they had never ventured under the roof of a structure. Hyenas? So far, none had frequented the camp while he had been there, as far as he knew. Slowly, quietly, he turned on his side and reached down to pick up his sheathed bush knife from the floor. Equally slowly, he slid his legs from the sleeping bag. Sitting motionless on the bed, still in a state of heightened alertness, he listened for other noises.

Dawn would soon be breaking. If there was a lion outside, it would be best to remain hidden in the tent, with the ability to react if necessary.

Gideon waited. And waited.

A half hour later, the first tentative ha ha ha cry of a pair of hadeda ibis was joined by the yelping call of a fish eagle, sounding the dawn. Waiting until it was light enough to see, sure enough, it didn't take long to find what had moved the chair. Boot prints circled his tent, twice. From there, they headed a few yards towards the chitenge. From the continuity of the prints, he could see they hadn't stepped up onto the concrete floor. The emphatic dig of the toe and heel marks showed the prowler had stood for a while, looking at his tent. From there, the prints led around the side of the structure before they headed in the direction of the upstream *dambo*.

A tingle prickled the skin of his arms. The prints were those of cross-stud boots.

The chair had not been bumped. It had been moved, purposefully, to taunt him.

As Gideon examined the tracks, the shivering echoes of almost-forgotten pleasures tickled at his mind, giving him virtual goosebumps. It was like a recovered alcoholic finding himself in the middle of a desert with nothing to drink except a bottle of whisky.

Waves of excitement and trepidation were being triggered by the anticipation of hunting the most dangerous of all creatures: a man. That old addiction thrill, wanting to be on every major operation of his unit. The exhilaration of facing extreme danger, and dodging it. Those who have never experienced such a sensation cannot comprehend the power of its motivation, the ecstasy of snatching life from the certainty of death. He could still hear its echoes like the voice of an old muezzin calling the faithful to prayer.

The best tracks to follow are fresh ones. A sense of urgency took hold. The sun was already climbing over the rim of the wide arena. The humidity warned of another tumultuous late afternoon. It would culminate in paroxysms of thunder. Nothing could wash away tracks as quickly as a big thunderstorm. He had only a few hours to decipher the taunting signs.

The hunt beckoned its euphoric finger at him.

"Okay, I'll shut you up for a while," he promised Precious in his mind. "I'll find something to show you."

* * *

Whoever had left the tracks made scant attempt to hide them. Their originator was deliberately picking the softest, barest, most blatant dirt to leave the sign. The message was as clear as a newspaper headline: "I own this place. I do as I please. Follow me, if you dare."

The taunting arrogance was both vexing and exciting; the throwing down of the gauntlet triggered a long-dormant stimulation of a primitive part of Gideon's brain. Like a wild dog before it joins the pack on a hunt, he had to suppress yelps of anticipation—made more powerful at the thought of bringing back a morsel to impress a beautiful bitch.

The tracks led towards the shower block. From there, they angled across a clay, grassless patch, and the twin tracts of the sandy dirt road to the lodge. The backtracking was easy. The originator had deviated to climb and stand on the top of a bush-covered anthill mound where big acacia trees spread their boughs across the road. The stranger had stood there for a short while, possibly looking across the expanse of the *dambo* before approaching Gideon's camp. From there, the backtracked trail led to the lodge through an opening in the fence shielding the logistics area, then across to the vehicle sheds, indicating someone had been standing, milling around in the same spot where Gideon had first seen the old mystery Croc man and the jackal paw. To Gideon's surprise, the tracks led to the cutaway ramp of the boat launch where Eddie had been grabbed. Why would anyone stand on the edge of the river in the darkness? Had the watcher met someone in a boat or a canoe?

Across the channel separating the lodge from a small island, a hippo snorted. From behind came the sound of voices with the occasional high-pitched, tumbling laugh of a woman. The staff had arrived to begin the day. Gideon was surprised at the earliness of the activity. Although eager to begin tracking, some preparation was necessary. If the track became difficult, it would be better to follow when the sun was higher, its light able to reach deeper into shady areas.

He had no idea how far the tracks would lead, thus it made sense to first get something to eat. He would drink as much as he could before setting off. It would be hot, so lots of water was a must. He might find himself away all day. Taking something light to eat for energy would be wise. Turning away from the river's edge, he walked up to the kitchen.

There was a comfortable, African untidiness about the logistic area of the lodge, stemming from an enhanced hoarding trait developed as a survival shield. One never knew when one might need to cannibalise something—a bolt or a nut—from some obsolete piece of equipment. As Gideon moved towards the kitchen, he cast around for some section of metal pipe that could be cut into an appropriate length. He didn't feel a sufficient sense of danger that would oblige him to borrow the lodge's rifle. On the other hand, a long, thin metal baton would certainly afford some stand-off offensive ability. Maybe his belt-harnessed machete would be enough if he came upon a belligerent adversary. He wasn't seeking confrontation, only more clarity as to the tracks movements. Where did the guy go to? Where had he come from?

Gideon wanted a cup of coffee. He reckoned by now one of the workers would have placed the old black metal kettle on the equally old and black propane burners in the kitchen. Entering its gloom, his attention was drawn to the kettle's hiss. The kettle itself matched the simple austerity of the place. Its surface was scuffed and dulled by the myriad scratches gathered like battle scars from being rattled around in the back of vehicles bumping over rough roads. Letting his eyes adjust to the gloom, Gideon thought it could be a metaphor for his life: both of them banged up and scratched, but still able to get fired up and hiss at the world. Glancing around, another surprise awaited. In addition to the cook and two serving girls, Precious and Bright were standing back in the deeper gloom of the pantry. They already had big tin mugs in their hands, trailing teabag tags. Like Gideon, they were waiting for the kettle to boil.

"*Mwabuka byepi,*" they greeted each other.

"Good morning, Bright," Gideon said. "What are you doing here so early? Is it because a pretty woman is making the tea?" he quipped.

A flicker of annoyance crossed Bright's round face. Gideon like to tease. He sensed that some of the lodge's men wouldn't have minded if the crocodile had dragged Eddie to his demise, giving them a shot at Precious's favors. She treated his jibe with the same aloof indifference she did all the others.

Bright scowled, but his glare passed when he lifted the boiling kettle from the burner to fill their cups. "I'm helping the cook to take stock, to check how low we are on perishables."

Reaching his hand into a large box on the counter he took out a rusk biscuit. Then dipping it in his tea, he continued. "I may need to send a vehicle to Mumbwa for fresh vegetables, or eggs. Maybe a few other things. We have a late booking."

After stirring her tea and taking a sip, Precious set her mug on the cutting table. She disappeared into the pantry, coming out with a two-liter water bottle and two sandwiches wrapped in wax paper, as well as a small paper bag held in her hand.

"You will need these."

Gideon was taken aback. How in the world did she know he was heading out? Like a pair of startled cats, the two other kitchen girls scuttled out the doorway. The cook moved quickly into the large storage room at the far end of the kitchen. He was joined by Bright, where they busily began taking stock. It was as if they preferred not to hear what Precious had to say. With a roll of her eyes, under her breath Precious explained like a teacher to a child.

"The *nganga* was here again last night. He spoke to Kings. I didn't see them, but I heard their voices. I guessed that at some stage he would come to check you out. To poke and prod you, testing, looking for what kind of muti you possess that thwarted Eddie's sacrifice. I came here early. I saw you following tracks. So I knew that you were responding, going to go after the nganga to find out about him before he discovers your weaknesses. Remember what I said about the *mwaabi*! They say the most powerful *muti* comes from those with white skins. The Crocodile could be sniffing if your sort of whiteness is as good for *muti* as those from *mwaabi*. So you will also need this."

She handed him the paper bag. As Precious walked back out the kitchen doorway into the sunlight, Gideon turned to see Bright come out the pantry and looked for his reaction. He was ducking out of the way, avoiding Gideon's questioning stare. With his back to him, Bright deliberately wiped the surface of the counter where sugar and coffee had spilled. Reaching into the paper bag, Gideon pulled out its contents: a long leather thong with small river-snail shells threaded along its length.

"Bright," he queried. "What do you make of this?"

Bright opened his mouth to speak, but instead gave a slight shrug of his shoulders while pursing his lips, indicating that he didn't know.

"Bright, something weird is going on. Now all I get is orders from Precious, and for some reason nobody wants to speak about it." He pointed his finger accusingly. "That includes you!"

Bright shrugged again before turning away to wipe the counter.

Gideon stared at the back of his head. "I asked you a few days ago about that old man who appeared out of nowhere. Something strange went on there. Something unusual involving Precious, but you avoid my questions."

Leaning with his back against the big cutting table in the center of the kitchen, with both hands stretched out sideways and holding its edge, Gideon waited for Bright to finish cleaning the spillage. As Bright crossed over to the sink to rinse the dish cloth, Gideon again spoke to the nape of his neck.

"Precious said she confronted that old man because she is betrothed to Eddie, but the way she behaves, it doesn't seem that she is interested in Eddie. Which is really weird."

Bright didn't look up.

"Both of us know that despite that obedient bullshit she pulls in front of you, she is made of much sterner stuff than the others around here. You hinted at it yourself when we last talked."

There was still no reaction from Bright.

"So what kind of fucking game is everyone playing around here, trying to suck me into something that I don't want to be involved in?" With growing exasperation, Gideon repeated himself. "There is something weird going on. Why is nobody willing to speak about any of this bullshit!?"

Slowly turning to face Gideon, Bright reluctantly spoke. "There are whispers. You know how it is in the bush. There is always the influence of the nganga. It is like baboons in the trees at night. When they sense a leopard is on the prowl, they all keep very still. They don't make a sound. They are afraid if they do, it will attract the leopard."

"Why are they scared to tell me this?" Gideon asked.

Bright raised his hand to silence him. "Everyone knows that there is a strange *nganga* on the move, a powerful *nganga*. No one is sure if he is here to do good or evil, but we know he is prowling around, looking for something. Everyone is nervous. If they react, it might attract the attention of the spirits. Bad things might happen to them." Folding his arms over his chest in a gesture bolstering his authority, Bright went on. "We know who the *ngangas* are in this district, all of them from Mumbwa to Kasempa, even beyond to Solwezi. But nobody knows who this one is. As you yourself saw when Eddie was attacked, he appears from nowhere, then disappears. Rumors are that he flies on the back of a hyena. They say only the most powerful *ngangas* have the skill to tame the hyenas, to feed them special potions that allow them to fly."

Listening to these explanations, Gideon wondered, as always, at how deeply entrenched witchcraft is in African culture. Even this efficient and effective manager of a high-end tourist operation was influenced by it to some degree.

Bright stared up at the thatch of the roof as he spoke, then cast a quick glance at Gideon with a wry pursing of his lips before raising his gaze again. "The people feel that *muti* has been spread by this strange *nganga*. When Eddie was caught, they could see that it was bad mischief. However, it was not clear if this was the price of the mischief or its appeasement. Everyone hoped, and believed that it would have ended there, with Eddie being sacrificed." Lowering his gaze, Bright stared at Gideon. "That is when things went wrong. They say." Bright continued to stare at Gideon. "That is why people are afraid. They don't want to speak to you because you interfered. You got in the way of the spell, as it was happening, despite the *nganga* arriving to claim his sacrifice, and telling you not to meddle. Now, like the baboons hiding in the thickest leaves at the very top of the trees, not moving and not making a sound, the people are watching to see what happens next. They are nervous. They don't want to get caught in the *nganga's* revenge. So far, nothing has happened. People are saying it is because you must have strong *muti* for protection. Very strong."

"You've got to be joking," Gideon exclaimed.

Bright shook his head. "No! Even though you are a *mzungu*, the people know you grew up in our culture. The stories they tell say you have survived where others have not. Even before this event with Eddie, there was some mystery whispered about you, about some *penga*, some madness. Now, after Eddie, there are more whispers about your power and *penga* madness. That is why people are nervous of speaking to you. They are afraid, not just of the *nganga* but of you as well. It is bad enough when baboons feel there is a stalking leopard below in the darkness. They freeze, but it is worse when there are two."

Bright's broad, round face held a look of steady intractability. Gideon recognized it: a look filled with a resigned acceptance of fate meted out by spirits bridging between the magical and the everyday.

"One more thing." Bright hesitated before speaking again. "It's not just me. The people have noticed that Precious has been talking to you. That worries them. They saw that she has the power to make the strange nganga back down. They know who her father was. As I told you, they talk that she has inherited some of his power. But, they ask, do the two of you have enough power to chase that nganga away permanently? How is it going to end? Will everyone have to pay?"

"Where the fuck is Moses when I need him?" Gideon muttered under his breath.

"What did you say?" Bright asked curtly.

"Nothing, just talking to myself." Gideon answered. "I was thinking about someone who can help me."

For the first time ever, Gideon found himself in this strange position. Instead of people clamming up and things being hidden from him because he was an *mzungu* outsider, it was precisely the other way around. His insight status prevented him from being privy to the background chatter. He felt honored. He meshed closely enough for them to overlook his pale, outsider skin, making him one of them. He was an actor on their stage, not sitting in the audience with witchcraft providing the script. So? Should he speak the lines as presented, take a more raucous role, risk being caught up in the plot as it threatened to spill off the stage? Gideon had no belief in their witchcraft, or did he? Everyone assumed that he did. Damn it. *Ngangas* and girls with snail shells. Maybe he should play along; show that he actually did possess strong muti. As an ex-army officer, he was familiar with the power of symbolism when it came to leadership and influencing others.

Gideon gently fingered the delicate spirals of threaded shells in his hand. Putting down his mug, he tied the ends together. As Bright and the cook watched, with the girls looking on from beyond the kitchen door, he dropped the strand over his head. Retrieving his mug, he walked into the early morning light.

Precious was nowhere to be seen. The cook came out of the storeroom and began to fuss around the kitchen again. Looking across at the big, brick bread and pizza oven, with the office and the river behind it, Gideon noticed the two girls returning to the kitchen.

Hmm, Gideon thought. The stalker has gone, and the creatures can move again.

12

November 16

It is spellbinding to watch a pointer in flowing stretches coursing the fields, searching for the invisible ether of a scent borne on the breeze. Suddenly, with sharp abruptness, the dog's bounds jerk to a halt. It transforms; tail raised, foot cocked, nose extended, pointing with all the quivering directional tension of a drawn bow. If the nose of a pointer is spellbinding, the mind of a master tracker is magical; the only manner to describe the mix of art and alchemy of its intricacy. Unlike a scent in the nose of a dog, or smoke in the eye of an observer, it is in the mind of a master tracker that the magic is made.

A track's thread must be mentally pieced together, synthesized from a myriad of details, changing every second as the eye of the tracker moves, reaping and gathering a plethora of information, registering how the bush is, comparing it to how it should be, noticing a depression here, a bent stem of grass further on, a broken twig, a plucked berry, the darker color of a fallen leaf, the distant alarm call of a bird. The basics can be taught, but there are rare individuals who from birth are given the keys to a knowledge locked away from mere mortals. They can sniff out the signs in an odorless landscape.

David Maritz

"Where the hell is Moses?" Gideon mouthed the words to himself as he set off.

Moses was one of those magicians. An absolute asset when on the hunt for men. His uncanny way of knowing when they were close, contact imminent. It gave a huge edge. Having walked behind him many times, watching him point to this clue or that, Gideon was confident that his own basic proficiency would allow him to follow the footprints of the mystery man, but he surely missed Moses now.

The open, treeless expanse of the Shalamakanga *dambo* stretched lazily southwards until its spongy soil dribbled its rain stores into the Kafue River. A bird in the sky would see how the dambo stretched into four long sluices, each curving west like the open reach of an eagle's talons. One claw hooked at the artery of the main road, making it flinch westwards. It was as though the talons were attempting to grab at whatever scuttled past on the road.

So far so good! The ease of the tracking had allowed Gideon's mind, like his feet, to flip over the possibilities. Reaching the shank of the *dambo* where it widened into the pad spawning its tributaries, a mixed herd of puku and impala raised their heads sharply from their grazing in the open grassland. They looked on with some curiosity before scampering away. It was heartening to see how the numbers of these animals had increased from when they had been subjected to blatant poaching. This was reflected by their relatively tame and unconcerned behavior, tolerating vehicles and even humans on foot.

Lowering his gaze from the antelope, it took little effort to pick out the form of the boot prints, especially if Gideon walked on the verge of the twin tracts as they headed along the southern lip of the *dambo*. The thin shadow of their indentations were etched by the bright rays streaming in from the sun where it hung like a banzai flag in the eastern sky. The mystery man was simply following the lodge's secondary access path back to the main arterial. Gideon was breaking the first rule of bushcraft, heading a long way out into the bush alone was never a good idea when hunting an unfriendly quarry. He should have taken a buddy. Nasty stuff can happen quickly; one does not want to be alone without a helper in these situations. There was always the risk of snakebites and elephant charges, but nothing as dangerous as an unfriendly human. However, in the risk-reward balance, he needed to act fast if he wanted to get a jump on things, to take the initiative. He justified the risk by telling himself that his quest was not confrontational. He was seeking clues to the what, where and how.

The mysterious man's indirect taunts were bullshit; they angered him. Gideon didn't need Precious needling him to get himself fired up. He assumed the taunting was designed to test and scare him. The old *nganga* probably thought he would be an easy target. He surely didn't know details of Gideon's mercenary past, if any. Few people did. Obviously the old *nganga*–and Gideon assumed it was him that he was following– had knowledge of the lodge schedules and procedures. With no guests, he would know that there wouldn't be an armed game scout around to accompany guests on game walks, or to go with Gideon on hunts. It didn't matter anymore. Gideon was on the hunt anyway. Reaching up, he fingered the shells of the small leather strand around his neck. He pulled a face. What the hell. If it helped, so be it. In any case, he would be careful. The bush had not changed significantly for thousands of years. Out here he wasn't at the top of the food chain. He couldn't out-bite a lion or outrun an elephant; definitely he could not out-fight a younger, fitter man. Not without a better weapon.

Gideon walked quickly along the dirt strips of the road skirting the lower side of the *dambo*. Jutting out of the bush line was a small copse, at the center of which a dead tree thrust the fingers of its bare branches up like the wizened hand of a witch. Sitting, sunning themselves at the extremities of these spindly fingers, was a small flock of secretive green pigeons. In unison they took flight as he passed by. The beautiful birds flew back towards the river, the olive emerald of their wings flickering behind the brushed grey of their napes, the bright highlights of their yellow leggings showing even in the shadow of their disappearing tails. Protecting such riches of nature made the risk worthwhile.

* * *

The boot prints led unconcernedly, step-by-step, along the bumpy center of the twin-strip road. Initially it appeared that their lack of concealment was a deliberate flaunting. Now after following a good distance, the disregard for concealment still apparent, Gideon wasn't so sure. Was it simply that, or a haste to get to a rendezvous out at the main road? Gideon chuckled. Maybe a hyena waited to whisk the *nganga* away. Gideon wished he could believe in anything, even flying hyenas.

For Chrissakes! All that belief bullshit. The only time he had gotten close to believing in anything was his own mortality, when someone was shooting at him—and even then it was sporadic because of all the ducking and diving and shooting back.

He followed the sign at a fast walking pace. Great tracking is all about persistence with minimal pauses for rest. Only the best can follow like a dog on the scent. He wasn't one of them, so despite the clarity of the sign, occasionally he would lose it and need to scout around to relocate it. Thus, where possible, he walked a lot faster to catch up. It was exhausting; he would not be working in a relay of trackers (as they sometimes did back in the bush war) if the pursuit went on for a long time. There was the strain of the mental on top of the physical. It would be harder if the target didn't want to be followed, and was engaging in evasive tactics to hide his tracks. What was the *nganga's* game? Gideon sensed he would find out more once the tracks reached the main road. Would he be able to out-think his target? Moses said that was how to be the best. Get into their head. Know if they were to go around the right, instead of the left side of a thicket. Learn if they were more likely to choose thicker bush to move through. What idiosyncrasies did they have? The excitement pushed

Gideon along, urged him to get inside the mystery man's head; try to predict what he would do next.

Gideon walked fast, breaking into a jog when the ground hardened, making running easier. By the time the lodge's dirt-strip road and the prints he was following reached the main arterial, Gideon estimated he had gained almost half an hour. At the junction, his target had paused to mill around, as if looking back at his path. This gave Gideon another few minutes gain. From there, the *nganga* resumed steady progress north along the verge of the main road, walking at a regular pace. There was nothing hurried in his gait. Gideon could see the heel of the imprints was not accentuated, indicating a relaxed pace. Correspondingly, there was no deep toe print; no rock across the ball into the spring of a rapid step. The tracks hugged the road's softer verge, where it was spotted with tufts of grass. This made the sign easier to follow, suggesting its creator was loathe to be detected by passing vehicles. The tracks kept to the edge of the road, allowing the old man to quickly duck into the bush if a vehicle came by. Evidently this had happened here and there.

Gideon followed the occasional faint footprint in the patches of dust where it was undisturbed by traffic. The crushed and bent grass signed the direction. Following the footsteps wasn't difficult, but required concentration. He tracked the prints until they reached a disused quarry. Here the mystery man had stopped and waited, until he had been joined by others. Mixed in were three different sets of prints. These had more conventional print patterns than the nganga's boots. There was another surprise: one set of prints was significantly smaller than the others. A shoe had been taken off to clear an annoyance. Its lateral shoe print was deeper dug, indicating a side-to-side adjustment to keep balance on a one-legged wobble, obviously not successfully because, alongside, was the imprint of a bare foot where it had been briefly placed to keep from falling over.

The female foot generally has a greater bow between the heel and the ball. This was such a print, delicate and slender.

David Maritz

What the hell was the mystery man doing amongst this bunch, which included a woman? As he contemplated this quandary, without undoing the shoelace, Gideon tugged off one of his own leather veldskoen shoes to shake out the fine grit that had somehow slipped into it.

It took a while to figure out what had gone on in the quarry. New tracks led in from the north to meet in a confused jumble, as if the group had moved around during a discussion. Gideon was unsure how long they spent together. Half an hour? The female prints were concentrated in a patch. She hadn't moved much. The others milled around hers. Why was she hanging back while the men interacted? From there the spoor—mentally Gideon was using the old Cape Dutch term for track sign, led out towards the road where vehicle tracks cut in to the entrance of the quarry.

The biggest surprise was waiting. The *nganga's* tracks had halted a few meters from the vehicle, then crossed the quarry to head away from the road and into the bush. The others hadn't come to pick up the *nganga*. Whatever the case, Gideon figured he was now only two hours behind his mystery man. But why and where was the old sod now heading?

The tracks led off into the trees towards the east. They would be easy to follow through the longer grass, whose bend would be obvious to indicate direction. A short distance later, the signs led through thick vegetation before opening into the head of a large *dambo*. Gideon recognized it as the *dambo* which looped in a wide sweep across the top of the Shalamakanga until its breadth is squeezed by the bush line into a ribbon, where it seeps into the Kafue. Tracking progress became slower. The *dambo* grasses were shorter, coarser; their springy toughness more resistant to the snapping and crushing than the shade-etiolated grass beneath the trees.

Hugging the bush line, Gideon noticed that this section was a favorite resting place for puku, which were dotted across the grassy spread. The antelope had lain on patches of grass, compressing them, so that tracks hardly made any impression. Gideon had to carefully search from one flattened midden to the next. By now he had followed the tracks to a point in the dambo's sprawl where it curved southeast towards the river. The sun was angled steeply above the horizon, its warmth nudging the air into a breeze which tumbled across the dambos like kids running onto a playground.

The difficulty of following the tracks across the trampled middens left Gideon oblivious to his surroundings. A distant snap of a branch caught his attention. Stopping to listen, he heard nothing more; so he resumed scanning the grass and stubble, but with a heightened awareness for sounds. Then another cracking sound from a bigger branch breaking drifted in from the bush ahead. That sort of sound could only come from one source: elephants were up ahead.

The herds here were big. A single matriarch could lead up to fifty cows, calves and young bulls. They had learned that to survive the poachers' ambushes they needed the experience of the oldest and wisest of the cows. Gideon was acutely aware that the wind was carrying his scent towards the animals. He wasn't king of the castle out here; better get downwind from them as soon as possible. The young bulls and cows with calves were likely to be aggressive. They wouldn't distinguish his scent from that of any poacher. Both would be dealt with in the same unforgiving way.

The elephants were slowly working their way along the tree line, coming towards him as they fed, breaking off branches to chew on the leaves. The herd had obviously been to the river to drink. Now they were heading back inland. If Gideon ducked into the trees, he would still be upwind as they passed by. His best option would be to jog back, then cut across the dambo to the opposite tree line where he could safely wait for the herd to move past. If, that is, they kept to their overall direction.

Retracing his path, he crossed over the *dambo*. Keeping inside the opposite tree line, he waited until the herd and its last stragglers had moved on and upwind. He was about to cut back to the other side when, looking down at a sandy bare patch in the shade of the trees, he spotted a familiar boot print.

David Maritz

Gideon was elated! The detour around the herd had inadvertently taken him ahead to where his target had looped back. Picking up where he had left off, Gideon followed the fresh tracks, which headed over the shank of the *dambo*. From there, they headed back in a shallow loop towards the strip road near where he had started in the early morning. Reaching the road this time, they again headed to the main road. But now the tracks weren't keeping to the direct path of the ruts. They were occasionally meandering to the side, as if checking, or following something else. Where he had earlier deviated to look at the pigeons, the mystery man's tracks followed his own. It took a moment for the obvious to strike him.

He was being tracked. The hunter was being hunted!

There was a simplicity in the way the cross-pattern of prints pressed their faint mark deeper into the sandy outline of his. Standing transfixed, he scanned the imprints as his mind hurried over the implications. The big loop had been a setup, a way to get the better of him.

So what now? Had he been led into a trap?

His only advantage was that with the shortcut forced by the elephants, he was ahead of the game. His stalker wouldn't yet know that Gideon had discovered his deception. What was the stalker's intention? To lead him into his killing-ground?

Crouching to inspect the tracks, Gideon noticed the inverted shape of an ant lion's funnel in the sand: an ant had fallen into it. The ant lion, hiding under the grains at the bottom of its trap, began to flick sand. Soon the ant would suffocate under the grainy flicks.

Gideon broke off a stem of grass to help the ant, his empathy stemming from a sense that it wouldn't be long before he felt virtual flicks over his own head. There would be no saviour to drop a rope from the skies, allowing escape from the middle of the broad, grassy *dambo*. If he was to get out, it would be with his own resourcefulness: surprise the surpriser. In adversity or conflict, he had learned the hard way that the more aggressive adversaries usually win.

Something didn't add up. Was this real aggression he was facing? Or was someone messing with his mind? If it was an intended ambush, why had it not been sprung at the quarry, when there were two or more of them? Why had the *nganga* done a complete loop-a-loop which allowed Gideon to come upon the tracks, to let him know that he was being followed? Was this deliberate? It didn't make sense. Surely this couldn't be a deadly 'catch or be caught' drama. He and the *nganga* were no longer mario-nettes, dancing at the end of strings, manipulated by political ideologies blowing across Africa. If it was a mind game, now that he had got a jump on things, maybe he could switch and mess with his target's mind.

So what to do? Keep following the tracks to catch up from behind?

Gideon crouched and watched the ant clamber up the grass stem out of its tiny prison.

Should he double back and confront? Or wait in a stationary ambush?

Glancing across the road strips he noted how a thin stem of grass imper-ceptibly rose from where it had been pressed into a footprint, its torsion lifting it up from the moist stickiness of the soil. The print was less than half an hour old. The shortcut had gained Gideon an hour and a half. He would be more likely to surprise the *nganga* if he kept following hard, rather than doubling back.

He quickened his pace, moving briskly along the dusty ruts like a speed walker. With his mind floating, his eyes automatically picked up the sign of the prints. He had been lucky: gaining an hour and a half on a moving target isn't easy. The *nganga* must have proceeded down to the river and then back to the road line through the thick bush. The maker of the spoor hadn't counted on the elephants forcing Gideon to cut across his big loop. Now speed was of the essence.

A bateleur eagle rocked across the skies, its wings set in its characteristic dihedral. Vulture-like in its habits, it was a magnificent flyer, barely flapping its long, pointed wings in its direct flight. Gideon envied the bird's ability to cover the ground so rapidly, to see so far ahead. It certainly wasn't sweating, nor was it feeling the weight of a water bottle rubbing into the small of its back, bumping along in time to the cadence of rapid strides. Gideon stopped momentarily to watch the eagle cross the *dambo*, its wings rocking like the pole of an acrobat.

'Bateleur', another disappearing relic of an older, more romantic Africa. Now given a new name: a short-tailed eagle. What a fucking bland name! How LeValliant, the flamboyant Frenchman who bestowed the name, must be turning in his grave. All the bullshit political correctness eradicating ties to an old colonial past, even in the names of the birds.

"Whatever!" he said out loud. "Who really cares? So long as the eagles keep flying."

It took a few seconds to register what his eyes had already noticed. There was a third track in the dust, a vaguely familiar track, which he couldn't quite place.

With his mind now fully engaged on the signs, he backtracked a few meters to where the third set of tracks joined from the southwest. Gideon had a chance, if it was only himself and the mystery man. But two of them? No. This wasn't someone willing to simply mess with his mind. It would be foolish to find out what would happen if he caught up and confronted a pair with nefarious intentions. It wasn't worthwhile finding out.

Turning on his heels, Gideon cut into the bush to the south. At a fast pace he moved in the direction of the lodge.

It wasn't long before the heat and his thirst caught up. He was walking too fast. Despite the urgency, he stopped to avoid the risk of muscle cramps. Taking the water bottle from his backpack, he gulped down its contents while searching his memory for a match to the new boot print. At least the empty bottle wouldn't dig into his back when he ducked and dived under low branches, or around the outstretched clasping fingers of thorn trees. As he hoisted his pack, from nearby came the snap of a branch.

It couldn't be from elephants.

Someone was following, moving fast.

At a half jog, half run where he could, Gideon angled back to safety. Anxiously, he considered if he could make an adequate stand if anyone caught up. What if the follower was as young and fit as he had been when he'd chased men through the bush? At his age, he couldn't outrun a fit, young pursuer. His mind raced over what to do if he couldn't make it to the lodge before his pursuer caught up. Suddenly, he stopped running. Turning around, he slowly retraced his steps. Only one person wore boots with unique prints like those.

Missionary boots, they used to call them.

13

November 16

At the western rim of the sky, the sinking sun inexorably slid closer to its collision with the expanses of the Kalahari Desert, whose dust burnished its halo a richer gold. Even further away, the echo of the sun's distant quenching in the Atlantic hissed softly through the breeze-ruffled branches overhead. Night fell fast in the tropics. This sudden plunge into darkness often took the uninitiated by surprise. The branches feeding the fire at their feet spiked out like the spokes of an old wagon wheel. Slowly the glow receded as the stub embers dropped their ash. Occasionally a pocket of moisture, trapped in the semi-dry timber, snapped sharply when its steam burst a cloying cell, cascading sparks to where their sandal-clad feet stretched towards the warmth.

They'd been sitting together at the periphery of this glow for some time. There was no need to talk: all catching up was done. They sat, letting their thoughts drift. The fire's mesmerising magic molded their minds into a trance-like state, the erratic and repetitive flicker of the flames brushing away their contemplations, emptying their thoughts of logic and reason. All that remained were the gentler senses: the image of the flames dancing, the warmth on their shins, the softness of the air on their arms, the pressure of their bodies in the camp chairs, the sounds of the night. They were at one with a jackal yipping intermittently, excitedly, hysterically. The little dog was motivated by its emotions, not words.

Food? A bitch in heat? Gideon wondered. Lucky devil if it's the latter.

Gideon's thoughts were motivated by feelings rising from the depths of his subconscious: feelings, if examined, hinted of a satisfaction no less profound than that of the jackal's yips. After all, he now had an ally in his hunt for the Crocodile lurking in the people's minds.

He watched the fire's hub burn back, leaving a wider ring of ash. Taking turns, each man would stretch a leg to nudge a spoke back into the center of their shared combustion. They sat mesmerized, watching the flames lick resurgent, like the jackal's cries. There was no need for words: they had the yips of their reunited souls. Small licks of light pushed away the darkness enough to let Gideon make out Moses's features. His old platoon sergeant had aged better than he. The flames' warm hue reflected off his ebony skin, imparting it with a wrinkle-free smoothness. Any blemishes were removed by the shadows. His features, polished by firelight, revealed facial muscles tightened across his cheekbones, spreading down to flex with his lips, suggesting a toughness resisting the rigors of time, burnished into agelessness like the leather of a cavalry saddle. In a strange way, age had made Moses a more handsome man than the one Gideon remembered.

Gideon lowered his eyes back to the hypnotic flames, leaning forward as he spoke. "The last I heard he was up in Nigeria." Gideon drew his focus back from the fire's subtle grip. "I saw this in a post from one of our veterans."

Moses stretched his arms languidly above his head. Looking up lazily, he dovetailed his fingers with palms facing up at the swathe of the stars, which gave the impression of the full moon cradled in the basket of his hands. He flexed his body in relaxed contentment, embracing the unaccustomed stillness of his torso, sitting in this position since sunset. "Yes, he is there a lot. Eben is probably the most senior consultant to the authorities in their fight against the Islamists." Lowering his arms, he folded them across his chest. "I was part of his team. At least they got it right. They had the balls to hire the right type of advisory group. You know what they call us these days?"

It was a rhetorical question.

"We are no longer mercenaries. We are now PMCs: private military contractors. The Nigerians were clever enough not to use foreigners who had never fought on this continent, and who don't know how things operate here.

"Sheesh!" Gideon retorted with a slight hiss. "PMCs. All this political correctness bullshit." There was bitterness in his voice.

Moses went on. "We went into West Africa with two hundred men plus Nellis and his gunship. We sorted it out. Then the media gave the word 'mercenary' a bad rap, because the eighteen thousand UN guys who had done squat-all found themselves with peace but nothing to keep."

"Yes, I heard you were with that group. The lads said you folks did amazing work, including the head of the Brits who came in after you, but the lowlife politicians puffed up their chests when the danger was over."

"You and I and the others," Moses chuckled. "We may have been on the losing side of our Bush war, but that wasn't because we weren't good soldiers."

"Yup," Gideon said. "We had to be to beat the Russian Cuban cabal. Compared to them, you must've gone through those scumbags up there like a knife through butter."

"We did, but that was part of the problem." Moses pushed another branch onto the fire. "We were fighting bands of drugged thugs, many still children with machine guns, crazed with savagery, moving around mutilating anyone they found. It was on a scale that was hard to imagine. Sickening. We had to kill kids. The line between good and evil got blurred. I couldn't take it. Everything about it had mixed up morality. It was horrible."

Gideon listened as he sat quietly staring at the embers.

Moses was lost in his memories. "It was hard not to mete out punishment. Some did. That made it easy for the politicians to point their fingers at us. Some of those kids were only thirteen, as young as my son. How can you kill them? You have to. Kids with machetes and guns: high on drugs, hacking off hands, feet, ears, lips, for the fun of it, for some scumbag to get rich off diamonds." Moses voice trailed into silence.

"I thought about joining your gig." Gideon leaned forward to stir the ashes with a long stick. "Instead I got an offer from one of those ex-Rhodie SAS guys to help bodyguard a Lebanese head honcho: a cushy job, good conditions, good pay, surrounded by pretty Maronite girls – until someone blew the boss to bits with a car bomb. Luckily, it was my day off." Gideon chuckled.

A lion roared somewhere upriver.

"Eben is smart," Moses said. "I'm surprised he hadn't thought of this gimmick earlier. You have to admire the marketing gurus. They need mercenaries like Blackwater. So call them something else. Say they are in the PMC business. The voting mob won't figure it out."

"Yes," Gideon agreed quietly. "It sounds like they're talking about an elderly home-care gig, or something that happens to a woman later in life. The PC pussies would be too embarrassed to ask what it really stands for."

They chuckled.

"You still talk like a soldier," Moses commented.

The lion roared again. Somewhere downriver, a hippo snorted; strange it had not left the river to feed; maybe a cow with a newborn calf.

David Maritz

"By the way," Moses spoke from the hush of night, "whatever happened to Sophia?"

"Wow. You remember her?"

"Of course I do! You were smitten with her for as long as I can remember."

"It's a long story." Gideon folded his arms across his chest and leant back. "She asked me to never contact her again. I let her down too many times, she said. She'd found a reliable man, she told me. Then she disappeared; never answered phone calls, or letters, or the occasional email to see if I could get an echo out of her. Nothing! Just one big bugger all!" He drew in a deep breath. "That was a long time ago. But amazingly, a few days ago out of the blue, I got a text from her. Where she got my number, I don't know."

"Are you going to meet her?" Moses asked.

"I haven't answered her text yet." Gideon said. "Seeing as she made me wait twenty years, I can make her wait a few more days."

"Is she still important to you? If so, you should strike while her iron is hot."

"That's the point," Gideon said. "Whose iron is hottest? I'm seeing a woman in Lusaka. She's great. I love being with her. I rent a great space from her, and she has become part of the benefits. So why piss on a fire like that?" Gideon hesitated.

"But what?" Moses asked.

"You remember that feeling you get when walking into a good killing ground? You don't know what it is, just that something is telling you to watch out?"

"Yes," Moses said, "I remember it very well."

"I get that sense with Claudia, the girl in Lusaka. On the inside she is all sugar and honey. On the outside, she barely recognizes me. So I don't know. She is far more integrated into the fast-paced modern city life than I am. I just get this sense of unease. So I'm tempted to answer and make contact with Sophia. But would it be any different? It didn't work then, so why would it work now? Unless we have both changed. Which we probably have, if she's had anything like the sort of knocks I have in the last two decades. And you, old buddy, what about you?" he asked. "At the end of the war I remember you were married with a kid. What happened to them?"

Moses rubbed his chin. "You have a good memory." Moses said. "Like you and Sophia, that was a long time ago. My kids are nearly finishing school."

"And your wife?" Gideon asked. "What happened to her?"

Moses kept stroking his chin. "She died. Malaria."

"I'm sorry." Gideon said awkwardly.

"It's okay. It's been a long time."

Nothing more was said for a while.

Gideon leaned forward and pushed a stick into the fire. "Father Xavier mentioned something about you marrying somebody else."

"Yes." Moses answered slowly. "That is also a long story. I married her sister, in a traditional way. She and her family helped raise our children. They were Tongas. They were a large family, my foster family. They moved up out of the valley to north of Siabonga when Lake Kariba was built and flooded the valley. The clan was big; brothers, sisters, half-brothers, aunts, uncles. Tongas have more than one wife." Moses picked up a twig. Breaking pieces off, he threw them into the fire. "Growing up on the mission, my best friend was from there. Why he was at school in Lozi land is another story. I would spend holidays with him down on the edge of Kariba." Moses threw the stump of his twig into the fire. "His uncle taught me to track. On the edge of the lake, fetching water, is where I met the sisters. Later, I had good money. I could pay. I could support. So I married them both."

"Two wives!" Gideon exclaimed. "Hell, I couldn't even manage one. Not even girlfriends. Probably still can't. Heck, handling women for me has always been as complex as trying to figure out what to do in this messed up new world." Gideon looked at Moses carefully.

"Are you still married?" Gideon asked. It was Moses's turn to fold his arms over his chest as he tucked in his chin as if defending himself from a punch.

"Yes." Moses tucked his chin deeper. "But I haven't seen her or our children for a very long time."

"Why?" Gideon asked.

"The Tongas lived on both sides of the Zambezi before the British came with their colonies. The family on the south bank of the river fought them during the bush war. Their relatives on the north helped them. That war left deep feelings. When they found out I was fighting with the South African Buffalo Regiment, they kicked me out, even though I was fighting in Angola."

"Shit, that sucks." Gideon commiserated. "What a fuck up!"

"In Africa God gives with one hand and takes with the other," Moses said.

Gideon listened to the lingering sadness in Moses voice. He had touched a sore spot. "I'm sorry," he said.

"I was on my way back to see if they had forgiven me when I got your message. Father Xavier said to be a good man to many, be a good husband to your wives, and a good father to your children. Grow your heart to feed them all. It will be good enough for God."

"You are right." Gideon said. "But out here with all the tough skin, it's hard to dig through it to find anyone's fucking heart. The bad thing is that the women around here have the toughest, thickest skin of all. But now old buddy," Gideon changed the subject, " it is time to turn in. Tomorrow, I will take you upriver for a quick survey of the area. We can meet some neighbours involved in the anti-poaching gig."

Rising, moving towards their tents, Gideon said, "I will certainly need your help to do some tracking and chasing. Rest assured, we will be on moral high ground here, fighting for God's great green earth without any women in the way."

14

November 17

The ash of the previous night's fire lay in spiked, powdery shadows. From the tip of one wooden stub, a strand of translucent smoke rose as straight as the stem of a bulrush until its wispy resolve faltered. Its spirals mingled aimlessly as they disappeared into the smooth morning air. The gusts of late winter were long gone. There was little possibility that a puff would fan an errant ember across to the dambo's long grass, but taking no chances, Gideon pushed the stub into the sand, smothering it. With its blunt end, he stirred the ashes to dissipate any glows still lurking in the powder. Even in the dawn dimness it was evident that the rains had been absorbed into a blush of green vitality; winter's dusty dryness swept away by summer's flush. Overhead, the air was rippled by the braying calls and pulsing swish of wings as a gaggle of trumpeter hornbills spread out upriver from their roost in the dense riverbank trees.

Earlier, well before any hint of dawn, there had been the hiss of the gas cooker which gently pulled back the cloak of slumber while Gideon lay wrapped in its comfortable folds. Moses, as he had always done, roused first. Gideon lay listening to Moses's quiet steps as he filled the little pot of water before putting it on the gas ring. Then came the click of a spoon as ground coffee was ladled into the French press, followed by the clink of mugs on the table. Deep in the warmth of his sleeping bag, Gideon heard

Moses grunt an acknowledgment after he said, loud enough to be heard, "There's a box of rusks at the back of the *chitenge*. Top shelf." Moses hadn't forgotten how to make a good cup of coffee. That was one of the most important rituals in the bush – no matter when, where, or how.

Rousing, shoulders hunched, Gideon stood with his hands pushed deep into his pockets. The front that had herded the thunderstorms to the north had left cooler air behind like dust settling on a road. Cicadas would begin their shrill screeching as soon as the sun warmed the air. Already the sounds of birds were everywhere: a black-headed oriole, issuing a late courting call.

Gideon had introduced Moses to the lodge staff the day before. Now as they headed across to the complex, they exchanged the customary *'Mwabuka bulongo'* (wake well), with a few of the staff sweeping the pathways. Crossing the footbridge over a shallow gully bordering the *chitenge* lawn, they could hear women's voices coming from the kitchen. The draw of friendly chatter was augmented by the smell of cooking. It was enough to make Gideon glance at Moses.

With a nod, Gideon commented, "Smells like something that needs to be checked."

In the kitchen's gloom, they experienced a moment of shyness as three young kitchen maids working there adjusted to Moses's imposing presence. Their awkward reticence was soon dispelled by the smile and the warmth with which he greeted them in their native Kaunde language.

"Mwabuka byepi?" asking politely if they had woken refreshed.

With giggles, they responded saying that if they didn't want dogs sniffing around the kitchen this early, they shouldn't cook bacon.

Their sly scrutiny was evident in the way their gaze lingered when Moses wasn't looking. It affirmed Gideon's judgment that Moses was still a handsome man, having aged so benignly. Gideon's own pale skin hadn't stood up to the rigours of the African sunshine as well as Moses's brown leather; like papyrus, it didn't take long to wrinkle and crack when not shaded. It helped that Moses was younger by quite a few years.

Gideon couldn't quite identify it. Moses's allure had much to do with the broadness of his shoulders and friendliness of his smile, but there was also something exotic, hard to pinpoint: a slight Hamitic refinement of his features. These gifts were not lost on the girls.

Gideon wasn't averse to riding the coattails of Moses's popularity. Not only were the men presented coffee, but surprisingly each was given a sandwich of thickly cut fresh bread, liberally smeared with butter, embedded with slices of crispy bacon.

The group's conversation, with its spirit of flirtatious banter, was too fast for Gideon to follow, so he headed outside to finish his coffee and go over the mornings plan in his mind.

What better way to do this than to traverse the area by boat? Gideon would take Moses upriver to meet their neighbors, who also had a vested dog in their shared conservation hunt. Returning for more coffee, Gideon picked up his binoculars, then headed to the boats tethered in a haze lingering over the water. Glancing up, he saw Precious following him to the river's edge. She stood on the deck above as he loaded a boat. Tucking the oars out of the way against the gunwale, he added a small anchor. Placing the binoculars under the prow, he checked that there were life jackets plus two full water bottles.

"What's all the activity in the kitchen about?" he asked.

"Some unexpected guests will be arriving." Precious regarded him contemplatively. "We only were told about them last night. Bright left for the village to pick up an assistant chef and a few more casuals."

"When will they arrive?"

"In three days I think."

"How long will they be staying?"

She shrugged her shoulders. "You will have to ask Bright."

Flicking coffee dregs into the river, Gideon leaned over the gunwale to scoop and swirl his cup clean as he quietly acknowledged the river god. He was tempted to make the sign of the cross: saintly patience might be necessary, because two-stroke engines can be as temperamental as teenagers, and equally reluctant to rouse in the morning. It was best to get things stacked for a quick start, so the first kick of action happens before realization sets in, and a stubborn lack of response ensues.

Pumping the ball valve of the fuel line to clear air locks, Gideon pressed the engine primer. He cranked the throttle handle open and closed twice, a ritual that seemed to help. He set the throttle a tad post-idle. Taking a deep breath while bracing himself, he hauled on the starter chord.

Nothing.

Another lunging haul.

A third and a fourth followed.

With an amused look on her face, Precious leaned forward, elbows resting on the deck rail, her chin cupped in her hands, settling herself for some entertainment. To appease the river god, Gideon did make the cross sign while scowling his annoyance. He cranked the throttle again to give the carburettor a suck of air. Biting his lips with effort, he hauled back as hard and quickly as he could. He was losing his belief in the benevolence of whatever god he needed to appease.

One more time.

Hallelujah! With a cough, the engine ran for a brief second, only to die out in an erratic flutter, like the wings of a headless chicken. With invigorated zest, and to catch this wind of fortune, he quickly hauled on the chord. The engine caught again. It spluttered unevenly for a few moments, then grudgingly stuttered into life, shivering with a reassuring buzz as it heated up.

His trust in the river god briefly restored, Gideon looked at Precious. He gave her a thumbs up. She straightened. With a toss of her head, she disappeared across the deck toward the kitchen, disappointed at missing the entertainment of his godless cusses at uncooperative machinery.

Gideon's small boat, with its fifteen-horse motor, was tethered between a similar and a much bigger boat, both lodge owned.

Moses arrived and walked lightly down the steep bank to untie the tether from the exposed roots of one of the trees shading the deck.

"So they let you get away!" Gideon pulled a theatrically surprised face.

"Oh stop," Moses retorted. Stepping aboard, he held onto a root until Gideon nodded his readiness to move.

Flicking the engine into reverse, Gideon twisted the throttle. The propeller cut into the water, making the motor hesitate under its new load, sliding the boat backwards from under overhanging branches. The current caught the craft, pulling them further out until he gently gunned the motor while turning the engine to point the prow into the flow. A pair of white-crowned plovers stood clinking their alarm from atop an outcrop of rocks, the only feature to disturb the broad waters before they split to slide past an island opposite the lodge. Beyond the rocks and the plovers, a few hippos from the local pod popped their heads above the surface like curious children, exposing lumpy snouts and stubby ears, their eyes set midway between. The huge animals swivelled their heads like periscopes on submarine bodies as they followed the boat's progress. With chesty snorts of spray, one by one, they ducked under the water. This local pod was of little concern – unlike those on the Lunga, where the pressure of poaching was greater; hence the nervousness and aggression shown by those dangerous beasts. Turning his attention back to the river, Gideon opened the throttle further. As they left the hippos behind, the flat surface of the river was wrinkled by the drift of the current as it tightened behind them in anticipation of pushing past the island opposite the camp. With the recent rains, the river had risen, making navigation easier. Gideon wasn't as proficient at threading through channels as the lodge guides, but with deeper waters flowing well, he felt confident enough to raise the boat's prow over the broad hippo pool, which would lead him past the first upstream island.

From here there was a change in the character of the river. Islands stood in deeper, narrower, faster flowing water, the eddies and swirls indicating big boulders lurking beneath the surface. Between two such islands, Gideon pointed the boat through a gap into a faster-flowing channel. Cutting back the throttle, he let the boat drop off its plane. Caution was needed to look out for the big standing swirls hinting at underwater obstructions. He didn't need a propeller strike or a broken blade.

Moses pointed to the riverbank. Gideon slowed until the boat stood still in the current. They sat in silence, watching a bushbuck ram moving with mincing steps through the thick undergrowth at the water line. His flanks were flecked with white; his throat swatch contrasted strongly with his dark fur and even darker underbelly. The buck was crowned with a pair of tightly swirled horns.

"What a beautiful creature," Moses murmured to Gideon. "Created by God in heaven."

Briefly Gideon's soldier humor resurfaced.

"Is that the same God who made the croc that caught Eddie?" Gideon waited for a reaction. "To God's credit," Gideon went on, "he has made me this heaven, and I haven't yet been kicked out." Then he added, "The only improvement is if God upgraded me into a bonobo chimp, so I can swing around the trees eating figs and being pandered to by the ladies."

Rolling his eyes, Moses glanced back at him. "Gidi, God won't kick you out of the real heaven, at least not yet. With your silly sins, God likes to play with you." Moses chuckled. "Do you think His hand was not with the engine this morning? For some reason, He likes you. Which is surprising, because unless you have changed radically, and none of us do, you probably already behave like a bonobo, at least when it comes to ladies."

"Piss off," Gideon laughed back. "You are jealous!" Gideon tugged the engines tiller sharply to dodge around a stump sticking up in the flow. "What can I do to have Him stop sending old mystery men to mess with me?"

Moses threw up his hands in mock frustration. "Learn to pray for your soul."

The stern wiggled its way over the eddies like the sway of a belly dancer's hips. Beyond the channel was a broad, flat section of river distinguished only by a half-submerged outcropping at its center, which seemed out of place. It was adorned with the straggly litter of flotsam left behind by last summer's floods.

"We are going to meet a great conservationist who has shot more animals than anybody I know," Gideon called out to Moses.

The boat eased past an island into a wider stretch of water. With no rocks to stir its flatness, the unbroken reflection of the clouds marched away on the river's broad mirror. Gideon felt confident enough to gun the engine, lifting the boat into a plane. He licked his lips, and felt the rush of air cooling them in their speed.

Half an hour later, they nosed into a cove with a small concrete jetty. Beyond it, tucked under a grove of huge trees, was a bush camp: the headquarters of the Lunga-Lushwishi hunting concession. Edging the boat into the cove, Gideon spoke to Moses.

"This place is run by Alan and his son Roger. They have held the concession here for over a decade. By doing so, Alan has saved this huge area, which had been overrun by illegal settlers coming to fish and hunt. Contrary to what the bleeding hearts will tell you, hunters are probably the best conservationists. They preserve habitat so there are things for them to hunt."

Moses nodded. "Yes, you're probably right."

"All those bleeding hearts get bent out of shape whenever an animal is shot, but they think nothing when the concrete of a development is poured, killing everything there for the next thousand years or more."

"Gidi," Moses shouted back over the engine. "You should become a believer. You wouldn't get so bent out of shape. God created it all, and nature will bat last."

"I hope you're right." Gideon cut back the speed.

Moses raised his arm, pointing to the side. "The eagles are here to greet you."

A pair of handsome black and white raptors winged away from the trees. Catching a thermal, they swept into tight circles.

"African hawk eagles," Gideon said. "That's the third time I've seen them on this section of the river. They must be nesting somewhere in the area." They watched as the birds gained height. "As a falconer, I have always wanted to hunt guinea fowl with one of those eagles." He nodded his head in the direction of the big birds.

The raptors were soon out of sight and with a scant forward motion, the boat twisted sideways in the swirl of a back eddy. Reaching under the prow deck, Moses took hold of a mooring rope and stood up, waiting to throw it to a young woman walking across the lawn towards them.

"What is so special about Alan?" Moses asked.

"He's shot more animals than anyone I know, at least elephants: probably hundreds of them. In my humble opinion he is one of the greatest conservationists I have met."

Moses tilted his head with a questioning expression in one raised eyebrow.

"Alan once worked in the parks department in the old colonial regime. That's why he shot all the animals. He was responsible for culling rogues. But more importantly, as he rose higher in the ranks, his position let him push through legislation protecting many areas, which are now national parks. He's preserved more habitat than anyone else I know. Conservation is all about preserving habitat and environment."

Flicking the engine into reverse, Gideon tucked the stern of the boat against the jetty. Moses tossed the rope to the woman, who pulled the prow along the side of the dock, and held the gunwale as Moses tethered the boat to the mooring.

"*Mwabuka byepi*," he greeted the shy smile of the dockhand. "Are the bwanas here today?

She gave an "*Ehe*" of affirmation. They followed their helper across broad lawns to the older brick structures tucked into the shade of a copse of big trees. From there the lawn spread out, leading out of a gap in the scrubby undergrowth. To their right, beyond the lianas hanging from the trees, was a view of river rapids. the roiling sound of the water provided background to the duet call of a pair of bou bou shrikes. A paradise flycatcher with its long russet-red tail flashed past.

There was an air of tiredness in the color and tidiness of the camp. The obvious swept cleanliness of the surroundings could not hide the occasional split in the brick work at the base of a half wall. Further along a cracked concrete platform looked down onto a lower wooden deck above the river.

"This place has been here for a while. It's not as fancy as our lodge, but then most hunters aren't as picky, as long as they can bag what they have come for."

The dock tender asked them to wait while she informed Bwana that they'd arrived.

"*Twasanta*," Gideon said to her. Thank you. He was surprised by her impeccable English accent. It was oddly out of place.

As they waited, they took in the ambiance of the place. Underneath the low-hanging branches of the trees, a section of the riverside deck was visible. From its direction, above the rush of the rapids, they heard voices. Some of the discourse was loud and emphatic. They didn't wait long. An elderly man, tall and slim, appeared around the edge of the shrubbery. He was wearing khaki clothing which fitted him like a second skin. Its fabric was faded and well worn, but its tidiness, draped austerely over his wiry frame, gave him a regal air. His hair, though not the thick crop of youth, covered his head like a mop, his sideburns darkening before they merged into his beard.

Three things always stood out about Alan. First, the length of his big bushy beard, the color of which contrasted starkly against the silver of his hair; its tangled thickness unable to hide his seemingly permanent grin. Second, if his disarming grin couldn't command attention, his booming voice soon would. Gideon always thought Alan should have been an opera singer. Third, he was always barefoot; a trait for which he was locally famous.

Alan greeted Gideon warmly, who then introduced Moses.

David Maritz

"Moses is my sidekick. We go back a long way. He and I spent years on the wrong side of the *Chimurenga* in Angola." Gideon knew, given his history, that Alan would understand his reference to *Chimurenga*, the word for insurrection. "Moses is here to help me figure out about some witchcraft stuff in our area."

Alan had a vibrant, rich way of speaking: "There's talk about it here as well." He shook hands with Moses in the traditional African way; clasping hands on the down movement, then as the hands lift up, momentarily wrapping thumbs. "*Bwerani bwanji*," Alan addressed Moses in fluent Nyanja.

Moses's usual deadpan expression flickered with recognition. Here was a *mzungu* of a different ilk – one of those few who could speak an African dialect as faultlessly as a native. Gideon thought how this was the real new Africa – one without color or creed.

"Good to see that Gideon has someone to keep him out of mischief," Alan grinned at Moses. "What will you be doing?"

"Tracking. Trying to see if I can find out things for Gidi."

"Good luck," Alan joked, "I've found it hard enough keeping track of Gidi with his wanderlust, let alone those he gets involved with."

"Hey," Gideon exclaimed half-heartedly. "You'll give me a bad reputation."

"That was praise," Alan interjected. "I wish I had the energy and zest for life you've got. It seems chasing stuff keeps you young. Let's see if you can catch a man this time."

They all laughed.

"You are all jealous." Gideon said.

15

November 17

A raucous shout of laughter rolled up the slope from the river. Alan nodded his head in its direction.

"We have a real pair of 'dodgies' this time: a father-son combo."

Another set of loud guffaws buffeted the stillness.

"Not since I guided Escobar back in the eighties have I come across a pair like these two." Alan nodded again in the direction of the laughter. "Actually, Pablo was a breeze once you got used to the sidearms and bodyguards."

Gideon raised his eyebrows. "Really? You guided Escobar?"

"Yes. Compared to our current duo he was quite a gentleman. He flew in with his private jet; no passports needed. A bit further north from here, mind you, out of sight, out of mind you might say, and he paid very well: cash!"

Gideon chuckled. "So much for Interpol and all that law-and-order stuff."

Alan made a wry face. "What did I care about the morality of someone selling cocaine to stupid people? Money is not political or racist out here. When there's enough of it, it can buy anything. And if you are invited to these bad boys' table, it's best to accept the invitation, or else one may find oneself on the menu." Tilting his head towards the river, Alan indicated to follow. "Come. Let me introduce you to our pair."

Approaching the deck, they could see three figures. To one side was the customary serving table, covered with a cloth, sporting a vibrant African motif. Opposite were six comfortable camp chairs set in a half-circle facing the river. Three of the chairs were occupied. Gideon immediately recognized Roger. His dark brown hair and bushy beard, like his father's, couldn't hide the roundness of his face. The son was much shorter than his father. Gideon surmised that Roger must've inherited his face and stature from his mother, including a propensity to follow—which, knowing Alan, Gideon also imagined was necessary if one was to constantly cope with Alan's drive and energy.

It was not yet midmorning, so the table sported what was to be expected at this time of day. There were the flasks, jugs and cups laid out to make coffee or tea. Beside these was a woven basket containing toast; another held freshly baked muffins, both covered with a gauze cloth to keep off insects. Alongside lay cutlery to spread the butter, marmalade or jam in the glass jars. All the elements of a light bush breakfast—and all of it untouched. On the opposite side of the table, somewhat forlornly, stood an empty whiskey bottle, with another of vodka, half empty. An ice bucket and crumpled soda cans completed the picture of a different type of indulgence.

Standing up, Roger moved across to meet the new arrivals. With a handshake, he greeted Gideon as warmly as had his father. In the same fashion, Gideon introduced Moses, who was just as warmly welcomed. Then with a broad sweep, Roger gestured towards two other men who remained seated.

"Let me introduce our guests." Roger paused. "Alexei."

A man with dark eyes and a face whose pudgy shape and dark brown hair bore a vague similarity to a shaved Roger, nodded back at them.

"And Vladimir." Roger indicated an older man of a slighter build than his companion. Although seated, it was evident that, like the young one, he was not tall. His sparse fair hair was closely cropped in a military style. It wasn't obvious if the thinness of his hair was as a result of its cropping, or because he was going bald. Gideon extended his hand for a friendly shake.

Vladimir didn't rise from his chair. Instead, he lazily raised his arm to give the offered hand a perfunctory, listless clasp as he briefly drifted his small, piercing blue eyes over the newcomers. He accompanied his glance with a nod of his head and an indecipherable grunt, issued after he had already turned back towards his companion, to whom he began to talk in what Gideon assumed was Russian. Gideon ignored the rudeness and introduced himself anyway.

"Hi, nice to meet you. I'm Gideon." He waited politely for Vladimir to finish speaking to his companion. When the man swivelled his eyes back, Gideon addressed him. "This is my partner, Moses."

This time it was Alexei who interrupted Gideon's introduction. Speaking, again in Russian, to Vladimir—who didn't even grant an acknowledgment before replying to whatever Alexei was saying.

After answering his son, he peered at Gideon. His empty gaze lingered long enough for Gideon to realize that the piercing effect of his blue eyes emanated not so much from their color, but from the pinprick constriction of his pupils, expanding the hue of his irises. An abrupt breeze eddied towards Gideon, bringing with it the smell of stale whiskey which even a subsequent half bottle of odorless vodka couldn't suppress.

Sheesh, Gideon mentally exclaimed. The asshole's drunk, and it's only eight in the morning!

David Maritz

"Can I offer you coffee or tea?" Alan invited them to the table. "Feel free to have some of this toast, or a muffin." He added that the coffee was freshly filtered, not that instant chicory knock-off stuff.

While Alan poured the coffee, Moses and Gideon helped themselves to the table's bounties.

Moses commented to Gideon. "What a lovely setting this place has."

Beyond the leafy shade over the deck and swaying fronds of the river grass, the morning sunlight reflected off the water rippling across the rocky shallows in a spray of glitter. In the background, like a musician practising for a performance, the call of a red-eyed bush dove rose up and down its repetitive scales. Its melody blended with the river's burble as seamlessly as background music mingles with the murmurs of a crowd waiting for a maestro.

Gideon wondered if the two foreigners appreciated the halcyon splendour of the setting.

"Yup, a great place for breakfast," he replied to Moses. "And we are getting it for free, making it even better."

"I want more drink." It was Vladimir who spoke. "Vodka," he added.

Roger obliged, handing him a glass, then filling it half full until Vladimir lifted it to clink on the neck of the bottle. Gideon watched in amazement as Vladimir raised the glass. Tilting his head back, he poured its contents down his throat with no more than three gulps.

"*Nostrovia.*" Gideon felt obliged to give a cheeky toast.

"You speak Russian?" Vladimir fixed his beady eyes on Gideon.

"No," he replied, "I know a few words, but I can swear in Russian."

A smile touched Vladimir's lips, but not his eyes. "Where did you learn Russian curses?"

Gideon couldn't help himself: the temptation to tease a rude drunk was too compelling. It brought back the old barroom brawl army days. Who more appropriate than a Russian adversary, those old-time enemies?

"I had a Russian girlfriend," he lied. "*Youb tvoju mat, idi nahui*, she would say to me, or *Idi v pizdui.*"

Vladimir snorted, turning to say something to Alexei, whose face also glimmered with a smile. "Where was that?"

"Oh, it was up north a long way and time ago," Gideon said. "I was scared of her: she was bigger and stronger than me, but she taught me many useful things—not just to swear."

"What did she teach?" Alexei's voice was deeper than Vladimir's.

"She taught me how to milk a cow." Gideon hesitated. Their indifference to his introduction annoyed him, giving impetus to his taunts, but he had to be careful. He didn't want to upset their hosts by offending their clients. That was the challenge: to make his comments seem innocent even as he got the rude asshole's goat, to make him bleat. "She said she didn't like teaching tricks to the men back home. They had no manners, even with a cow."

Vladimir's flattened boxer's nose bore testimony to a pugnacious past. Probably, like many of his countrymen, he had an astounding ability to be a functional drunk. It was clear that on this beautiful morning Vlad wasn't fully sober, and hadn't been for a while.

Gideon knew there were two types of drunks: the stupid silly or the nasty aggressive. His gut feeling was that Vladimir fitted into the latter category.

Out of the corner of his eye, he saw consternation on Roger's face. It validated that he was dealing with a nasty sort of drunk, so he backed off.

"Actually," he mused out loud to soften the dig a tad, "I remember now. She was from the Caucasus region, only sort of Russian."

"Are you hunters?" Alexei asked. Unlike Vladimir, he spoke good English with a minimal accent.

"No," Gideon replied, "I'm working here under a contract to train scouts to save animals so that you can shoot them."

Vladimir, unsure if Gideon was being sarcastic at his expense, glowered at him.

"Is this the first time you have been in Africa?" Gideon asked Alexei.

"No, we are here many times. We are involved with mining in Tanzania and the Congo. This is the first time we are in this country." His expansiveness suggested that Alexei was the other type of drunk.

"I want more vodka." Vladimir spoke. "I want vodka and cola."

Turning towards the bar which was further back above the deck and across a small lawn, Roger beckoned to the barman.

Glaring at Gideon, with a flick of his head toward Moses, Vladimir said, "Tell your boy to bring me cola."

Gideon made a mental note. He was correct. Vladimir was the nasty kind. "I beg your pardon? I'm not sure I heard you correctly."

Vladimir's escalation caught him off guard. Grudgingly, Gideon had to give him credit: the guy knew how to fight. Don't underestimate these fucking Russians. Both Alan and Roger sprang up, stumbling over themselves to diffuse the situation. Not being on his own turf, Gideon backed away from the confrontation, but Vladimir had gone too far. Vladimir was drunk and he was not, but the Russian was still sober enough to know in Africa which buttons to push. Here they were less offended over their women, but racial slurs—that was fighting talk.

Gideon picked his next sentences carefully. Here was an ideal asshole in a perfect state to teach manners, or have fun doing it even if nothing is learned.

"Vladimir, have you ever invited your wife out to Africa, shown her some of the great sights and places here?"

Vladimir eyed Gideon suspiciously, unsure of where things were going. "*Nyet*," he replied without elaborating.

"I'm curious," Gideon asked. "What is your wife's name?"

When Vladimir didn't answer, Alexei answered for him. "Natasha."

"And you, Alexei: would you not like Natasha to visit?"

Alexei shook his head half-heartedly. "She is not my mother."

With that information, Gideon could go for a good body blow without riling Alexei up; no need to jerk both their chains.

"Natasha!" Gideon said admiringly. "What a coincidence. I once had a dog named Natasha: a big fat lazy old mongrel bitch with a sloppy tongue and missing teeth." Gideon didn't stop himself from turning the screw one more time. "Oh boy, I loved that dog except when she farted on my bed. Her farts were eye-watering, but what can you expect with a name like Natasha?"

A flush of red in Vlad's face showed Gideon's verbal punches had hit their mark.

Gideon stood and said to Moses, "Now that we've finished our coffee it's time for us to go."

The slur of alcohol was detectable in Vladimir's voice. "Before you go, tell your flat nose to bring me Coke."

Moses set his cup down on the table. For the first time he spoke to the elder Russian. "Vladimir," he said softly, "Alexei asked if we are hunters. My friend Gideon said he is not. That is not quite true. He is a very good hunter. So am I, which is why I am here. We hunt men." Moses moved his gaze to Alexei, and then slowly back to Vladimir. He crossed to the barman standing with a cola bottle in his hand. Taking it from him with two fingers, Moses swivelled smoothly like a stalking cat. "Vladimir," he hissed quietly, "I have hunted many Russians. In Angola, they were easy to find, and even easier to kill, because they loved their vodka." The menace in his voice was clear. "Today I am a religious man, so now I bring you your cola instead of a bullet." Handing over the bottle, Moses smiled at Vladimir's baleful glare as he beckoned for Gideon to follow.

Alan and Roger trailed after them. Gideon and Moses would take their leave, and offer apologies at the dock.

16

November 17

Leaving the hunting camp, they continued upstream, gingerly navigating a section of narrow channels where the river had split apart like paper through the blades of a shredder. Here they were outside the boundaries of the national park, travelling between Alan's concession and a huge piece of private land.

Stopping at the old unoccupied camp there, Gideon explained to Moses: "The sons who inherited this place don't have their father's passion. Since the old man died, they've been looking for a buyer. Rumor has it that a wealthy foreigner is interested. They're the only ones willing to spend that sort of money. The new African rich don't fully trust the places they came from."

Moses laughed. "What a fucked-up war we fought: the winners simply replaced the previous thieves. If you got rich from corruption and stealing your country's wealth, why would you invest back where someone else can steal from you?"

Beyond the old guest camp, they ran upriver until they approached the edge of Alan's hunting concession, where the river broadened into an expansive flood plain. Gideon gave a wide birth to a nervously snorting pod of hippos. He didn't want to get near shallow water with the prop mired in mud, and a big resident bull deciding to charge.

He raised his voice above the buzz of the motor. "This is as far as we'll go. The border with the tribal area isn't too far upstream from here, which is why these hippos are nervous. They've had plenty of bad experiences with humans."

Cutting the engine, he let the boat drift slowly with the nudging current. Beyond the hippos on the north bank, a huge herd of elephant came down to drink, at least seventy strong.

"Well," Moses glanced at Gideon. "Alan is having some success with his anti-poaching efforts."

"He is effective," Gideon replied. "He set up a network of informers."

After watching the elephants drink, sucking water with their trunks and squirting torrents into their mouths, Gideon pushed the engine tiller gently away from his knee. The prow swung in a wide circle. The boat moved faster as its bearing meshed with the current. Heading slowly downstream, they passed the hunting camp. They waved to the shapely young dock lady standing on the jetty, indicating that they were not stopping. Gideon couldn't help thinking how well spoken she had been. Hers was an accent and charm that went with a private education. What the heck was she doing working at this remote place?

The Russian pair still sat on the riverside deck, whiskey glasses dangling from their fingers. They rose unsteadily when they noticed the boat, then sat down disinterestedly once they saw who it was.

"Maybe they are expecting someone prettier," Moses commented.

Their unsmiling stares faded into the distance, as did Gideon's thoughts about them.

"Be careful of that place." Gideon pointed at a rocky hillock pushing its black basaltic crown above the tree line along the river. "If any poor sod is running the risk of getting sand-bagged by a woman, that is where it will happen."

Moses stared at him.

Gideon explained. "The view brings out romance in spades up there. The only escape is to drop dead from a heart attack."

"So your heart must be in good nick," Moses tossed back at him. "If my memory serves me, you ran that risk more than any of us. A leopard doesn't change its spots!"

"Hey," Gideon chuckled back. "I just play possum before I get whacked. It either scares them away or they are all over me to bring me back to life."

They laughed.

"It sorts the husk from the chaff."

Turning serious, Moses said, "Be careful my friend. You're getting longer in the tooth. Your ticker may be more delicate than you think, especially your emotional one."

"True, but why not make hay while there is still some sunshine left?"

Gideon remembered the first time he had experienced the hillocks magic. What was her name? That short, stocky ball of fun when he first got here two years back. Bright had asked him to escort her. Jenny? Judy? The guest who wanted to be escorted up there by the exotic magnetic grizzle of a game ranger. Was it him, or the place? The blue of the river ran full, and everything had been emerald green and touched gold by the setting sun. He remembered a thick mop of black curly hair bobbing on a pretty head, everything swaying – her breasts, his resolve. Was it Africa's savagery, or its beauty that affected the morality of those who spent enough time in its embrace. Who was he to judge anyone's motives, or use a yardstick from another time or place. The war in Angola had long ago dismissed his youthful naivety. Months later, a text, *Eden came into the world December 22. Mother and daughter doing great. A Christmas present.*

For whom? It was better to let sleeping dogs lie, especially when the bark in the background was of a husband. But even so, like so much on this continent, the curiosity was always there. It still vaguely niggled at his conscience.

"Ahh, to hell with it!"

"What?" Moses responded.

"No worries, I was just thinking to myself." Gideon went back to explaining to Moses about the black hillock they were passing. "The view from up there is stunning, especially when the bush is green after new rains. I call it Eden's Outlook." Idling the boat's engine, drifting closer, he let the current do the work.

Looking back at Gideon, Moses nodded his head towards it. "Let's check it out. You've made me curious."

"Okay, but watch out that you don't succumb to its spell." Gideon laughed at the face Moses made. "First I need your help to sort out the other weird bullshit going on."

He gunned the outboard to swivel the boat's prow to find a mooring spot.

Soon, after a vigorous scramble up a steep slope they were absentmindedly chewing on stems of elephant grass as they sat admiring the view. The scene was beautiful: emerald *dambos* pinned along the blue ribbon of the river. Moses sat perched pensively on a pinnacle rock.

"So what do you make of that delightful pair we met this morning?" Gideon asked Moses.

"Those Russians are not hunters," he said. "They're hiding something."

"Yes," Gideon replied, "but they must be wealthy. Only the wealthy can afford to pay the trophy fees and taxes to hunt big game. Roger said they'd booked the camp for a month, costing a fortune: two grand a day each before trophy fee taxes."

"The young one said they were involved with mining."

"Yes, he did." Gideon tried to remember what had been said. "They must own a fucking gold mine to afford staying for a month." He looked up as a bateleur eagle took off from a dead tree across the river. With rapid flaps of its wings, it spiralled skyward into a thermal. "The Russians don't strike me as being interested in the bush, or concerned with aesthetics and the environment. It doesn't look like they've done much hunting, if at all. Alan said they were dodgies, whatever that means, so there must be something weird about them, just sitting around, getting drunk, waiting for something to happen – which I doubt will be the Messiah riding in on his donkey to save them."

Gideon tossed his chewed straw aside. He picked a fresh one, then nibbled at its spongy base. "I wonder where they get their money? Very few of the rich I've known were alcoholics, except those who made theirs the old-fashioned way: by inheriting it."

Moses grinned and nodded. "Gidi, you must have met more of these types than I, but I sense something strange with those two, mainly the older one. He has an air of dereliction, that same sense you get when you see a lone zebra wandering around with a big herd of wildebeest: something has lost its way, or it doesn't fit with its own crowd." Moses paused, then went on in a sly way. "Sort of like you."

"Hey," Gideon remonstrated. "Speak about yourself. I'm not derelict. Yet."

Moses chuckled. "Look at you: alone, mostly keeping yourself company, no house, no pension, no wife, just an occasional fling when the opportunity presents itself, like one of those lost zebras." Sensing he'd touched on more truth than intended, Moses became conciliatory. "I won't suggest my situation is better than yours. We've both lost what we spent our lives fighting for. I bet that Russian is the same."

Gideon stood. He threw a stone far out towards the river, hoping to hear it splash into the water. "The difference between me and that Russian," he said, " is that booze has him by the balls, and mine still hang free."

"Lucky for the ladies," Moses quipped slyly.

"Piss off," Gideon tossed back, then threw another stone at the river. Deep down, he knew Moses was right. He changed the subject. "We met Russians in Angola. My guess is that Vladimir is a peasant, with only his old inertia keeping him pointed this way. Too bad he is sucking his son along in his wake. Those Russians were as tough as nails, and useful if facing the right direction. So I wonder who is pointing their way, and what for?"

Moses agreed. "Maybe they should look for that girl you told them about: Natasha. She could try to teach them something useful, like how to milk a cow."

They laughed.

"You certainly flushed his crap when you pulled his chain with your comments. We do have something in common though. I bet, like us, he doesn't have a home to go back to."

Gideon heard a surprising wistfulness in the way Moses spoke. "Huh?" he exclaimed. "What happened to that village with your wives and your kids?"

"It's still there," Moses replied. "A home is where you have a family who welcomes you, but things have changed. No one welcomes me, so I don't go back for long. I had two of everything: homes, fathers, wives. I thought it would last forever." Moses hesitated. "We all change. Without a wife next to you to make changes seem trivial, you end up surrounded by strangers." Gideon waited for Moses to continue. "Father Xavier is a father to me. He welcomes me, but a father is not a family. For us Africans unless you have a family you have nothing. That is why I want to go back. Why I hope those who suffered and were bitter from the war and the old colonial way have forgotten." Moses kicked at the dirt with the toe of his shoe. "At least my children don't care about the past. As for the future," Moses put his hands together as if in prayer, "the Lord will take care of me."

Gideon replied caustically. "You're lucky. You're only excluded from your village. I'm excluded from this whole fucking sub-continent. I'm a *mzungu*. If I wait long enough, everyone will forget that white men are the ones to be kicked. They'll switch to the Chinese who are flooding in, taking over this place." Gideon flung a third pebble, harder this time, out at the river.

"Anyway," Moses said, his head resting in his hands with his elbows on his knees, talking more to himself than to Gideon. "It's all in God's hands."

From far away, across the river, deep in the national park, came the sound of a gunshot.

"Did you hear that?"

Moses nodded.

"Come on. We need to get to the scout camp."

Scrambling down from the hillock, they leapt into the boat. Gideon hauled on the start chord as Moses shoved the bow into the current. Gideon gunned the engine, keeping the skim of the boat to the center of the channels while nudging it around submerged rocks and logs where he could.

The river forced them through a labyrinth above the twin islands; they had to be obedient to its flow. Then where it spread into broader swathes, Gideon gave screaming head to the engine's fifteen horses, praying to his river god they wouldn't have a prop strike. If they could get to the scout base before mid-afternoon, they'd have time to head out in the direction they heard the shot. Quick preliminary scouting before nightfall would give the best chance of catching any poacher.

"Why don't you ask the scout leader if we can join his team?" Moses shouted above the noise of the engine.

Gideon hesitated. It meant that his original plan of showing Moses the lay of the land would have to go on the back burner. In two days Gideon was scheduled to move to the southern iTezhi Tezhi part of the park to train another team. Before he'd left, he had hoped to squeeze in a road trip to Kikuji, the future lodge site on the Lunga River where the cement bags had been slashed by the author of the threatening note. But the gunshot put a stick in the spokes of that plan. Improvisation was called for. What better way for Moses to get a feel for the area than joining a scout team? Observing, hearing first-hand explanations from the scouts. "That's a good idea," Gideon shouted back. "If they'll allow it. Otherwise, you'll have to go on your own, because I'm scheduled to do some training down at the south end of the park. I need to do some prep before then."

Moses shrugged. "So what? I'm a big boy, old and ugly enough to take care of myself." He winked.

The flow of the river took the boat wide, towards its south bank. A few minutes later the deck of their own host lodge came into view. Snorts from the resident hippo pod assailed their ears.

"Stop at our camp. I'll grab my pack," Moses called out. "We can scrounge some food from the kitchen. All I need is some tins of sweetened condensed milk and peanuts for energy, like we used to do when we traveled light and far on Deep Ops."

Throttling back the engine, sweeping into a curve, Gideon brought the boat into the current and against the bank. A wave from Precious as she stood on the deck greeted them. Twenty minutes later, Moses was back with his pack. Precious handed him a package of food to store in the boat. Then a few of the kitchen ladies joined Precious to wave and call out Kaunde goodbyes.

"You have admirers!" Gideon teased.

Moses gave a dismissive flick of his hand. Opening the throttle, pushing the boat fast, they watched a fish eagle fly overhead with a big pike in its talons.

"Hey!" Gideon shouted over the engine, "let's see if we can make some poacher's life as miserable as that fish."

It wasn't long before the pontoon cable came into view. They waved to its crew sitting idly in the shade of the trees, waiting for a client needing to cross the river. Gideon pulled into the northern bank of the river where they secured the boat onto a low branch. They had traveled fast: it was mid-afternoon. Musekela, the lead scout, was standing at the top of the bank. Gideon quickly explained about the situation with the gunshot. He introduced Moses as his helper in the training mission, tentatively suggesting that Moses accompany the scout team. To his surprise, Musekela readily agreed when Gideon explained that Moses's specialty was tracking.

"If you want to see a real professional, watch him."

"Give us a half hour to get ready," Musekela said. "Will you go to Lunga island, below the confluence, to pick up one of our scouts at the fly camp there?"

"Okay," Gideon replied. "That's good because it will give a chance to show Moses a bit more of the area."

Pushing the boat into the water, it only took a few minutes heading down-stream before they were in the shadow of the ridge which dominates the area, where the Kafue River punched through the barrier, with its high, brooding cliff looking down on the confluence like the hollow face of an old witch.

Fast skimming in the boat soon got them to the fly camp. A quick expla-nation was given to the scout. He clambered aboard. As they passed back upstream beneath the witch cliff's face, Moses motioned with his head to look up. "At the top," he shouted.

Squinting, shading his eyes with his hand, Gideon finally saw what Moses was pointing at. It was hard to detect, but among shrubby vegetation covering the hill, like unkempt hair on the head of an aged beggar, stood a motionless figure. An old man, his camouflaged clothes blending with the background as he made an unambiguous sweeping gesture with his arm.

"Go away!" he indicated.

17

November 18

The rusted frame of the park scout's Cruiser creaked gingerly along a rough game-viewing road as it led loosely upstream north east, towards the Lukamga Swamps. In doing so the road sometimes pinched between a hillock, dipping its flank into the river, or at others it respectfully swayed back inland to hedge around the damp marshy spread of a dambo. The team's six scouts had never seen anything like it – this method of scouting for tracks. It was a technique Moses had learned from the bushman trackers serving in the army in Angola. Sitting on the scratched and dented engine hood with his feet on the winch drum at the front, Moses could pick up signs even with the vehicle traveling at speed. If the poachers had come from the north, as most of them did, they would have crossed the river somewhere. If so, they would also have crossed the road to get deeper into the park from where the sound of the shot had emanated. The other likely possibility was that they had floated in with canoes from the tribal areas to the east. In both cases, their endeavors would be multi-day affairs, entailing a temporary night base. The fact that Gideon and Moses heard the gunshot deep in the park at midday suggested that this was the case. If so, such a base would be within reasonable distance of the river for its drinking water. With only an hour of sunlight left, if they were to get a jump on a pursuit, this was their best bet of finding a start point. It was a trade-off. A quiet foot patrol would give greater stealth, but

David Maritz

it would be slow and take time. Considering that the Land Cruiser had a good muffler and could barely be heard further away than a few hundred meters when running at low revs, Moses felt that it was worth the risk.

With a raised hand, Moses signalled the driver each time he detected an anomaly in the sand and grass at the side of the tracks. Most weren't human. Three sets were but they were old, the imprints only surviving the recent rains because of protection from tufts of lodge grass bent over the road strips.

"When was the last time you had a patrol here?" Moses asked Musekela.

"About two weeks ago," he replied.

"I can see your tracks," Moses pointed at the set, and Musekela nodded.

It was when the vehicle was nearing the edge of the national park, where it bordered with the private reserve, that Moses quickly raised his arm again. The scouts were astonished. They were good, but not as good as this. Off to the side was a small, flattened patch of grass, with a faint crumpled tuft between the strips and another on the other side.

Moses indicated the grassy indents. "Someone has jumped from one side of the road to its center, and then to the other edge." Sliding off the hood he began to carefully scout around.

Musekela opened the cab door.

"Wait! Stay in the vehicle," Moses ordered. "I want to look for other signs before we disturb them." Like a pointing dog, Moses edged back and forth as he picked up the 'scent'. "There are four of them," he stated. "You can see from the way the grass has risen back up that they are about two days old. Probably made when they entered the park. When you track these, focus on the grass, not the dirt. The tracks in the dirt will have been washed away in the rain. But the bending and breaking of the grass won't.

The tracks from yesterday and today will be clear, as they will be after the rain two nights ago. Okay, everyone can get off the vehicle and we can begin," he said.

By now there was only half an hour of daylight left.

"I suggest you track these people until dark, then come back here to sleep next to the vehicle. Without your sleeping stuff you will move faster. You can head out before dawn to pick up the tracks where you left off." Moses looked at Musekela questioningly. "If it's okay with you, I want to continue along the road to see if I can pick up anything else. We can meet back here after nightfall."

Moses had a hunch, even if they had penetrated deep into the park, the tracks would head back towards the river. Poaching parties traveled light, for speed and to be able to carry their spoils back out of the park. They only carried enough water for daily walking, unencumbered by non-essential weight. This meant that they probably had an overnight camp close to the river.

Musekela gave orders to his team. Shouldering their weapons they set off southwards into the bush. At a fast, almost jogging pace, Moses headed on up the track road.

As the dusk sucked away the last of the daylight, the straightening flick of a grass stem caught his eye. It was where a reach of thicker bush proliferated on the higher ground before it eased back to touch the river. It formed a good corridor, obscuring vegetation for anyone who wanted to move closer to the river. It was also where four sets of tracks had crossed the road.

This time there had been little attempt to hide the crossing. The tracks were fresh, very fresh. The trampled grass was still rising back up even as Moses watched. It was a good sign. Moses sensed that these poachers would be relaxed and unsuspecting. They had been in the park for two days, and had probably got what they wanted. Their carelessness in not hiding their tracks showed that they were on their way out. It would be easier to get close to them; but if the scouts did not catch them before dawn, they would be gone. Tracking in the dark wasn't possible, the half moon would only rise around midnight. However Moses knew that fresh tracks heading towards the river meant that a temporary base could be close. It was now a matter of very careful movement, which would let him check out his gut feeling. Moses would use his ears rather than his eyes to hone in on his targets. Patience would pay off. Lynx-like, he carefully, silently, moved forward, stopping every few meters to listen. A hyena yodelled not too far away, followed by the yips of a jackal. Probably the scent of meat hanging on drying strings in the trees had caught the attention of the carnivores.

Meter by slow, stealthy meter, Moses placed his careful footsteps, one after the other. With slow, smooth motions he crept forward. Nothing could draw attention as easily as a jerky movement, even in the dark, or the snap of a twig beneath a misplaced step. He was counting on them no longer being cautious. They would talk softly amongst themselves, give a laugh, a cough. Or there could be the sound of breaking branches if they had made a fire. If they had built it in a shallow pit to hide the flames, the shimmer of its light would reflect on the leaves of overhead trees; there would be the smell of smoke.

It would be a patience game, and Moses had plenty of that.

It took nearly two hours for him to gradually creep through the stygian darkness towards the river through the half-kilometer of long grass, bushes, and around the large tree trunks of this section. His senses were at their peak. He was now close to the river. If the poachers had made a camp, it had to be close. But maybe he was wrong, and there was no camp after all.

A twig cracked to his left. He froze. Animals only snap twigs and branches at night when they are being chased. He stood barely breathing for some minutes before resuming careful progress. There was the faintest sound of another twig snapping. This time to his fore. All his senses now focused on a point ahead. Something was moving.

Was this a trap? Were they waiting?

A flash stabbed through the darkness, and a thunderous roar ripped apart the tense cocoon of quiet. Moses instinctively jerked back in shock as the echoes of the sound rumbled back from the distant hillocks. It took a few seconds for him to realize what it was. Only a large powder shot from a muzzleloader could produce that sort of flash and sound, the full-throated, roar of a poor village poacher's homemade weapon.

A flurry of movement rustled about in front of him, accompanied by low excited calls.

His instinct was to flee. But he held himself; his training and experience had taught him that running away from trouble was a bad thing.

Watching it unfold, he realized that the commotion was heading along the upstream bank of the river. Voices continued calling to each other. The beam of a small penlight held by someone at the center of the activity gave an edge of clarity to the scene. In its light, three men bent over something. With the adrenaline subsiding, Moses raised his binoculars to see if he could make out what was going on. In the faint and erratic light beam he saw that the men surrounded an animal. Holding its hind legs they dragged it along the ground.

It was a hyena.

As carefully as he had approached, Moses cautiously withdrew, moving faster and less cautiously the further he was away. Back on the game-viewing tracks, he half-ran, half-jogged the few kilometers back to the scouts' vehicle.

David Maritz

The scouts were spreading their blankets, preparing for sleep. They roused at the urgency in his tone.

"Yes, we heard the shot," Musekela said.

"It was strange," Moses explained. "They were very quiet, and if they had not shot a hyena I would have stumbled right into their camp." Moses began sucking on the hole he had punched in a tin of sweetened, viscous condensed milk. "I think that their quietness was to get the hyena to come in close before they shot. They used a muzzle loader, which is not accurate. So they had to let it get close."

"But why shoot a hyena?" Musekela asked. "These are strange poachers."

Moses unfurled his blankets. Turning to Musekela he said, "I have a lot of experience with catching people off-guard from my time in the military. If it was me, I would go in before dawn when they are still drowsy and half asleep. They will least expect any interference." Moses didn't want to get Musekela's back up by challenging his authority. "What do you think if our watch wakes us at 4 am?" he asked. "It will take us about an hour to get there so if we leave here at four thirty, we should be there and in position by five thirty, and ready to rush them."

Moses need not have been concerned. Musekela was happy to follow his advice.

He set the watch to wake everyone at 4 am.

In the darkness, each of the men held a cup of hot sweet tea in his hands. It was clear that Musekela was not going to give a pre-operation briefing. Why should he? He had never engaged in combat operations. For him, policing was simply chasing after a few poachers whenever he stumbled upon them. Even this predawn operation was foreign to him. Moses was again worried about treading on Musekela's toes.

"Do you mind if I give a briefing?" Moses asked.

Looking into the tin cup he held as he swilled it, Musekela said, "Go right ahead."

Facing the group, Moses began.

"We should try to catch this group when they are still sleepy. There are four of them and seven of us. I will lead the way in single file, because I know where they are. Before dawn we will have good moonlight to get close to their camp, but not too close so that they don't see us. A hundred meters should be enough. At that stage we should spread out in line-abreast, and pair up. Count your steps as you spread out. Twenty paces between. We will wait there until it gets light enough to see each other when we are that twenty paces apart. Clear your throats and blow your noses before we start so that there is less chance of a cough or sneeze as we get close. When I give the signal, we rush them as fast as we can. We should be on them in seconds. If they detect us before then and start to run, we must rush from wherever we are. We will work on a buddy-buddy system. Each pair will have one man focusing on getting handcuffs on the target and the other holding and getting a target's hands behind his back. The first pair should grab the closest man and so on. You all know how to give a choke hold if things get rough. If not, I will demonstrate it and we can practice it now. I will be the only one alone to tackle a suspect. Once you have handcuffs on, push the target down onto his back, and help anyone else who is still struggling. It is hard to stand up if your hands are tied behind your back. Cuffed suspects will not be a problem. If they do manage to get up, push them down again. There's no need for violence unless they try to shoot at us. But from what I saw yesterday, they are armed with muzzleloaders. I don't think they will have time to load once we are charging at them. Any questions?"

There were none.

David Maritz

An hour later, as a faint glimmer started to lighten the eastern skies, Moses left the grassy edge of the *dambo* with the scouts following single file. He entered the thicker obscuring bush where the poachers' base was located. They had walked silently and easily so far. By keeping to the open grass, Moses had taken the group to within a few hundred meters of their target. But with the dawn approaching, getting any closer out in the open grass would risk discovery. Ducking into the thicker bush, Moses slowed their progression, signalling to everyone to be careful where they stepped so as not to snap a twig. He need not have worried; the scouts' bush craft was excellent. They moved forward soundlessly. It wasn't long before Moses pointed giving a thumbs-down signal. Their target was ahead. The scouts quietly spread out. They waited in tense silence. The trees and bushes slowly emerged with greater definition from the gloom. Then, with a wave of both hands, Moses gave the signal.

The bush was filled with the thump of running men as they crashed through brush.

It was a complete surprise. The first startled shout of warning came from a poacher when the scouts were almost upon them. Two of them threw off their blankets and were attempting to stand as they were tackled. The other two didn't even make it that far. It was over in less than a minute. As the tension ebbed out of the scouts and they hooted their success, in the background Moses caught the fading sound of breaking branches. Standing still amidst the flurry Moses listened carefully. Someone was running away, with the sporadic sounds of escape fading towards the river. All around the scouts exclaimed in disbelief. Hanging from the trees were the skins of hyenas, jackals and a serval cat. In another tree was the skin of a python. In a third a wire loop had the paws of these animals strung on it. A separate loop even had two vulture heads. A fourth held animal tails. It was a very unusual poacher's camp. The exuberance of the scouts dissipated as they examined the loot.

Moses paid no attention. Holding his machete, he chased through the thick underbrush in the direction of the disappearing sounds. There had been a fifth man. Unusually he had slept away from the others, thereby affording his escape. The path of the escape was easy to find; it had crashed through the grass and brush. It led down to the river's edge, where the tracks disappeared. In the mud it was easy to see that the boot prints had a unique crosshatch patent at their center. They led to a shallow line, indicating where a traditional Makoro dug-out canoe had been beached. It had gone, leaving two behind.

As Moses stood looking down at the river's water, from a long way away, across the river, came a cackle of laughter.

18

November 21
Elephants

Ducking under it, Moses held the long thorny branch of a 'wait-a-bit' thorn bush until Gideon reached him. Then he moved on as Gideon caught it to stop it flicking back in his face. Now back from his training sessions to the scout teams in the south of the park, Gideon had joined Moses on a sleuthing foray. They were weaving carefully through thick bush looking for any sign that may have been left behind by cross-hatched boot prints. Earlier that morning, Precious had taken Gideon aside when he came in to scrounge an early morning cup of coffee. She had heard a stranger talking to someone last night, she said. It was near the staff quarters. She couldn't make out who it was.

"Kings maybe?" Gideon had asked.

"Maybe."

When she went out to check, they had gone.

"It is good that you have found your feet here so quickly." Walking behind him, Gideon spoke to Moses as his old sergeant moved ahead with his alert eyes constantly taking in everything. "I've just found out that I need to go down to South Africa to help with a dog and pony show."

"What for?" Moses queried.

"My boss says he needs my help. Our main donor will be out from Germany. He wants a progress report. So my boss wants me there for back up."

Moses led the way between a series of dense copses. From there he moved out into spottier shrubbery which formed the transition between the thicker canopy and the grassy terrain bordering the arc of a big *dambo*. With some unfathomable algorithm, he wove their progress in and out of the bushland features. Obviously he felt it would give the best chance of detecting the tracks of someone hiding theirs.

"Why do you need to speak to this guy?" Moses asked.

"Governments seldom budget enough for conservation," Gideon explained. "However, there are those who care. The trust I work for tries to fill some of the gaps. So the old 'tin-can' needs to be shaken under the noses of rich folks. A big part of my boss's job involves schmoozing. For some reason he thinks that I add value. I must be the tame baboon that he pulls out to add a wild flavor to his funding requests."

"A good description." Moses interjected.

Gideon didn't answer. He was preoccupied with carefully releasing a straggly branch where its thorns had hooked his shirt.

"At least he cut off your tail," Gideon detected the smirk in Moses voice. Now he needs to fix your bark."

Heading back into thicker bush they walked in single file.

"I hate it, and I am not good at it. These corporate donations are a way of buying absolution from their guilt in sinning against nature. "Gideon spat to the side to indicate his displeasure. "Conservation is all about habitat, and development is guaranteed to fuck up habitats, no matter how hard they try to spin its eco-friendliness."

Moses nodded sporadically to indicate he was listening, while searching for those little anomalies.

"These corporate types believe that we aren't part of nature, that we can piss on it, cut it up, dice it and cover it and grind it away. Sadly, they are part of the billions of good intelligent folks who believe that this world is given only to humans by a God."

"Hey, watch out," Moses spoke back tersely at Gideon. "I am one of them. But I am one of those who respects what God has made for us. If I wasn't, I wouldn't be here with you now."

"I grant you that." Gideon said, "but you have to admit after what both of us have been through that we are the most murderous, destructive creature to have ever lived on planet earth."

Moses stooped to peer carefully at a cluster of dead leaves lying scattered across a small sandy patch. Gideon waited until they started walking again.

"It is our murderousness that has made us so intelligently destructive. Our ancestors regularly killed each other when squabbling with neighbouring groups. As you and I know from Angola, staying alive and unhurt when you attack another bunch takes skilful cooperative intelligence, especially if they are able to kill you instead. That has been as true in Angola a decade ago as it was back a hundred thousand years ago in the Olduvai Gorge. We had to be better than them to be successful. We had to be smarter to plan, adjust and communicate when things changed or went wrong. As leaders we needed to be especially smart. Benign to buddies and fierce to foe." Moses paused to pick up a pinch of soil in his fingers. He rubbed this gently in the palm of his hand and sniffed at it.

"What are you doing?" Gideon asked.

"Something had a piss there. I was checking if it was human."

Gideon had to admire his partner. "For Christ's sake, Moses, how many times did you have to sniff to figure out the difference between human and cat, or dog or whatever piss?"

"A lot," he replied.

"You should get a medal for that."

Moses clapped his hands theatrically as if to applaud himself.

"I bet, back in the good old cave days, that after a scrap, you didn't get a cheap medal, you got a share of the spoils. The only spoils three hundred thousand years ago were a few stone tools and their ladies. Like today, the clever ones, the leaders took the best and biggest lion's share. I bet it didn't take them long to get their share into the family way. The babies resulting from such a hoo-haa inherited the genes of the clever winners, not the dead losers. If you repeat that scenario enough times over hundreds of thousands of years, you get a clever, coordinated, communicative killer primate. Basically, old buddy, you get you and me."

Moses didn't stop scanning the ground, but Gideon heard his chuckle.

"All that hogwash that mankind is peace-loving is bullshit. Nothing gets us as riled up as a good fight, which we sublimate these days as team sports fighting for territory. Shit, look at the sport of rugby."

Moses did respond this time. "What about rugby?"

David Maritz

Gideon cleared his throat and spat to the side again. "They even symbolically rape the loser's woman. A phallic ball is kicked between the upright spread goal post legs while the losers stand dejectedly behind the white line prison, and the home crowd goes wild with excitement. Soccer isn't much better. Have you ever wondered why it is so popular? It speaks to that same old urge.

Moses gave another dismissive snort. "Gidi, you have an unusual take on life."

"You bet I have. You will be amazed at what ideas have been swept into the gutters because they are not polite enough to talk about. But you and I have been the dumb ones. Look how we got fucked around by some big bullshit patriotic idea, put right in the middle of the road for us to admire. You are doing great stuff we were told, keep it up and the whole nation will be thankful for your efforts and sacrifice. And then when it is all over and we see the big picture, we find out we were on the wrong side and get nothing. The ideas were for all to admire, while the action was in the gutters, where we still are. Look at us out here being scratched by thorns and bitten by tsetse flies and mosquitoes."

Moses kept moving, searching for clues. He glanced back. "These days you seem to be pretty comfortable with life in the gutter."

It was Gideon's turn to laugh. "You are right. It is amazing the interesting stuff one can find there. All the stuff that gets swept there, people, ideas, things."

"So why don't you call your boss and tell him that you have important stuff to sort out, and you can't make it?"

Gideon sighed as he picked up a dead branch and tossed it aside. He was walking fast to keep up with Moses. "My boss is a good guy, so I feel obliged to help him when he asks. If it wasn't for him I wouldn't have this job, so I owe him."

"Can't you get him to bring the donor out here to see first-hand?" Moses asked.

"Apparently not. The donor schedule is too tight." Gideon was short of breath from talking while walking fast. "I need to be there to keep the boss focused on what we need. If not they will start speaking conservation babble. Buzzwords like sustainability, carbon footprint, carbon credits, clean water... blah, blah blah... all the shit that sounds fancy, but nothing happens with it except meetings, and academics putting up slide shows. They won't talk about snares, and poisons, and catching bad *ngangas* who are frightening scouts from doing their duty. Or making charges stick, so that poachers don't get to be part of a game of legal musical chairs. Or about habitat preservation with villagers letting their cattle and goats encroach on the protected areas, and then settling there and making it almost impossible politically to remove them. But enough of donors."

They were now walking back along the dirt track that led in from the main road. They had executed an extended circle north up beyond the edge of the upper *dambo*. From there, they headed down southwest close to the main road, and now were moving back southeast, towards the lodge. As they walked, Gideon continued to talk. Moses's eyes never seemed to leave the ground, always searching for sign and tracks.

"Do you think the old crocodile guy is playing games with us?" Gideon asked.

"Of course he is." Moses stopped to examine a faint depression in the sand. "He is playing mental guerrilla tactics. Now you see him, now you don't. He is trying to mess with our minds. His strategy is successful with the lodge staff," Moses continued. "One of the kitchen girls told me that the finds of the poachers' camp has somehow leaked back to the lodge. Everybody knows that it was witchcraft muti that was being gathered. "Something big and potent. But why, and for whom? It has some of them on edge."

A long, slender slither of dark grey rippled out of the grass on the other side of a bare clearing in front of them. For a few moments their gaze was mesmerized by the beady black eyes at the sides of a bullet shaped head. A forked tongue flicked curiously in and out of an evil grin. It observed them, and then, finding them wanting, all they could see were the grey dimples of its scaly skin sliding away.

"Who got a bigger fright?" Gideon asked Moses. "Us, or that big old mamba?"

"That is strange!" Moses exclaimed. "That is the third time I have seen that snake. It wasn't scared. While you were away doing your training I have been this way a few times. Each time I have seen that snake. It must live in a nearby anthill burrow. But even stranger is that the tracks of the *nganga* also pass this way. He stops and mills around here." Shaking his head, Moses carried on walking. It was getting late.

The terrain had gently risen to the high point in the woodland, which marked the midway between the two adjacent arms of the *dambos*. These ran back towards the river, where they joined, one below and one above the lodge. Here the vegetation was even thicker, with clusters of broadleaf shrubs tucking around the shady areas of the big trees like sycophants to royalty. One of the biggest copses they passed had a lucky bean tree at its center.

Gideon called to Moses to slow for a moment as he searched for a few of its beans. "We need some of these."

The unique candelabra shape of a big euphorbia was beyond it, and Gideon walked fast to catch up… but with thirty meters separating them, suddenly there was a crackling, snapping sound. Out of nowhere too young bull elephants crashed through a gap between two vegetative islands.

Gideon had faced elephants before. The worst thing was to follow instincts and run away. He froze behind Moses, who was between the elephants and himself. They couldn't outrun an elephant. There was nowhere to hide. The elephant sense of smell is so acute, they would scent them out if they hid in the tangle of a thicket. There wasn't time to climb a tree. Even if they could, the pair would be upon them before they had scrambled high enough. With the dexterity of its trunk an elephant could pick them out like a monkey picks a berry.

Moses, with his arms spread wide, stood motionless, facing the trumpeting charge of the leading elephant. Behind it the second young bull, not quite as aggressive, veered to the side, where it hung back. The first bull pulled up short, only meters from Moses. Flapping its ears and trumpeting screams with its raised trunk, it was unused to having primates whose scent it hated standing their ground.

Its blustery body language broadcast its indecisiveness. Fight or flee?

In the sudden stillness, Gideon could hear his panted breaths and the beat of his own heart. With redirected aggression and raised trunk, the bull shrieked another angry trumpet, shook its head, and kicked up more dust with its feet. But it didn't advance.

Facing it squarely without moving, Moses gave a little upward flick of his spread arms showing the elephant where he stood that he was not going away. The movement wasn't startling, but the elephant reacted with a jerk of its head. Moses's wave signalled that he was not submissive. 'I am here, I am big, I am wide, and I am not scared of you, so watch out.'

It was enough to rattle the elephant's confidence, who had never encountered such strange behavior. Its fight turned to flight. In its haste to get away, the elephant bumped into its partner as it wheeled around. Together they crashed away into the undergrowth. The stomp and swishing sound of their feet rushing through the grass, augmented by the snapping cracks as they barged over shrubs and trampled through the undergrowth, gradually faded.

David Maritz

It'd been a while since Gideon had felt that heady adrenaline rush, and its weak-kneed aftermath effect. They looked at each other. "I'm glad to see that your nerve is as steady as ever!"

Moses shrugged. "All in a day's work."

From a long way away, and yet distinctly audible over the fading sounds of the elephants departure, came the cackle of an old man's laugh.

They looked at each other again, this time with raised eyebrows.

"He laughed like that after we raided the poacher camp," Moses muttered. "He thinks that he is clever. But he will make a mistake, and we will get him."

"Maybe," Gideon replied. "I don't like this game he's playing. Jesus. Our guy has taken a leaf from some strange bush recipe to mess with our minds. Snakes, elephants, crocodiles." Gideon let his annoyance show. "I don't like the snake part."

"Yes," Moses agreed. "Our old guy is into major *muti*. No wonder he has the locals shivering with fright."

"Well, my buddy," Gideon said. "I'm glad you have shown you have more nerve than his 'special' agents."

Moses grinned. "It is good to have God on your side, so stick with me."

19

November 22

As Precious walked from the squat, box-like staff rooms and along the narrow path leading to the kitchen, there was nothing but the soft crunch of her footsteps to dent the silence. The crescent of a waning moon hung in the eastern half of the sky, with its light etching the shapes of the tall trees and low bushes in monochrome starkness on an ambient canvas of silver luminescence. She loved this time, when the night held its breath prior to the birth of a new day. Its pregnant heaviness imbued a special creativity in her imagination. The night's shadows were like pencil sketches stacked against the walls of her mind, waiting to be painted with the colors she would soon pick from a palette filled with the light of the newborn day.

She didn't feel the twinge of anxiety that was present when there was no moonlight. At such times, her progress along the path had to be found by the feel of the grass at its verges brushing against her shins. She knew that, like a big cat, the unknown prowled the bush most actively when it was cloaked in complete darkness. On such occasions she could wait for Charity or Nora to rouse, to have their company on this short walk. But she was always loathe to do this; she was aware of her own aloofness when it came to the other girls at the lodge. She preferred to rise even earlier, and join Gilbert. He rose before anyone. He would don his clothes a full hour before dawn to head over to the pizza oven outside the kitchen. There he would blow on last night's fire and pick up its embers. With another bucket of kindling, he would methodically move down the line of chalets, lighting a fire at the base of each of their wood-fired boilers, ensuring there would be hot water for morning showers.

However, now in the bright predawn moonlight, Precious didn't need someone's presence to allay any anxiety about the unknown. Everything was bathed in grey-scale clarity. She took the kidney-shaped shadow of a monkey bread tree's pod and replicated it in repetitiveness down her mind's eye, alternating them in reds and bright oranges on the ruffled silver of the grass below the tree itself. She then stripped away the ruffled shine, replacing it with a weave of the long shoots of the elephant grass plucked virtually from the patch she was passing. With the big gaudy pods of color on the fabric it would have to be that of a summer style printed on light linen. And for the winter, she would take away the monkey bread, maybe leave the tight straw links to augment the warm weave of a heavy tweed. Her imagination seldom stood still. She was born to fill the shadowy space behind her eyes with designs and patterns inspired by even the simplest things she noticed around her.

Suddenly a flicker of movement froze her thoughts, scattering the bright pods hanging in her mind, whispering a warning. She stopped, standing still. There was a rustle in the grass ahead. Hesitating, she held her breath. Her body tensed, ready, its primeval instincts tightened to the verge of flight.

Everything was still.

A flicker of movement caught her eyes as she scanned her surroundings. Straining to see, the silhouette of a warthog moved out of the grass into the path. A piglet followed.

Precious felt her relief ease into a weakness in her legs as the adrenaline faded. She moved again, one gentle step in front of the other. Gidi claimed that the area around the lodge held the highest concentration of warthogs in the national park. He couldn't give any reason for this, but said that in many ways it was a blessing, because even though the warthog itself could hardly be picked for the centerfold in the lodge's brochures, their abundance attracted some unique predators. "We are not the only ones who like bacon," he joked.

The warthog had stripped the imaginary creations from her mind, replacing them with am image from a week ago, when as Precious had walked between the chalets, a martial eagle had flashed out of nowhere as a hog and her two piglets nibbled the lawn. Precious had stood motionless, watching the drama as it unfolded meters away, the little pig squealing its agony as the eagle mantled over its victim with spread wings, footing and crushing its talons into the little hog's body. After subduing its prey's struggles, the huge bird looked up. Noticing her, in its fright it abandoned the piglet to fly up into a nearby tree. She had backed away slowly leaving the little piglet squealing pathetically, its body punctured. With a crippled front leg, it wasn't able to follow its mother as she bolted. From the inside of a chalet where she was not noticed, Precious watched the eagle return to carry the helpless little creature, still squeaking pitifully, up to a bare branch, where the majestic bird tore off chunks of flesh, until the piglets screams subsided into silence. But now, Precious set aside the gory images and watched as the mother hog and possibly her remaining piglet, with flagged tails, turned to trot away into the moon shadows.

She reached the kitchen. There was still enough charge in the solar batteries to power the lights, revealing the pots and pans stacked on the shelves and the kettle on the stove, the heating of which would be her first task. Then her thoughts flowed through her hold on a broom's handle as she mindlessly brushed the few crumbs left from the previous eve's activity into a dust pan. The hiss of the kettle changed its tone into the rattle of boiling water.

With Gidi away, Precious wondered if he would be replaced by Moses, popping in to scrounge scraps of company and coffee.

Swathed in the dimness, and wrapped in the sound of her broom and the fading whisper of the kettle, Precious considered the *mzungu* man. How many opportunities had he squandered to end up as a footloose wanderer – not much different from the men in her village, stoically facing and accepting life and its capriciousness? He was too old for her! Or was he? She was by far the oldest of the female staff here. But whatever it was, she sensed a dependability beneath his forlornness. She could count on him to help get to where she wanted to go. There was an allure about him. But it was best not to play with fire, no matter how tempting. She had watched an occasional guest do so, they could snuff the consequences when they left. She couldn't.

Precious had been at the periphery of the safari business for long enough to know that December was the start of the slow tourist season. It is when the usual clients hunkered down in the cold darkness of their northern winter. Further discouragement was that, unlike the plethora of long, bright and mostly dry days of the northern summers, the Central African summer was aptly named the wet season. December was when this wet-ness began in earnest. The summer deluges produced the impassable mud on the roads, even as their warm, wet vitality made the long grasses and the leaves on the trees unfurl like a low, green fog, obscuring the animals from any viewing tourists. Precious knew that African tourism was about animals, not greenness. Despite this being the case, she knew that it was not unusual for the lodge to be filled with local guests for the few days between Christmas and New Year, even though the long dirt road between Mumbwa and the Lubungu pontoon was barely negotiable, even with a 4x4 vehicle. Neither the rain, nor the poor state of the road, could keep the local wealthy away. They had 4x4 vehicles, and they were the ones with the winches, ropes and expertise to extract themselves if stuck in the mud. What was unusual was to have the whole lodge booked by a single client from mid-November to the end of the year, with an option for another two weeks. It was also unusual to have it booked for so long by someone who had little interest in taking time off to celebrate a Christian holiday. But then, Africa was often full of contradictions. The name 'Mohammed Bahadur' showed on the booking sheet.

She knew of him. His reputation stretched as far west as Mumbwa, where the small Indian community dominated the town's commerce below the tall spire of its mosque. Maybe it was them who whispered the sketchiness of Mohammed's reputation. Whatever its origin, it was even known in her village. Or perhaps it stemmed from the way he had pushed his fingers into some of the local community's pies. This was no mean feat, given the close-knit nature of that community, knit so tight that the locals joked they were inbred.

Precious had also heard of his passion for hunting, and that he had a controlling interest in some of the more productive hunting concessions across the country, particularly in the east. Rumor had it that his quota of trophy animals was higher than most, which was why certain officials had slightly larger rolls of pudge rippling above the tight collars of their jackets, and their wives wore more extravagant jewelry.

Precious wondered if it was lucky breaks or hard work that had given Mohammed his wealth? Had he cheated along the way? Bribed his way to affluence? She was seeking a role model to help her get to where she wanted to go.

Swathed in the dimness and the sound of her steps and the brush of her broom, she considered her unique brand of solitude. Was being Mushala's daughter a lucky break? She knew the whispered stories of her father. After his death, her mother's fate hadn't been much above that of a warthog, on its knees rooting in the mud, scrounging for scraps. Precious had seen this fate suffered by so many of her peers in the villages. 'Hewers of wood and bearers of water', fates virtually biblical in nuance. To which should be added bearers of babies.

Where could one find a husband who limited his aspirations to not more than two children? How often had she seen her peers, even the most ambitious, have their aspirations smothered under their maternal obligations to care for a child, and another, and another, until their dreams were lost in the cries of children, the chopping of wood, and splash of water from a communal pump? In the villages, the age of consent was largely biological, not statutory. 'She has grass, we play ball,' was the adage. And most girls had enough grass by the age of fourteen for the game of life to begin. She had not been an exception.

Was she wrong to resist the pressure to be a possession? To be purchased, to be bred like a cow? Her final resistance was yet to come, when Eddie came to claim the bride he had bought.

There was a certain perfidy in her actions. But what other way was there? Being betrothed to Eddie, with his connections to the chief, had opened the door to a job at the lodge; her first step towards a different future. She knew that she was special; it was reflected in her aloofness. For her, not all of the social laws applied. Not that she had chosen it to be so. She knew from the stories, and self-realization, that her obstinacy came from her father, as did her acute sense of injustice – perceived or real. She had inherited his focus and determination to resist wrongs where they affected her. Luckily, she got her logic from her mother. If he had been able to reason, her father wouldn't have died with a bullet through his eye and another in his chest. His body wouldn't have been displayed for all, to show the people that the power and magic of Mushala was over. He would have understood the futility of his cause. But, was it over or not? After all, it was the legacy of his lingering spells in the minds of the people which was both a blessing and a curse. It rendered both Precious and her mother relatively untouchable. People were wary of messing with Mushala's women. Nobody knew what spirit lurked in their shadows. What kind of ether had he become? Would his ghost haunt those who messed with his women?

Nobody knew.

No man was bold enough to take Mushala's widow to wed. And an unsupported woman in the village leads an austere life. However, an unwelcome nuance was that sometimes these 'limbo' women found themselves selected where tradition must be fulfilled. Mushala's spirit could hardly object if one of his women were chosen to be at the center of a ritual, even if unwillingly picked. And at the age of fourteen, Precious could object even less. It was pointless asking why, after all the times her mother had balked, fate had finally proved too powerful. Why had her mother not resisted more fervently as it wrested her daughter from her protective embrace? Precious wondered – if she had screamed out loud, would her cries have been as futile as those of an abandoned piglet? Instead she had wailed silently on the final eve of the annual 'Juba JaNsomo' festival when the early grass had already started growing on the field of her life. Despite her terror, she had resisted the hypnotizing effect of the hours of chanting, clapping of hands and stamping of feet. She had not heeded the urgings to let go and subside into trance. How was it that she had been uncannily afforded the break that changed it all? Was her father's spirit still with her, listening to her wails of misery?

Luck comes in strange forms, even as a Seventh Day Adventist. Such an honoured festival guest had incurred a severe penalty for showing disrespect. His religious morality balked when presented with a fourteen-year-old virgin as a consort for the eve. A special gift, courtesy of the festival. That clash of cultures reflected in the amount of the fine of his refusal. And by the next year, she was no longer pristine enough to be a gift, condemned to a customary life hewing its wood, bearing its water and babies. Instead, the guest gave the precious child a magazine to placate her nerves before sending her back to her mother. It was a magazine left on a coffee table in the guest's home, in the far-off city, by his wife. He had picked it up to read a political article, whose catchy phrase in small print on the cover had caught his interest.

But it was not the catchy phrase which captured the young girl's attention; it was the sumptuously dressed woman who dominated its cover. The Vogue magazine was filled with color and clothing, brimming with fashion and style. It overflowed with ideas so radically different from those of the bush, of the huts of the village, of the tin cans of water to be carried, dirt floors to be swept with a grass brush, and corn to be crushed and cooked into porridge. The images fanned the glow of her ambition, kindling a desire to paint the colors and flickering patterns taken from her

David Maritz

village and the bush, and splash them across the equator to form a new patina in the fashion of the world.

Now she felt that fate had again laid another stepping-stone in her path, even if this time it came in the unexpected form of a tall, slender, broad-shouldered atheist. She would manipulate him into embellishing her chances, as she guided his seemingly aimless steps.

She would mingle their destinies – at least for a while.

20

November 25

Even though only in his mid-forties, it was clear why Ulrich Richter headed up the banking consortium, providing a substantial amount of the funding for the Nature Trust's conservation efforts. He was impressive. Gideon was aware of his ruthless reputation. He knew what Ulrich looked like, having sat, unspeaking, in a small audience at a presentation given by Gene, his boss, on a previous trip down to South Africa.

This was to be their first formal meeting.

Ulrich's chiselled Teutonic looks and tall, fit physique could easily have starred in one of Leni Riefenstahl's old propaganda movies. The conservation trust's operations in the Kafue were only a small part of Ulrich's corporate sponsorship in Africa. Although directed by an independent board, with Gene as the chairperson, it was the size of Ulrich's donations that gave him so much sway over the trust's activities. It was his brutally efficient attention to the smallest detail that had earned him his position and reputation. Now it was their turn to endure the piercing gaze, or glare of his critical eye... Heaven forbid!

The tension was palpable in Gene's voice as they waited for Ulrich's arrival.

David Maritz

"He has an uncanny ability to pick on things we haven't thought through properly," Gene explained.

The meeting venue surprised Gideon. The South by South East had once been a popular small conference center. It had all it needed for its purpose. A neatly delineated parking area stood adjacent to a sprawling Cape Dutch style façade, its white walls stopping below the russet of a terracotta tile roof. A generous, tidy reception foyer led into a wide, high-ceilinged conference hall and equally sized dining area, with a kitchen set to service up to fifty attendees. Off to the side, an adequate smoking bar for post-conference socializing opened out through big glass doors onto expansive and well-tended lawns. The lawns were partially shaded by large exotic trees, and bordered by bounteous flowerbeds resplendent with zinnia, cannas, and numerous other splashes of color. Located well to the east of the city, the venue's approaches were increasingly choked by the growing squatter camps which fester at the peripheries of most Southern African towns.

It was only when Gene mentioned that Ulrich was an avid light sport pilot that Gideon understood the choice of this venue. It was a fifteen-minute drive from a local airfield specializing in that sort of flying. With his pedantic daily schedule broken up into quarter-hour granularities, Ulrich would come to the meeting directly from early morning flying.

As Gene and Gideon waited in the sparsely furnished hall, a single long table was set at its center, with a chair placed at its head and two others halfway down its sides – one for himself and one for Gene. Through the window, they watched Ulrich's arrival. He held a large canvas sports bag as he quickly got out of the sleek chauffeured car, and disappeared into a small change room on the edge of one of the tennis courts. A few minutes later, precisely on time, he emerged. He was no longer wearing casual jeans and a sports jacket, and instead was dressed like a German banker. He hung his tailored charcoal suit jacket over the back of his chair, and Gideon could see that the cufflinks of his delicately pinstriped and immaculately pressed shirt were in the form of small silver elephants. The only other deviation from the conservative exactitude expected from a man in his position was a bright yellow tie. It was dotted with little hooded falcons, a nod to an elite affiliation with the sport of kings. Gideon set aside an impulse to tell Ulrich that he himself was a falconer. The man probably wasn't the type to be affected by gestures of commonality.

The meeting began cordially, with Gene offering introductions and talk about the lodge and its surrounds. Ulrich spoke impeccable English, but with a clear German accent, as if designed to differentiate himself from them. From the light discourse, Gideon discovered it was Ulrich's stay as a guest at the lodge a few years ago, where he had enjoyed the fishing, which resulted in the corporate funding.

After a few minutes of banal banter, it was down to business. Gene gave a report on the financial side of the operation, how much was being spent on salaries, fuel, provisions, equipment and training. His report on the training methodologies followed, the number of game scouts who had completed the program in the last year, and what the future goals were.

Then it was Gideon's turn.

It didn't take long for the banker in Ulrich to start asking about metrics. He was interested in numbers and statistics. How many more animals per square kilometer were there today? What was the ratio of animal increase to scout presence on the ground? Gideon said he was aware that success needed to be measured, and it attempted to do some very basic metric taking. Once a week, he told Ulrich, he had counted the number of puku alongside the roads which skirted a few of the dambos in the area. He presented these figures.

"But what about the other types of animal?" Ulrich asked.

"That's more difficult," Gideon said. "It's harder to count the species that are not found in the open grasslands. This would only be possible if one did a comprehensive camera trap survey."

"Why has this not been done?" Ulrich wanted to know.

"Budget and time," Gideon replied. "My mandate was to train games scouts, not to do game surveys."

The sour look on Ulrich's face indicated that Gideon's answer didn't find favor in his eyes. Gideon suspected Ulrich regarded him as cheeky; that he wasn't showing sufficient deference. This was confirmed when Ulrich went on to suggest that if he had been doing the work this aspect would have been addressed. He icily asked how much it would cost to do a proper survey to get him metrics. Gideon replied he would investigate the costs, but that it was unlikely he would perform the survey.

"Why not?" Ulrich asked with a sharp edge.

"Because I am not an academic," Gideon replied. "Surveys would fall under the category of research. I would have to apply for a research permit, which given my non-existent academic qualifications, I probably wouldn't get."

Ulrich snapped back coldly. "Then maybe we need somebody more qualified than you to do the job." To rub it in, he continued. "My son has completed a degree in ecology, maybe he would be more suitable."

"Maybe he would," Gideon said with as much dislike in his voice as he could muster.

It was clear that this banking guru was accustomed to clicking his fingers, and having everybody spring to his bidding. He was obviously not someone who had spent much time dealing with the clumsy, inefficient, and intricate workings of African bureaucracies. He wasn't aware that getting permission from government departments in Africa wasn't something predictable or guaranteed.

Gideon sat still, looking unblinkingly at Ulrich.

A work permit for his son! Hmmm. The asshole had no idea how long it would take, or how much bribe money would be required. But, he shouldn't delude himself – if his rich-kid son wanted the job, he was sure his daddy had enough money to pay any bribes, or grease the palms of the 'fixers' to organize a visa. In his case, money would not be the issue. Rather, it would be the black and white purity of his principles that would get in the way. Gideon wondered how willing Ulrich would be to risk staining his records with the pragmatism of the blurry grey strings that often need to be pulled to get things done on this continent.

By this stage Gideon deemed it pointless to mention the issues most bothering about the work on the Kafue. He doubted there would be much place in Ulrich's world for witchcraft. It was clear that there would be scant chance for further funds to train additional scouts until he could get him his metrics. If Ulrich wanted him out of the way, he would leave it entirely up to his privileged son to educate him.

Gideon had served in the army long enough to recognize the sort of puffed-up HQ theorist, full of self-importance and scant experience of field reality. So going for broke, he continued. "Your son, like you, wouldn't know how to put up with all the larger bullshit of Africa or the local crap to do the job".

Gideon succeeded in not only pissing Ulrich off, but also his boss.

It was with subdued anger, tainted with a sense of hopelessness, that Gideon watched a good-looking young African woman, dressed in a neat driver's uniform, hold the door open for Ulrich as he paused to wish Gene a goodbye and praise him for a job well done before getting into the silver Mercedes.

Ulrich didn't deign Gideon any parting nicety, except to say, "Remember I like metrics."

"I'm sorry if I messed it up for you," Gideon apologized to Gene as they watched the Mercedes pass through the gates onto the road.

"Hell!" Gene burst out in frustration. "You certainly know how to bite the hand that feeds you."

With the tension of his anger receding, Gideon regretted his impulsive reaction. "I said I'm sorry. I will make up for it somehow."

"How?"

Gideon pinched his lips. "I don't know, but somehow."

To cheer himself up, Gideon let his mind dwell on what waited when he headed back north. He wanted to connect the dots blurred by time. A deviation to where it all began, the yardstick of his life, a place and a person. Everything since then judged as better, or worse than the metrics, set so long ago between some hills and a girl.

Sophia had texted that he was welcome to visit.

* * *

As the escalator carried him down into the check-in hall, Gideon thought how it must be the name change which was behind the substantial facelift that had been given to Johannesburg's O.R. Thambo airport. The euphoria and fanfare of majority rule in South Africa was now a distant memory. But to give credit to the engineers and refurbishers of this face of Africa's advancement, only now, many years later, were the first signs of the African malady beginning to show. In the airport, here a stationary walking conveyor belt was blocked with a strip of yellow tape, over there a window was cracked, and in the underground parking a ticketing machine was not functioning. Prompt and regular maintenance is not an African forte. Its people are so accustomed to stepping over cracks that mostly they seldom notice any flaws, and the cracks only get wider the further north one travels.

However, the Mugg & Bean coffee shop on the intermediate floor between the A and B terminals was still full of vibrancy. Being a ubiquitous franchise across the country, Gideon was familiar with its fare.

He had time for a latte. He chose a table close to the greeting podium where two giggling waitresses stood. One broke away to follow him, and casually slid a menu his way, asking disinterestedly how he was. Catching her off-guard he answered with a, "Not dead yet."

The boredom on her face changed to a broad smile as she replied with a, "That's good."

Since it was midmorning and he knew he was headed north to a place of politically squandered dearth, he decided to spoil himself by ordering a latte and a slice of chocolate cheesecake. Who knew if he would find a slice of anything good up there.

"God bless the new, well-fed shape of Africa," he muttered to himself as he watched the shelf-like pout of the waitress's rump flick away with his order. "It must be the leftovers."

Scooping off small nibbles of the smooth, turgid cake with a teaspoon, he tried to remember how long it was since he'd last been to the city where he was headed. Fifteen? Eighteen years? Would he recognize the place? Sophia? Would she and the place be as unrecognizable as this airport? At least she would answer to the same name, unlike the airport with its reflection of politics.

Gideon looked at his watch. It was a short international flight; he would soon need to join the scrum in the hall serving the high numbered A-gates. Those gates more resembled a third-world bus station than an airport.

David Maritz

The atmosphere was warranted, because that was what it was – from here, all passengers were bused to the aircraft. And they needed to be there early.

After taking particularly long to slowly chase the last mouthful of the cake around the plate, and using his finger to surreptitiously aid it into the teaspoon, he checked the bill and added a generous tip, more for the Rubenesque eye-candy provided by the waitress than her unhurried service. It was an hour and a half to take off. Time to go. He gathered his laptop and carry-on bags and headed for the escalator down to the security check and immigration.

In Africa, as in many places, it is seldom wise to leave items of value in a bag checked into the hold of a commercial aircraft. It is best to travel as check-in-light and backpack-heavy as possible. The downside of being laden with carry-on was that the security checks, which were often cursory, still required the inconvenience of unpacking items into the scanner trays.

Gideon clenched his teeth with annoyance. The security crew had halted the scanner as they chatted about something that had nothing to do with the contents of his backpack. Looking back as he waited for his goods to start moving again, he registered the figure standing beyond the scan point. She was also waiting for her bags to move with the conveyor belt. In the shuffling wait in the queue to the check point, she had obviously stood unnoticed behind him.

The first flick of his eyes caught his attention in a breath catching way. Casually and surreptitiously, he let his gaze drift her way as he removed his laptop and kindle from their trays, more slowly now, as she passed through the scanner, his eyes absorbing the outline of her elegant figure.

She was as dark as a Dravidian, the tone of her smooth skin complementing the simplicity of a sleeveless dress fitting her like the fur of a cat. The only concession to color was the silver necklace which glistened out from under the coal silk of her hair cascading down onto her shoulders.

It was those bare shoulders which really caught Gideon's attention.

Drifting out from under her dress and along her arms was the finest tattooed filigree imaginable. Etched onto the amber of her skin, stylized fronds tumbled down her shoulders, onto her upper arms, brushed behind her elbows, and reappeared with delicate simplicity back onto her forearms, until the wispy tendrils teased to the edges of her wrists.

From the fineness of her features and the darkness of her eyes, Gideon knew she must be of exotic origin. Being in Africa, she was probably from the stock of those from the Horn of Africa who, long ago, followed in the footsteps of the Arab slave traders. Or from those kept in chains and mixed with those masters. Still stealing glances at her in the next queue, he was unsure if it was the artwork, or the dark hinted romance of her face and figure which was more arresting. She was as dark as any African enigma, with eyes as black as those of the Queen of Cush, and ebony skin tinted with the copper from King Solomon's mines.

Gideon mentally whistled to himself as he picked up his stamped passport and moved on, leaving her still waiting in line.

Hurrying to the far end of the airport shopping mall and down to the 'cattle' gates, the gate bus queue was already moving as he joined it, with the first bus full and ready to depart for the aircraft for the flight north to Bulawayo. Handing his ticket to be checked, he looked across at the next queue over.

The Queen of Cush had just joined its melee. It was for a flight to Lusaka.

21

November 26

The crowd at the foot of the mobile stairs slowly fed itself up into the plane, as a few yellow jacketed officials lazily flapped their arms at the periphery like exotic herdsmen tending a flock of goats. With the area shared between domestic flights, and the short international hauls, and with the Joburg-Cape Town route being one of the busiest in the world, the apron was a buzz of activity.

Moving into the aircraft, Gideon asked a plump, dark-haired woman to let him slide across to his allocated window seat. Then settling down for the short flight northwards he politely introduced himself.

"Hi, I'm Gideon."

The woman nodded back. "Hi, I'm Rochelle. Are you heading home?"

"No," Gideon said, "just visiting. A quick stop on my way up to Lusaka. What about you?"

"Bulawayo is home for me, " she smiled back.

The climb out of Johannesburg was bumpy, setting the tone for the rest of the flight. The air, spurred on by the blazing sunshine, buffeted their aircraft as it rose, sucking moisture up with it, so high that the jet-stream blew the cloudy crowns sideways like the hair on the head of a windswept girl. Gideon peered out the window at the top of one of these huge vapor anvils.

"It looks like we can expect a thunderstorm this afternoon," the woman commented. "We could use it. We never have enough rain these days".

Gideon smiled at her. "So things haven't changed. That is what they have always said."

"Really. How do you know?" she asked.

"I grew up there. But I haven't been back for twenty odd years."

"That's exciting," she said. "What's bringing you back?"

"I'm going back to connect the dots. To check how much the yardstick to my life has changed."

"That's a strange thing to say. What do you mean?"

"I'm going back to meet someone who once was an important part of my life."

A few of the passengers glanced around nervously as the aircraft rocked its way through the sky. Gideon settled back in his seat with his thoughts and watched as the Limpopo river slid past under the wing. He thought how north of the Limpopo is where the real Africa started for him.

Half an hour later, as the plane dipped its nose, Gideon buckled his seat-belt and looked out the window to see the old familiar thorn brush land-scape rushing under them as the aircraft crossed the runways threshold.

David Maritz

* * *

In the hillside suburb, the tall endemic trees mixed in with exotics to shield the eye from the worn drabness of the old houses. Here it seemed Rip Van Winkle had fallen asleep. Behind their fences and high walls, the houses stared out at the roads like geriatrics from the veranda of a hospice.

Leaving suburban stagnation behind, Gideon noticed the lethargic blanket covering the peripheries gradually lifting the nearer he got to the city's heart. It was a hybrid awakening. The skeleton of the old colonial city, with its wide streets renamed in honor of revolutionary heroes, still had the same hollow-eyed store fronts staring at cracked, uneven pavements. Little had changed. The new crowds, resembling ants looking for scraps on the bones of a skeleton, wandered the streetside pavements while avoiding hawkers' wares spread out on blankets. The hawkers themselves crouched on their haunches, backs against frugal storefronts, haranguing passersby while attempting to entice the unwary into making eye contact. Gone was the cosmopolitan color of the crowds. The old tint of Caucasians, Greeks, Lebanese, Jews, even Indians had been replaced by an monotone ebony. Old Lobengula's people had reclaimed their pre-colonial capitol.

Why in the world would Sofia want to come back to this place? Gideon wondered.

Reengaging with the city of his boyhood, he left his rental car near the museum gardens, and walked the distance to the address she'd sent. He joined the swarm of people spilling off pavements, haphazardly crossing roads with artful disdain, dodging between a clutter of minibuses, motorbikes and bicycles as everyone noisily squeezed their way to wherever. Getting closer, anxiously he quickened his step. The enigma, with its big brown eyes and strawberry blonde braids having ignored his pleas for two decades, now beckoned irresistibly. Would he recognize her emerging from those old scars of the heart? Or would she be wrinkled like the sidewalks of this city? Would she dangle possibilities from the window of her castle, then clip her golden braids as he climbed?

At the address which he had long since memorized he knocked on a heavy wooden door. Through the small glass pane at its center he was beckoned in by a young curly-haired less, a secretary maybe? The office was large, divided into cubicles, none of them occupied. The pleasantly plump young girl asked if he was there to see Sophia, and when he said, "Yes" she pointed across to a side door.

Stepping across and after another tentative knock, from its dim interior, for the first time in over twenty years Sophia smiled at him. Here it was, that moment he had dreamed of in a thousand ways, a thousand places, a thousand moods. Those dreams painted in hues of scarlet, crimson, gold an indigo. Now washed away in the simplicity of the setting, the poignant beauty of the soft flesh color of a shy smile and the dusty brown of her eyes, below the faded strawberry tint of her hair, still crowning her head like the halo he remembered. The eternal summer of his memory confronting the autumn of reality in a poignantly wonderful way.

She led him into her office, allowing him to talk about his life as if it were a job interview: kids, career, places, events. She offered tea. He declined. It was her turf. He was the intruder.

His emotions were like the back tug of a wave pulling the sand of his certainty from under his heals. He wanted to say, "Let's get the hell out of here."

From her outline, her contours were as ample as always, even more sumptuous where they curved over her bosom. From motherhood, maybe? The shadow of her beauty was still etched in the creases of her face, augmented by tendrils of worry reaching out from the edges of her lips and the corners of her eyes.

The homely young girl crossed from her desk, knocked and came in to ask if she could collect something. With a frown on her face Sophia snapped back at her. "Can't you see that I am busy?"

David Maritz

It caught Gideon off guard. He hadn't expected to see the old imperturbable aloofness replaced by something else. Impatience? No. There was an air of bleakness.

That was where he first detected the despair. Sophia was accusing, making it worse with a hollow laugh. His heart went out to the girl. He wanted to say, "You are doing just fine sister."

With the naivety stripped from his eyes Gideon looked about more carefully. The office was without cheer. Her long black dress reached high up her neck. A barrier blocking any happiness sneaking out with her wane smiles when he managed to get her to briefly forget the weight of the world. He tried to remember her big soft, surprisingly weightless breasts, and the beautiful bell shape of her hips, how they spawned the curves of her thighs. But the bleakness smothered his memories.

"Do you have pierced ears?" The crown of her hair covered her ears.

From his pocket he took out a folded envelope and handed it to her.

Opening it a pair of earrings fell out onto her desktop, They were delicately crafted from three lucky beans each, strung together with a wicker of fine wire.

"I made these for you," he said.

Sophia took them and lifting the locks of her hair threaded the hooks through her earlobes.

"I no longer wear jewelry," she said. "Except this ring."

She took it off and showed it to Gideon. On the inside it was engraved 'HK'

"I take it this is from you father?" he queried.

"How did you know?" she questioned.

"From the initials." He said. "Wasn't his name Henry? Henry Kowalsky." Gideon searched for a smile on her face.

"How is he?"

"He died last year," she said. "I miss him."

"Wow he must have been over ninety. "

"Yes, he was a tough man", she spoke softly. "You had to be to survive the concentration camps.

"I am sorry," he consoled. "How are your mother and sister?"

"They both passed away a long time ago." She answered flatly.

Gideon tried to shift their conversation to lighter matters. But it kept drifting back into the bleakness.

She saw herself as a victim of her own character. She chose the same kind of men in her life, she said. Men who let her down. Men like him.

"Were there others?" Gideon asked.

"Yes," she said.

"Still?"

"No," she said.

Gideon said he didn't want to upset the equilibrium of her life in any way. Where was the bright, happy, impulsive girl he'd once loved? She said she remembered their time as if it were someone else's. She wondered that she was the age of her daughters now when all that happened. Not him. He remembered everything. But it was claustrophobic, discussing the past in this bleak place. With the bright colors of his memories gone, his urgency to get out grew.

"Come on, let's go for a walk," he suggested.

* * *

Almost two and a half decades before, in this same park, amidst its once-floral opulence and hot humid air, for a brief hour they had sat side by side. Unknowingly for the last time, Gideon had embraced her magnificence. Then, with a casual "See you soon," they had parted, with the wars that changed the face of Africa intervening.

Now, they were walking under the big trees of the city park next to the old municipal swimming pool. The grass needed cutting, its growth spurred by the summer warmth and the advent of the rains. But mowing was not a high priority on meager city budgets.

"This place is so messed up. The roadblocks, the potholes, the power outages, the lack of civic services, running water. Doesn't it get to you?" Gideon asked. "Why the hell did you come back here?"

Sophia took her time. "This is where I feel at home. The highveld down south always felt foreign. I'm not married, my daughters are in Australia. An inheritance pays my bills, with a bit left over for indulgence. I have a few good clients down south. With the internet reaching here, I can work as easily here as anywhere. Yes, there are inconveniences, but it is relatively safe in this backwater, compared to a lot of other places in Africa. I love the old atmosphere of the suburb where I live. It has barely changed since we lived here. The houses are the same, the gardens. Yes, the trees are now huge, but that adds to their charm. More importantly," she emphasized, "home is where you have good friends. I have two great friends from school days here, who never left, even with the war and troubles. Having special friends close by is crucial for happiness." She studied him carefully. "Wouldn't you agree?"

"Absolutely."

"So I came home."

"Why did you contact me?" he asked.

"It was an impulse. Your name came up in a conversation with someone here who knows you and our past. "

"From what you say you seem to be comfortably settled here. But are you happy?" Gideon asked.

They kept walking.

"Yes, for now."

"For now? That isn't a very good endorsement of the future. What's wrong?"

"One of my friends is emigrating, and the other is thinking of moving to the eastern part of the country to be close to her son." The bleakness that had left her voice crept back in. "It will be lonely here if they both go. And you? Are you happy?"

"I guess I am," Gideon said, "But I still have a nagging sense of alienation and a desire to accomplish something important in life. If I squint down on this part of the world, I see myself for what I am; one of the pale-skinned dregs left behind and now blamed for Africa's woes. This makes it difficult to get to do anything great, especially when my youth was wasted fighting a losing battle. I can't help feeling that I am a pale scab on the dark skin of Africa, attempting futilely to heal some of its wounds. But nobody is going to thank me, or admire my achievements – if any."

Sophia smiled at him, "Except maybe me."

Gideon narrowed his eyes as he looked at her. "Hmmm."

"Don't you wish for just peace and quiet?" she asked him.

"Yes, but with whom?"

"Me."

Gideon looked at her closely, unsure if she was joking. Where was all this new openness coming from?

"I have been lying for years in a dark riverbed of life, with all my edges knocked away. Some of the knocking done by you."

"You deserved it," Sophia threw back.

Gideon dipped his head. "Whatever. Now destiny has tossed me into a backwater, another shallow, murky pool of my existence. Admittedly it would be nice to have someone there beside me. But what I have learned from the new Africa is that you cannot have it all. There is always a croc-odile waiting to burst out of the slime to grab a leg, and drag me beneath the surface of history."

Sophia laughed. "My bite is not as bad as a crocodile's."

Gideon nodded, "But from what I remember, those bites still hurt."

Reaching the far end of the park, Sophia turned to him. "Come. Let's start back. I have another meeting at the office in a short while."

"Okay," he said.

"Oh, and another thing! How long are you going to be in town?"

"Three days," he said. "I want to visit a few other old friends while I am here. Also go out to the Matopos hills."

"Where are you staying?"

"At the old Churchill Hotel."

"Why don't you check out and come stay with me?" she suggested. "I have a big house. And we still have a lot of catching up to do. You can tell me all about your murky pools."

"I would love to!" he replied.

* * *

The warm night air drifted in through the open windows. There was the occasional flutter of a moth on the screens as they tried to fly in, attracted by the single lamp that glowed on the small table beside Gideon. They had ended up sitting on an old couch, out on a section of her veranda which was protected by insect screens. Slowly over the course of the evening, she had moved closer. She was tucked in snugly next to him, her head leaning on his shoulders and her legs folded under her. Over the dinner, which she had cooked herself, and the course of the evening, their conversation had drifted over the past decades.

"So what exactly do you do up there?" she asked. "I know it's something to do with scouts and anti-poaching. But what exactly?"

"It has taken a while to work out a concept that everyone, from top to bottom, can understand." Gideon explained, "I call it the Bang Concept.

The 'bang' being when a poacher kills an animal. That is what traditional anti-poaching has focused on. With limited success. I've expanded this to the pre and post-bang, to make it easily understandable. What happens before and after a poacher kills an animal is often more important for anti-poaching success than the 'bang' interdictions, which get the publicity."

Sophia ran a finger down the inside of his arm, as the slow revolutions of the big ceiling fan brushed its faint relief from the warm night air over them. "Tell me about it," she said. "It sounds interesting."

"Well, the pre-bang is developing intelligence networks and gathering actionable information. We focus outside of the park. Most of the poachers live in the surrounding villages. Everybody knows who they are. The trick is to find informers who will let the scouts know when the poachers leave the village, and if they're lucky, where in the park they are headed. Predominantly this is small scale, opportunistic stuff to feed themselves and their families bushmeat delicacies. Then there are the large operations, with intermediaries which stretch to the cities and even across the borders into Angola or the Congo. From there, things may reach further into big cartels. Here, there are two flavors. First, the commercial supply of venison to local city markets. Venison, or bush-meat as it is called, is considered a delicacy amongst the Africans, who are the customers and consumers. Add to this a certain amount of poaching for animal parts for the witchcraft markets. Second, more insidious and where the big money comes in, is the poaching to supply the fetish or stature items to the Asian markets. Rhino horn, ground to a powder, as a male aphrodisiac, or elephant ivory to carve works of art, or signature rings to be used as stamps on legal documents. Add to that Pangolin scales to be made into a soup delicacy. Once again, close to the park, the locals know the movements of the vehicles bringing in strangers and taking out the goods. Here, park scouts need to work with the police and even Interpol. How to develop rapid response liaison protocols is what I focus on. Corruption notwithstanding," Gideon continued, "anti-poaching operations are basically law-enforcement activities with apprehended poachers going through the justice system. This is where the 'post-bang' stuff is important. Collecting evidence, processing crime scenes, preparing for trial… unless done correctly, this results in a revolving door for the poachers. They get out with a slap on the wrist and are back on the hunt the next day." Gideon lifted his arm and let it drape over her shoulders.

"Wow!" she murmured. "You have been a busy boy. You will have to invite me up there and show me firsthand."

"I like being busy." Gideon reached over and turned off the light.

22

November 23-30

Precious paused her sweeping of the *chitenge's* tile floor. From under its roof, she watched the approach of the sleek Land Cruiser. Virtually unheralded by the quiet purr of its engine, the dark, dust-covered vehicle glided to a halt in the small gravel parking area across from where she stood. The almost soundless arrival meant that the welcoming group had to scramble to be in time to sing and clap hands. She looked on as the occupants stepped from the air-conditioned the vehicle into the afternoon heat. Each was offered a glass of cool juice on a tray, together with warm hand towels to wipe away any dust and sweat. It was the lodge's welcoming ritual.

Later, replaying the scene in her mind, Precious realized that the personalities and relationships of each of the guests was apparent from the moment they stepped forth. Bright had pre-briefed the staff. The guests were to be a father and daughter and her friend. The father was a fine-featured man who, although a lot taller, had an uncanny resemblance to a Somali store owner in Mumbwa. Later, Precious was to realize that his height was masked by a tendency to stoop forward as he walked. His lean, sinewy physique had an air of austerity to it. An unusual trait were his quick movements for someone so tall. It brought to Precious's mind the sly quickness of a jackal scavenging in tall grass. As for the two women, the shorter one – the Jackal's daughter – was lighter-skinned than her father. The mop of her boisterously abundant, wavy, raven hair was gathered and pinned up in a barely manageable swirl above her head. Precious wondered as to her full heritage, not quite matching her father's. An Indian mixture, maybe? Her companion, tall and fair-haired, effused an ebullient spontaneity, backed up with a quick laugh and expansive movements, her excess energy lavished on whatever was at hand. Here the father handed back his empty glass with barely a nod, whereas the tall woman loudly expressed her appreciation.

"Oh, darling, that was just what I needed!" She gave each of the surprised waitresses a wide-armed hug, before twisting away with a swish of her hips and a trailing drift of an arm and leg.

Precious came to realize that the aloof indifference with which the father treated the waitresses reflected his general attitude to life. For the most, the staff barely existed. He had an expectation of service, with scant need for reciprocal politeness.

However Precious was fascinated by the ebb and flow of tension between each of the group, which soon became apparent in postures and body language. Not to mention the contrast in their appearance and aesthetics. The physical frugality of the father, behavioral abundance of the friend and of course the delicate tattoo on the dark daughter's arms. Precious had never considered the body as a canvas for artistry. What made it more interesting was its bearer being the daughter of a man whose rigorous observance of a prayer schedule showed him to be a devout Muslim. Was the tattoo to spite the father's conservatism?

Overall, during the next few days the guests settled in.

It was the alcohol veto, Precious noticed, which put a definite dent in the tall blonde woman's bubbliness. In the late afternoon she sat enjoying a gin and tonic on the riverside deck when one of the staff would requested that she take her drink elsewhere, because "Mustafa was on his way", and she would scowl and mutter to herself before flouncing off to her chalet. There she would sit simmering on its deck.

"Yes," Precious heard her say to her companion, "I can understand your father's sensibilities, but we are not in Mecca. We are out here to enjoy ourselves and to get away from the crap, like we used to. It bugs me that I have to be told how I must celebrate!"

The short, dark daughter would agree, half-heartedly defending her father by adding "But we are his guests. And he is not around most of the day."

Which was true, and made Precious wonder where he went and what he was doing.

"So what? Let's transfer to another lodge," the blonde friend had replied in a vexed voice. "I hear that there is one further downriver. I can afford it. We don't need your father's generosity." Precious watched as the blonde sipped her gin and tonic and reached across to touch her dark friend's shoulder, "You and I, darling, we need some of that old buzz back in our lives! We don't need your father dampening our fun along the way."

* * *

It was his tiredness which lowered his guard. Add to that the interference of the rustle of leaves shivering in the light breeze, and snorts of the hippos. The big beasts were inordinately noisy, grunting and squealing at each other, with a good deal of splashing about. A cow was in heat, and the dominant bull was being challenged by an aroused subordinate. Even so, it was unusual for Moses to not pick up on the approaching footsteps.

"Hello!"

He whipped around like a stalking cat having its tail pulled.

"Sorry!" she exclaimed. "We didn't mean to scare you."

Moses looked up sheepishly. A tall, fair-haired woman with a wide smile was staring at him curiously.

"When we go by," she said, "we wondered who stays here." She looked around. "I'm Lauren, and this is my friend Narina." She indicated a shorter, dark woman standing at her side. With her legs set apart and her toes pointed slightly inwards, the tall woman removed her cap, shook her head to loosen her hair, then threaded the ponytail of her long blonde hair back through the cap's opening. "If you don't mind my asking, what is your name?"

"Moses," he replied.

"That's unusual," she said. "Sort of old fashioned. Do you like it?"

Moses was surprised at her effrontery. With a deadpan face he said, "I like it because I can easily remember it."

The blonde wasn't sure if he was joking.

"It suits me. As a baby I was abandoned on the banks of a big African river, so what name could be more appropriate?"

The look on her long, but pleasant face was quizzical. "Seriously?" she asked. "Where was that?" Her lips moved on the edge of a follow-on question, but raising his hand Moses cut her off.

"That is a story for another time."

"Have you been here long?" she asked.

"Personally I have been here for about ten days. But my partner Gidi has been here for two years. He works here. How about you?"

David Maritz

"Four days." She craned her neck to peer behind Moses to see what was on the floor of the *chitenge*. "There's only so much viewing and sitting around that one can take." She flicked a hand with frustration. "Can you suggest something?"

"How much longer will you be here?"

"We're not quite sure; it isn't up to us!"

"So who is it up to?"

"My father." It was the dark girl who was looking at him intensely. The wavy mane of her coal-black hair cascaded down her back in unruly freedom, complementing the sparkle in her brown eyes and the dark ebony copper of her chamois-smooth skin.

"May I ask what may affect his decision?" Moses asked politely.

"You will have to ask him," replied the dark one.

Their glances at each other hinted at some tension.

"Are you here on holiday?" he asked.

"We are. He isn't," the tall blonde explained. "Narina and I are celebrating our freedom." She said this with emphatic satisfaction. "Well, at least I am!" She raised her hands above her head, pointing at the sky, while giving a little skip of pleasure. "Free at last! My divorce is settled and final." Lauren looked past Moses. She stepped up onto the floor of the chitenge and looked around. From there she walked over to a tent, opened the flap and peered inside.

A nosy type, Moses reflected.

"Narina has been footloose for a while." Lauren looked hesitantly at her friend before going on. "She was given her freedom together with a nice big present to go with it. She has been free for long enough to start taking it for granted."

Moses saw how the dark woman surreptitiously rolled her eyes.

"Did you also get divorced? Moses asked her.

"Her husband conveniently died," Lauren answered in her stead.

"Oh, I am sorry," Moses said.

"Don't be sorry. It was headed for a split anyway."

Moses didn't quite know how to react. "That is the strangest reason for a safari."

"If you say so," the blonde replied. Then indicating Narina, "We have known each other forever. Since high school actually. We have always shared the big events in our lives. So why not celebrate like this?"

A smile flickered across Narina's face as Lauren bubbled on.

"It wasn't too long ago that Narina returned from some godforsaken South American place. Her ex was from there. Someone over there did her a favor by making her a widow. So we decided to join her father, and come this way."

Moses was surprised by her flippancy.

"So!" Lauren asked him caustically. "Are you going to let a woman stand around, or will you be a gentleman and offer us somewhere to sit?"

Making a shallow bow, Moses said, "Be my guest." He led the way to the wooden table and chairs under the *chitenge* roof.

"Isn't there any place less formal?" she exclaimed. "We get all the pampering and formality we need at the lodge. I only need a gentlemanly camp chair and a good drink."

Moses gathered three folding chairs and beckoned them to follow him between the thick riverside trees down to a little sand bar. "Don't get too close to the water," he warned, "crocs can leap quite a way out to grab you."

It was one of those lovely late afternoons, where the sound of the rippling water mingled with that of the zephyr tickling the leaves. Their presence distracted the hippos. Their ears and snouts barely above the water, the animals suspiciously eyed the people on the bank.

Lauren laughed out merrily as she commented on this, "They look like children hiding after being caught doing something naughty."

Moses nodded in agreement. "How have you found your stay at the lodge?" he asked.

Settling into one of the chairs and stretching out her long legs, Lauren spoke lightly. "Great, but the best part has been being with Narina, catching up. It has been ages since we could really laugh at some of the stuff we got up to. At the lodge," she continued, "the hospitality has been fantastic. The location, the food, the showers, the beds, and the guiding. But we are ready to move on. She again looked at her friend, who only shrugged and pursed her lips. "I need the bustle of the city," she said. "I wouldn't even mind spending some time in Lusaka. They say it is booming these days."

"Where is home?" Moses asked.

"Oh, I have a lovely little penthouse apartment right in the heart of Cape Town's docklands. Have you ever been there and seen what they have done?"

Moses cast his mind back to the days he had spent on a military training course not too far to the north of there. "Not for a long time," he replied.

Lauren waved her hand as if to emphasize her point. "I miss the bustle of the city and its perks, and I love looking out of my window at Table Mountain. The Cape is such a beautiful part of the world." Lauren made a little sad-face frown, and then brightened right back up. "So, tell us Moses, what do you do out here? The staff at the lodge said you are involved with anti-poaching." Her tone changed to give staged emphasis, "That sounds so exciting! Do you have to do wild chases like they show on the Discovery channels?"

Moses shrugged. "As I said, I haven't been here long. My friend asked me to help with some problem he has."

"Do you go on patrols?" Lauren asked.

"No. My friend does. He goes with the scouts he is training to see how well they are assimilating his lessons."

"What sort of training does he do? And can we go with you?"

Moses shook his head. "I don't think that would be a good idea. I don't patrol, I work alone. I track people, find out what they have been doing."

Lauren looked at him imploringly, "Oh, I'm so bored, we've done all the game drives that they can offer, and we been up and down the river on the boat. I don't like fishing, and I'm on my last book, so we need something interesting to do." Looking at her friend, Lauren sought support. She winked at him. "It you are as good as you say at chasing people, I'm sure you could give a gal a run for her money."

Ignoring the comment, he turned to Narina. Her reticent quietness strummed a harmonious chord in his mind. "Are you also bored?"

David Maritz

"Yes!" Lauren replied vehemently for her.

Moses scratched his cheek. "Can I offer you a cup of coffee?"

"How about a gin and tonic?" Lauren asked.

"I don't drink alcohol. All I can offer is coffee, tea, or I think there may be some soft drinks that my friend Gidi has stashed in his tent. Would you like me to look?"

"What?" Lauren expressed her incredulity. "This is the first time I've ever heard of a bush teetotaller." Tilting her head inquiringly she said, "What is the matter with you?"

Moses smiled. "I was raised on a mission. It's because of their values that I don't drink. My partner here, Gidi, also doesn't drink. But for different reasons. Life and alcohol knocked him down so many times, he finally decided that it would be better to fight only one demon at a time, so he gave up the alcohol."

Moses was aware of dark Narina gazing intently at him. "I wouldn't mind a soft drink," she said quietly.

Somewhere deep within him, an unfamiliar responsive chord quivered.

Lauren stood and linked her fingers, then pushing her arms out in front as she stretched back on tiptoes, she said, "Well, I will leave you two to your soft stuff. I'm heading back to the lodge. Maybe Tarzan will be there waiting with a knock-me-down G&T."

* * *

It was the third time she had stopped by his campsite in the late afternoon, "Just catching up on the local flavor," she said.

Twisting in her chair and peering over her shoulder Narina watched Moses carefully duck under the liana braids drooping from the big river trees. In one hand he clasped a French press and a small jar of powdered milk. In the other he held the handles of two large plastic mugs, with a small packet of sugar scrunched in the crook of his arm. Settling into his camp chair he set the paraphernalia on the sand at her feet.

"I apologize for the lack of elegance, but how do you like your coffee?" His glance caught her coy smile.

"A half teaspoon of sugar," she said. "Just enough to take the edge out of the bitterness, and the same amount of powdered milk to bleach it brown."

He handed her a mug. The hippos snorted as he poured his own.

"Are those hippos still fighting?

"Yes. They are like us," Moses said, "they can get pretty intense over their ladies. They can fight for days, even wounding each other so badly that they may die, or be unable to defend themselves if attacked by lions when out of the water at night." Moses spooned sugar into his mug. "Please don't criticize how much sugar I take." He looked up, "It is a bad habit. I like mine bitter, strong and sweet, because then like life, it has the bitter and the sweetness mingled together." He chuckled at her sour face. Moses took a sip. "That's how my friend Gidi describes it. He really loves his bittersweet coffee." Moses leaned back in his chair and they sat listening to the soft hush of the river in between the raucous outbursts from the hippos.

"It sounds like you and your friend work well together. Where is he at the moment? Narina kicked at the sand with the heel of her shoe.

"He went down south to give a report to the people funding his training program. He should be back in the next few days, so you may get to meet him."

"What sort of training does he provide?"

Moses shrugged. "As I mentioned, I have only been here a short while, and I have concentrated on tracking people, to find out what they are doing. So I haven't sat in on Gidi's training sessions. From what I understand he is focusing on how to prevent poaching before it happens and what to do afterwards. He calls it the 'pre and post-bang' stuff."

Narina looked away to follow the hippo's splashing squabbles.

Moses took in the silhouette of her face. As she lifted her cup to her lips, he let his eyes drift down her arm. They followed the fine floral tattoos on the amber of her skin, tumbling down her shoulders, onto her arms, brushing behind her elbows, delicately reappearing to tickle the edges of each wrist.

She turned back to look at him. "So what exactly do you do if your job is to track people? Are you tracking the movements of poachers once they are in the park?"

"No, not poachers specifically. There is something else going on, which neither Gidi nor I can quite understand." Moses picked up and tossed a pebble into the slowly flowing waters beyond their feet. "Gidi thinks we may be seeing the start of a turf war in our area. It seems that the clue to it all is held by a single man. It is this man who I am following."

"Have you found out much?"

"Yes," Moses said quietly. "But it is making the picture more complex." He sighed, "But anyway, Gidi will be here soon. I can tell him what I have found so far. He will figure it out."

"You have a lot of confidence in him!" she stated with a surprised purse of her lips.

"Yes I do, I have been with him in many tough situations. He always manages to sort things out and get us out of trouble. He was a good officer." Moses paused. "One of the best in our unit, which was one of the best in that war."

"I am curious," she asked, "how much do they pay you to do this work?"

Moses laughed, "Nothing."

Narina raised her eyebrows in surprise. "Then why are you here?"

"I'm not all that sure. To help Gidi. I was in the area when somebody told me he was looking for me. I was between then, and here, and there."

"What does that mean?"

"I have been away for a long time. I'm going back to where I had a family."

She sensed his reticence. "You don't have to tell me if you don't feel like it."

He looked up at the sky. The buzz of pleasure talking to this woman threatened to fade into those wisps of sadness, which unless he fought them, still seeped into his soul.

Another raucous set of grunts came from the hippos.

"Oh boy! They certainly do fight a lot."

"Only when they have something worth fighting over," Moses said.

After a while the hippos settled down. Moses began speaking.

"First there was the war in Angola. Afterwards I was a mercenary. So was Gidi. It was good and bad, depending how you look at it. For me it started as a crusade, which was good. Later I was being paid for stuff I could not

David Maritz

identify with. That was bad." Moses threw a stick hard enough to land way out in the middle of the river. It made the hippos turn their heads and eye them suspiciously. "It got back to my broad family that I was not fighting with whom they thought. They assumed I was with the forces of one of the Angolan factions, Savimbi's UNITA. But actually I was with an Angolan volunteer unit, 'Os Terriveis', led by South Africans. We did a lot of fighting with Savimbi. We had the same enemy, the Communists. For me, it didn't matter who I was fighting with. The South African unit paid better than Savimbi, and I had families to support. But many in my extended family still had bitter memories of war. Any association with the South Africans was unacceptable. I wasn't welcome back. Even after the wars ended." Moses sipped his coffee.

"So what happened?" Narina asked hesitantly.

"I stayed away. My children were raised with aunts, uncles, cousins. At least when they got older, I would arrange to meet them in Lusaka."

"What about your wife?"

"My first wife died of malaria and her sister doesn't want to see me."

"You married two sisters!" Narina said in surprise.

"It is Africa. You must know that traditions are different here. Amongst the Tonga, my adopted tribe, having more than one wife is common."

"Of course," she answered, "I have been away for so long, how things differ gets painted over and forgotten."

Little plops spread across the water in front of them. "A pike must be on the hunt for little fish," Moses commented.

"How many children do you have?" she asked.

"Four. Two sons with the older sister. A son and daughter with the younger. I have good contact with all of them, but mostly with my daughter. Now that my children are grown and about to spread out into the world, I hope that with my children on my side, they can help me make peace with my big extended family. The times have changed. The emotions of the independence struggles have dissipated …"

"Wow," Narina said, "that is so tragic."

"Not really. At least I have realistic hope. But these hopes will have to wait a bit longer, because I was on my way back when I got Gidi's call for help." Moses stretched in his chair. "I am luckier than my friend. I am able to be satisfied with what God gives me."

Narina looked at him curiously.

"I think that many who fought on the losing side have been left forever searching for relevance. When you fight in a war, you get to build intense bonds with the others in the unit. Your fear of dying is less than the fear of shame for letting down your unit and the others, not so much the ideas it is fighting for. When you lose the whole war, everything becomes a failure, including those bonds with the others. You lose yourself. It all gets destroyed inside. Especially when you have nothing to go back to. The new Africa didn't want him. The soldiers like him returned to a very different country after the war. They were at the back of the queue. They even had their pensions taken away. I was lucky. I spoke Portuguese and was a volunteer. I was fighting outside my country, so apart from my family I had a country I could return to where I am welcome, even if I had lost a family."

"Do you still have contact with those in your old unit?" Narina asked.

"Yes, some of them, that is why I can see what has happened." Moses looked at Narina hesitantly. "I haven't talked about this with many, and I don't want to bore you."

"No, please go on," she said.

"After our bush war most of us lost dreams, careers, sense of worth and belonging. It is very hard to get that back. So Gidi is still searching for that sort of stuff. Not finding it, he is becoming like a dog. He moves to the next emotional bowl before he has licked the old clean."

Narina folded her arms across her chest. "You must know him very well."

"Yes, we spent years together in that war. You get to know people intimately in those conditions. I think he escapes his loss and loneliness by working out here, caught between the past and the future." Moses flicked the dregs of his coffee into the river.

"And you?" she asked.

"I am different," he shrugged wryly. "I have Africa on my side. I still have a home that has not changed to go back to. It is just that it has taken longer than I expected. I am a believer, and I believe that things will turn out well. I have God on my side. Gideon has none of that, which is why he is still searching, moving from bowl to bowl. At least he hides away here in the bush while he searches his heart, and is not hiding in a bar, looking in the bottom of a bottle for relevance like so many of our comrades."

"Yours has been a very different world to mine," Narina said.

Moses changed course. "I'm curious, what business is your father in?"

"I'm not sure. He has fingers in many pies. I am not privy to what he does. But whatever it is he is doing over here, I hope it will be over soon, because I can sense that my friend Lauren is starting to annoy him."

"Why is that a problem?" Moses tilted his head questioningly.

"My father is an old-fashioned type; he doesn't tolerate women who he thinks don't know their place." She took the last sip of her coffee, and set her mug down on the sand. "Lauren is one of those independent sorts. I hope we can be away before things get out of hand."

"By the way," Moses stood and picked up the two mugs, "You have an unusual name."

She smiled. "My mother gave it to me; my father was away. He came back too late to interfere. The name was given to a bird in honour of a naturalist's mistress."

"I know, that is why I asked," he said.

"A beautiful bird. Rare. But we find them here."

23

November 30

Tipping back and stretching in his seat, Gideon felt a sense of emptiness as the aircraft crossed the Zambezi River back into the Africa of his soul. Looking out the window, far below, the sun reflected off the form of Lake Kariba as it snaked up the Zambezi Valley. Gideon suddenly felt it to be the long arthritic finger of nYami-nYami, the river god, pointing disrespectfully up at him.

"Fuck you!" the god indicated.

Was this land as fickle as the faded love of a woman? Was it inevitable that the changes time wrought on the land and relationships would need more nurturing than he could provide? The reunion had been a step back into another older time, in both place and person. Filled with poignancy and the ache of what-ifs, it had twisted torturously over the past. Weaving, stitching, darning the holes and rips, culminating in an ending – insistent, intense, loud, long, with more not an option. Yet full of ambiguity. But time had filtered out the old hint of a cigarette habit from his memories. Only in the darkness of the night, with an expectation of kisses as tender as the memories, were the sugar-sweet lips replaced by the stale taste of nicotine. Was the gap too wide to reach over and hold hands, stepping into the future?

"*Iwe, Muzungu!*" he could hear the cranky old god shouting up at him, "Like the skin of a snake, they will all shed you."

Surreptitiously, so that his fellow passengers wouldn't notice, from his window seat, Gideon raised his middle digit back at the hoary old sod. "Go fuck yourself," he muttered back under his breath.

The feisty old bugger's attitude kindled a slumbering awareness of the enigmatic essence of Africa towards him, the sense of indifference, like a futile relationship with an uninterested woman. Once gone, no matter how persistent the effort and gifts given, the response was seldom more than as for a token in a candy-bar machine, if one was lucky.

Waiting for his bags, there was a text from Claudia. A friend was occupying his room for the night, but would be leaving early in the morning. She had booked him a place for the night. A shuttle would be waiting.

He didn't mind, she was always so thoughtful. He was grateful and appreciative for the priority she afforded him in her inner life.

It being the late flight into Lusaka, he cleared out of customs after sunset. He was pleased to be collected by the pioneer shuttle, taking him to a comfortably rustic camp on the outskirts of the city. In an atmosphere of old, soothing Africa, listening to the cries of the night apes and the hoots of the spotted eagle owls in the trees above his chalet he could digest it all, and mentally rinse away the sweet taste of guilt from a bite into a candy bar.

* * *

Claudia purred her pleasure as he massaged her neck and shoulders. It was a ritual he performed each time she returned from the office, and after she made them both a cup of tea.

David Maritz

"You are back to being colorful again," Gideon stated. "Does that mean you're no longer dealing with that problem client?"

"Yes, thankfully we only occasionally have to meet with the brutes from across the border. My partner on the project is good to work with. Together we get things done. It is those we deal with who are occasionally the problem. Like you, he says he prefers me in full color."

"Who is that, your boss?" Gideon asked.

"No," she replied. "His nephew. Most of the time the nephew works for his father up in East Africa. But he is here to get the Congo deal done with me. His father is originally from Somalia, but moved to Zanzibar as a youth where he met my boss Mohammed's sister. Hence the family connection."

Gideon flicked his hand at the fly that was buzzing annoyingly over her head.

Lying on the couch with her head in his lap, Claudia twisted slightly to face him. "It's an interesting story. When the Indians were kicked out of Zanzibar after Independence, old grandfather Buhadur moved here." She closed her eyes with the pleasure of Gideon's manipulations. "Africa needed logistics which crossed borders. He had his sons set up in different countries. Angola, Botswana, Kenya and Mozambique. He himself moved here with his eldest son, my boss. They brought the trucking business they had run in Zanzibar with them. It is a combination of caution and risk in each of the sons which has allowed the business to thrive. Ahh, that feels so good." Claudia half opened her eyes as he kneaded her shoulders.

As she rolled her head slowly with the pleasure of his kneading, he asked, "How does this affect what you do?"

"Like the smell of meat attracts a hyena," she replied, "some scent has caught the attention of the most adventurous of the clan. He is uncurling one of his long tentacles, in the form of his son, to test the air across the border. He sees opportunities where others see chaos. He thrives where the rule of law is scant and danger scares others away. He likes to get what he wants. His son is like him. But in a more refined way. Because it is a family alliance, I have been tasked with temporarily working on this project to scan the fine print and count the chips." Claudia rolled her shoulders with pleasure. "Actually, you may get to meet the nasty brother-in-law. My boss made him a booking for over a month out at your place. Something to do with other business."

"Will his son be out there with him?" Gideon asked.

"No," Claudia murmured, "we have too much to do back here and up north."

"It sounds like you admire both of them, the father and the son"

"I do," she said. What they do isn't for the faint of heart though. A lot of areas in Africa are pretty unruly. One has to have guts to operate there. At least I don't have to cross the border. All I have to do is dress formally sometimes, informally at others. It gives a psychological edge. Why not? They all take notice of me. I like that."

"I bet they do," Gideon replied with an edge of sarcasm. "And of course, for the right reasons."

Claudia sat up. "Now it's your turn to tell me what you did down south. But not here."

Switching off the light and taking his hand, she led him across the room.

24

December 1

Shrieks of happiness were welling out of every movement she made, with the raucous excitement of a child on a playground. Logic was superfluous. The heart is both the seeker and the sought. It was ridiculous, hopeless and wonderful all bundled into a tangle of emotions – a rollercoaster of delight sweeping her along, unheedingly deaf to her half-hearted pleas to slow down. The midday sun, pouring relentlessly onto the *dambo's* surface, quickly dried its clay crust. A cloak of short grass hid hippo footprints pressed through this surface into the mud. Narina was oblivious to occasional stumbles into these soggy traps.

"Am I going mad?"

The figure striding before her moved smoothly, confidently through the grass, occasionally snapping off a longer stem, unconsciously picking it apart the way an old man may finger his worry beads. Vainly, she tried to conjure up some annoyance at the unexpectedness of it. How did this happen? So far out in the wilderness, with no warning.

His movements were mesmerising. She forced her eyes down, away from his lithesome strides. Unlike her, almost god-like, he never faltered.

An exclamation of "Goddam holes!" came loudly from behind. Narina turn to offer commiseration to Lauren, stumbling a few meters further back. As she did, Moses pointed to a flitting flash ahead.

"That is a Painted Lady." He pointed to the fast flutter of a beautiful insect with wings dappled in russet-reds and black, with here and there a fleck of white. It landed on a patch of damp ground in the shade of the bushes at the tree line. "It folds its wings when it lands. As you can see, the under-wing is very different; the freckled greys blend it into the background. It is a fast flyer with a high wing loading. It makes this up by rapid wing beats."

Yesterday, as had happened each evening for the last few days, Narina had succumbed to the temptation to wander over to Moses's campsite before darkness set in.

She could no longer pretend it was simply a welcome change from hang-ing around listening to her friend complain of boredom. In contrast, in his quiet way, the conversations with Moses as they sat on the little sand bar were far more interesting. She hoped the staff could keep her secret. Her father would be furious should he discover her infatuation, just when he thought she was returning to the family fold from the grasp of a non-be-lieving marriage. Her father's hopes for a pedigree would once again recede. She couldn't bear her father trying to intervene as she reached for the sky.

Yesterday, Moses had offered to lead her on a walk into the park. They would cross the river with the boat, he said. On the other side, it would be a short hike. Only a half hour each way, over the open flood plain, across the big dambo, followed by a short climb up the low hill looking back at them from across the river. Everything he wanted to show her could be found between here and there. They could have a picnic lunch at the top of the hill.

"The view up there is beautiful," he'd said. He would show her some-thing different.

David Maritz

"What?" she had asked.

His reply was so unexpectedly unusual. Like much else of him. "Butterflies," he answered.

"Where did you learn about them?"

"From the books in the little library at the mission where I was raised," was his nonchalant reply. "Africa is rich in butterflies. Few people pay them much notice."

It was intriguing. Like everything about him.

A stumble brought her back to the now. Reaching the edge of the pitted grassy ordeal, Narina felt she could lift her head without risking a faltered step into a hippo hole.

Quite a hike. Easy for him, but not for her or Lauren, who had demanded to tag along.

From the grassy spread of the *dambo*, the three of them moved into the tree line where a patch of clay soil stunted the vegetation at the foot of the hill.

"That one over there is a Pansy." A colorful butterfly, with yellow splashes bordered with black and a violet spot in the center of the lower wing flitted past. "You can see how it resembles its gaudy floral namesake. I won't bother you with Latin names; you won't remember them anyway."

Narina stared at him; mesmerised, captivated. The tall, vibrant abundance of him, packed into lithesome lean luxury, held together with taut muscles rippling beneath a smooth, ebony surface. His description of butterflies added to his aura of uniqueness. It was gentle delicateness emanating from a frame of subdued strength. The soft sound of his voice, its accent a mixture of the English lilt of Africa modulated delicately with a faint foreign trace. She must ask him about it.

Conscious of staring too long, she caught the curious manner he returned her gaze as the flush colored her cheeks.

"The one flying past over there," Moses pointed, "with the long narrow wings, is an African Monarch. It is similar to the American Monarchs which migrate down into South America. Here they don't migrate far, although many of the butterflies engage in smaller intra-African mini-migrations."

Struggling up the slope of the hill, Narina stop to catch her breath as she lagged behind Moses's effortless strides. Joined by Lauren, both of them rested from their exertion in the shade of a tree halfway up the slope, even as Narina tried to come to terms with her runaway emotions. Moses himself said that being raised at the mission was reflected in his life. She wasn't a believer, but coming from a Muslim family, their differing attitudes would be a spike in the wheel of any shared destiny. So how could it work? Long ago she had emotionally flown the dogma of her family's religious coop. She was proud of her independence, expressed in her quiet, determined rebelliousness. She wasn't as extroverted as Lauren, but she was as focused about it. It was one of the reasons the two of them got on so well together. She thought how it had been with a sense of spite that she had tattooed her arms, even in the face of her father's ire.

That was then. Now, how could she dash their raised hopes again? If she gave in to her heart, what would her extended family think? What would they say if they saw her falling in love with another unbeliever – this one even worse than the first in a different way; little more than a wandering pauper? At least they said her ex had left her rich with a bounteous Caribbean trust untouchable to others. With maturity she had learned it wise not to needlessly offend family sensibilities. Just look at what had happened to Moses and his family's break-up over differing beliefs. Religion and politics: equally dangerous.

Continuing her slow climb up the hill, her reverie was cut short as Moses stopped abruptly.

"That one over there is called a Guinea Fowl. It holds its wings open when it lands, unlike the Painted Lady. You can see how its steel grey color, sprinkled with fine white spots, gives it its name, after that of the bird."

Continuing up the slope, there were Cabbage Whites, Common Grass Yellows, and Leopards, the last so-named due to their spots. Moses also pointed out a Citrus Swallowtail, and some African Whites, as well as Gaudy Commodores and Round-Winged Orange Tips.

Narina was astonished. Where did they all come from? All these unnoticed insects. How could he remember their names? It was so impressive.

"I never noticed all the sorts of butterflies before," she said.

"They are everywhere, if you look," he answered.

The slope was deceptively gentle. Behind her Narina could hear Lauren muttering about the steepness, and that she had not worn the proper footwear. It served her right for insisting on tagging along. It wasn't the short, easy hike she had envisioned that could be done in sandals.

Ahead, and higher, the slope eased gradually into the dome crest of the hill. Shallow shelves of dark brown basaltic rock stretched between the anaemic trunks of spread-out trees; a sign of scant topsoil. Behind these terraced shelf edges, and tickling at the feet of the next, was a covering of short wavy grass giving the hilltop its deceptive appearance of round, parklike smoothness. The soil had been stripped away from the hill's rocky cheeks by the punches of time. The open spacing of the trees on the slopes meant that although they were out in full summer greenery, their leafy heads didn't obscure the horizon. If anything, like a giant gallery, they framed the vistas spreading out as far as the eye could see, proffering a magnificent view out over the Kafue River laid out in long, lazy loops below. On one of the layered rocky terraces near the crown of the hill, pulling the back pack off his shoulders, Moses announced it was their picnic site.

"Now we will wait for two of the most beautiful butterflies to show up. They have been frequenting this spot lately."

"What are those?" Narina asked.

"Wait and see."

It wasn't long before he pointed to a big, triangular-winged butterfly flitting between the branches overhead.

"That is the Foxy Charaxes. To get a good look you will need my binoculars. They are very quick, and are always at the tops of the trees."

Lauren reached for his glasses first.

"Now, let us hope that the one I really want you to see pays us a visit. It is territorial, and up here is where they often hide in the shadows between the rocks. They sip the moisture in the leaf detritus that accumulates there."

Moses reached into his backpack and took out three bottles of water and three cellophane wrapped sandwiches.

"Wow, you give the full service!" Lauren said. "I'm impressed."

Unwrapping their sandwiches from the cellophane paper, the two women sat on a big rock admiring the view.

Moses kept scanning the area. After a while he said. "I am sorry, every time I have been here recently I have found them, but not today."

Narina appreciated his frankness. What did she care about a single butter-fly? Already he had lived up to his promise of showing the unusual. The warmth of the sun and the satisfying fullness of the food made her drowsy. Lying back on a patch of softer grass, she closed her eyes.

Should she share her mental state with Lauren? No, absolutely not. Lauren would laugh. They were here to get away, not to get closer to men, she would say. But it had been two years since she had felt the embrace of a man. Her husband had drifted away from her long before he was murdered in the cartel wars. She had been his showpiece from the moment they met. Only later did she understand that he had come to Africa to set up one of Escobar's safari hunts. Her attraction to him was nothing like what she felt now. She was shocked at how the man moving next to her quickened her breath.

Did he notice?

The images cavorted dreamily across the inner glow of her closed eyelids. They chased in a heavenly wilderness, dashing between the flowers, hiding behind the blush of big bushes. Hoping he would find her, then giggling and laughing like a schoolgirl. Inexorably swirling towards his center like a leaf in a whirlpool, with all its giddying consequences. He should chase her, catch her, hold her, trap her, have his weight press on her, his strength, his protection.

It wouldn't be possible. Their lives had followed such completely different trajectories. Apart from this brief intersection, they were on journeys to separate realms of the future. But her heart leapt remembering how his quizzical stare had questioned not so much her motives, as her emotions. Had he detected her futile struggle ever since his gentle kiss? That soft, sensuous press and linger of their lips as they parted on that second evening. His smiling face pushed itself into her mind. His face, unlike and yet faintly like hers, with a delicate refinement. Their mismatch would be an issue in the extant racial consciousness of this continent, with her hybrid pedigree, a mix of Africa and India. That admixture which gave her a unique beauty, she was told; the reason her ex-husband had wanted her as a trophy. The pout of her full lips, the waviness of her long, boisterous mop of hair. The gloss of her skin covering a shape as perfect as a vestal virgin. Yet she felt how they matched, the refine of his face. Its lines as slender as his tall physique, as mysterious as the difference in his accent; something faintly inherited from her own mix of Zanzibar and Turkana origins. She was waiting, hoping, silently begging for him to catch her wrist, swing her around, dance her off her feet, whisk her away to a paradise. She wanted him to carry her to a promised land, where they could kiss, caress, conjugate, like no lovers had ever done before.

"There!"

It was his emphatic exclamation which brought her back to the present.

"Over there." He pointed.

Neither Narina nor Lauren saw a thing. "Where?" they asked.

"Next to the rock that looks like it is leaning against that tree trunk." Moses motioned with his hand. "Directly below it. There is a leaf stuck upright into the sand."

"Okay, where is the butterfly?"

"Keep looking," he said.

With a lazy, languorous motion, the leaf unfurled. A splash of creamy abalone was daubed at the center of a dull grit canvas hung in the shadow of the rock. Like the blink of a cyclops eye, there was a transformational flick.

"Wow!" Lauren exclaimed in wonderment.

"So there you have it, I doubt that any lodge guest has seen one of those. They are harder to find than wild dog or Serval cat."

With a silent snap of its wings it was gone.

"You have been graced with a bushland gift. A Mother of Pearl. Now," he said, "we can go."

25

Somewhere, Sometime

The old man sensed that this homecoming was different. From the top of the shrub-covered riverbank, people peered down at him. Too many to count. Smiling up at them, he waited for a small truck and a motorbike to disembark. Why were they quiet? The pontoon crew had also been unusually subdued when he boarded; they hadn't extended their customary jovial greeting.

Pushing his bicycle up the incline of the riverbank, he greeted the crowd with a tentative hello, accompanied by a friendly waving gesture of his hand. He was answered by a soft collective murmuring, like the sound of the wind moving through the dry winter grass. A wispy anxiety crept into the old man's consciousness. But gathering his resolve, he pushed on. If you ignored them, they didn't exist.

A woman stepped into his path. He knew her well; like all of them, she was from his village.

The first rock hit him in the stomach.

Shock flashed across his wide-eyed face. He recognized his neighbour's wife as the stone-thrower.

David Maritz

She shrieked, "Kill the witch!"

Her scream unleashed the silent menace in the crowd. Howling like a pack of dogs they hurled their stones.

Turning to run back towards the river, his bicycle clattered to the ground. He managed no more than a few strides before a rain of stones hit him. Two found the back of his head, pitching him face forward. He made no effort to cushion his fall, being senseless before hitting the gravel. Shrieking as they rushed towards him, the crowd encircled his shrivelled figure, clad in long grey pants and white shirt whose vintage matched his shoes, worn for so long that if anyone cared to look past the frenzy, they would see how the heels were worn. But the horde didn't care about shoes, or anything else. It didn't even care that he had lived amongst them for over sixty years, and that as a schoolmaster he had dressed in the same grey pants, white shirt and scuffed shoes during the four decades he had stood in the classroom teaching them the rudiments of arithmetic.

Now all they saw was a witch.

The prone figure spasmed and twitched as its devil spirit was expunged. It was the only way to get rid of the evil divined by the trancing pallbearers at yesterday's funeral. Bearing the coffin on their shoulders, the possessed carriers had shuffle-jogged to the doorway of the old man's shack, thereby signifying who was the devil behind the recent deaths.

Then it was over.

As if to draw its breath the crowd fell silent, pausing momentarily to take in the consequence of their frenzy. With a collective sigh, everyone began to gabble in excited relief as the tension oozed away like the brains and blood from the broken body. The face which had smiled up at them only minutes before was crushed beyond recognition. There was a certain, subdued shame amongst some of the crowd. But there was nothing they could do about it, because such things are the ways of the spirit world in the old traditions of Africa.

26

December 2

The staff hadn't seen anything like it. Later, Bright was to say he had witnessed something similar, but it was years ago at another lodge. It began at sunset as a Land Cruiser pulled into the parking spot across the foot bridge from the *chitenge*.

"Madame," a waitress had addressed Lauren, "the master is arriving. You must take your drink elsewhere."

Everyone heard Lauren's furious response. "To hell with this hypocritical bullshit!"

The kitchen staff rushed out to join the other onlookers. They gawked as Lauren, drink in hand, strode up to Narina's father who was flanked by two other men who looked at her in baleful silence.

"Mustafa," Lauren addressed Narina's father, "I am letting you know that as of midnight tonight I am no longer your guest." Her voice was icy. "As of tomorrow I will be paying for my stay here. As such, I will do as I please. One of the things that pleases me is a good gin and tonic, whenever and whenever I want. To hell with any restrictions, religious decorum, or whatever. I will be staying here only as long as it takes me to organize transportation away from here."

Mustafa glared at her with his fists clenched. Listening to her announcement, the other two eased up and grinned. One even gave a mock clap.

As Lauren flounced past them the other toasted, "*Nazdorovie*," which she acknowledged with a raised glass as she angrily strode on, answering him with a "Cheers".

As she crossed over the foot bridge towards the chalets, the younger of the two newcomers followed the elder ones toast with a loud wolf whistle.

The staff saw how she turned, raised her right arm high in the air with a clenched fist and middle finger pointed upright, as she shouted back, "Fuck off, you asshole!"

Now, hours later, Lauren sat on the porch of her big thatch-roofed chalet. Perched on the remnants of an old anthill, it was comfortably shaded under a small cluster of huge acacias. The hand-slashed grass surrounding it afforded a park-like appearance to the view towards the river. Being the last in a line of similar structures, the short stubble beyond it quickly blended into the longer dambo grass. From there, the parklike openness stretched a kilometer upriver towards the campsite, where Moses would be preparing his dinner.

Lauren was leaning back in one of the padded wicker chairs with her feet comfortably crossed on a coffee table. Next to the overlap of her legs on its top was an empty glass together with the picked-at remnants of her dinner. The reason given for the earlier room service was that Lauren had a 'bad headache'... she needed a break from socialising at dinner with the others. However, from the flash in her eyes, even from a distance Precious could see lingering traces of her earlier anger.

David Maritz

It was a warm evening, despite the breeze remaining from a late afternoon thunderstorm to the north. As Precious stepped up the low wooden steps from the paved pathway, Lauren uncrossed her long athletic legs to lift her feet off the table. She still wore her afternoon garb: a pair of short cut, loose denim pants, with an old, faded tank top, leaving her shoulders and arms as bare as her legs. This attracted the mosquitos whose tiny, erratic flights were refracted in the light of the overhead bulb. Appearing as quixotic as specks of backlit dust, the insects made drifting forays on her bareness. A tube of insect repellent lay on the floor; possibly why she hadn't yet resorted to the protection of long pants and the unfurled sleeves of a shirt.

For the last week, Precious had witnessed the growing tension between the guests, specifically Lauren and Mustafa, and even between the two women. Narina was squeezed by her ties to her headstrong friend on one hand, and loyalty to her authoritative father on the other. As she moved up the steps onto the chalet deck, Precious was aware of the piercing look in Laurens eyes. She guessed that Lauren's 'immodest' attire may have been more motivated to annoy the ascetic Muslim man than to provide expanses of provocative skin for the benefit of the mosquitoes. Precious set down a replacement for the gin and tonic, then began to clear the dinner service.

"Thank you, sweetie."

There was something inviting in how Lauren pronounced 'sweetie'. It intimated an openness to more than the usual client-servant relationship. But Precious was hesitant to respond. The staff were trained not to get 'close' with the guests. All the same, there was an edge of curiosity in Precious's mind as she considered Lauren. She looked carefully at the tall woman smiling at her. With her long hair pulled back in a ponytail held in a wooden hair band, and flanked by earrings delicately carved from the same ebony, Lauren appeared sophisticatedly elegant, despite the simplicity of her clothing. How did she do it?

Precious replied with a polite, "My pleasure."

As she turned to head back down the steps, Lauren called out, "No wait, don't go. It's too quiet out here. Stay, let's talk."

Hesitating, wanting to find out more, Precious gave in hesitantly to her curiosity. She turned back. Maybe Lauren needed some moral support now that the adrenalin of her anger was abating. There had already been the soothing effect of the first G&T, and the further calming effect of the night's solitude, and the calls of a night ape in the tree above her chalet. She was obviously in a better mood.

Hearing its swish in the branches, Lauren said to Precious, "That cute little thing has been keeping me company. Have a seat." Lauren reached out, taking hold of the armrest of the other wicker chair, and pushed it over to where Precious stood. "I've watched you working. I wonder why you are still here."

Precious sat down, stiff with a sense of social unease. "Why do you ask that I should still be here?"

Lauren shrugged. "I am curious. You seem out of place."

"Is it not obvious? Did you not drive all the way out from Lusaka?" Precious asked.

"Yes, we did," Lauren nodded. "I wish we could drive back tomorrow. But what's that got to do with my question?" Lauren leaned forward to stretch a slender arm towards her drink.

In tandem, Precious placed her elbows on her knees, making a spire with the tips of her fingers touching under her chin. "Madame, once you leave the city, apart from the token policewoman at the roadblocks, how many women did you see driving cars, or trucks, or even riding bicycles? How many did you see wearing business suits, and carrying briefcases?"

Precious hesitated. "Did you go into the Mumbwa market? No? There are hundreds of women carrying babies on their backs, and baskets on their heads, and trudging kilometers back home, or waiting by the side of the road for a bus."

Lauren swilled her glass, making the ice in her drink tinkle against its sides. "So?" she asked. "What has that got to do with you?"

"Madame, I am from a village which makes Mumbwa look like a hive of modernity. My job here at the lodge allows me to escape from the life that is expected of me."

Lauren stared at Precious in silence before speaking again. "I have noticed that you are older than the other girls. I understand Africa. I'm curious. Do you have a husband who allows you to work away from home?" Without waiting for a reply Lauren continued. "I have also noticed the little necklace of snail shells you wear, and how you braid your hair, coiling it up on your head on both sides. It is so different and appealing. Not only that, when I walked back behind the kitchen, I saw you were wearing a beautiful dress. I wondered where you got it."

Precious smiled back at Lauren, "Madame, I am not married, and I made the dress. It is what I want to do with my life, and why I am here. This place and this job is my chance to escape the life that waits for me in the village. Maybe one day I will find a client who is young and unmarried, who will take me away."

"Really!" Lauren motioned dismissively with her hand, "Do you really think that some prince will carry you away?"

Precious replied with slight annoyance at the dismissive tone, "Two years ago there was a waitress here, Sera. And a young man from Croatia married her and took her away. But I agree, the odds of it happening twice are slim. There aren't many young, handsome, rich and single men visiting here." Precious gave a hollow laugh for emphasis. "But what other hope is there?"

She added wryly, "I do not have much time left. A man here is paying lobola to my uncle for me. I don't want him, but Bright the manager here is part of the family, which is why I got a job here. Once the payment is finished there will be pressure on me to marry. To tell the truth," she continued, "at times I have been so desperate I have contemplated running away. I have read about the boat people crossing to Italy, and how they seldom get sent back to Africa. But I digress." Precious took a deep breath. "My job here, and the success of this lodge, is important to me."

"Why is that, if you want to get away?" Lauren asked.

"Madame, my passion is designing. I love clothing, jewelry, make-up, everything. I want to be a designer. For example, I am curious to find out about your earrings and hairband. I want to be the African equivalent of Coco Chanel or Alexander McQueen. But at my age, with no money, I will never get to the dream of being close to the big fashion centers. So I have set goals at least to get away from my village, with its old way of living. If I can get to Lusaka, or Livingstone, with all its tourists visiting the Victoria Falls, and if I can afford to live there, it will be enough." Precious became agitated. She sat up straight, wringing her hands.

"My plan is to convince Bright, and the owners of this lodge, to set up a gift shop. In that case, I will have the women in the village weave and make my designs. Dresses, shirts, skirts and trinkets, jewelry, all of it. My salary is not enough to go places. But if I can make most of the items to sell in a gift shop, I can."

Lauren had drained her gin and tonic by the time Precious finished her explanations. "Yes, I will agree that the right spouse can be a great help," Lauren cut in. "I have been dating an Indian man in Cape Town. He is a dream to be around, compared to my ex-husband. He is so different from the plain sexism, as with this old-fashioned bastard we have here with us. So there are some bad and some good ones." Lauren raised the base of her glass to drain its last drops.

"Did you say you are from Cape Town?"

"Yes."

"Oh, Madame, I have seen the pictures. It must be a magical place!" There was a pause, "What does the Madame do there?

Lauren looked closely across at the woman sitting opposite before answering. "I run my family's yarn and cloth import-export company. It is one of the oldest and most successful in our country."

Precious felt herself catch her breath as, undetected, a flush of excitement widened her pupils.

Lauren picked up her empty glass. "Please stop calling me 'Madame'. My name is Lauren. And why don't you fetch me another of these? And something for yourself." She hesitated, "Ohhh, while you are about it, put it on the tab of that old bastard, or one of his ex-Communist friends. Then come back here and let's talk more about that beautiful dress that you made, and I will tell you where I got my ebony hairband."

27

December 3

Lying next to her in the 'zero-dark-thirty', which comes long before the earliest of the roosters of Lusaka commence their crowing, Gideon considered how Claudia unconsciously compensated for the transgression of his relationship rules.

Rule one was never have a lover ten years younger than himself. Rule two, never have a lover living further than twenty minutes away, because when these rules were being formulated, it was more tempting to pop the top off a beer than waste 20 minutes getting to any favors. Now, decades after he had formulated them, Claudia fitted well within the brackets of the first. But she certainly didn't conform to the second, seeing as she lived a half-day trip from the Kafue River area of his operations. However, she amply made up for it with the curves of her comforts. Her spooned figure fitted to his as closely as inter-locking jigsaw pieces. Sleep with her was bliss; it made up for any and all other mismatches. Next to her, he finally felt he had a home—both physically and emotionally. Yes, she kept him at a public distance, but that would change. Of that he was sure. Her pleasure with his presence becoming more overt each time he came back to the city.

Now he hugged her warm body and placed a last kiss on her still sleepy forehead. Then he reached down beside the bed to gather the clothing that had been discarded as hastily as the paper from a birthday present. Tiptoeing out and closing her bedroom door behind him, he quietly crossed to the kitchen where he turned on the kettle. It would be tight if he wanted to cross the city from east to west before the morning traffic escalated to a choking crawl. But a good cup of coffee was worth the wait. Standing naked, he spooned the coffee into the French press and poured in the water.

Letting the coffee draw, he began to pull on the pile of clothing he had dropped at his feet. Tugging his shirt over his head, he saw that the grab of his socks from under the bed included a little something else.

He immediately recognized it for what it was. He had some of the same.

It was torn open along one edge.

Riveted in place, it took a few moments for the implication to set in. It couldn't be. He had just spent the whole night feeling her unabashed intimacy.

He walked back across the room to open the bedroom door. Halfway there, he stopped. Only when ambushed should one react impulsively. It would be counterproductive to burst in and demand an explanation of what an open condom packet was doing under her bed. Through the sudden thunder of his emotions, a small voice called out, How dare he? if he did. Sauce for the goose, sauce for the gander. Did he really want to know? Certain things were best left alone until the confusion had cleared, allowing realities and truths to be discussed frankly and openly.

He was still riveted with shock. He had been so sure of himself, returning with a finger on the balance, tipping it towards the promise of a newer hybrid Africa. Finally letting go, moving on beyond the old sedate suburban houses of yester-year with its nostalgic pleasures. The decision to move beyond the past, to commit to this little brick cloistered Garden of Eden with its curvy, smiling Eve, had given such pleasure.

"Goddammit," he swore as he continued dressing.

No wonder she had booked him a place last night at Pioneer. He should have reminded himself that the story of Eden is not only about Paradise. It is also about a fucking snake. How long had he been stupidly oblivious of something slithering around this cottage?

His fucked-up story of Africa. There was always a reptile coiled up in some dark corner.

Clenching his fists and biting his tongue Gideon reminded himself that he had a job to do. With his cup in hand and mind still racing, he crossed the courtyard to his vehicle. His first stop would be Chilanga.

* * *

At its inception in the colonial days, the HQ of the Wildlife Authority was established outside the city limits, in a cute little village. It even hosted a zoo which took in and attempted to rehabilitate injured and orphaned animals. Today, the ugly sprawl of the city has overrun the area. The nearby cement factory spread its dust over the vicinity in symbolic scorn at efforts to preserve nature. It behooved Gideon to know and be wary of not only the power and politics of a German banker, but also that of the department who issued his work visa. It was particularly important as he sought to get additional scouting patrols. He was aware that wildlife conservation frequently involved egos and manipulations as back-stabbing and counterproductive as national politics. When outside donor money was added to this brew, it made for a mouthful that needed to be chewed and swallowed with care. Standing on toes had to be avoided. His friend in the department had advised that Gideon work with other donor organizations. When he had arranged sufficient funds and commitment, he could get back to him, and his friend would see about setting up meetings with higher-ups in the department bureaucracy.

David Maritz

Gideon's sidestep on the way back to the Kafue was in an intelligence-gathering spirit. He would have a good chat with a few of his 'buddies' at the central HQ. He could glean from those in its trenches what they knew about high-level politics. Find out who he could work with, or who to gather strategic information from. For a moment, Gideon thought bitterly of how banker Ulrich—who held the purse strings of his project—had no idea about the complexities and behind-the-scenes actions required for successful conservation efforts out here. He bet the banker's son, with his degree in biology, wouldn't have any clue how to work the politics of an African bureaucracy. Oh well, that was life. Let the assholes replace him and see where they got.

Sharing a bunch of bananas purchased at the side of the road and a few bottles of cola was all that it took for his best 'insider' contact to fill him in. The contact was still unsure exactly how some of the big foreign endeavors fitted into the picture.

"Yes, all these people," he said, "they think that they can come in here and run things. But you know the politics of Africa, it is rough. Here it is a contact sport. The higher-ups are not willing to give up power, and more importantly they are unwilling to give up the profit from favors."

Sitting with his contact in a side office at the HQ, Gideon exchanged pleasantries as he was given a handwritten sheet bearing a list of names and numbers.

"These are the ones, both inside and outside the department, who can get things done," the contact said. "They are not necessarily the official people."

Gideon thanked him for his insights and shook his hand. Then as he started his engine, a vehicle entered the HQ gate and parked across the lot. He recognized Claudia's boss at the wheel.

What was he doing here?

The thoughts of Claudia, which he had managed to push out of his mind while talking to his contact, came flooding back with the clutch of a strange terror: the searing horror of loss.

Claudia's boss would be too old. But who was the snake? The younger partner who she so enjoyed working with? A brute who responded to formal attire, disguising intentions? Those intentions, how spontaneous had they been? How persistent? Not knowing produced a sensation so intense it was hard to breathe. It was all he could do to not walk across and confront the older man and ask questions. He must bide his time. Get a perspective. Learn what it is like to have the shoe on the other foot. Here he was attempting to preserve Africa's Gardens of Eden, and yet of necessity it meant preserving everything that was to be found there—the twisting, twining, undulating coils of the snakes, as well as the pawing, panting yips of jackals. Gideon would have time to agonize over how to respond, if at all. Never prioritize intentions, only capabilities and actions. That had been a principle as true in the war as in all other forms of competition since. What were Claudia's intentions? Sophia's? And what were the capabilities he faced with them?

* * *

The sun had dropped below the western horizon when Gideon peeled a few notes from the wad of kwacha in his pocket to convince the pontoon crew to make one last late crossing. Then, in the beams of his headlights, driving along the dirt track skirting the lodge's small parking area, he noticed an unfamiliar vehicle. Flipping through his memory, he recalled Precious mentioning a late booking. Drawing closer to their campsite, he saw that Moses had the embers glowing in the firepit. The fire spread its welcome on his forearms as he stretched his palms towards its glow.

It felt good being back in the bush. With all the changes to the Africa he'd known in yesteryear, he hadn't yet been robbed of a few of its old pleasures. A campfire, the sounds of the night creatures, and a unique friend with whom he had shared so many intense times.

"You're a star!" he said when he saw the tin beaker tucked into the glow of the coals, where it was hissing on its way to boiling the water.

"It wasn't hard to guess you would soon be here. The air is very still tonight. Sounds travel a long way. I heard your vehicle as it came through the *dambo* on the other side of the lodge."

Crouching, Gideon rubbed his hands together close to the fire. "I'm hungry. All I ate today was some tough stuff at the Mercy store in Mumbwa. It was a yard chicken. They boil the fucking thing with a brick in the pot, and then they served me the chicken, and the brick to someone who wanted something tender. Have you already eaten?" Gideon asked.

"Of course I have! I didn't think that you would make it across the ferry. But if you make me half a sandwich I will join you."

While Gideon was slicing and garnishing the bread, Moses prepared the coffee.

"How did it go down south?" Moses asked.

"Not so good. It's hard to tell with Germans. The main donor is a puffed-up prick. He wants metrics. His time scales are unrealistic. I suspect he wants to show off to his board of directors about how many poachers were caught, animal numbers rising, all that. But a herd of impala doesn't flick out of a cash machine like a fistful of Deutschmarks. I requested a budget for camera traps to start some sort of measurement. But that will take years to get results. I'm not sure if he has the patience to continue the support until we have proof that our efforts are working. In the meantime I think they will keep funding for another year or two, maybe. After that I don't know."

A fruit bat peeped rhythmically in the tree overhead.

"I was cheeky to the asshole. So I don't think I made friends. As they say, 'friends come and go, enemies stay forever'. So we will see."

Staring at the flames, Gideon rolled his thoughts back over how life had been a long sequence of 'don't knows'. Claudia swept back into his mind, flooding him with a shock of feelings as he tried to suppress his latest 'don't know'.

He didn't want Moses to notice.

What the hell. Why did things get messed up so fast, without warning? Had he been too blind? Taken her too much for granted, and missed the signs? Realistically how could he expect to keep her attention when he only saw her every few weeks, while she moved in her social circles?

"Goddammit," he muttered quietly under his breath.

How could he get off this latest upheaval swinging his life around like a cat by its tail?

Across the river came the warning cough of an impala, followed a few minutes later by a distress bleat. In reverence to its sacrifice, they sat silently listening to its last gurgles of life. The culmination of a leopard's successful stalking.

"So tell me, what did you find so far?" Gideon asked. Focusing on the witchcraft would help distract his anxiety.

Moses scratched his cheek. "A few things, but it wasn't quite what I expected." He frowned. "We know that there is an old man messing about with witchcraft. For some reason he is inciting and stirring up the local population, with rumors, stories, and the usual stuff that presses superstitious buttons." Moses leaned down to set his mug on the ground. "This individual isn't from here, although he is familiar with the area. So why is he here, why now?"

Gideon nodded agreement.

"I wanted to find out if this guy was a genuine *nganga*? If he was, he would have a place where he could communicate with his spirits. African beliefs keep their spirits close, not out beyond the galaxies. So where could this be?" Moses cracked his knuckles. "I had a hunch that the area around the confluence of the rivers, with its hills and cliffs would be a good place to start looking, especially since we saw him shouting at us from the top of that hill."

Gideon rose and pushed the beaker pot back into the fire.

Moses went on. "The scouts showed me where at the foot of the cliffs a mental man had lived in a scrape under the trees for years with no shelter. They also told me the rumor of a white farmer, who bought gold and buried it on the hills above the cliffs before he died. All these things give the area a significance when it comes to superstitions. It is where a *nganga* would gravitate if he wanted people to take him seriously."

Gideon handed Moses a biscuit from a pack.

"It didn't take too long to find a cave." Moses continued. "It had been used ritually for a long time. There were totems engraved on the rock walls. From the tracks on the ground, it was obvious the place was visited frequently. But for some reason it took a while for our *nganga* to visit when I was staking it out."

Gideon pulled a long, dour face. They both listened to the hoot of a spotted eagle owl. "He walks in to his cave, using different routes, as part of his efforts to hide some of his movements – but not all. Now you see him, now you don't. Why he does this I'm at a loss. I suspect he is trying to set a narrative to the locals who probably cannot track his hidden movements like I can. He arrives from further away on a bicycle, which he hides in thick bushes near the road." Gideon used his hat to hold the hot handle of the beaker of boiling water as he lifted it off the fire.

"The old *nganga* travels on his bicycle at night, when there is little chance of meeting a strange vehicle. He regularly meets people at the abandoned construction quarry on the road. He doesn't trust whoever he meets there. He waits and watches them for a while before showing himself. Pretty gutsy given the presence of lions in the area. One of those who he meets often is Kings. We already know that from what Precious tells us. She has heard them talking, and we see the *nganga's* tracks. However, some of the meetings are out at the quarry. I followed Kings one afternoon without him seeing me. He met the *nganga* and someone who arrived on a motor-bike. It didn't take long for them to start arguing loudly. Suddenly Kings punched the bike rider hard in the face a few times, knocking him to his knees. Kings then kicked the guy in the face until the rider was cowering on the ground, with Kings shouting at him to get lost and think about some offer or other."

"Jesus!" Gideon exclaimed. "I was right about Kings being dangerous. That is why I haven't confronted him directly too much."

Overhead branches rustled and shook as a night ape sprang between boughs. Crickets creaked everywhere.

"A few nights ago, I got close enough to recognize who else the *nganga* was meeting. That's where things got confusing." Moses stood and paced around the fire before clearing his throat and spitting into it. "He meets the Russians."

Gideon snorted. "I should have known they were up to something. It was staring me in the face. They show up, and the shit hits the fan."

Moses crouched and rearranged a log on the fire.

"During one of the meetings, a young woman was with them. She didn't say anything, just stood to the one side." Moses stirred the embers again with a stick before sitting back in his chair.

"So what do you think is going on?" Gideon asked. "What's with the girl? Remember I saw a woman's tracks at the quarry. I bet she was there with the Russians back then."

"I don't know. Obviously they are involved. They have been here for a month. From what I hear, they never hunt. They are up to something."

A series of high-pitched, throaty yelps came from across the river. A side-striped jackal had started its evening search for food. Somewhere beyond it came the trill of a scops owl.

"It would be worth trying to coax some information out of those two sons-of-bitches!" Gideon said to Moses. "Maybe we should eat our pride and revisit them, and kiss their asses." He kicked at a log which had burned back from the fire. A shower of sparks arched into the air. "The best way to get information out of those two characters is to get them motherless drunk. We should figure out how to get them over here and give them free booze."

Moses cleared his throat again. "That might not be a bad idea. Most of the guests at the lodge right now don't drink too much alcohol, so maybe Bright could spare us a few bottles of whiskey at cost."

"Have you met the latest guests over there?" Gideon asked curiously.

"Yes, a strange bunch. A father who travels around a lot, leaving his daughter and her friend hanging loose in the wind."

Moses spoke nonchalantly, "The two women stopped by here a few days ago. They are bored. They are lookers. One of them is really beautiful."

The wistfulness in Moses's voice caught Gideon's attention. He stared at Moses, who kept looking down at his feet. "Moses!" he teased, "We're going to have to get you out of the bush if you start talking like that. We can't have you going bush-mad."

Gideon ducked as Moses threw a mock punch at him.

Christ, Gideon thought. When it came to affairs of the heart, little did Moses know that the joke was on himself.

28

December 4

G ideon suggested, "How about fresh fish for breakfast?"

"Sounds good to me." Moses responded. "I haven't had it in a long time."

As the sky added a trace of orange to its palette, beyond where Eden's Outlook punched its basalt fist up from the riverbank, Gideon tucked the boat behind a mid-stream jumble of rocks capped with a shrub which clung with admirable tenacity to a crack in a boulder. It was a wonder how it survived when it was tugged mercilessly by the summer floods. This obstinacy offered a good place to secure the boat's line.

Gideon couldn't help feeling an affinity for the plant's stubbornness. Africa is a tough place to live, he thought. Especially when something is trying to pull up your roots.

On either side of the outcrop, the river spread out to a wide, lazy drift before again gathering energy and forcing its way through the constrictions of the downstream rapids. The regular wrinkles of its flow hinted at a flat riverbed beneath its shallow waters. Gideon knew that large rocks were sprinkled across its even expanse like currants on a bun. With the boulder's edges rounded by the river's rub, he hoped to find a few big 'robbie' bream fishes lurking in their lea.

"Here, try this one. I have had success with it in water like this." He handed Moses a deep purple rubber worm flecked with chartreuse speckles.

Standing in the stern of the boat, Gideon cast his line across the current towards the bank, while Moses flicked his at a shallower angle on the other side. His hands went through the motions of the flick, twist and turn, casting and retrieving the lure. Like a violinist's dexterity after countless hours training with a bow, Gideon was at one with the water, with the world beneath it; together with the world he was molded for by nature. Wrapped in its perfection, the connection ran not from the mind but from some very deep, primitive place in the soul. It ran down his arms, through his hands and fingers and into the long artificial extension of nylon and carbon fibre, ending in the soft, latex rubber synthesis beneath which lurked an enticement as timeless as the eons. It tugged him back to this bushland and these wide African rivers. It was the same bond and emotions as those of his ancestors when he felt a little tug; the flutter of a fish. The strike which set the hook was as instinctively immediate as any buzz felt by his long-disappeared predecessors. He knew with an uncanny sense of awareness that he was good at what he did. But was his audience able to recognize his competence? How could an audience of one understand the nuances of the African bush from gazing at spreadsheets in an opulent banker's office in Munich?

Honed by war, together Moses and he were as professional a bush team as any on this continent. No duo was more capable of discovering the strange flows of the last few weeks, or would be more able to set a hook into the gums of any witchcraft's maw. But would that far-away banker give them the time to find the boulders behind which the nganga hid? And what about the lump in his heart? Would he have time to find what hid behind that? He had tossed its despairing complexity back and forth much of the night, until giving up the dilemma and drifting into sleep, exhausted. What was more important – the big gambling flashes of youth, or the small cautious intimate acts of maturity? Both lurked – shockingly, unexpectedly – under the surface in the stream of his life. Again, with mentally clenched fists, he set aside his anxieties, considering how it didn't take long to land three nice robbies and a big purple bream between them.

"Okay old buddy," Gideon said. "Time for breakfast. One each. We can have the other two for dinner. Or we can ask the ladies at the lodge to make fish fingers. They are good at it. Also," he teased Moses in hollow fashion, "while we are there, you can show me that new lady friend. With my experience," he teased him, "I am better at judging beauty than you."

"Piss off!" Moses scowled.

Gideon smilingly admonished him. "I bet they didn't teach you how to give the finger at the mission."

* * *

It had rained hard far to the north some days earlier. That water had now reached them. Heading back to the lodge, Moses raised his voice over the rattle of the engine. "It looks like the water has come up half a meter overnight. Just as well we are not camping on a sandbar."

The river was tinted with the cloudy opacity of fine soil flushed from denuded land to the north. Not even the Lukanga Swamps could filter out the consequence of the upstream overpopulation.

"Who knows what the river will look like in a few decades, when the swamps are finally overrun by too many goats, chickens, and people with scratched out patches of maize." Gideon spoke more to himself than to Moses.

The river's muddy surge pushed the vestiges of its clear winter water out of the way. It's waxing vitality surged on until eventually it would tumble down to mingle its mud with the Zambezi. Thereafter augmented by the energies of the Sanyati, the Luangwa and the Shire, the waters would inexorably carve deeper, wider scars into the cheeks of Africa before bleeding into the Indian Ocean. The water's silt was the color of a changing land. Why did he care? He could do nothing about it. He wondered if Ulrich was underwriting any upstream mining projects.

Gideon throttled back the engine, making a wide half-circle in the channel to turn the boats nose into the current, edging it across towards the mooring point below the deck.

"We had rain around here while you were away," Moses said, "Which was why it was hard to track the old *nganga*. The tracks kept getting washed away."

As Gideon edged the boat into the river bank, they could see Precious waving at them from the lodge's deck. As they approached, she moved down to meet them, catching the mooring rope thrown to her to pull them into the bank. She extended a hand for Moses as he jumped ashore, where he secured the line.

"We have come to ask a favor," Gideon called out. "We are looking for an expert cook who can fry these fish for us."

He held the fish up for her to see, two per hand, fingers through their gills.

"Nice ones," she admired. "How much are you willing to pay?

"Nothing, we are both broke," he said, straight-faced.

"In that case I can't help you!" she dismissed them with a wave of her hand. "Unless you are willing to barter."

"What!" Gideon exclaimed theatrically. "Are we back in ancient times?"

David Maritz

"Aren't you, here?" she teased. "Bartering should be second nature for the ancient like you."

"Ouch," he said. "Okay, what if you make them into fish-fingers and we share?"

"Deal," she said. "Come on up."

Gideon walked up the little gully beside the *chitenge*. Reaching its platform, he glanced across to its far end, where he noticed the two women sitting on the couches. He nodded a greeting in their direction.

"Show us what you have there!" A tall, fair-haired woman called across to him.

He looked at her for longer than he should. She was hard to describe without contradictions. Sitting slumped back in the couch, she appeared slight and slender. Then with the fish still held up for display, he looked at her more carefully as she stood and walked towards him. She was wide hipped, with a tall, proportionate figure. Reaching out to touch one of the fish, the faint rippling of the muscles under the smooth skin of her forearms hinted at an active, athletic lifestyle. Her long face was not unattractive. Her fair hair was gathered in a ponytail, pulled through the opening of her cap. This gave an impression of youthfulness, even though she clearly was straddling middle age. Standing before him, he realized that her slender appearance came mainly from her height. She was nearly as tall as him, and he stood at 180cm.

"What beautiful fish," her voice was surprisingly girlish, but it's tone and measured cadence held a hint of confident authority. "When I fished with my father, we caught some of those."

"Really!" he exclaimed. "Do you like fishing?"

"No, I don't! I hate the feel of those worms squirming around when you are getting them on the hook."

"Actually," he said, "we caught these with lures."

No longer interested in the fish, she looked unblinkingly at him. "My father was a doctor working at out-of-the-way bush clinics. He had a passion for fishing. We did a lot of it."

"If so, you should come out fishing with me."

"Fishing is boring," she said dismissively. "Like most fishermen."

Gideon smiled, but said nothing. Like Precious, this woman knew how to punch below the belt. He had better be careful.

Pausing and looking around, he saw that Moses had drifted towards the far side of the chitenge, where he was deeply engaged in conversation with the other woman. Moses was leaning forward, smiling and gesticulating to emphasize his points. Their conversation was animated, punctuated by peals of mutual laughter. It was obvious that they were well acquainted.

Oh boy, what is with this guy? Two peas in a pod, Gideon thought. His attention was fixed on the arms of the woman interacting with Moses. He had seen them before. Those delicate tattoos which teased down off her shoulders, down her arms, and flowed behind the elbows to curl around her forearms and brush the edges of her wrists, a narrow frond reaching out to tickle the middle finger of each hand.

As Gideon gawked, she turned to look at him, reacting Moses's frown at the surprise on his face. She was as he remembered, small, catlike, beautiful, with long wavy hair as black as sin, and a figure as sumptuously languid as the stretch of a sphinx.

The tall blonde woman noticed the flash of recognition in Gideon's stare. "Hey, don't be rude! I'm talking to you," she exclaimed loudly, dragging his attention back.

"I'm sorry, I got a surprise when I saw your friend. I've seen her before."

"Oh yeah? Where was that?"

"She was standing next to me at the security check at the airport in Joburg. It's hard to miss those tattoos!" Gideon introduced himself to the blonde. "I'm Gideon, Gidi for short."

"Yes, I know, we've had your background filled in by Moses. As you can see, he has a fan." With her chin she pointed across the floor. Then she extended her hand. "I'm Lauren. My friend over there is Narina. You can call me very bored for short."

Gideon raised his eyebrows in mock surprise. "What's the matter? Don't you have enough to do here to keep yourself entertained?"

"No!"

She placed her hands on her wide hips with an emphatic flourish. "We have been here for ten days, which is about six days too long for me. That isn't what I signed up for."

"So what's the deal?" Gideon asked.

"Our stay seems to be sort of open-ended. My friend over there, Narina, her father sets the schedule. Doing what, I don't know, and don't care, because whatever it is, he doesn't spend too much time here."

"That's too bad," he shrugged. "I can stay here for weeks and not miss any other place."

"Well, then you're lucky. I don't. I like having a lot of people around, with the bustle of civilization. Usually I have Narina on my side to fight her father. But as you can see, lately she doesn't have quite the same motivation to leave."

They watched Narina and Moses, their laughter punctuating the gaiety of their chatter.

"Maybe you should reconsider coming out on the river with me."

"If things carry on this way I will." Lauren turned back to face Gideon.

He stretched his arms above his head. "Moses said you were here to celebrate divorces, or something like that. Which is pretty unique."

"That's right," Lauren nodded. "But lately Narina prefers celebrating with her new friend."

"Oh really? I arrived back late last night, so I didn't get a full briefing."

Lauren pursed her lips, "Hmm, acting shy is he? You spoiled the fun. From the sounds of it, there has been nocturnal sneaking back and forth extending the socialising. Them acting like a pair of teens. Who would have believed it! And I am stuck watching all this unfold."

"You sound jealous," he teased.

"I am! At least it would give me something to do. Actually, I admire Moses's courage, Or maybe it's his stupidity." She gestured towards him again.

"What do you mean?"

"Narina's father can be a nasty type. "Now here she is, all a-twitter around your man, as if he was carrying the ten commandments."

"But what's that got to do with Moses's courage?"

"Her father is protective of his beloved and only, but wayward, daughter. Outwardly he's a strict Muslim. I doubt he would appreciate knowing that his precious daughter was busy falling for another non-believer. Especially when it appeared that she was heading back into the fold after an ex-husband conveniently got himself shot. More importantly, her dead ex left her with a lot of money in a Caribbean trust account. More money than even her son-of-a-bitch daddy could dream of. I think that daddy was entertaining thoughts of her financing a few of his riskier deals. I doubt he would be pleased to see someone he'd consider a pauper to get between himself and his daughter's windfall." Lauren lit a cigarette and took a long draw. "More important were his hopes that she would provide him an heir with a pedigree he approved of." Exhaling the smoke from a deep drag, Lauren went on. "I think that he would find it hard to reconcile your friend's missionary tainting." Another deep draw on her cigarette, and she blew a smoke ring in the direction of the giggling couple. "All he would see is a penniless, footloose, fancy-free wanderer."

"Interesting," Gideon said quietly. "But if things do develop, Daddy will find Moses doesn't scare easily."

There was that narrowing of Lauren's eyes. This time she aimed her smoke ring at Gideon's face. He didn't flinch. "If you get my drift," she purposefully flicked the ash of her cigarette onto the floor. "Your guy is brave to sniff around that promised place like a jackal looking for scraps."

"By the way," Lauren altered course, "Moses tells me that you are quite a man of the bush. How about taking me out on one of your patrols? I could do with some exercise. They don't want me to go out jogging alone here. Too many pissed off elephants they say."

Gideon hesitated. "I doubt you would like the patrols. We go out for days and rough it. If you find it hard to put a worm on a hook, I don't think a patrol fits your flow."

Lauren fixed him with an unblinking gaze. "Oh my, a real tough guy we have here!" Leaning forward she again blew a smoke ring at him. "You will have to find out how tough I am.... For your information, there is a difference between something slimy, and something tough. My ex thought he was tough, but he wasn't, which is why he is gone."

"Okay," Gideon hesitated. He was treading at the edge of the envelope. "How about the heavens? Would that keep you from getting bored?"

A glimmer of a smile appeared below her narrowing eyes. "Maybe I would like that. Let's see if you have what it takes, tough guy."

Precious came walking through the gap in the fence carrying a big bowl. "Gather around. Bring your coffee and loaves. A false prophet caught some fish and an angel cooked them."

Lauren turned and followed Precious. "I'll try some of those if you don't mind."

Gideon stared curiously at the sway of her hips and ponytail as she walked away.

"Sheeesh, a real man eater!" He thought.

29

December 5

"Come on old buddy, we have work to do."

Moses had been sleeping lightly. "What's going on?"

Gideon turned off his flashlight. Behind him were the first hints of dawn. "One of the lodge staff has come over to tell me that the guards at Kikuji heard shots yesterday. They sent a guy on a bicycle to tell us. Quite a feat with all this rain and mud"

"What do you want to do?" Moses asked.

"Be assertive, go after them!" Gideon answered. "The problem is that the scouts at the pontoon base are out on patrol right now. So we need to pick up a few off-duty scouts and do a follow-up patrol. I know where one of the team leaders lives. If we can find him, I am sure he can get an improvised team together."

Moses had already started dressing.

"I'll get the coffee going. It'll take a few hours to get to where he lives from here. With all the rain we have had, it'll be a bit of a bugger getting there, so we will have to skip breakfast."

* * *

The gravel road between the Kafue and Lunga rivers had held up remarkably well considering the scant maintenance it had seen over the past decade. As it drifts north, where it meets the Lunga River, it dips down into a gap carved into the river bank. Here the big metal ferry's drawbridge is pushed up onto the gravel by the momentum of the approach.

Moses stood beside Gideon, facing the cab of the vehicle, his elbows resting on the hood as he looked down and scratched at a few pebbles with the toe of his shoe.

"If I had to start a war in this part of Africa," Gideon said to him, "Sunday morning is when I would begin shooting."

Pausing the scratching of the gravel, Moses turned his head to look at him with a quizzical grin on his face. "Why?"

"Very little shooting would be necessary," he muttered, "it would all be over in minutes. All those buggers over there are still so hungover, they wouldn't even be able to find their guns let alone their goddamned rifles."

"For Chrisssakes," Gideon said. "Remember how Sergeant-Major Oliveira would make new recruits grab their package and repeat, 'this is my rifle, this is my gun, this is for shooting, this is for fun'? These buggers are so wasted they couldn't even point their guns out their pants to piss. I wonder where those sods managed to get enough hooch to get so motherless? I bet they started bingeing on Friday."

As they watched, a lethargic figure appeared at the top of the opposite bank. He slowly carried a big blue plastic canister down the slope and out onto the pontoon's platform. He then equally slowly began to pour its contents into a funnel inserted into the tank of one of its swivel engines.

Moses went back to scratching the dirt with his toe.

A second figure, still rubbing sleep from his eyes, followed the first down the bank. He stepped aboard and waited for his peer to finish filling the other engine. Fishing a rag out of a scruffy plastic can, he used this to wipe a dipstick to check the engine's oil.

"Why do things in parallel, when you can waste more time doing them serially?" Gideon said. "If this was anywhere else, you would assume that these clowns were union men being paid by the hour."

He dug deeper into the reserves of his patience. The first man walked slowly up the slope and headed away until the top of his head disappeared into the long grass at the side of the road. "What the hell are they up to now?"

Moses turned around and called out across the river, and a few sentences were shouted back and forth in Kaunde, before he turned back to Gideon.

"The book. They have gone to get the man with the book."

Gideon shook his head. Despite growing up in Africa, he could never quite get the rural African attitude towards time and their deep reservoirs of patience.

He and Moses had spent so many years together on operations, whose success depended on meticulous timing, and yet Moses always had a longer fuse than his. Fuming was a waste; there was nothing to do but wait for the crew to get its painstaking act together. The concept of customer service didn't reach up this remote stretch of river. Especially not on a Sunday morning. Gideon could hardly contain his impatience. It seemed that his urgency was being thwarted deliberately by the pontoon crew's lethargy. Leaning against the front of the Land Cruiser, Gideon slapped at an annoying tsetse fly. They were bad today! The bothersome flies fanned his impatience.

With the pontoon still moored on the far bank, and the road on the other side of the river in an even worse state, Gideon wondered how much longer it would take to gather a team. On the other side, the road's condition quickly deteriorated. Being outside the park and with more traffic, the havoc was wreaked by the big trucks churning the surface as they moved copper ore from a nearby Chinese-run mine. Not even the South Africans, let alone the Chinese, could build a dirt road to stand that sort of punishment. Their efforts became a quagmire each time it rained – and it had rained a lot. The huts comprising the extended village where the scout lead lived dribbled down that mud bath in a desultory fashion. It was with no pleasure that Gideon contemplated three or more hours crawling through the slosh, with the diff-drive locked and the vehicle in low-ratio, looking for enough sober scouts to make a team. His only consolation was heading back, he should have a complement of strong men to push the vehicle through the mud, if necessary.

His annoyance was distracted by the sound of engines as two vehicles drew up behind theirs. To his surprise, the Russian pair were in the first. As they came to a stop, he noticed that they were accompanied by a good-looking and smartly dressed young woman. She looked familiar. Peering more closely through the grime on the vehicle's windows, Gideon recognized the well-spoken dockhand from Alan's camp.

"Good morning. This place is getting crowded!"

The two Russians responded warmly enough to Gideon's greeting. Alexi nodded at Moses, who raised his hand in a perfunctory salutation. Vladimir on the other hand glared back when Moses called a "Good morning" across the roof of their vehicle. He still harboured a grudge.

David Maritz

Alexei mumbled evasively to Gideon's query as to where they were headed. Something up north a way, 'to check it out'.

"Hunting?" Gideon asked. "Surely not. You will be outside the game management area."

"*Nyet*," Alexei replied, "we also do some consulting."

"Are you still at Alan's camp?" Gideon asked, to which Alexei answered in the affirmative. Gideon whistled, "That must be costing a pretty penny!"

Alexei smiled with a shrug. "We have a good client who pays well."

An occupant from the last vehicle walked towards them. He stopped and beckoned to Vladimir, who walked across and bent his head forward and cocked his head sideways as they conversed in quiet tones.

The newcomer's full head of thick, curly African hair was tinged with grey, indicating that he was older than his good physique suggested. He had a light way of walking, rising a tad on the balls of his feet with each step and leaning forward, accenting the incongruity of stylish shoes more suited for a city office than a muddy journey in this bush backwater. He cut a fashionable dash against everyone else's drab khaki. His neatly pressed white cotton shirt tucked into long charcoal trousers, held up by the clasp of a woven leather belt sporting a silver buckle.

"A fancy-pants," Gideon commented quietly to Moses. "Who the hell is he trying to impress?"

There was something Hamitic about the man's sharp hawk-like face, suggesting an origin further north up Africa, with a touch from an ancestral dabble with an Arabian concubine.

Gideon lifted his hand and called a good morning across to the man, who didn't respond. Turning to Alexi he asked, "Is that guy with you? Not exactly a friendly type!"

Alexei looked surprised. "Haven't you met him yet? He is staying at your lodge."

It was Gideon's turn to be surprised. "Really! So he is the Mustafa I have been hearing quite a lot about lately. No, I haven't met him. I was away. I only arrived back two nights ago, and he has not been around. He's nothing like what I expected. Quite a dapper chap. He must be a hit with the ladies with his fancy dress."

As the man walked back to his vehicle, Gideon peered intently after him, imagining the fire that must erupt when he and Lauren occupied the same space.

"So what does he do with you?" he queried.

"He is an investor."

Alexi moved across to join his father, who had beckoned him over. They were joined by Mustafa. Gideon was tempted to ask the Russian pair about late night meetings with a mystery man. But it would be stupid to let them know that they were being watched before he had found out more about what they were up to. Was Mustafa mixed up in what was going on? Gideon let his mind roll that proposition around. The Russians were here on an open-ended extended stay, and so was Mustafa. That in itself was curious. Now add to that discovering them travelling together, and Alexei describing Mustafa as an 'investor'. It built on the intrigue.

Gideon walked across to the other side of the Russian's vehicle and tapped on the window where the young woman was sitting. She rolled it down as he greeted her.

"This is a surprise to see you here," he said. "What brings you this way?"

"I am so excited," she answered, "these men have a contact who is a foreign executive. He is looking for a secretary for his office in Rome."

"Really?" Gideon exclaimed. "Are you sure this is genuine?"

"Yes, of course it is," she said, sounding offended. "They have organized my passport and have even provided me with luggage for the trip." She pointed to a sturdy modern backpack with thick comfortable shoulder straps on the seat beside her.

"So are you going for an interview, or do you already have the job?"

"I am sure I have the job. I will meet the executive in Solwezi and then fly with him to Lubumbashi in the Congo. From there to Europe."

"Congratulations!" He gave her a thumbs up. "I hope it works out for you."

Turning away, he watched as the group of men broke up. The newcomer returned to his vehicle, driven by what Gideon assumed was a driver, who held the door open. Thinking back, Gideon remembered Alan mentioning that the Russian pair were involved with mining. Their lack of interest in hunting now made sense. They were at the hunting camp for its convenient luxury while they worked in the area. On the face of it, everything looked legitimate. But why the night meetings with the nganga, and other strangers? And what was this stuff with young woman and jobs?

Detecting Alexei's reluctance to talk, Gideon walked down to the river's edge as the first thump of the single cylinder diesel signalled life. Flywheel spinning, it billowed black smoke across the water like a squirt of squid ink. Everyone's attention was drawn to the pontoon as it crept across the river.

Moses, who had sauntered over to speak to the young woman, returned to their vehicle. It was an opportunity for a last leak. Gideon walked back along the road to where the underbrush encroached on the waiting area. Here he would be obscured from view.

By now the early morning's shadows were retreating back under the tree branches, exposing the vehicles to the sun's heat. The fancy-dress new-comer stood behind his vehicle. He was obviously too warmly dressed. He had taken off his long-sleeved shirt to pull an under vest up over his head. Tossing the vest through the open window, he picked up the shirt again. As he fumbled to find the sleeve openings, Gideon caught a glimpse of his upper torso. The front of his lean, bony chest was covered with the welted tautness of a big scar. Its pale blemish contrasted sharply with the dark chocolate of his skin. It was as if boiling oil had been poured down from his neck and across his chest in a widening splash until it puddled out to one side over his belly.

It was a striking scar, and an unusual shape.

* * *

It had been a big herd. Chewed and discarded branches lay spread over a wide swathe. The herd had crossed the road only a half hour before; some of the dung piles still had steaming wisps of foggy vapor. At least Gideon had managed to collect six scouts in less time than anticipated. So now there was nothing to do except bottle his frustrations.

He brought the snout of their vehicle to a stop before the fallen tree, and stretched back in his seat with an annoyed abruptness.

If they did nothing about it, the tree could remain across the road for months. It was too large to be summarily dragged aside, and the bush on either side was sufficiently accommodating to allow a detour. If he pioneered a skirting path, his tracks would be widened with successive vehicles, following sheep-like. Each set of wheels would press into the sand and mud until their trenches were impassable. Then others would circle further out, surrounding the obstacle with rutted rings of inconvenience. Moses looked at him with mild curiosity, waiting to see what he would do. Switching off the engine, Gideon took out his knife and started cleaning the dirt from under his nails, left there from an earlier dig of mud from around the wheels.

"Can you tell the scouts to cut the tree?" he said. "The government pretends to maintain the road, like it pretends to be paying all the scouts' benefits, so we may as well get our money's worth."

He watched as two of the men raised their sinewy, ebony arms and drove the flared blades of their bush axes into the woody flesh of the fallen tree. Each swing was as precisely executed as the wrist pivoted chip of a golfer. Angled first from the left than the right, or the top after the bottom, working in successive patterns, each bushmaster chopped their wedges until all that was left of the tree's creaking groans was a shapeless pile of chips and hacked branches. With its lofty crown now at the bottom of the pile, a gracious giant of the woodland was no more than firewood. Watching its transformation from grandeur to scrap, Gideon was touched by a feeling of sad reverence, which morphed into darker contemplation. Looking beyond the butchered tree, he gazed down the length of the road until it drifted away before being buried under the canopy of the woodland far ahead.

"Only when something special is gone, one realizes how exquisite it is. But by then it's too late." Gideon was half talking to himself. "Often it's our own stupidity that doesn't recognize what is special, and easily lost. Like this tree, and the elephants which pushed it over."

"Hey! Speak for yourself," Moses said. "I am not stupid. But what are you getting at?"

Looking down, Gideon started cleaning under the nails of the other hand. "Once it's gone, all that's left is a pile of chips."

"My word!" Moses exclaimed. "The philosopher in you is certainly on a coffee buzz this morning."

Gideon paid no notice. "Loyalty and fidelity. What's the difference? The bush is loyal to us, even though we cannot count on its fidelity. It's always fucking with us; it never loves us back. But it doesn't discard us. At most it leaves behind a pile of chips. I can reach out to touch what I love without guilt, smell its smells, feel its sweat on the skin of my arms, its hair brushing my legs as I walk, the sound of its breath in the rustle of the leaves."

Moses made an indifferent face. "Oh boy!" he cocked his head. "Who kicked the cot of your philosopher this morning? He looked at Gideon pointedly. "What has gotten into you?"

Gideon let his inner anguish fade into the background. He couldn't put his finger on what had unwrapped the moody thoughts. It wasn't just the chopping of a tree, or his shaken connection with womanhood.

The scouts were clambering back onto the vehicle. Was he jealous of the happiness in Moses's voice? Why could it not be like that for him as well? Goddammit. Why couldn't he find Moses's clarity and simplicity of choice?

Gideon let out the clutch.

Glancing back in the rearview mirror at the forlorn pile of chopped branches and chips, it struck Gideon how quickly the sedate order of life could be turned upside down. Suddenly there it was, the source of his unease. Upside down, it was just as Father Xavier had described it.

That scar. Mustafa's scar.

* * *

"Why are you suddenly so quiet?" Moses asked.

Gideon concentrated on negotiating the primitive bush track from the main road to the new lodge site. It led westward through thick wooded patches interspersed with open marshy sections. They were forced to skirt far out around these waterlogged *dambos*, as well as cross two deep washouts before they could get to the Lunga River and the construction site. It was past noon by the time they reached the river. A short boat ride got them across where they were greeted by three guards. There was yet barely any evidence of the future Kikuji luxury lodge. Its *chitenge* would be at the foot of a gigantic mahogany, towering its ebullience over that of its peers. Under the tree, blocks, metal sheeting and other construction material were piled onto a platform over which a wooden framework held up a canvas tarpaulin. The guards were using this as their campsite shelter.

From the guard's description, the shots had been close. Gideon was worried that there was a message in their proximity. Shots alone would suggest a hit-and-run operation. But if they also found snares, it would imply a mock of authority. A 'catch them if you can' deliberate taunting arrogance. 'We will be back to check the snares', it would imply.

After speaking to the construction crew, he and Moses crossed back over to the east bank of the river and joined the scouts on a short patrol downriver to see if they could find the tracks of the shooters.

It didn't take long to discover the first snare.

A well-worn game trail led down to the river through a break in the undergrowth. On both sides, cut brush was piled loosely to funnel any hapless animal towards a wire noose stretched across the trail. It was a flagrant throwing down of the gauntlet. Gideon tried to remember the wording of the warning note, left here, which now seemed so long ago.

"Moses," he said, "what do you think? It looks like somebody is playing games with us. Like we did in Angola, 'tempting' with small bait for others to follow our tracks, so we could hammer them when they walked into our ambushes."

"Yes!" he replied. "But that isn't the motive. It might be that they want to scare us away."

"Why would a snare scare us?"

Moses instructed the rest of the scout team to continue searching. "Come," he said to Gideon. "Look at this." He pointed to where the snare was tied to the tree. "There is witchcraft involved."

Stepping closer so he could see whatever it was that blended with the bark, Gideon saw that the wire was slipped through the vertebra of an animal.

"That is from a jackal," Moses said. "It means that the *nganga* is watching. Sneaking around at night. Looking for a soul to snatch." Moses let his words sink in. "I suspected this, so I looked for it." The small bone was pressed into the flaky bark of the tree. He untied the wire strand and put the bone in his pocket. "It is not good if any scout is worried about following these people, like if they think that witchcraft is on the side of the poachers. If there are more of these bones, we need to find and remove them. We don't need the word getting out that the poachers have a *nganga* on their side everywhere."

"Damn!" Gideon exclaimed. "All I need is a few more scouts to get spooked and disappear."

"When is the team at the pontoon base due back from its patrol?" Moses asked.

"Tomorrow." Gideon hesitated. "Maybe the day after, they generally carry only a day's food and water, allowing them to spend a night away before returning. Why do you ask?"

Moses gestured across the river. "I will go with the scouts tomorrow and look for signs further down, on this side of the river. But I think that you should get back to the pontoon base and have the scout lead there send out another team up towards us. We can meet in the middle, and get to the poachers quicker if they have headed downriver."

"Okay," Gideon replied. "I'll head back first thing in the morning and get that ball rolling."

Moses looked at him. "You seem upset. Why?"

"Oh, it's just that I'm pissed at this bullshit, starting with the asshole in Germany. He has no idea how witchcraft affects a lot of people out here. He holds the purse strings to my job. It may be on the line if we don't get to the bottom of this stuff soon."

Gideon shrugged. "Let's go on a bit and see if we can find more of these nooses."

If Moses only knew the extent of all the upside-down issues. But why distract from the task at hand with his latest inverted-down dilemma.

30

December 6

There was only the swish of the grass brushed aside by their legs and the soft crunch of the soil beneath boots between the far-off, repetitive calls of a ring-necked dove and the soft chatter of a honey guide. The little bird trying to get their attention would have no luck today; the scout patrol was steadily moving south along the river's margin.

Stretched out in line abreast   formation to increase the chance of detecting tracks, or finding snares, they moved with purpose and in silence. Not having to concentrate on following a track, Moses walked slightly to the side and rear of the formation. His mind and soul basked in the pleasure of walking with the team and his thoughts. He was at one with the world. He had spent his life moving with men. Mostly peacefully and uneventfully, but sometimes with deliberate purposeful strides toward strife. Moses hoped it would stay calm, but one never knew what would happen if they came upon a group of armed poachers. Man was made in the image of God. Ever since Father Xavier showed him how to shelter in the shadow of that image, away from the heat of evil, he felt comfortable dealing with those with whom he moved—carefully choosing some and rejecting others. The old priest had taught him to be practical about his faith and service. Sometimes it was necessary to slap back even while turning the other cheek. It was why he had spent his life fighting, even killing,

David Maritz

to preserve the shades of God's goodness. That world had not spared much time or space for the affairs of women, definitely not understanding how they can take over men's hearts.

Yes, he had married early; barely past his teens. It had been arranged. She was fifteen. Despite his youth, he already had the money to pay her family's lobola price. Traditional African marriage was about practicalities, not so much luxuries of the heart. Even so, it was his first real confrontation with the blend of his upbringing on both a mission and in a village, presenting ideological dilemmas which had ruffled the surface of his equanimity ever since. His attempts to reconcile old African conventions with the ideas of the church.

His marriages had been good practical choices made on his behalf, the sisters. His hesitation to marry both overcome only when Father Xavier said for him to remember that he was named Moses for a reason. That the ways of God didn't change over time; only man's interpretation of it did. An old, vengeful father could slap, even as the Son turned the other cheek. There was a time and place for everything. The struggles on behalf of that God had been far away. Angola, West Africa. He was always separated by space and time from his wives' womanly ways. Malaria took one's spirit away, distance and disapproval the other. With it went all the sadness that follows death and rejection, and children still crawling and walking towards their future. Luckily, grandparents and family were there to help raise the children he hardly knew. At least the pay in his unusual career had been good, and they had all benefited from that abundance.

But now this newness!

"Narina!" Moses silently mouthed her name. "What a beautiful name. Given to a beautiful bird two centuries ago to honor a Frenchman's Khoi-san mistress."

Father Xavier always said, 'God works in mysterious ways'. Because of that, on a whim, he had answered Gidi's call. Leading to this mysterious glimpse of a promised land. A flood of abundance, affecting every facet of his life. The unaccustomed elation of it taking him completely by surprise. He had always been driven to impress and prove himself to men. Never had he sought the approval of a woman. Where did his compulsion to find favor in this woman's eyes come from? The approval of men was nothing compared to that of this girl. Her shy smile hinting at her interest in him. His pleasure at impressing, bringing little gifts. A string of lucky beans, a bouquet of wild flowers. Such joy! Her glow was easily kindled. Like hers to him, his presence brought her happiness, triggered in the small things he said, the little favors he performed. Showing the insignificant trivia of the bush, tracking a tortoise, where to find the lilies of the field, an ant colony on the march, find her namesake, the beauty of a bird in a thicket. How was it that after tracking mystery men all day, when otherwise he was heavy and tired, that his gait increased its alacrity? An effusion of pleasure, knowing that at sunset she would appear, to sit side-by-side with him on the sandbar at the edge of the river with the fire at their feet, talking about the meanderings of life, listening to the snort of the hippos. Telling her the snippets of his hidden Africa, its sun, its shade and its darkness. The happiness was so new.

When he realized she was interested in him as a man, blinkers were stripped from his mind's eye. He saw her in a new light. So sudden, watching her come closer. He couldn't remember—was it the second or third time she visited his camp? With her hips like bells, the catlike way she walked making her flare of hair sway so that it brushed her shoulders above the tightness of her top. It opened the gates to his heart. It was an awareness of her being. Strange. It felt so utterly good. Sitting before the fire, their feet resting on a big log as they laughed, inching closer, until her toes touched his.

The flare of the heart was immeasurably more intense than the flame. Swirling with sweeps of passion reaching up like a full moon poised to sprinkle its silver over the deficits of his splayed desire, he had tried to haul on the lanyards of his billowing emotions.

To no avail.

Tumbling into the ebb and flow of her tides, his mind flowed between the moon and the sun, spilling over a surreal stage of unexpected chance. His imagination pointed its shivering way towards the heat of her magnet. He no longer drifted east or west with the tug of passing fancies. Fabulously abandoning escape, his stretches into the future were accompanied by breathless pants of hope. How could one even contemplate a plea for forgiveness with the perfection of how she accepted him, as willingly and excitedly as he could ever dream? With the speechless ease of a daydreamer, a drawn out sigh of submission had heralded his headlong plunge into that cradle of creation. The shadows of goodness are always dappled at the edges Father Xavier said, as long as one made sure there was enough sunlight for the flame lilies to flower.

As Moses walked, his thoughts were brushed aside when his eyes caught the familiar cross-hatch boot print tracks of an old, grey-haired *nganga*. They came into focus as if to deliberately tread on his joy, in the same way Gidi's words had as he departed in the morning.

"Moses, that woman is not suited for you." Gideon had said.

31

December 6

Despite being tired from the long day with its early start, and most of it spent slogging through the mud of the roads, followed by the short patrol down the river, Gideon hadn't slept well. His dilemmas, now exacerbated by the image of the scar on Mustafa's chest, kept cropping up in his mind, leading to the same dead end. The indecision was foreign. He had always been a good tactician, able to make decisions and take snap choices when things changed, or went wrong. These current options weren't the sort he was familiar with. Pull the trigger, move this way or that. Here the issues were murky.

Dammit, why did this stuff have to pile up?

He wished he could pass on the choices to a God. But he couldn't. He had to take on that role here. Between his African culture and the Old Testament, Moses could find justification for two wives, but not sleeping with a sister. Gideon was certain that if he told Moses his suspicions, they would surely both lose. Moses would leave before they had solved the witchcraft problem, and, of course, Moses would lose the new love of his life.

Should he shut up and watch stoically from the side as Moses and Narina continued to deepen their emotional bonds? The poor bugger, just when he had the resolve to go back and confront the past, attempting to reunite with his lost family in the aftermath of losing the two women who had borne him children.

Christ! That had to count for something!

Narina would be the third loss, almost before its blast had begun.

Despite his bravery on old battlefields, Gideon found himself facing a new reality: his emotional cowardice. At daybreak, leaning out the window, and before starting the engine all he could say was, "Moses, I don't think that Narina is meant for you. You should think long and hard whether or not you two are suited to each other."

Gideon knew his advice had been shallow, platitudinal advice. Cowardly, side-stepping advice. He had seen the shock and anger on Moses's face.

Gideon inwardly asked himself how the heck once again things had become so messed up so fast. Why was he still trying to fix problems that he hadn't created?

The heck was he still drawn to the people and places like this? Was it to escape further back behind blighted relationships and the obliteration of an identity? Or an attempt to shape a future as a reflection of an unrealistic ideal of how it should have been? Or perhaps it was simply the only home he had ever known, with all the emotional impossibility and heartbreak if he abandoned it.

Gideon had lost track of time as he drove. Proceeding down to the scout base at the Lubungu Pontoon, he saw that Dima's patrol had not yet returned. There wasn't anyone there to give an update. If they had not returned by tomorrow, he would head into Mumbwa and ask Ernest for some backup. Leaving the scout base, he returned to his camp above the lodge. The buzz of the cell phone in his pocket brought him back from his musings. He had reached the umbrella of the lodge's satellite Wi-Fi. The pent-up messages streamed into the instrument, announcing their arrival with short sharp shivers.

Stopping where the road skirted the kitchen fence, he scanned the texts. Maybe there was something important to deal with before he continued back out of Wi-Fi range up at his campsite.

There was.

Gene, his boss, wanted to talk. It was important he said. He was willing to fly up to meet and speak about it in person. There had been an official complaint. Someone he worked with had filed it. He wanted to discuss things before reporting back to the trust's board. With the engine running Gideon stared at the message.

"What the hell! Who would file a complaint, and what was it about?"

He engaged the gear and began to drive on past the lodge. A flutter from under the *chitenge* roof caught his attention. It was the silhouette of Lauren's hand, stretched high above her bare shoulder as she energetically waved at him. Backlit by the afternoon light in the cool gloom of the chitenge, she wore a tank top and faded cut-off jeans.

Hmm, he thought, today's been suntan time for those nice long legs and arms, below a bit of burnishing for her shoulders. Why not catch up with her before he headed out with scouts, or to get others from Mumbwa early in the morning? She was fun. He needed something to get him out of his funk.

Stopping, he shouted across at her that he was going to clean up and would be back in an hour. Parking his vehicle in its usual spot in the shade of the big trees behind his tent, Gideon crossed to the shower block. He washed the sweat from his face and hands before walking back to his tent to get a fresh change of clothing.

David Maritz

It was as he was about to unfurl the flap covering the entrance to his tent that he noticed the figure. It stood very still in the shade under the roof at the far end of the small campsite chitenge.

For what seemed an eternity the two men stood looking at each other without moving. In actuality it could not have been more than a few seconds.

"What do you want?" Gideon spoke first.

Kings let his crossed arms drop free and hang at his sides. "I have come to give you a final warning," he said. "The crocodile has been patient with you. But you ignore his warnings, those he gave you directly, and those that I have passed on."

Gideon held Kings's stare for a while before replying. "To hell with you, and your crocodile man!" Gideon felt his temper rising. "Who do you think you are coming out here giving warnings? I'm here to do a job and that's what I intend to do. So take your warnings and put them where the monkey keeps his nuts." The muscles of Gideon's jaw were clenched so tight that his words came out as a hiss.

They glared at each other.

Kings stood with his legs slightly apart and his head lowered as he opened and closed his fists, flexing his fingers like a bar-room bully preparing for a fight. The lines that usually formed between his eyebrows deepened, accentuating his glare. "If you would stick to what you should be doing, everything would be okay," Kings said. "But you do not; you listen to that woman. You invite her across here. You listen to her and you want to impress her. You do what she asks. You carry out her meddling. Then you even bring in others to help with your interference."

"What the fuck are you talking about?" Gideon exploded. "Something strange is going on here and if it involves gangs and their poaching it is my business, and I will listen to anyone who can help me understand what the goddam hell is happening. I will speak with, listen to, and get help from whoever I want."

"Stay away from that woman." Kings growled. "She has no business dealing with old, ugly men like you."

"Listen to me, my buddy." Gideon let the sarcasm seep into his voice "Are you telling me this because you are the one who wants to impress her? Do you think that she will be impressed by your bluster and bullshit?" Gideon could tell that Kings was not one to think logically. He knew that if pushed a bit more Kings would pop, and potentially burst into violence. "Listen Kings," he said, "I am not interested in Precious as a woman. I am not going to get in your way if your think that she is attracted to you." He let his words sink in. Then the old officer training kicked in. Gideon realized he must defuse the situation. An open war right now would only get in the way of finding out what was really going on. Consciously forcing his muscles to relax he said quietly, "Thank you for your warning. I will think about it."

Kings continued slowly clenching and spreading his fingers.

Gideon stood silent, still, ready to punch. But the tactician in him knew it best not to yet make a complete enemy of the man. Better to let Kings think that he had been intimidated. Life here at the camp would be very uncomfortable with a war going on. Better to let Kings bring more rope, so all that would be needed was a hanging.

"You have been warned for the last time," Kings said. Turning on his heel, he stepped out from the shade where he had been standing and walked away across the open *dambo* grass.

* * *

David Maritz

Gideon was still flushed with anger as he walked to the lodge, but a good shower and a fresh change of clothing helped put him in a more approachable frame of mind. He wondered what had long ago broken the branch of a big leadwood tree standing at the edge of the lawn between the *chitenge* and the kitchen. Maybe the tug of an elephant's trunk? A thunderstorm's billowing downdraught? Whatever it was, the break had healed in a hollow, glove-sized aperture. It was sufficient space for a pair of Arnot's chats to raise a family – a seemingly safe spot; but this was their second attempt. What became of the prior brood? Maybe a ground squirrel's dash and snatch up the tree trunk, or had the squeaky, begging clamour of the chicks caught the attention of a mamba? Had the snake surreptitiously slithered along the branch, peered its big black unblinking eyes into the gloom, and opened its wide grin to swallow the pink chicks, even as they blindly begged for food? But fate was on the side of these latest chattering youngsters. They owed their domicile to the presence of lodge guests back in September, over springtime nest selection. Being chats, their parents had more tolerance for the presence of humans than the black-collared barbets, whose greater aggression would otherwise have won the struggle for nest real estate. Persistence and adapting to the upheaving reality of changing circumstance had been the secret to success for these little creatures. So should he learn from them?

But (so much for the scolding of the cheeky little black and white birds) it was Lauren's figure out on the deck that drew his attention. Just then, an unusually boisterous rush of air buffeted the tops of the trees. It tumbled down the slope towards the river, shaking the shrubs that grew in the gully alongside the chitenge. Rising, the wind playfully pushed at the woven reed matting along one of the walls, before snatching his floppy hat and tossing it into the long grass in the gully. Bending to retrieve it, he noticed an unfamiliar vehicle partly obscured beyond the nearest chalet. With his faded cloth crown back, Gideon acknowledged Lauren's breezy, "Welcome back stranger."

Behind her, two figures were slumped in the large lounge chairs.

"How did your mission go?" she queried. "I looked for you last night. You didn't tell me that you would be away."

"It was an emergency," he said.

"So what! In that case you should have invited me."

"There was no time, or room for you."

"Whatever. Your loss."

They crossed to the beverage table tucked against the now-limp matting of the chitenge's wall.

"Tea, coffee or juice?" she asked.

Gideon's gaze drifted across to the new figures. One was leaning forward with her elbows on her knees, her chin resting on the knuckles of her hand as she held a phone in the other. Her companion's elbows were splayed on the chair's upholstered armrests, also with phone in hand. Neither looked up to notice his stare. The cascading jet-black mane of the smaller of the two framed a finely fashioned face, sporting a bounteous mouth whose pouted lips were coated with red lipstick so startling it rendered her theatrical. Her dark eyebrows gave her a stylized hieroglyphic look. The other woman was equally striking. Her hair, although not as full, found its dark chestnut abundance tinted auburn with golden highlights. Her big, hazel eyes set wide apart below pencil-thin eyebrows spanned a high bridged nose. Hers was a profile stolen from a Minoan vase. Both were far too skinny for Gideon's taste.

Gideon nodded surreptitiously in their direction, as under his breath he asked Lauren, "Are they your friends?"

"Not mine. Companions of Mustafa's friends. There is no need to keep your voice down. They don't speak English."

David Maritz

"A pretty pair," Gideon admired.

Noting the wide golden bracelet adorning the hand of the darker one, and the light elegance in the purple flow of her close-fitting dress, he muttered, "A fancy pair! Do they think they are going to an opera? An expensive pair I should imagine."

Lauren snorted as she led him out onto the deck. "Wait until you see their partners. Hideous. One tall, the other short and pudgy. Right out of a comedy script, covered in bling."

"Where are they?"

"Across in the office with Mustafa, speaking to Bright about something."

Now that she had pointed it out, if he listened carefully, Gideon could hear faint voices coming over the thatch fence from the logistic area.

Waving her hand in the direction of the glamorous latin women Lauren said, "It seems that the two men are going to dump these delights here and head off shortly with Mustafa, coming back tomorrow or whenever."

Indicating the women again, Lauren continued. "You're right about them being high maintenance. But who cares?" she said, "Whoredom is just another form of bartering in goods and services. And in a capitalist world, what's wrong with that? Usually it's called marriage."

"Wow!" he had touched a nerve. "You have strong opinions."

"No, I have experience, which breeds realizm, calling a spade a spade."

Moving out onto the deck, with more exposure to the vagaries of the wind, Gideon pulled his hat tighter onto his head as they sat talking and listening to the rustle of the leaves, and the ripples of the river.

"I may be heading in to Mumbwa early tomorrow," he said. "I may need to ask the head warden to send a patrol up the west side of the Lunga River."

"If you do go, please, please take me," she pleaded. "I need to get the hell out of here and back to my hustle and bustle, even if I have to stay at some flea-bitten motel for a month before I can catch a bus. Sitting around doing nothing but bump into Mustafa is driving me nuts."

They sat on the deck for some time discussing the unusual activity he had encountered the day before. Lauren bet that if he dug deep enough, Gideon would find Mustafa and his friend's manipulating puppets tying those vertebrae to trees.

"He's a jackal," she said, "a master at manipulation. Most people don't know what he's up to, or that they are snared in his mesh. Now he's wooing big money. As you said, that pair over there don't come cheap."

"What do you know about them?"

"Not much, only what Narina told me. They have been staying at a lodge downstream a way. But they now want to be closer to the action. Whatever that means." Lauren shrugged. "They are South American. Narina speaks their lingo. She lived there until someone shot her guy. I suspect he was connected to this lot. It makes one wonder."

"Hmm. Interesting," Gideon hummed.

Lauren scoffed. "Mustafa has dual motives for inviting his darling daughter and myself out here. It is convenient to have her around to translate."

"Not what I would have guessed," Gideon said. "Africa certainly has a way of making strange bedfellows."

"Having her as translator is why Mustafa doesn't want us to leave," Lauren grumbled.

"How have you and Narina remained friends if you have such a poor opinion of her father?" The surprise on his face showed.

Lauren sighed. "It's a long story. We were at school together. We had a strange relationship. I was a teacher, fresh out of training college, when she became the head-girl. Her mother had recently died in a car accident. She needed consolation. I needed a friend. It was this unusual give and take between us that bonded us together, and has kept us ever since."

The intensity of the voices from over the fence increased. Gideon tried to hear what was being said, but the words were scrubbed by the rustle of the river.

Lauren went on explaining. "Her father was seldom around. So I never really had to deal with his Jekyll-Hyde personality." She inhaled deeply on the cigarette dangling from her fingers. This time she blew two smoke rings in Gideon's direction. He suggestively skewered both with his middle finger. He could give and take. She smiled and touched her lips with the tip of her tongue, before drawing on the cigarette again.

"Okay," he said. "If we go into town, you'll have to get up early."

"Thanks!" she said. "Supposing you will get me out of here, I'm inviting you to dinner over here tonight. It will be your last chance to show me some of the magic you make around here."

As Gideon walked across to return his empty cup to the coffee table, he noticed three men walking through the gap in the fence. He recognized Mustafa from the meeting at the ferry. The other two were as Lauren had described; comic contrasts. The one a short, stocky man with a round, jowled face made more oval by a small mouth surrounded by facial hair trimmed down into a goatee. He had the saddest eyes. The second was a tall man with a short neck, giving an impression of hunched shoulders. His rough, spiky hair surely confounded any neat trimming. It gave a shaggy look to a face, which seemed primitive due to prominent brow ridges and small, piercingly dark eyes. His untidy visage was exacerbated by cheeks ravished by the pockmarks of youthful acne. The men were dressed in far more subdued attire than their lady friends. Jeans, sneakers and large, checkered cotton shirts ensured that they would not stand out in a crowd. The bling wasn't quite as Lauren had emphasized it. Their nod to flash was a heavy gold chain on one, and the large-format signature rings worn by his short, stocky companion.

32

December 7

Gideon's bush khakis were no match for the women's elegant attire. Their dress suggested that they were all from a more refined class. But so what? He could hold his own equally well with paupers or princesses such as these. During the delicious, well-served dinner, his conversation was directed mostly to Lauren sitting beside him, while Narina interacted in Spanish with the other gaudy pair. Maybe because she was spurred on by successive glasses of merlot, Lauren extended her already extroverted friendliness. Her knee kept bumping and pressing against his under the table as they talked about how a sliver of the moon had risen, with its reflection shivering off the river waters.

Leaning over to him, she whispered in his ear, "It has been a while since anyone has shown me the stars." He assumed it was partially the wine that had her continuing in a sultry voice. "How about it, big boy? Show me what a hot shot you are."

Responding with teasing ambiguity, he replied. "I'm up for the challenge. You'll have to be the judge if I have enough spark to light a fire."

Lauren kicked him under the table. "Oh, yeah! I hope you know a bit more than basic bushcraft."

Gideon winked at her. "Back in the army we didn't have GPS to get to where we wanted. I still don't. You'll have to wait and see if I can still show you enough of the heavens. Get into some comfortable clothes after we finish dinner. I will meet you outside your chalet. Bring a blanket."

A faint smile found the corners of her mouth.

"Come on," he said. "Finish your wine. The show is about to begin."

* * *

"I present to you, the Milky Way!"

There was no need for Gideon to point out the huge, powdery swathe cutting across the sky.

"What you see is a pittance of the universe's stellar dust, swirled into the dotted flatness of our galaxy's disk, and stretched into countless billions in its spiral outreach. Beyond this star-packed swathe, we are looking from here to eternity." Gideon let her take in the majesty. "It's our celestial city! Please excuse my flowery language. It always fills me with awe."

The rasping, wood-saw grunts of a leopard came from the tree line behind them. They had spoiled its hunt. On the softer, sweeter grass at the verge of the *dambo* there were no puku and impala. Instead, Lauren and Gideon lay side-by-side on blankets spread on a patch of cropped grass. Where they lay in the middle of the treeless expanse, they were afforded an unobstructed view of the night sky.

"If the heavens have been at the heart of so much old poetry," he said, "imagine how much richer it would be had those bards been inspired by southern skies. Too bad they thought that the world was flat. They had no idea that their northern view looked out at the bland galactic suburbs, instead of back at the neon of this awesome city center."

"It's so beautiful. You're right, it looks like the distant lights of a giant metropolis!" The whisper of Lauren's voice at his side barely rose above the crickets creaking in the stubble. Lying on their backs looking upwards, he had tucked a fold into the blankets to provide a small cushioning wedge where they could rest their heads. The insect chirps mingled with her subdued breathing as she soaked in the heavens.

Gideon swept the beam of his flashlight up into the darkness. "All this heavenliness splashed across the sky. It's where we live in the universe. We have billions of neighbours. Everything that you can see with the naked eye is part of our galaxy. "

Lauren spoke in wonder. "I've grown up in Africa, and I never paid much attention to the skies."

"It's splashed with such splendor that it is hard to imagine, and even harder to describe. A visual feast so sumptuous that it seems squandered on us mortals. All of it held together by a black hole so strong that it pulls billions of stars, some of them thousands of times larger than our sun, into a circle which would take a hundred thousand years to cross even if we could hitch a ride on a light beam. Our paltry slot is two thirds of the way out on a spiral reaching out into nothingness."

"All this beauty makes me imagine things."

"You are not the only one. The stars have always been the catalyst for ideas. I love the ancient Greek mythical reasoning the best. Some claimed the mist of those billions of stars to be from the breath of Zeus, his lustful pants flapped triumphantly across the skies by his swan wings as he ravishes Leda.

Others said it is from the squirts of milk from Hera's big boobs, as baby Hercules nips her nipples."

Lauren laughed. "Too bad we are so prudish we can't give explanations like the ancient Greeks."

Gideon pointed his flashlight to the east. "That region over there, where it is glowing brighter, is the center of our Milky Way. Our sun has only done a quarter revolution around it since the dinosaurs went extinct sixty million years ago."

They lay listening to the distant trill of a scops owl, and the five-part rise and fall of a rufous-cheeked nightjar. The stillness and the sounds of the night beneath the splendor of the stars seemed to be having its effect on them both. The magic of the moment covered them in a cloak of shared intimacy.

"This majesty," Gideon stated, "is a speck in the even bigger plethora of billions of other galaxies, spread across the universe so far away in time their light is only now reaching us."

A hyena cut in over the trilling of the crickets with its long mournful wail, providing a lonely backdrop to his otherwise freshly elevated mood.

They stared into the heavens until a shooting star cut its shimmering trail across the sky.

"The heavens have guided me well in the past. Maybe they will in the future." Gideon pointed downriver with his light, the beam picked up in the reflected flecks of flying insects. "Do you see those four stars?"

He waited until she murmured her acknowledgement.

"That's the Southern Cross. It is the crux of bush navigation, and has shown me the way many times."

The eerie sounding rise and fall of the hyena's yowl's wafting across the river modulated with Lauren's quiet ummms of appreciation.

David Maritz

Pointing to a faint red star he said. "That is Antares. It is a thousand times larger than the sun!"

"You are a good teacher," she whispered.

"Thanks," he said. "I go to a good school."

"Is that why we are lying here?" she asked.

He waited until a jackal ended its yammering.

"Yes," Gideon said, "but even here I'm sure I won't find all the answers to some of my questions."

"Such as?"

"Oh, big-picture stuff. Morality, loyalty, fidelity. What is learned out here, lying out under the stars and listening to nature, is different to what is taught sitting in a school desk, or in the front pew of a church."

"Do you care?" Lauren asked.

"Yes, sort of," he said. "There are different winners and losers depending on who does the teaching. But then that isn't new."

Gideon pointed the flashlight around to check that there were no unblinking red eyes behind them. Lions' eyes. The lonely howl of the hyena drifted across the river.

"There's my teacher talking," he laughed. "There is an element of truth in my words. After the war in Angola, with all the moral ethical yardsticks snapped and tossed aside, with the reasons told to us for fighting discredited, a lot of us were left adrift. Some grabbed at religion, others the bottle, others like me pulled in our heads and went to fight elsewhere. We still don't trust conventional morality. We've seen how it's manipulated. So maybe it isn't so bad to take a few ethical lessons from a hyena or a jackal. Their sense of right and wrong has served them well for millions of years."

Lauren laughed again, "Narina's father probably has your same teacher. So why are you fretting? As long as you know who eats who." Lauren turned on her side to face him. He could barely make out her features, as he cut the flashlight.

"Who cares about philosophy right now?" she said. "Follow your nature. Surely you should've learned what is good and bad by now."

33

December 7

Pan's sister couldn't have skipped her fingers over a flute as softly and sensuously as those which danced to and fro along the stretch of his excitement. Touching, teasing, tripping over scintillating streams, she splashed her melody over everything with waves of wonder.

On the blankets spread beneath the inky canopy of a star sprinkled sky, in long silence they gazed up at the heavens. As slumber is oft heralded by a gentle dream, it began with a whisper. Perhaps it started earlier, when the two fingers touched the back of his hand. Or maybe it began when he didn't move it away. He couldn't remember.

"So big boy," the whisper was so quiet it was barely audible, "what about your promise of those other stars?"

He was taken aback. Yes, he had picked up on her double entendre earlier, but everything about his suggestion had hinted at nothing more than flirtatious fun. Stars of the heavens, yes. Of the mind and body? No. Not yet.

"Not here, not now," he murmured.

Her fingers rose from the knuckles of his hand. Slowly, delicately, they walked up his forearm. In the darkness only a light touch indicated their movement. Spiderlike? It didn't matter, the progress was deliberate and steady. Up his arm, over his shoulder. From there inching down his chest, across the fabric of his shirt. He felt her roll onto her side to more easily extend each step by finger-step down over his belly and onto his thigh. Reaching his knee, they paused before slowly turning to retrace their path. They stretched cautiously up his thigh, then poised motionless before the loose opening of his short leggings.

"So, big boy. Are you as bad as you are big?"

"Probably not as bad as you," he whispered.

"No, probably not!" she echoed, "Sometimes I'm a bad girl, a delightfully bad girl."

Inflection points are those moments in life when, due to seemingly innocuous choices, one finds oneself ending in unexpected circumstances. If he had risen and left then and there, things may have been different. But he didn't. Somewhere far away, a voice echoed in his mind. Would she be his Madonna, or he her whore? And in that moment of indecision, those fingers slowly, stealthily crept into the deeper darkness, urged on by the hemlock of naughtiness to make the choice for him. Her lips was so close he could feel the warmth of her breath as she whispered her words, which together with her touch, burrowed under the fabric to fan the embers of their fire.

Taking his hand, she guided him gently. "Touch me there!" her soft hiss commanded as her teeth gently nibbled the lobe of his ear.

The tree of mindless bounty in the Garden of Eden, with its petals spread like the wings of a night moth, held the nub and nuzzle of it. At the same time, those fingers moved over its fruit with the dexterity of that flute playing nymph, tantalizing, caressing to the brink of mindless euphoria.

David Maritz

Like so many mice, his enchanted resolve followed in the footsteps of her piping.

"You are a dog," she hissed as he delved. "You think you can have everything on your terms."

"If I am a dog," he countered, "you are a bitch; a gorgeous bitch."

"Thank you!" she giggled softly, "I will take that as a compliment. But now it is time for the music to begin."

As soft as the night she murmured, "Let's see if the jackal in you can howl at the moon."

Then, lost to time, like confetti at an astral wedding, the Milky Way sprinkled stardust on their delight.

* * *

It was the dew soaking through the woollen weave of the blanket which woke him. Instead of fluffy comfort, it drooped its damp chill onto his bare limbs. But his refuge had not yet been disturbed. Gideon's reluctance to rouse was a tribute to the primitive comfort of the tufted grass on which their blankets were spread. It had kept them cradled for hours. The chill of the dew was cushioned in his sleepy awareness by the jumbled recollections of the night, mixed with the gentle reassurance of her breathing beside him. These were augmented by the sounds from the grass, the trees, and river beyond. Blinking up at the dawn sky revealed how the stardust was slowly being swept west by the morning maiden's broom. Gradually after completing her sweeping, she polished the darkness with successive patinas, initially a deep orange blush on the eastern cheeks of the sky, then slowly she rubbed through the rainbow on the way to daybreak's blue. Somewhere along that progression, his attention was drawn to measured footsteps. Too regular to be those of a grazing hippo, it didn't take long to confirm the source. Tucking his head backwards to flip his view of the world upside down, out of the predawn glimmer, Gideon saw the figure of Precious approaching.

A flash of shyness tugged at his emotions. He had been caught consorting with a guest. He immediately pushed that feeling aside as his pragmatic instincts reasserted themselves.

Precious walked up to where they lay. Squatting down in the way of Africa, with outstretched arms loosely clasped and her elbows resting on her knees, with her quiet voice matching the morning, she greeted him.

"*Mwabuka byepi!*

"Gidi, before you leave, I need to talk to you urgently."

Rolling onto his side, he propped himself up on an elbow as Lauren roused. Blinking to open her eyes, she answered Precious's "Good Morning."

"What is it about?" he asked Precious.

"The word from the village is that one of the scouts on patrol with Moses has been identified as a witch."

Gideon stared at her. "They will kill him if he goes home."

* * *

A flask of filtered coffee stood on the table, which was covered by a cloth decorated with a colorful ethnic motif. The rest of the morning fare was on its way, lemon cream biscuits, or maybe diminutive pancakes next to a jar of honey. A box of Cornflakes stood beside a basket bearing toast. The slices were wrapped in a serviette to keep them warm. Complementing

David Maritz

them was a jar of jam, and of course the milk, sugar, tea or instant coffee, and orange juice, to complete the offering.

The air was so still as he looked across at the firepit that Gideon could hear the chatter of the waitresses in the distant kitchen, busy laying out serving trays. When the platters were set on the bright, zigzag colors of the table-cloth, it was too bad that it would be superfluous effort. He suspected the current lady guests had long ago forgotten any involvement with breakfast preparations. Without their male consorts to shake them awake, their only response to the sounds of dawn would be to wrap themselves tighter in the comfort of their sheets, until the coffee was cold. Even Lauren had returned to her chalet.

Precious waited at the firepit as he went back to his tent to shave and wash his face. He donned a light sweater to ward off the faint chill left behind by the damp blanket.

Returning afterwards, seeing Precious standing next to the fire waiting for him, he felt no guilt helping himself to the bounty on the table, especially as it was Mustafa and ilk who were footing the bill.

"Can I make you a cup of coffee?" she asked.

"Yes, thank you."

Her mug was already half drained. She topped it up while preparing his. He stood behind her tall, assertive outline, and listened to her directives to Nora and the other waitresses as they laid out the trays. He watched how effortlessly she assumed unopposed authority. Mushala's daughter! She would handle the service, she told the others. If any of the guests showed up, she would ask for their help. Now with only Gideon around, there was no need for their presence, she said to the two waitresses.

It was obvious she didn't want them in earshot.

Gideon and Precious were alone again.

"So?"

Cradling her mug, she moved to sit on one of the wooden chairs beside him. Why was it that when talk of witchcraft was in the offing, her hair seemed to be arranged symbolically. Her braided coils wrapped loosely around her head like a charcoal crown, the tassel ends licking her ear like the flickering tongue of a serpent. She looked up at him as she blew a breath to disperse the steam rising from her cup. "There is bad witchcraft in the village."

"What do you mean by bad witchcraft?"

"It is much feared. It is rare. But when it appears, it involves powerful *muti*. It scares the people badly. They call it *'mumone'*."

If she had deigned to catch him this early in the morning, he needed to take her seriously.

"Okay, what is it? And why is it so feared?"

"*Mumone* happens when men carrying a coffin at a funeral are possessed by spirits. They slowly jog towards a particular hut. When they get there they stop at the door. Asked afterwards, they don't know anything about it. It is this pointing of the coffin that is feared. It tells the people who is the one to blame for the death. Someone living in that hut has been possessed by a devil."

Gideon looked up to see one of the other girls approaching. Precious waved her away without a word.

"Recently a young village woman died under strange circumstances. Her funeral was yesterday. The men carrying the coffin were possessed by spirits. They stopped at the door of Musekela. He is the leader of the scouts

David Maritz

you deployed to the Lunga area. Such a *mumone* has not happened in our village for many years. But, back then, like now, the person identified as a devil was not home at the time. The villagers knew he would be back. So they waited."

Precious took a sip of her coffee. "As he walked off the pontoon, they stoned him. That is what will happen to Musekela if he goes home."

"Precious, how are you sure about this?"

"I'm sure because, although it has not happened at our village for many years, it happened recently in a village further north from here. In that case it was also someone who worked in this area. People are getting scared. They are beginning to say that there is powerful *muti* being used in this area. They will be too afraid to work here!" She rose and placed her cup on the table. "If that feeling becomes widespread, this whole place will shut down. We will all lose."

34

December 7

"We won't be going to Mumbwa. An urgent issue has come up which I need to take care of."

Lauren stared at him in petulant dismay. "Are you kidding me?"

"No, Precious brought me the news."

Gideon gave Lauren a brief outline.

"So what are you going to do?"

"I need to speak to Moses," he said. "He understands how to deal with these issues better than me. Firstly we need to make sure that Musekela doesn't return to the village until we've figure out some options."

"Like what?" she asked.

"Maybe we can get Muskela, and then his family to move to another area. I am not sure if the evil spirit that they will say has possessed him is location-specific. Moses will understand this stuff."

Gideon scratched distractedly at the welts from the tsetse fly bites on his legs. "If you are going to go and look for the patrol and Moses," Lauren implored, "can I tag along? I can't stand waiting here with nothing to do except listen to Narina speak Spanish to the other two. I don't even have her father around to focus my annoyance on! He and his ugly partners are out doing who knows what."

Gideon took off a sandal. A thorn had penetrated its rubber sole, deep enough to be felt by the heel of his foot. "That isn't a good idea. If the scouts have already started to sweep downriver I may need to follow them for a long way. It may take two days to track and catch up, with another day to get back to the vehicle."

"Well," Lauren replied, "even if they are heading down to the river's confluence, which is closer to here than there, surely it will be quicker for you to come back here instead of walking back to get your vehicle?"

He used his belt-knife to dig at the broken end of the thorn. "Yes, but so what! It just adds complexity. You will be one more thing I have to worry about."

"I would still like to tag along to see the new lodge site," she said. "If they are already headed south to the confluence, and you have to track them, why don't you let me drive your vehicle back here? It will be closer and faster, instead of wasting time retrieving it."

Gideon started to dismiss her suggestion, then checked himself. He looked at her carefully. Her persistence was annoying. But she made sense. "I thought you were a city-comfort craver. Do you think that you have enough tomboy in you to stand roughing it?"

He was purposefully trying to annoy her. He wanted her to react. He wanted an excuse to turn her away.

"I take your monikers as compliments!" she coolly held his stare. "You have not seen anything yet! I left my ex because he couldn't keep up. I hope you aren't like him."

"Okay, we'll see. You can drive from here to Kikuji. If there is enough boy in your tom, you can drive the vehicle back. If not, you will need to stay until I return, with the tsetse flies biting you, *n'shima* to eat and river water to drink. The real bush deal."

"That sounds perfect!" she eyed him coldly.

Sheesh, he thought, I'd better watch out. This woman would be hard to scare away! The fight in her bitch may be bigger than that in my dog.

It didn't take long for her to allay his concerns about bush-road driving. It was how she handled the long gear lever, palming it to and fro with the open flat of her hand, like an old-time long-distance trucker, and the smooth easy slip of the clutch, with confident, timely snatches of a gear shift when the wheels needed more power in the sand.

"My uncle owned a fleet of ex-army trucks." Lauren spoke breezily; she had got her way. "Do you remember those big green squat-nosed trucks, with a hatch in the cab roof? I was thirteen when my legs were long enough to reach the pedals. You had to pump twice and double de-clutch to change down without grinding the gears." She was in her element. Her self-assurance palpable. "I learned to drive on those big old Bedfords. Not many kids can say that today, not even tomboys." Lauren glanced across at him as she accelerated up to the sweet spot, where the syncopation minimized the shudder of the wheels over the ruts. She was enjoying scratching at his scepticism.

As they drove, his appreciation of her ability deepened.

Halfway between the Kafue and Lunga pontoons, the main road made a gentle sidestep where it angled across a rocky dyke delineating the Kafue

Basin on its eastern flank and the Lunga on the west. It was as they headed through this feature that he again broached his nagging quandary. "Last night, there was a reason I brought up the subject of ethics and morality."

"Oh really?" she said, "I thought it was to justify your ethical outlook on life and admiration of a monkey's morals."

"Hey," Gideon complained, "that's unfair."

"Don't get me wrong," she said, "I admire that you've even thought about these things. Most men never consider the ethics of anything, let alone act on those thoughts. That you have situations where you need to confront them shows that you are either an interesting guy, or have an interesting life, or both. I like that."

Gideon looked at her, smiling smugly. "Or I have interesting friends."

"True!" she agreed. "But what was the other reason?"

"Selfishness," he said. "Can selfishness be justified if it has a greater good?"

Lauren glanced at him curiously. "But you weren't being selfish last night. Unless you feel you were having more fun than I was, which wasn't true." She glanced at him again. "Or you were feeling guilty about breaking some implied promises to some other lady friends."

"There is some of that," Gideon said.

"Well, you have no reason to feel guilty on my part. I'm not stupid. I know exactly when I'm taking a risk. Which is how the best things are found in life."

"Actually" Gideon interjected. "Mostly it is an issue with our friends."

"What do you mean?"

Gideon looked out the window watching sightlessly at the big bushland trees resplendent in fresh green spring leaves roll past. "Moses and Narina are half brother and sister."

Lauren kept driving without reacting. "What? Are you joking?" she asked.

"No. I'm not." Gideon said quietly. "Moses's mother was raped by someone with a big scar on his chest. Mustafa has that sort of scar, with the shape of an upside down map of Africa."

"Aren't you jumping to conclusions?"

"Maybe," he said, "but it's more likely I'm right. Look at Moses. He has that refined Somali in his features. He's not a typical Tonga or Lozi. Also, what is the likelihood of a scar like that on another person's chest?"

"Yeah," she said, "but stranger coincidences have happened."

"But that's where my question on selfishness comes in. My selfishness," he answered. "I personally don't care what happens between them, or if they should be made aware of being half siblings. If anything, African life has taught me to be pragmatic about issues, including right and wrong." He grinned. "You see, there is a benefit to having a hyena as a teacher."

Lauren slowed down and moved her hand on the stick shift, easing into a lower ratio as she coaxed the Cruiser through a washout in the road. "Are you worried about Narina getting pregnant?"

"No. I couldn't care much about the biological issues. A chihuahua was once a wolf, a cow was once an auroch. It didn't take our ancestors long to figure out that an auroch with big udders if put to her sons, and grandsons, would produce daughters who also had big milky udders. I feel no more qualms about this than I do about a breeder producing champion dogs with wobbly back legs. I couldn't care if Narina and Moses had a kid with recessive squinty eyes."

"For God's sakes!" Lauren exclaimed. "With that attitude, what can possibly bother you?"

"Firstly," Gideon said, "my concern stems not from my godlessness, but Moses's faith. He would never forgive himself if he found out the truth, and even worse, that I hid it from him. If he knows, he will leave, to avoid sinning. For various reasons, Moses has an Old Testament take on religion. It takes him quite a distance. If Abraham and others can have at least two wives, such as biblical David with eight, including knocking up a married woman and sending her hubby off to be killed, then it is okay for Moses to do some of the same. But the Sodom and Gomorrah incest thing is a no-no. Secondly; this is where my selfishness comes in. I need his help in bushcraft, and his cultural insight on how to handle difficult situations like this one. Saving the bush and its wildlife is all that I have left. I need his help for a bit longer."

Lauren let him talk on.

"I wasted my youth fighting doomed wars. Those like me are screwed. The bastards down south have even taken away our pensions. We face closed doors all over the place. I am too old and too white."

"You sound bitter."

"I am."

"Why don't you just let it all go?"

"And do what?" he said. "If I was younger I would. Now I don't have time on my side."

She shrugged again, unconvinced.

"Lately it seems I have a German banker glaring at me, threatening to toss me out of the only home I have."

Lauren pulled a face. "You are being awfully bleak."

"No," he replied as he slapped at a tsetse. "I am being realistic. There is a risk of Musekela getting killed. If so I will get tainted by association. Not only that, yesterday I got a text from my boss that he wants to speak to me. Someone has put in a complaint."

"What about?"

"I have no idea. But one thing can be certain. If I let things pile up too high, I will lose. At my age, all that will be left is to get a job as a parking attendant in some slummy grocery outlet in some crappy city down south."

"Oh, stop being so negative."

Gideon laughed. "Jesus! Do you think I'm joking? The truth is even worse. No woman wants to lie in the grass with a parking lot attendant. Not even you."

"Oh, stop taking it too far," Lauren sighed. "You never know."

"Whatever," he said. "I guess I have answered my dilemma. I can't let Moses go just yet."

* * *

He shouldered the backpack. He would be traveling light: a waterproof ground sheet, which could be formed into a tent in the event of rain (thankfully the forecast was for dry weather), and a blanket to ward off the dawn chill. Only two liters of water – he should not be far from the river to replenish. Some biltong to chew on, and four cans of ultra-sweetened viscous condensed milk and peanuts for energy. He slid the sheath of his machete onto his belt, nodded a goodbye to Lauren, and watched her drive away.

The scout's tracks were easy to follow. They were blatant about it. It was excellent anti-poaching deterrence. Poachers, or anyone with nefarious intentions, tend to avoid areas where the footprints of authority are evident. Gideon didn't stay with their tracks for long. It was apparent that the scouts' intention was to patrol down in a line, moving abreast out from the river's edge. He didn't plan on staying close to the river. There the thick riverine vegetation made it too difficult even for the animals to get to the water. Over the millennia, well-trodden pathways cut through these tangles down to the drinking spots, forming ideal places to set snares. The scouts obviously had some members checking these game access routes for traps, while the more inland members were looking for the tracks of those who had done the setting.

For the first few kilometers south of the new lodge site, the river made two big westward-bending sweeps, like the ears of a rabbit. Instead of diligently following the patrol, Gideon decided he would take a shortcut across the hare's neck, thereby getting a jumpstart of over half the distance to catch up, assuming they had proceeded that far.

Further inland, walking through the bush was relatively easy. Here the porosity of the sandy aeolian soils enabled the rains to leach the nutrients. The trees weren't as spectacularly tall as in other parts of the river basin. In addition to spreading the trees and bushes, the soil's paucity added an edge of sparseness to the grass cover beneath the relaxed leafy canopy. Every now and then, like gentle waves rolling onto a shallow beach, the trees slowly broke their uniformity to subside into a froth of successively shorter shrubs, which finally found themselves with spent energy at the edges of the open dambos, their drowned roots wallowing in water trapped by impervious clay. There, it was easier to spot tracks. He was confident that with his shortcut gambles wouldn't take long, or it wouldn't be too difficult to catch up.

It was heartening to note that already the indirect early efforts of their conservation, even if only yet in the form of lodge construction, were having an effect. The animals were returning. On the edges of the *dambos*, a few small groups of puku antelope dashed away at his appearance. In the bushy in-between stretches, a scattering of impala did the same. It wasn't only the small antelope who were coming back; a big kudu bull laid its long corkscrew horns along its back as it dashed away through the thickets. Even more heartwarming was a small herd of sable antelope. It would take a while before all their skittishness was assuaged. But that would probably only occur once regular vehicle traffic was doing the rounds, with the purr of diesel engines and the reassuring clicks of cameras replacing the poachers' gunshots.

Walking fast brought out the sweat on his back. The air had warmed quickly, carrying enough moisture to make it muggy. But there was a mindless pleasure to the walking. There was a oneness with the natural world. Communication with oneself no longer needed the medium of speech. Instead, the subtle reversion to an ancient state was infinitely more calming and reassuring. Sounds, smells, sensations welled up in the mind as images, where they flickered or surged, then faded as if in a muted game of destiny. There was the exhilaration of being, like an animal at the edge of fight, or flight.

Finally, an hour before sunset, Gideon picked up the fresh tracks of the patrol. A section of woodland opened into a clear vista stretching parallel to the river, where its floodwaters overspilt its banks and filled the flatlands along its sides. In the distance, he could see two members of the patrol about to head into the next wooded section. He increased his pace. Halfway across, he startled a pair of wattle cranes. With guttural croaks of protest, they opened their huge wings and ran a few paces to gain momentum. They gracefully slid up into the air and stroked in a half circle to settle down to his rear. A member of the patrol had entered the riverside shrubbery as Gideon drew near – close enough to call out to them. They all swivelled to stare at him in surprise. The scout who had disappeared into the thickets walked back out and joined the others in returning his wave.

"*Mwane!*" Gideon greeted Musekela directly. "How goes it?"

Musekela pointed to a scout standing behind the group with a sash of wires drooped over his shoulder. "We have saved a lot of animals," he said. "Many of these snares were freshly set."

"Great work!" Gideon gave praise. Then added, "Where is Moses?"

"He is following a track."

Gideon was surprised. "Alone? Isn't that dangerous to let one man track one of these poachers? There will be others and he will have trouble."

"Yes, I know." Musekela answered testily. "But this track was not like the others. It came in from the side, alone, and then left alone." He pointed off to the edge of the riverbank. "We are still following the main tracks of those that set the snares. They are somewhere ahead. If you go over there, you will see the tracks. Four of them."

Musekela gestured again to emphasize his point. "Moses insisted that he followed this one alone. He said he knew who it was. That he could handle the tracking. That it would be better if he were alone."

Unease settled over Gideon. A feeling from long ago, yet remembered – the foreboding when one senses the killing ground of an ambush. Gideon had learned the hard way not to ignore those feelings. But now, not knowing where Moses was, how could he react? Would he have time to push a stick into the spokes of whatever witchcraft was waiting for Musekela if he went home?

Gideon realized that at this stage it was pointless trying to follow. Things were unfolding too fast. He needed to focus on keeping Musekela from going back to his village.

"Since it is almost dark, we are going to stop here," Musekela said.

"Okay," Gideon said. "When you finish this patrol. I want you to wait at your base for me. I have something very important to discuss with you."

Musekela nodded.

"I will see if I can follow Moses."

Gideon had no intention of doing that. His best choice was to get back to the lodge and wait for Moses to show up. Hopefully before Musekela finished the patrol and tired of waiting to meet about 'something important'.

35

December 8

Leaving the still sleeping scouts swaddled in their blankets, Gideon strode towards the pot providing the ink gradually conveying golden definition to the high upper branches. He picked the easier, more open spaces between the thickets. There was no need to slow down to search for tracks or signs. He was not following the loops of the river; instead he followed an oblique compass bearing, which would halve the distance back to the lodge.

Walking fast, the quartering breeze quickly dried the sweat off his cheeks, but not the dampness between his shirt and backpack. Nevertheless it was invigorating. The msasa trees were out in emerald effrontery, their leaves fluttering everywhere like miniature flags in a gigantic bush parade. The rain had refreshed everything into abundance. Even the yellow grass had been tinged green. Thankfully in many places the grass had not yet grown much since it was burnt down, making walking easy. Lauren had been right. It had been quicker to let her drive his vehicle back, and for him to cut through the bush on foot, rather than walk back to the Kikuji construction site and drive the long loop back.

By early afternoon Gideon was standing outside the kitchen, drinking a cool, thirst-quenching glass of orange juice handed to him by Precious.

Stopping only to take out his water bottle and to eat a handful of peanuts, it had taken nine hours to walk the remaining thirty kilometers of the diagonal between the Lunga and Kafue rivers back to the lodge.

From across the straw fence, he could hear the sound of heated conversation from the *chitenge*. A higher-pitched male voice, Mustafa's probably, interjected and interspersed itself between deeper-sounding Latin accents. It wasn't loud enough to follow, but the undertone of disagreement was clear in the way their remonstrations cut in and clambered over each other.

Gideon's silent gesture of 'What's going on?' was answered by Precious saying, "They've been arguing for over two hours. They chase us away anytime we go over there, even Bright".

Taking his glass, Precious asked if he wanted more. "Madame Lauren said to tell you that she is at her chalet, and for you to stop by."

Gideon barely managed to thank her before she twirled back into the kitchen. Genuinely twirled, executing happy little circles between the hops and skips that edged her closer to the door, where she skipped up the steps and disappeared inside.

Weird, was the only word that came to mind.

Gulping down the last mouthfuls of his second glass of juice, he followed her in and set the glass down in the sink. She was humming a tune to herself. They were alone. She moved about happily.

"What has got into you?" he asked.

"I am happy."

"Why?"

"Because I got the present I have been waiting for."

He looked at her carefully. "What is it?"

"I'll tell you later."

"Why can't you tell me now?"

"I don't want to jinx it, and there are still a few details to work out. Some of which you can hear them arguing about over there."

"Hmmm," he hummed. "Since Christmas has come early, what about me? Do you have a spare sock for me?"

"What do you want put in it?"

"I am sure you can guess," he winked.

She looked at him intently for a second. "Okay, since I got mine early, I will give you yours."

Taking his stubble-scratchy cheeks in both her hands, then raising on her toes to reach him, he felt the wide full sensuousness of her lips. There was a momentary hesitation of their slight parting before the tip of her tongue press between his own startled pair. He couldn't help himself, his arms encircled and pulled her against him. It felt so good. Then as he came out of his shock of surprise she wriggled free and scampered away with a giggle.

"That is enough," she said. "Remember you are too old for me." From the doorway she turned and said impishly, "but Lauren isn't." And added, "And she is waiting for you."

He was still off-balance. It must have been wishful thinking that detected a hint of jealousy in her voice. He walked the long way around to Lauren's chalet, giving time to get his composure back and better to avoid the growling dogs in the *chitenge*.

Lauren was lounging in a chair on the chalet's deck. As usual her long legs were extended, hooked one over the other, resting on the coffee table. With her arms stretched out like her legs, elbows drooped on the armrests, the rim of a tall glass dangled between her thumb and middle finger.

"Well, well, look what the cat dragged back!" she exclaimed. "How was your adventure?"

"Not so good," he replied. "I found the scouts. But not Moses. He has gone off on his own."

"What's bad about that?"

"It's never good to be alone in the bush when hunting men and you can be outnumbered. There was a group of them, and one track left, and Moses followed it. But I've seen him go out on his own and come back safely so many times I can only trust it will be the same now."

Gideon rubbed the stubble on his chin. "So I haven't yet spoken to him about how to deal with the Musekela witch thing. I left Musekela and his guys heading downriver. Now I am counting on Moses getting back here before the scouts finish searching and return to their base."

"Is the patrol going to check with you when they get done?" she asked.

"Yes, I told Musekela that he absolutely has to give me a report in person before he heads back home. It will buy me time."

It wasn't just Precious; Gideon also detected a change in Lauren's demeanor. She was smiling more readily, and generally exuded a happier, more relaxed attitude.

"Can someone give me one of those happy pills that everyone around here seems to be sucking?" he asked. "What's made you so bright and bushy-tailed all of a sudden?"

David Maritz

"There are changes around here," she stated. "It seems that everybody is heading out of here in the next day or two. I'm not quite sure what the details are. The two Latin men will be chartering an aircraft to pick them up at the hippo camp airfield, down river. But they don't want their fancy ladies along with them. They have told Mustafa that he needs to transport them back to Lusaka, together with all the baggage. Wherever it is they are going, it will be a quick trip, and the men will be travelling light." Lauren took a sip from her glass. "It is more important that the Latin pair have their driver and vehicle waiting for them in Solwezi when they return, than running a shuttle into Lusaka. Of course Mustafa isn't exactly overjoyed with this. It seems the Latin partners don't regard him on an equal footing. He is resentful of their attitude. They are treating him like a servant, he says." Lauren smiled widely. "It is lovely to see him having to swallow some of his own medicine." She gave a happy laugh. "What makes it even more of a bun-fight is that the Latin ladies aren't happy either. They resent being sent back alone. But they have even less of a leg to stand on. Apart from Mustafa feeling like a taxi driver, their two lovely ladies have a lot of luggage. To add insult to injury, the men want that, and all their own junk taken back and sent on the commercial flight to wherever with the women. They are still arguing about this. Mustafa also doesn't see himself as a baggage handler." Lauren reached down and scratched her calf. "The bloody mosquitoes got me good last night. Anyway," she went on, "I have left them to poke each other's eyes out. Actually I think I contributed to their bad moods to some degree. For a while I also let Mustafa know that I wasn't happy with being squeezed between loads of luggage. The Latins couldn't understand why he wasn't able to shut me up." She giggled. "They are not fans of democracy." She leaned back lazily. "Giving them all an earful has done me the world of good."

"Too bad I didn't see that fight," he said quietly.

"Actually I've enjoyed myself while you were away." She took out a cigarette from a pack on the table, lit it, and inhaled deeply as if to underline her newfound pleasure. Looking pointedly at him she said, "I tried out a bit of your jackal tactics and nipped at their heels. None of us want me squeezing between the luggage, the beauties and Mustafa's scintillating personality." She made no effort to hide her sarcasm. "So if you're going into Mumbwa soon, I would prefer to squeeze in with you. You can give me another lesson in your animal ethics." She laughed happily.

"Christ!" Gideon felt a twinge of guilt. "How do I get sucked into these situations? But okay, that's fine," he said. "I still plan on going to Mumbwa to ask for an extra patrol up the Lunga, and to speak to Ernest about Musekela."

"Great," Lauren beamed at him. "By the way, there is another major development that you probably haven't heard of."

"What's that?" he queried, noting her raised eyebrows and the roll of her eyes.

"As you probably know, Precious has a fascination with fashion."

"Yes," he replied, "I've seen her designs. Damn good stuff. She told me how she wants to get out of the bush, and that this place was going to be the catalyst for making it happen."

"Well," said Lauren, "she may have been granted her wish."

"What?" he exclaimed. "What are you talking about?"

Lauren took a long swig of her gin and tonic, and switched the glass so it dangled between the fingers of her other hand. "One of the Latin men has also noticed her talent. He said for her to come along on their air charter."

"Really! You must be kidding," he exclaimed disbelievingly.

"The guy told her that he will be meeting a contact up in the Congo who produces clothing for Europe. If this guy likes what he sees, maybe she can do some designs for him, claimed our Latin hero."

Gideon slapped his thigh. "That explains her weird behavior when I got back."

Lauren laughed. "Plan B is to have Mustafa come back and fetch her and put her on a commercial flight from Lusaka." She laughed again. "That really put pepper up Mustafa's nose. In the meantime they are awaiting the confirmation of the type of charter aircraft that will pick them up. If it is big enough, she will be going along."

"That is incredible!" he stated. "Almost too good to be true."

Lauren grimaced her face. "With Mustafa mixed in, it probably is. But there's no telling that to Precious, she is beside herself with excitement. Even Bright has been swept along in the jubilation. He is sending her with a driver up to the village to fetch her passport. As far as I know, the three of them are booked into Hippo Lodge tomorrow night. That is where the charter will pick them up."

* * *

Precious appeared unannounced at the edge of his campfire's umbra. She was wearing her uniform in the same rakish fashion as he remembered, what now seemed like ages ago when he first heard her ululation. The long coil of her hair was woven and drooped down her back in the same style.

"Gidi, I have good news." She pulled up a camp chair and sat opposite him, leaning forward with pent-up excitement. "I'm going with Luigi and Jose to Lubumbashi in the Congo."

There was no point telling her he'd heard this already. Why spoil her excitement?

"So what is it, Precious? It must be something big, if it makes you dance when you give me orange juice."

Precious laughed, "I'm so happy I can hardly believe it. Luigi has a contact in the Congo who has a factory making clothing for a big chain in Brussels. He will make an introduction for me with this man. Luigi says this man is always looking for new designs. I may even go to Brussels if all goes well."

Gideon said. "It is good to know that you are on a first-name footing with those two."

She didn't catch his sarcasm.

"What do you know about Jose and Luigi? Do you trust them? Have you asked Luigi for the name of the company? Maybe we can check it out on the internet later tonight, when we have enough bandwidth."

Precious regarded him indignantly. "Jose and Luigi are Mustafa's business partners. If he trusts them I think I can do the same."

Gideon held his tongue. Better to say nothing about what Lauren thought of Mustafa, or that with the angry arguments earlier, they didn't appear to be such great partners.

"No, I haven't had time for that. Bright has been very good. I thought he would be upset. But he even offered to send his vehicle with me to fetch my passport. I'm so glad that I applied for it two years ago."

Who am I to put a damper on her enthusiasm? he thought. "So when are you leaving?"

"As soon as I get back tomorrow afternoon. We will move across to Hippo Lodge and spend the night there. Bright made the booking for us."

"And when are you coming back?"

"I'm not sure," Precious said. "I think it won't be more than a week. Luigi said that they only needed a few days in the Congo to wrap up what they are doing. But it may also be longer if I go on to Europe."

To distract his unease, he said, "Well Precious, let's celebrate your luck with a great cup of coffee."

"Okay," she laughed, adding, "maybe I will also meet Father Christmas up there, and I will bring you back another present."

"You coming back safely will be my gift," he said quietly.

36

December 9

It was after sunset that Gideon's wispy anxiety was brushed aside by footsteps heralding Moses's appearance out of the darkness. He didn't bother greeting him. "What in the world have you been doing?"

"I was doing what you asked me to do—getting the answers to your questions."

Relief mixed with annoyed impatience nudged aside Gideon's vexation. "Okay, I will make the coffee, and you can tell me all about it."

Drawing up a camp chair across from the fire's embers, he sat down. "It is complicated," Moses said. "Guess who explained a lot of it to me?"

"I have no idea. All I know is that Musekela said you had gone off on your own, tracking somebody?"

"Yes. It is as well I did, because it was he who explained much of it to me."

"Who was that?" Gideon asked.

"Your old friend, the crocodile man," Moses said nonchalantly.

"You are joking!" Gideon was astounded.

"Yes Gidi, I was in the right place at the right time. As they say, luck comes to those who look for it."

"So how did you get lucky this time?" Gideon queried.

Moses went on. "While patrolling down the Lunga with Musekela, I recognized the tracks of our old man. He had followed behind the poachers. He was just following them. Then at some stage he broke off and headed away on his own. As I tracked, I realized that he was heading to the quarry where he usually met the rest of the bunch. But this time it seemed to be a night meeting because it was already late in the day."

Gideon handed Moses a cup of coffee.

"Like novices, they met at the same place each time, which meant if I knew there was a meeting I could get into a good place to overhear what they were saying, before they arrived. Since it would be dark, getting in close would be easier. I moved fast, circling past the old man. I hid behind a patch of scrub. Getting close was worth it, otherwise we would still be following footprints, looking for nothing more than gangs of village poachers. Sure enough they all showed up. And I could hear much of what they were saying."

"What was that? Gideon asked.

"Well, to begin with I thought it was the Russians who were behind everything, and then I thought it was the Somali, but actually it is the Spanish speakers. They don't mind dabbling in ivory, but it is bigger things they are after. They are part of a drug cartel."

"What! You've got to be kidding!"

"No Gidi. We were both on the wrong track, looking for petty poachers. These people are extremely smooth. They are making it look like it is poachers behind their mischief. But it is much bigger than poaching."

"Have you met these Latins yet?" Moses asked.

"No," Gideon said, "I have seen them, but not spoken to them. They have not been around much. They are always out with Mustafa. I had dinner with the women who are with them. But they only speak Spanish. So I didn't speak to them."

Moses rubbed his hands together. "As you can see, these men are an ugly pair. But they have money, plenty of it. We can now understand who paid for the Russians at Alan's camp. But I am getting ahead." Moses paused to take off a shoe and shake some sand out. 'They talked about mining rights and getting people to sign them over. The Latin pair were upset about the slow pace of things. They wanted the old man to do things that he objected to vehemently. He was shouting about them messing with Mushala's ghost, a sort of sacrilege in his eyes. Tempers rose and eventually the old man angrily said he was quitting. Guns were drawn, and to their credit the Russian pair lunged across and stopped the Latins from shooting the old guy. By the time emotions had calmed down, the croc man had disappeared. I figured it was the perfect opportunity to introduce myself to the old guy. I knew where his bicycle would be hidden. I crawled away while the others were still arguing, then ran back to get there before him. He didn't seem surprised to see me. He had been expecting to meet the son of the white witch, he said. Whatever that means." Moses rose to fetch himself a biscuit, dunking it in his coffee before coming back and sitting down.

Gideon remembered Father Xavier's words: "The *nganga's* will know who he is."

Wiping his mouth with the back of his hand, Moses went on. "The old man, the Russians and Mustafa go back decades. As far back as the independence insurgency down south. The old man was a liaison official for the insurgents. He worked with Vladimir, who was a Soviet supply officer delivering the Russian weapons. Mustafa's family ran a trucking operation, moving their supplies around the region. That is how they first got to meet and know each other. Kings was a local poacher selling meat to all of them. Ever since, Mustafa uses the Russians as enforcers. He calls them in whenever he needs some clout to get things done. The Russians learned that witchcraft is often more effective in Africa than the sort of barroom brawl that they excelled in back in Russia. So they use the old man, with his potent affiliation with a mysterious cult adding power to whatever spells he casts. However if some muscle is needed, Kings is called in. The Latins are the Johnny-come-latelys to this dance with the devil. It seems that Narina's ex-husband was part of their organization. Hence the contact with Mustafa."

There was a warm air of contentment in the way Moses spoke. Gideon remembered that old pleasure in the wake of a job well done, together with the anticipation of free time to unwind. He wished he had the same feelings.

Moses continued explaining. "According to the old man, the scar-faced one is a cartel captain. The other short one is a business development guy. If we connect this with what Alan told us about Pablo Escobar, I bet scar-face was a young 'soldier' when Escobar came out to Africa. He probably remembered that in Africa they could do as they pleased. They knew how simple it is to get anything you want over here with their carrot in the form of plenty of bribe money, and a stick and willingness to knock people's heads off."

Gideon interrupted. "But why would they want to sell drugs here in the middle of nowhere? It doesn't make sense."

"No Gidi, it is about taking over mining concessions. They want a laundering operation. Dirty money will come in to set up a copper mine. They will pay fake or corrupt contractors huge amounts to run a money-losing operation. They don't care, as long as the overhead comes out clean. The

Lunga-Luswishi is ideal for them. It is out of the way, in the back route between Angola and the lawlessness of the Congo. The problem is that even though it is a poor grade concession, it is held by locals, who don't see any reason to give up their mining rights. And that is the source of our strange stuff. The Latins want to scare people into giving up their rights."

Gideon whistled.

"But they don't realize that African witchcraft, like other forms of religion, has purists who will not compromise their beliefs for money."

Gideon shook his head. "Jesus."

Moses nodded. "One of these is our old crocodile man. He is familiar with this area, and it is his insurgent roots across the Zambezi that brought the Mlimo in to stir and enhance the local superstitions. The intention was to use him to scare the concession holders so profoundly that they would sell their rights to the cartel front people." Moses stretched back in his chair and cupped the back of his head in his linked palms. "The old man went along with this as long as it was within the bounds of his own beliefs. I thought I may need to force him to talk. But that wasn't necessary. He talked freely once he settled down. Knowing Kings, you can now understand why he would want to go along with all of this. He is still not much more than a low-level poacher. He wants everyone out the way so that he can get back to his good-bad old days." Moses sat and thought about what he had related so far. "There was also something to do with Kings and Precious that was pissing the *nganga* off." Moses said. "Something about Kings buying her! But the big arguments in the quarry were about the Latins wanting more pressure. Things were not going fast enough for their liking. They wanted an example made of people if they didn't agree. Murder was on the table, disguised as witchcraft. Apparently this was too much for our crocodile man. You do not mess with the spirit of Mushala. I am not sure what he meant by that."

"Wow!" Gideon exclaimed.

David Maritz

"But that isn't all," Moses continued. "The Russians had a sideline recruiting 'mules' for the cartel. Young women who they would get to travel to various places on the pretense of getting them a good opportunity. The women were provided with doctored luggage containing drugs. They were expendable to check for easier smuggling routes to the various destinations." Moses leaned back and crossed his arms over his chest as he relaxed. He had done his duty, had unloaded his burden of responsibility. The sergeant was finished with his part. It was now up to his old officer to do his. "I am tired, I will sleep well tonight." A glow of pleasure spread over his face. "Before I turn in, I'm going to head over to check on Narina."

Unthinkingly Gideon blurted out, "Why can't you leave her alone?" His words came out too quickly and too harshly.

Moses looked at him sharply. "What has got into you? What has turned you sour?"

"I'm sorry," Gideon said. "I'm just trying to help."

"No you are not. You are jealous that you have nobody special in your life anymore, and have become a bitter, dried-up prune."

"Moses," Gideon tried to back out. "What I want to say is stand back a bit and see how things develop before jumping in head over heels. I am not saying call it all off. Just saying to take it slowly."

"What the hell is the matter with you?" Moses asked angrily. "Where is the risk-taker that I once knew? You were the one who always plunged into everything without a glance to the sides or rear to see what you were leaving behind. I came out here to help you, and all you can do when you see things going well for me is put a stick in the spokes of my happinesss."

He kept glaring at Gideon. "To heck with you. I've volunteered and done enough. Narina has money. She has suggested I join her in starting some tourist business up in Zanzibar. I'm going. You can stay here feeding your bitterness while we go on and have a good life."

"I'm sorry, really sorry I said that. I didn't mean it that way," Gideon tried to take away the sting from his words.

Moses sat looking at him. "You're on your own from now on."

Gideon moved to stand in front of Moses. He placed his hands on Moses's shoulders so that they looked into each other's eyes. "Moses! I am sorry, really sorry. I will never get in the way of you and Narina. I am sure you will have a great life together for a long time. That will make me very happy."

Calming down a tad Moses said, "I am going over to see Narina."

He was about to walk off into the darkness when he stopped. "By the way, guess who the main mineral-rights holders are?"

Gideon said nothing, but raised his shoulders to silently signal he didn't know.

"Mushala's family. There was something being planned with them that really pissed the old man off."

Gideon stared at him as the full implications hit. "Moses, I have news for you. You're not going to do much sleeping tonight. You have to help me one last time."

The surprise registered on Moses face. "Are you crazy? You give me crap and then tell me I have to help you. Are you trying to stop me from seeing Narina again?"

"No. I told you I will not get in the way. Your future is not for me to interfere in."

"So what and why do you want me to help you?

"We have to act fast. Precious is Mushala's daughter. They have already kidnapped her. Who knows what they will do to her to get her rights."

Gideon looked at Moses. "I need you to help me rescue her."

37

December 9 - 10

"Okay," Moses said, "but only if you stop hassling me about Narina. She is my gift from God, and the sooner you realize that, and concentrate on finding your own, the better."

"I have already given you my guarantee on that." Gideon said. "Now let's think about how we can get Precious away from those thugs."

Sitting down and leaning forward, Gideon stoked the fire with a branch. "The pontoon has shut down for the night. Our options are either wait until morning to cross with a vehicle to get to Hippo Lodge before their plane arrives, or head down by boat as soon as we are ready."

Moses wrinkled his brow as he thought about the possibilities. "We can't depend on the pontoon crew getting going early enough. But if we go by boat before dawn, we could catch them with a sneak operation while they are sleeping."

"Yes," Gideon agreed, "the problem is motoring on the river at night with its obstacles, especially through the rapids below the confluence. But it is our only realistic option. At least we should have good moonlight if the clouds don't come in. If we do it right we can get in close and out before they have a chance to interfere."

They sat staring at the fire.

"Hippo Lodge is about thirty kilometers downstream. If we motor slowly we should average ten clicks an hour. We will drift as we get close so they don't hear our approach. It should take three hours to get there."

Moses nodded.

"We can land upstream. I will stay with the boat and you can move in to do a reconnaissance to check for a night watchman. I doubt there will be. Like here, it is too far out in the bush for them to worry about human thievery. If there isn't one, you can move down to the river edge and flash a light. I will come in close with the boat. Otherwise come back. We can move in on foot, and pick the best escape path before we check the chalets. A half hour should be enough to search. We can start checking the chalets closest to their chitenge. The most likely occupied. Listen outside. Those two Latins are in their late forties, at some stage they will make sleep noises. If after twenty minutes we haven't figured out Precious's chalet, we will have to go in to check. If it comes to that, I suggest that you pose as a night watchman."

"What do I do if it's one of the Latins?" Moses queried.

Gideon hesitated a moment. "Say you have come to warn that there is a lion prowling outside. Tell them to stay inside until you give the okay. Be quick about it. In, out and on before questions can be asked."

"I see you haven't lost your creativity when it comes to operations."

Gideon was relieved to see a smile on Moses face. His sergeant was back.

"We will split the chalets between us. If you find Precious, shine a flashlight on your face so that she can recognize you quickly. If we are checking separate chalets, give a low whistle like a reedbuck so that we can converge to help. If she is startled, give her a positive narrative. No mention of kidnap or rescue. It could upset her. Say there has been a change of plans. Tell her that Bright got a call that their aircraft will pick them up from Lufupa further downstream. That her heroes have already left. Being nice guys, they let her sleep longer while they get things organized at Lufupa. Urge her to be quick. If she wants her lucky break she must hurry. We will count on a person's tendency to keep moving towards their hopes. Once we are away, we can let her know what is going on."

"What if things go wrong?" Moses asked. "You always said few plans survive the meeting with the enemy."

"We will improvise as usual," Gideon answered. "I will pick her up and carry her forcibly to the boat. If that happens, you should go to the far end of the lodge, where the road heads towards the airfield. Make a lot of noise and shine your flashlight to draw attention away from the river. I will take the boat back up to where we first stopped. I will wait there. You know the motto, as old as the Bible, 'by deception they made war'. That's how they got her into this mess, and by deception we will get her out."

Moses poked at the embers of the fire with a stick.

Gideon rose. "We will leave at one in the morning. I am going to check the boat. You can go and howl at the moon if you want, but I suggest you leave enough time for an hour or two of sleep.

* * *

Luck was on their side for once. The moon's phase being full, it meant that it would only set just before dawn, which would be fortunate as that was when they would have the secrecy of darkness as they moved between the chalets, if everything went according to plan.

Gideon cut the engine and let the boat drift silently past their own lodge. There was no need to rouse suspicions. Who knew if Mustafa and the Latins had satellite phones? Once they were beyond the silent lodge, Gideon hauled on its chord to start the boat's engine. Aided by the flow of the current, their progress was thankfully uneventful. The only time they used their flashlights was while they were swept through the rapids below the Kafue-Lunga confluence. Keeping to the better, right-bank passage, they both picked out the big rocks as best they could. With Moses calling out warnings Gideon maneuvered the boat with sharp switches of direction to get between the big surges squeezed up by the boulders. Despite this, they were still bumped about by some of the submerged monsters. But, as planned, the bulge of the gibbous moon hung half a finger above the horizon as they neared their destination. The outline of the structures was still distinguishable in amongst the obscuring shapes at the river's margin.

Cutting the engine, Gideon used a long punt pole to edge the boat towards the shore. In the distance he could dimly make out the strut of the lodge's decking when he pushed the prow into the bank. Stepping ashore, Moses took the tether rope, with its small anchor, and set it in the mud.

"Good luck," Gideon called quietly, as Moses silently felt his way up the steep incline and disappeared into the darkness.

It seemed ages before a double flash flickered downriver. The all-clear. Pushing the boat into the current, and again using the pole, Gideon guided it down to where Moses waited. He pulled the tether and set it so the boat's nose pushed up onto the muddy shore. Moving stealthily, he joined Moses on the lawn above the moorage. There was still enough moonlight to move around without flashlights.

He was familiar with the lodge. Its chalets stretched out upriver. "I'll take the first," he whispered.

Positioning himself outside a window, he listened. After a few minutes a muffled, sleepy cough came from within – a man's cough. Gideon moved across to where Moses was standing, still and silent in the dark moon shadows next to a window. With his mouth centimeters from Gideon's ear, he was barely audible as he whispered, "No sounds."

"Keep listening," he mouthed theatrically back. "I'll check the next."

A faint voice came from the direction of the staff quarters downriver. "Damn!" Gideon muttered to himself. They were already up to make coffee. Obviously the guests intended to leave very early.

No sounds came from within the chalet.

Cat-like, Moses moved back. "There is a mug on the table outside the chalet." he whispered. "It has a tea bag in it. I doubt their thugs are tea-drinkers... we should risk checking inside."

The first signs of dawn were on the horizon. Again, a faint voice came from the staff area.

"Okay, we have to take a chance. All we need is somebody to come along with coffee for these clowns."

Moses nodded.

The door opened with a soft creak as Moses tiptoed inside. Gideon watched from the doorway. A mosquito net was drooped down over a bed, its white mesh backlit by the flashlight's beam; the glare hiding whoever was sleeping under it. Moses panned the light around the room. On the bedside table was a strand of snail shells.

Quickly Gideon moved inside. "I'll handle this."

The figure of a woman startled awake as he reached under the tentlike net and gently shook her shoulder. "Precious," he whispered urgently. "It's me, Gidi." He pointed the beam of his flashlight on his face so that she could recognize him.

The figure responded with a sharp scream.

Instinctively, he quickly cupped his hand over her mouth. "Be quiet," he ordered. "There is a lion outside." He was thinking fast. "You need to pack and come with me. I don't want to upset the animal." Gideon lowered the beam of the flashlight onto her face. He couldn't suppress his shock.

"Oh shit," he exclaimed.

There was both fear and anger on the face of a strange woman. She blinked blindly in the brightness of the flashlight as she raised her hand to block its beam.

"Who are you?" she exclaimed loudly.

"I'm sorry, "he said, "I have the wrong person, I am looking for Precious."

The sound of her scream and her loud voice must surely have woken the dead – let alone anybody else.

"Do you know her?" he queried quickly.

"Of course I do," the stranger retorted, annoyed.

"Do you know which chalet she's in?" he asked. "I am the assistant manager here and only got in last night which is why we have not met. I apologize again for disturbing you." Gideon hoped his explanation would calm her down.

The woman looked at him suspiciously, then pointed down the line. "The next one along. The A-frame."

"Thank you," he muttered as he darted out into the night.

"Dammit," he hissed to Moses. "That wasn't Precious. There isn't supposed to be anyone here except the two Latins and her. But there is." With a flick of his hand he indicated for Moses to follow. "Come on, let's get to her before the stuff hits the fan. She's this way."

They ran across the lawn to the next A-frame chalet. Without knocking, he opened the door. There was no need for a flashlight. Precious was already sitting up in bed with the bedside night light on.

"What the heck are you doing here?" she asked in wide-eyed surprise. There was no longer the need to tell her to be quiet.

"We have come to take you back before you get kidnapped," he said urgently.

"What are you talking about?" Precious said in disbelief.

"I'm serious," he said trying to convey that tone. "Your Latin friends are not who you think they are. They are not your friends. They are trying to lure you away to hold you hostage. We've come to get you away."

"You are crazy," Precious's voice was rising in indignation; he could see the stubbornness starting to appear at her edges.

Things were getting out of hand. At this juncture, Moses stepped into the room.

"You too!" Precious exclaimed in surprise.

A deep voice with a Spanish accent came from not far away, "Is everything okay?"

"Really?" she exclaimed incredulously.

"Precious, do you think that Moses and I would show up here at this time of the morning for nothing? We have no time to waste, we must get going. Put on some jeans and a sweater and your shoes. I will pack the rest. We absolutely have to get moving."

The voice called again from the next chalet, "Is everything okay?"

"Damn!" Gideon muttered to himself. The scream of the woman in the first chalet must have woken everybody. He froze with his arm outstretched and finger spread to indicate for her not to move as he tried to think how to handle the situation.

"Tell him everything is fine," he whispered.

She called back, "Yes it's all okay." But added softly, "I think."

Gideon raised his eyes skyward and made a pleading gesture to the heavens. "Precious, let's get the fuck out of here quickly."

He tried to convey the urgency and seriousness in the quiet intensity of his words. A new, expensive-looking backpack was propped up against the side wall of a wooden closet.

"is this yours?" he asked and without waiting for a reply, he grabbed items of clothing and started to stuff them into the bag. "Nice bag," he quipped.

"What are you doing?" she asked angrily.

"I'm packing your bag so that we can get the hell out of here."

It was a mistake. He should've known better. Precious was Mushala's daughter. She didn't take to being pushed around.

"Hang on," she said. "I'm not going anywhere until I've spoken to Melody."

"Who the heck is Melody?" he asked. "Why do you have to speak to her?"

"She is my cousin, and she is coming with me."

"Oh my God," Gideon burst out in restrained frustration, looking at Moses, who shrugged back at him. "Why the hell is she coming with you?"

Precious's expression had turned into an angry pout. "She is coming because Jose and Luigi suggested that she be a companion."

Gideon had to think quickly. It was pointless trying to argue. Rescuing two women was a different beast. Glancing at the new backpack, a glimmer of an idea began to form in his mind. There was no time to waste.

"Okay," he said. "Hang on for a minute. I need to speak to Moses."

He gestured to Moses to follow him out.

"Bloody hell," he exploded under his breath. "Those bastards are going to kidnap both of them. I bet her cousin also has mining rights."

"What are you going to do about it?" Moses asked.

Without hesitation, Gideon said, "By deception we will make war. We will go after the logistics."

"Okay," Moses looked at Gideon questioningly. "Sounds good, but how will that work?"

"I will distract Precious and get her out of the chalet for a few minutes." Gideon spoke fast. "When I get her out of the way and distracted, I want you to sneak back in and grab all of her clothing and toiletries. Specially look for her passport. Stuff it all into her fancy backpack."

"Okay. Then what?"

"I will keep her talking and distracted."

He nodded.

"Sneak out while she is still distracted. Then take the pack down to the river and leave it on the bank. Do this quietly and as fast as possible. Make sure nobody else sees you."

"What is the point?" Moses asked.

"You will see," Gideon replied. "I will then try to get Precious to have Melody come out and join us. When she does, do the same thing with her stuff. I'm pretty sure I saw the same sort of backpack in her room." Stirring sounds came from the chalet where the man's voice had sounded.

"Once you have this done, come back and join us, and we can start the next phase."

The male voice again came from the last chalet. "What's going on? Do you need help?"

There was no time to lose. Going back into her room, Gideon saw that Precious had changed into jeans and a T-shirt.

"Precious," he said. "Your friends are getting suspicious. It isn't going to take long for him to come across to see what's happening."

"So what?" she pouted.

"I need a few more minutes to convince you. Can you go across and get your cousin to join us in the *chitenge*? I think the coffee should be ready by now. I heard the kitchen staff talking."

Precious shrugged reluctantly, but turned and walked across to Melody's chalet, with Gideon following. Barely breathing with the tension, mentally urging her to hurry up, he had to resist physically pushing her. Glancing back, he saw Moses slip into her chalet.

He stood outside listening to the two woman speaking in low tones. Seconds and minutes seem to drag by. The sound of their voices became more emphatic and strident.

"Damn!" he thought to himself, what if her cousin was as stubborn and strong-willed as Precious?

Gideon moved to the door and without entering he spoke in at them. "Precious, tell her that it is urgent. I need to speak to you both before your friends join us."

An annoyed, "Okay, okay," came back out the door.

After what seemed an eternity, Precious reappeared followed by her cousin. Gideon muttered a quiet "Good morning" to the other woman as he led the way across to the *chitenge*.

It was getting lighter. It had taken longer than he had anticipated and her protestations were louder than he had hoped. As he prepared cups of coffee, he looked back across the lawn towards the chalets, which were now hidden behind tall bush and scrub. Through a gap formed by the pathway, he caught sight of Moses giving him a thumbs-up. So far so good. He could always depend upon his sergeant. He was making it happen.

It wasn't with a moment to spare. A minute later, a man walked through

David Maritz

the same gap, heading towards them. The short, stocky Luigi; not in a hurry. Thankfully!

He stopped to light a cigarette. Keep it that way, buddy-boy, Gideon thought to himself.

Casting furtive glances towards the man, Gideon continued to prepare the cups of coffee. He spoke quietly and hastily. "Your two friends are foreign gangsters trying to get your mineral rights to the area around the lodge."

A look of incredulity passed over Melody's face.

"These men are dangerous. They are trying to lure you out of the country where they can hold and put pressure on you to sign away your mineral rights."

"Don't talk rubbish," Melody said in disbelief.

The stocky figure was walking across the lawn towards the *chitenge* when behind him Gideon saw Moses again appear in the gap and tumble his hands. The ready-to-roll signal.

"Okay," Gideon said to the two women. "I've told you what is going on. Now I have to get out of here before these two friends of yours try to get in my way as well."

Leaving the two woman in confused disbelief, Gideon turned and walked as fast as he could across the lawn towards the beached boat.

As Gideon hurried past, the pudgy-faced Luigi looked at him coldly. Gideon nodded a good morning. Behind him Moses beckoned from beyond the bushes.

"Come on. Let's get going."

The last few meters to the boat were done at a scramble down the river-bank. Getting away before the woman told the dark squat man what he had said to them was now essential.

"Quick," he called out to Moses. Pull the anchor. We have to get out of here fast."

Gideon hauled on the starter line, and gun the engine to pull them back out into the current.

"Where are the backpacks?" he called out above the noise of the revving engine.

"Below each chalet," Moses shouted back. Flicking the engine into forward, he swung the nose of the boat downstream to arc the boat in a plane towards the chalets. The bright olive-green of the two bags was tucked into the weeds at the edge of the river. As the boat's nose grazed the river bank Moses leaned out and grabbed each pack and pulled it aboard.

Twisting the throttle full open they were at a plane as they skimmed out into the river's wide reach.

The two woman and the man had followed them out to see what was happening.

Over the noise of the engine he could hear their shouts. "Those are our packs! He has taken our backpacks."

Seconds later there was a familiar snap, followed by the thump of a weapon's discharge. A bullet had just broken the sound barrier over their heads.

"That bastard is shooting at us," Gideon shouted to Moses.

Another snap followed, then a third.

The skimming boat was putting distance between them and the shooter. At this range, with a handgun, the chances of being hit were getting slimmer. Nevertheless, Gideon was glad when hugging the shore upriver they were hidden from view around a bend.

Gideon eased off the throttle, letting the boat's nose drop from its plane.

"Christ!" he exclaimed. "I'm getting too old to go around rescuing damsels in distress."

"But you just left them behind," Moses eyed him with faint suspicion.

"Don't worry old buddy," Gideon smiled back. "The ingredients are in place. Now we'll let that Latin pair do some of the cooking."

38

December 10

"What are you doing?" Moses didn't need to shout above the racket of the engine; Gideon had already cut the boat's speed as he edged towards the riverbank.

"I'm getting off here," Gideon said. "Go on up to the scout camp. Get as many scouts as you can fit in the boat to come back with you. Tell them that somebody at the lodge is shooting. Say that it is urgent."

"Okay. But I doubt I'm going to get back before the aircraft arrives."

"That's why I'm heading back to see if those two have cooked their goose enough for me to push a skewer through their kebabs."

Gideon angled the boat into the bank and jumped out. Then, shoving its nose back into the current, Gideon gave Moses a thumbs-up as he watched the boat's prow lift out of the water and power upstream. Moving carefully back towards the lodge, the adrenaline added a special buzz to his tense excitement. Gideon didn't want anybody to be aware of his approach. At least Precious was now upset. It would make her more obstinate. His new plan was partially counting on that part of her character. He wanted her stubbornness to dig its heels in and delay things, as she had just done with him. It would give time for Moses to get back with the scouts. It would be interesting to see if the gangsters could improvise if she poured too much salt in their stew.

Twenty minutes later, he was close enough to the outer limits of the lodge. The thick riverside bush made concealment easy. He could hear loud voices arguing. It was too far away to make out what they were saying, but from the sound of things, it was two woman shouting back at a man. Gideon carefully edged closer until he could see them standing on the lawn. Precious and her cousin were gesticulating as they argued with the stocky Latin, while his taller companion stood to the side.

"Go, girl!" Gideon mouthed.

Melody had the same fire as Precious. From their loud outbursts, he gathered they were not interested in continuing their travels without changes of clothing, cosmetics—and especially not without passports. The stocky man appeared to be running short on temper. They were going to come with him no matter what, after all the effort and favors he had done to set things up. He would get clothing and documentation and everything once they arrived in the Congo.

The Latins had done a better job than Gideon had hoped of showing the women their true colors. Gideon didn't stay to see how the argument developed. Carefully he retreated into the bush, and then covered the short distance to the airfield at a jog.

If the woman were forced onto the aircraft, the only place he could intervene was there. He continued up to where the road opened up onto its verge. This was where arriving aircraft picked up or dropped off passengers, or where the planes were tethered for a layover stay. Glancing around, he found what he was looking for. The key element of any ambush: the weapon.

The sun was now well above the horizon. Everything was peaceful. On both sides of the airstrip, emerald spot doves were harping their mournful, descending beat. Overhead in the spindly tree, a bulbul made its tripling call. It was a waiting game. He had time to think about life and what in the world he was doing here. A Band-Aid attempting to stop a new cut in the skin of Africa.

"Go now," she had said to him, and he had. Who would've believed this was where it would lead? Now he had to exercise his patience. He had plenty of that, when it came to springing an ambush. The final flush of excitement always made the wait worthwhile. His weapons lay out on the airfield apron. He had checked them, making sure he could lift each on its edge and roll it across the ground. They were spread out, so one would always be close wherever an aircraft came to a standstill.

The tied-down anchors were big, heavy wheel hubs with a metal ring welded on the outside surface, allowing a strap to slip easily through the loop up to the wing of an aircraft, holding it in place in the event of a wind squall. By judiciously spreading them around, he could quickly lift or roll one behind his target. His ambush would work best if the aircraft were a single-engine machine. If it were a twin-engine, there was always the remote chance of it being able to escape. At least he knew it would be a bigger one. Big enough to fit five: the passengers and the pilot. His plan would work best if the aircraft didn't have a belly pod.

Gideon wondered how Moses was getting on, and then mentally went through how to spring an ambush. He practiced rolling and kicking the big metal hubs. Feeling confident that he could handle that aspect, he thought through the what-ifs. Deep down, he knew he was engaged in one of the most ancient traditions of Africa: men outsmarting other men. To kill or be killed, a tradition hundreds of thousands of years old, which had spread with men to every corner of the globe, making them such creatively complex and competitive killers. Hopefully he could pull off his ambush without any violence. These days the law sometimes got in the way. But the buzz of tension was intoxicating. It was something that today few men in the world had experienced: when the taking of life is more exciting than the act of its making. There is nothing, absolutely nothing that made one feel more alive. The ultimate foreplay.

His tension was interrupted by the distant hmmm of an aircraft.

It circled twice before dropping lower and coming in over the river for a touchdown.

He crouched down behind the trunk of a tree so that nobody on the airfield could see him. As he did so, he could hear the rattle of a vehicle approaching from the lodge.

His luck was in: the aircraft was a Cessna Caravan, the workhorse of the African safari industry. It didn't have a belly pod, making his ambush even easier. Interestingly, from the numbers painted on its fuselage it was registered in the Congo, probably working directly for the cartel.

Gideon didn't dwell on this for long. He was more interested to see who the passengers were. The safari vehicle arrived with the four passengers sitting calmly on its viewing seats. To his surprise, gone was any evidence of their earlier friction. The two Latin men walked across to greet the pilot. The short one then walked back to the vehicle and exchanged a few words with the driver, and handed him what seemed to be a substantial tip, because he beamed broadly and thanked the short one effusively.

The vehicle then departed.

It took a minute before Gideon could see Precious point to the departing vehicle and ask a question. Then her voice rose in intensity. "Hey, tell it to come back," she shouted.

Suddenly the Latins each grabbed one of the women, who began shouting and screaming to be let go. As the girl's hands were held behind their backs, the pilot took out quick ties and zipped their hands together like a pair of handcuffs. Still struggling and shouting, there was little the women could do. The pilot opened the aircraft's baggage compartment, and the two men each pulled a woman across and heaved them up into it like sacks of flour.

Seeing the way Precious was being handled added an edge of anger to Gideon's resolve. It was now or never. His chance to spring his ambush.

As soon as the pilot and the two men climbed up the short ladders into the front cabin and closed the passenger door, Gideon sprinted out onto the airfield, keeping his approach directly behind the aircraft, where he could not be seen by those inside.

A slow turboprop whine grew in tempo and intensity as the pilot started the engine. The propeller turned faster and faster. Gideon frantically picked up one of the big hubs and carried it under the tail of the aircraft, where he dropped it on its edge so that it rolled. Then, laying on his back with his elbows dug in as braces, he began to kick the hub forward with his feet. Any moment now, the pilot would finish his pre-flight checks and release the brakes, letting the aircraft roll forward to line up for a take-off.

Trying to straighten its progress with a hard kick to one side, the hub fell over. Staying hidden under the aircraft's belly, Gideon scrambled to lift it back onto its edge and keep it rolling. Back on his back, he rolled it as far as the aircraft's mid-point. Wriggling forward on his butt and elbows, he kept kicking the hub forward with his feet.

The engine suddenly increased its tone. Any second now the pilot would release the brakes. All would be lost. With his hands gripping tufts of grass and elbows dug into the sandy soil for traction, he mustered all his strength to give one last desperate kick, pushing the big hub.

The aircraft had begun to move forward as the hub's roll barely reached the blur of the spinning propeller. But it was enough. There was a howling scream of twisted metal as the blades dug in to the hub's heavy steel.

David Maritz

He didn't wait to see the final result. He was scrambling back even as the hub was still rolling. Reaching the aircraft's tail, he leapt to his feet and sprinted back into the bush.

The wine of the turboprop engine receded into dramatic silence.

As Gideon crouched down behind a tree trunk, he saw the pilot open his door and climb down his ladder with loud exclamations of "*Merde… merde!*"

The two Latins followed the pilot. They started to jabber loudly between themselves. As the situation became apparent, the angry outbursts of the two thugs quickly escalated into shouting.

"You damn idiot. Why didn't you check?"

"I did."

"You didn't."

"I did!"

"You fucking well didn't!!"

Gideon couldn't help admiring his own work. What a perfect ambush. They didn't even realize it had been an ambush. They thought it was self-inflicted pilot carelessness for not checking a clear runway. Gideon certainly was not going to enlighten them.

They almost came to blows. It went on for a few minutes, until their shouts suddenly went silent, replaced by the sound of a vehicle.

It was the safari vehicle again.

It came hurtling down the road onto the airfield, bearing Moses and five other camouflage-clad scouts with AK-47s at the ready. It pulled up in a cloud of dust in front of the plane. Two of the scouts jumped out and crouched down, their weapons raised and pointing.

Rushing out of the bush to join the show, Gideon shouted for Moses and Musekela to stop anyone getting back into the aircraft. He didn't want the gangsters to attempt a gun-to-head hostage situation with the woman. Moses shouted to the Latins to stand still and raise their hands. He had somehow gotten hold of a weapon and was pointing it at them.

Unlatching and throwing open the compartment doors, Gideon saw that they were lucky. In the rush to get airborne, although they had cut the quick-ties on the girls' hands, they had not yet moved forward into the seats.

"Jump!" he shouted to them.

Aided by Musekela, they each grabbed a girl as they leapt down to the ground.

"Come on follow me, run!" he shouted to both of them. The last thing Gideon needed was for the Latin pair to try a desperate move. "Moses!" he shouted. "Take care of these clowns. I'm getting the girls out of here."

It was only after they had run a few hundred meters down the road that he slowed to a walk. The adrenaline was replaced with a sense of lethargic tiredness.

"Why did you go out to the airfield with them?" he asked.

Precious looked at him sullenly, but Melody answered. "After a big argument with us at the lodge, the men calmed down. They talked together a few minutes then came back and said we were right. Once we had recovered our clothes and passports they would send the aircraft back in a few days to pick us up. They asked us to go with them to the airfield and meet the pilot. We were to only fly with him. So we needed to meet him to be able to recognize him again."

"Now do you believe me that those guys were scumbags?" Gideon asked.

Precious kept glaring at him even as she panted to catch her breath.

"Oh, never mind," he said. "Let's go and finish the coffee that was interrupted earlier. Musekela and Moses are old enough to handle those crooks."

* * *

They were sitting at a table in the lodge's *chitenge*. Moses had just joined them. He reported that the scouts had searched the Latins and found their handguns—a forbidden item when carried undeclared into the National Park and fired. They were going to take them into the Mumbwa HQ and involve the police for further questioning.

"I'm being serious." Precious still had her glare, "Would you please tell me what's going on?"

Gideon shrugged, and was about to give her an explanation when Moses interrupted.

"Precious, I'm going to take you somewhere. I will show you something which will explain it better than any of us."

"Where?" she pouted.

"Be patient. It's a boat ride away."

Gideon looked at Moses curiously. This was unexpected.

"Okay, are we ready to go?" Moses asked.

An hour later, looking back south west along the flow of the river, Gideon thought how peaceful the scene was, with no hint of the morning's drama. Moses gingerly steered the boat through the rapids. It was easier this time. They could pick their path, and there was more control over the boat's speed as they powered against the current between the rocks.

Past the rapids and the big Lunga Island, Moses edged their way upstream to tuck under the head of the cliff looking balefully down on the confluence, its neck spreading back into the spine of the dyke. Beyond this, where the hunchback ridge sloped back down into the flats of the valley, Moses turned the boat into a little gap between some trees. He gestured for Gideon to jump ashore and set the anchor. Tilting the outboard engine out of the water, and standing up, he also motioned to Precious and Melody to disembark.

"*Ti yenge*," he said. "Let's go! I have something to show you. Actually, it is someone."

Gideon looked at him carefully to figure out if he was joking. Moses's air of secrecy was uncharacteristic.

"Don't worry!" A slight smile appeared on Moses face. "Soon everything will be clear." He turned and began to lead the way, ducking under the outstretched branches of thorn bushes, around the sprawl of bigger shrub clumps, and under the spreading branches of the trees which grew big in the little gullies eroded into the slopes of the dyke. In the steeper spots, they had to watch their footing where the rocky gravel, loosened by the recent rains, slipped under the rubber of their bush boots.

There was only one place he could be taking them, but why?

The cave wasn't very auspicious. Not being deep, and looking out upon a relatively non-descript vista, he wouldn't have chosen it as a likely site for a *nganga* to practice his magic. But the topography was what nature provided. Thus it was not so much the cave that filled him with surprise, rather it was the figure of the old, grey-haired man sitting in its recess. He was crouched flat-footed on his haunches, with the crowns of his knees caught in the crooks of his elbows, giving the impression that his long, thin body was bowed forward. His hunched shoulders dipped his head until the crane of his neck thrust out his chin so it almost touched his crossed forearms.

As they approached, Gideon could see he wore the same old camouflage uniform as was his dress on their previous impromptu meetings. He hardly moved when they came to a stop a few meters to his fore. Only then did he deign to look up—more the lifting of languorous, almost disinterested eyes, than the raising of his head.

Gideon opened his mouth to speak, but felt the faintest restraining touch on the back of his hand from one of Moses's fingers. The two woman held back uneasily behind them.

The old man lowered his head as if lost in thought. With the flick of an outstretched arm, he made a gesture for them to be seated. As the man again looked up, Gideon was transfixed by some of the deepest, cataract-clouded eyes he'd ever seen.

"I have been expecting you," the old man said.

"Old man, I don't know you, so I don't know why you should expect me."

"Ah, but you forget." His voice had a deep gravelly tone. "You are from the region of the Mlimo. You do not know it, but the Mlimo listened to your soul. The message to me from that oracle was that together we would save this place."

Gideon was nonplussed.

"Sit!" the old man commanded. They obliged him, settling opposite and cross legged, Precious and Melody still behind them.

"Aaaah," the old man shook his head. "I have been watching you. Seeing if you can be trusted."

"Old man, who are you to give me marks?"

Again Gideon felt Moses's cautionary finger press, this time on the side of his leg.

The old man ignored him. "As you know I came to these parts long ago, to build the airfield for the *Chimurenga*. For N'Komo's men. It was where they landed the supplies for the revolution." He looked at Gideon, "Do you know where that airfield is?"

Gideon nodded; he knew of the old, defunct, overgrown landing zone.

The grey-haired man cleared his throat and spat into the dust at his side. Then picking up a twig, just as Father Xavier had, he scratched parallel lines in the sand. He appeared to withdraw momentarily into himself like a tortoise into its shell. "I met the Russian there. We have helped each other for many years."

"Are you still working with him?" Gideon asked.

The old man stopped scratching at the dirt and looked across at him. "Yes, and no." He looked back down into the sand at his feet. "But I will not work with the other foreigners." He pointed with his chin up over Gideon's shoulder, to where Precious crouched to the rear. "They want to play with things they know nothing about. They want to mess with that woman who sits back there. The one who is guarded by the spirit of her father. They want to steal his gift to her." He scratched the ground again and said, "I watched you and your man. I saw that you were genuine men of the bush. I let your man follow me. I played tricks and tested him, like I tested you. Even though you are a *mzungu*, you have some spirits helping you. I don't know why, or where they come from. They have said you belong here, that you have come home. That you will stay here forever. The message from the Mlimo oracle was that I was not to thwart Mushala's spirit, or the white witch. They said she had sent her son to sort out the issues here, and he would bring his helper."

Both Gideon and Moses said nothing.

The old man lifted his head. Making a hacking sound, he sucked in his gaunt cheeks, and spat into the embers of the fire. A transparent tendril of steam hissed up, twisting and curling into the fleeting shape of a question mark. "You can go now," he said, "I have work to do." No longer looking at them, he made a dismissive motion with his head. "I must go and collect the poison of a mamba snake. Then I will make *muti* to take to the village to undo the damage that those outsiders are trying to do with your scout."

Moses stood and silently beckoned to Precious and Gideon to follow. They walked away in single file, in silence. Moses led the way, with Gideon to the rear and the Precious Melody pair between them. Gideon watched the sways of the women's hips as they walked with Mushala's spirit at their side, seeming to him as mysterious as the ochre images on a cave wall.

"Go now, before it is too late." And he had gone. Gideon remembered Precious's command to him from so long ago.

The dislodged gravel beneath their steps trickled down the slope like his silent thoughts. Home? That was what the old man said. Had the circumstances of this grey haired *nganga* interfering with their lives, released Moses and he from their states of limbo, both spatial and spiritual? Would they now be accepted back into their different faces of Africa, with these new, mixed tones? A sentence echoed in his mind: Father Xavier's last words to him as they parted weeks before.

"The Lord works in mysterious ways."

No shit, Gideon thought to himself.

David Maritz

39

December 10

Watching the boat's wake unzip the surface of the river behind them, Gideon couldn't suppress the anxiety lurking in the background. What sort of can of worms had all this opened? How far did it spread? Was Mustafa in on the kidnap plot? Kings? How long would the police hold the Latins? Cartels had a way of getting what they wanted, and pulling their people out of tight situations. Would there be trouble when the two girls showed up at the lodge? Would anyone try to intervene and grab the women again? Now that their intentions were known, might the cartels pull back and push elsewhere? Or might they turn things around on him? They could claim the women had accepted an offer of travel, of their own free will. On the surface, it could hardly warrant a charge of kidnapping. Only the final struggle, not witnessed by anyone except Gideon, need be denied on their part. After all, when the scouts arrived the girls were sitting unbound in the aircraft. In fact, the 'sabotage' which he had performed would probably be frowned upon more intensely in a court of law with a cartel-friendly judge. Their shots fired? They could say they were preventing a theft.

Heading upstream, past where he had seen the drowned zebra, Gideon had an image of its terrified expression. Africa had a way of catching the unwary in its mud and exhausting its victims until they can no longer hold their heads high. He was not there yet. But neither was he yet clear of its mud.

Approaching their lodge, as he sat in the boat's prow, Gideon indicated to Moses to take the channel on the far side of the island, away from the lodge, and head up to their campsite. He call across to Moses, "I want to lie low and get the lay of the land before we take the ladies back to the lodge."

"Okay," Moses acknowledged.

"They can stay with me at our camp, while you sniff things out. Who knew or knows what. Find out how everyone is reacting at the lodge. Did Mustafa and Kings know anything about the thugs' intentions?"

Beaching the boat on the little sand bar, Moses helped the women step ashore.

"Okay, ladies, while Moses checks out the situation, the price of your freedom is a good cup of coffee. I'll get the fire going."

Gideon watched Moses head across the dambo. He couldn't help thinking that he resembled a dog with its tail wagging.

* * *

Sitting on the sand bar, the rustle of the leaves overshadowed the sigh of a breeze between the branches and the water, sliding over exposed tree roots. For Gideon, after the tension and excitement, it was as if the whole world had slowed down to catch its breath.

Precious offered him a biscuit.

David Maritz

The drama had lasted all morning, and it was mid-afternoon when they arrived back at the campsite. Moses had been gone for an hour when Gideon stood and stretched. He was suddenly exhausted.

"I have been awake all night, and could do with some rest. I'm going to lie down. It's best you keep out of sight until Moses comes back to give the all-clear."

With that he headed for his tent.

* * *

It was towards evening when he woke to the sound of voices outside. Gideon identified Moses talking to Precious and Melody, with Lauren tossing in a comment here and there.

Rousing and straightening his sleep-crumpled shirt, he stepped out of his tent. "What is happening?" he asked.

The women were talking excitedly amongst themselves.

Gideon motioned to Moses to one side. "What is happening?"

"All is clear," Moses said. "It seems that Mustafa suspected something was fishy with the gangsters' offer to take Precious, but it was just that—a suspicion. Apparently things are getting ugly between Lauren and Mustafa. So it is good that everyone is dispersing tomorrow."

"The sooner they all leave, the better. I want my peace and quiet back." Gideon said, "I will gladly hand Mustafa over to you."

Moses ignored him. "What is your plan?" he asked.

"Tomorrow first thing I will head into Mumbwa and give my version of events to the police."

Moses nodded. "OK, I have a friend who is high in the central police in Lusaka. I could speak to him."

Gideon thought a moment. "That may be a good way to speed things up. The quicker we get these guys feeling that they are being investigated, the better. I don't want to give them lag time while the police here decide what to do. We should make a report in Mumbwa, so the authorities there don't feel that we are going over their heads."

But we will also have an unofficial meeting with your friend, where you can explain how serious things could get unless nipped in the bud."

"In that case I will need to come in to the city with you," Moses stated.

"Fine!" Gideon retorted. "It may be a bit of the squash in the cab with three of us in the front seat, but so what. Lauren will be pleased; she gets a lift all the way to Lusaka."

Gideon was about to step across and join the group of women when Moses touched his arm. "This evening and tomorrow morning I would like to borrow your vehicle."

"Why?"

"I want to take Narina up Eden's Outlook."

Gideon detected the intensity in Moses voice. He didn't hesitate, "Sure. Where is Narina?"

"She is getting ready. I told her I would pick her up after I drop Precious and Melody off at the staff quarters."

Presumptive, Gideon thought, but let the future be responsible for telling Moses the truth. Why should he be the one to spoil his joy? Be kind, he said to himself. Let him howl at the moon.

At the same time, Gideon felt a pang of envy. Why could he never find the absolute certainty of single purpose? What was it about himself that got pulled in different directions when it came to belonging to anything, either a woman or a place?

The fucking story of his life.

* * *

"Are you coming with us?" Moses was loading the backpacks onto the bed of Gideon's Cruiser. Precious and Melody had already climbed into the cab.

"No," Lauren replied. "I'll hang out here for a while." She turned back to Gideon. "So you had quite an adventure without me."

"Yup," he said, "I didn't want to disturb your angel sleep."

Lauren snorted. "Angel sleep! You would wake a hibernating bear if you thought you could get some fun out of her."

"Now, now," he said," I have kept you up enough lately."

"Have you heard me complain?"

Gideon laughed. "Lucky me. One of the good things of working out here is that I get to meet interesting and unusual people. And I mean that in a good way. Take a seat. I even have some gin and tonic stashed away for special friends on special occasions."

"Well that is nice," Lauren said, "I'm glad you look at me that way. By the way, I think the same can be said about you… 'unusually oddball' is how I would put it."

Gideon delved into a box at the back of the chitenge and came out with a bottle of gin and a can of tonic. Handing her the glass he asked, "Why oddball?"

"That is easy to answer. Look at you! Life has stacked everything to go your way. Tall, handsome, intelligent, educated, experienced, fit, charismatic, adventurous, good health. Anyone else would be rolling in assets and roots, wives, kids and maybe even a few grandkids already. Instead we see a footloose, fancy-free tumbleweed. Why? Why do you stay here?"

Gideon sat staring at nothing. "I am here because of not recognizing that the rug of old Africa was being pulled out from under my feet. That meant mostly I was at the wrong places at the wrong time. I was painted with the last brushstrokes of old colonial Africa which for me started north of the Limpopo River, not at the foot of Table Mountain. I grew up here with its people. I have played with Africa's children, hunted with them, fished with them, made slingshots to shoot birds with them. I have taken the scrotum of a slaughtered bull with them, and hit it against a log to stretch it, then blown it up to make a football to kick around with them. I have absorbed the color of their values and beliefs. But in many ways, it is my own culture's rejection of me that has kept me out here. The pull of the one, the push of the other. Now I find myself, as I said to you, being a pale scab on the dark skin of Africa, trying to fix some of its old and new wounds."

Lauren looked at him carefully. "So which is better? The new or the old?"

"Well, I don't know," he said. "At my age, we are who we are. It is difficult to change for anyone, not even ourselves. So I bury my head in the sand of this place. But at the same time I know that eventually scabs are scratched away, or fall off naturally. And you?" he asked, "Why do you stay in your Africa. What makes you tick?"

David Maritz

"What happens if you discover that my ticking is a bomb?" she asked, giving him a narrow-eyed look.

"In that case, what a way to die," Gideon smiled back at her.

Lauren laughed and linked the fingers of her hands behind her head. "Do you think I am shocking?"

"No. I find it refreshing that there are women like you in the 'new Africa.'"

Lauren shrugged, "I guess so."

"Don't you feel alienated by what Africa has become?" he asked.

There was only the distant sound of an electrical generator running at the lodge to fill the void of his question.

"Actually I love the new Africa," she said. "Its vibrancy, mixing of cultures. The breakdown of the old ways and the synthesis of new. It is the essence of my life. The changes of color, texture, shape, pattern. I get my inspiration from everything around me. I'm a decade younger than you, and that has made all the difference. I wasn't painted with the brush of old Africa."

"Yes, and you live at Africa's tip," he interrupted. "It has always been different down there. Even the rain comes at a different season, the winter."

"I agree." Lauren handed him her glass, "Can you get me another of these?"

As Gideon fixed her drink, she asked: "When was the last time you were in the Cape?"

"A long time ago." He handed back her drink.

She took a sip. "Then you will need to come and visit me, and I can show you how much more has trickled down there. But until then, my advice,"

Lauren said, "is not to fret it. Mostly we are magnets, and if one keeps the current flowing, something will eventually stick."

David Maritz

40

December 11

From the slow, inexorable creep of the water up the sand bar where he was sitting, it was obvious that somewhere far to the north it had again rained hard. Keeping an eye on the water level during the wet summer rainy season was something one had to pay attention to when living on the banks of a big river. Now, its gradual progression barely made it over the threshold of his consciousness. Instead, Gideon's thoughts kept slipping back to Moses's infatuation with Narina. Was there any similarity to his own experience of joy with a woman, which always seemed to fade into blandness and then sadness?

The transience of it all. It was a wonder that his dreams of Sophia had not crumpled like the wrinkles in her skin. But then she was part of that old, disappeared Africa, with little left of it except the small pockets like the one he was struggling to preserve. If he rekindled a relationship, would he find it to be little more than a transient pocket poached by independence and freedom, like everything else that had doomed his old expectations of permanence with both place and people? Would that be true for anything new? His old roots were now withered and unable to push deep into the generally barren soil of any new relationship. Was that what was happening with Claudia? His lack of presence opening her door to other possibilities? Or had it always been so with her, with him only now recognizing that status. After all, she had always seemed able to pick him up and put him down. Another of new Africa's signals that he wasn't welcome. It was with growing anguish that he contemplated his meeting her when he got to the city. Would Lauren have time to love anybody? Maybe love was overrated. It was good enough to be liked. Love was too restrictive. Should he tell Moses to watch out, make sure Narina really loved him enough to like him once the flush had faded?

Ah, to hell with the philosophising. Gideon kicked at a branch to push it into the river's flow. He shouldn't ever give up hope. What had the old *nganga* said? That this was his home. Finally, ancient Africa recognizing her adopted son.

Hearing a vehicle, he walked up the riverbank. This time it was Lauren who accompanied Moses in the cab. Earlier, over a cup of coffee well before daybreak, when he asked about Moses's plans with Narina, Moses had answered with a hint of sadness in his voice. He said he didn't know when next he would see her. He felt an urgency to squeeze all the bliss from the present. He wanted the sun to shine its rays on their happiness as they watched it rise above the horizon from the peak of Eden's Outlook. From there he would take Narina back to the lodge the long way around, up the eastern *dambo*, across the western edge, then down on the far side of the lodge. A last game drive. Something the two of them could share until they met again, the early morning sun backlighting the herds of puku and impala, with maybe a solitary reedbuck or a cluster of kudu at the tree line.

"Gidi, I want to show her that Africa you always talk about. A place untouched by man since the beginning of time."

Moses wanted her to travel with them as far as Mumbwa, but that would be disrespectful to her father, she had replied. In any case, there wouldn't be space for both Lauren and her in the cab. So this morning, time with her would be his last for a while. She would be heading up to Tanzania for some weeks. Who knew what her schedule would be after that.

David Maritz

As the vehicle stopped, Gideon noted the broad way Moses smiled. The dawn excursion must have gone well.

Lauren leaned her head out of the Cruiser's window.

"I hear that you are taking me all the way to Lusaka," she said with gay relief. "Why didn't you say so yesterday?"

"Yes," Gideon pinched his lips as he answered, "you are stuck with Moses and me for a while."

"I like that!" she grinned back at him.

Throwing his overnight bag onto the back of the Cruiser, Gideon squashed himself next to Lauren on the tandem passenger seat. She leaned across to peck his cheek with a little kiss, and announced loudly, "This is going to be fun."

With that, Moses engaged the gears as he turned the vehicle back onto the track out to the main road.

Passing the lodge complex, Precious walked out to the edge of the road and waved a goodbye. As she did, he heard his cell phone give a WhatsApp ping as they drove through the satellite dish's reach. Lauren and he were packed in so close together he couldn't reach into his belt pouch to take out the phone. No matter, he would check the message later.

Two other vehicles were waiting when they arrived at the ferry point.

Already waiting to load, with the engine running and air-conditioning on, Mustafa's Land Cruiser had its baggage portion piled to the roof. Narina sat in the front with her father. Behind them sat the elegant consorts. Mustafa was correct; they didn't travel light. Neither did their departed male partners, whose excess luggage obviously contributed substantially to the overload. Bags were even squashed between them on the seat.

"You are right," Gideon said to Lauren. "Mustafa must certainly feel like a taxi driver. They don't look too happy about their situation."

He wondered what they would think once they discovered their partners were sitting in far less comfort than they, being in the squalor of an African prison.

Behind them was a shabby, battered old Isuzu pickup. It had crawled out of the bushland from somewhere, and gingerly eased its sad, creaking joints down the long road to where it now stood second-in-line to load.

Giving it a gum-less gawk its tailgate had fallen off long ago. The back-bed was piled to the top, and then more so, with old fertilizer bags filled with who knows what; maize meal, kapenta fish maybe? Sugar? Tucked between the bags were scruffy plastic containers also filled with the necessities of bush life. Instead of a tailgate, a latticework of scrap metal shelving lashed together prevented everything from rattling onto the road. Beneath all of this, like the leached tail-feathers of a diseased peacock, some transparent sheets of corrugated roofing drooped out to the rear. Sitting on the fertilizer bags were two men and two women. Presumably a husband and wife in one case, and a grandmother and grandfather in the other. The driver sat in the cab. Two women stood next to its open door. The one was emaciated; probably a victim of AIDS. The other bore a fine figure, standing fashionably with a long, wide, copper-colored cloth wrapped around her waist.

Their plethora of boisterous children played tag between the vehicles. Their shouts and peals of laughter were annoying Mustafa. He looked angrily across at the parents as he spread his upturned palms, as if to ask why they were not controlling the kids. They of course stared blankly back, not understanding why anybody would find the rowdy play of children worthy of sanction. After all, African life was always full of noise and motion.

Gideon lost interest in the group as he remembered the earlier text ping.

He checked the message.

David Maritz

The sounds of the children faded.

Lauren and he were standing to one side of the bank, surveying the scene. From far away he heard her ask, "What is that over there?" From equally far away he heard her repeat the question as he reread the text message.

I am in Lusaka. Staying at Pioneer. Wanna meet? - Sophia.

"What is the matter with you?" he heard Lauren remonstrate. "Is your cell phone more interesting than me? Give me your binoculars", she demanded. "Take a look at that." She pointed to a small narrow strip between the bushes on the opposite bank.

Still preoccupied with the message, he took the binoculars back. Pointing them to where Lauren indicated, he saw what had caught her attention: a huge crocodile lay sunning itself on a small sand bar at the river's edge. But he still couldn't focus. Why now? Why here? Did she always have to catch him off guard?

Gideon shifted the binoculars to watch how the rusted hulk of the pontoon pushed its way across the river, following the parabolic path of its guide cable. Why didn't he have a line to lead him across the waters of life like this floating platform, and Moses with his religion? It would make it all so easy. North to south, south to north, back and forth with no east and west, or any degrees in between. No distractions which had so often taken him to nowhere.

As he watched, one of the ferry operators idled his engine, while the other reversed his. With gushes of black smoke and a shuddering rattle of its thumping engines, the hulk lined its nose up with the bank and ground to a halt. Waving his hand, the operator motioned to Mustafa to drive onto the ramp, where he was directed to move forward, and to squeeze to the side of the platform, allowing another vehicle to park alongside. Next the signal was to Moses to squeeze in parallel to Mustafa. Lastly, the scruffy little pickup, bending and buckling under its burden, lurched up onto the pontoon, with its occupants streaming in its wake.

With Gideon distractedly trailing behind her, Lauren and he boarded last. They held to the railing to avoid being bumped by the children's on-going melee.

The two engines thumped arduously back to life, and the passengers gravitated into groups. The Latin ladies remained in their vehicle with Mustafa and Narina. Moses, Lauren and Gideon stood on the ramp that was now the prow. The group of pickup travellers congregated at the rear. As the pontoon scratched its tail off the gravel, unable to help herself, Narina abandoned her father's Cruiser to join Moses. The thump of the engines pushing them across the water only seemed to excite the children even more. They continued playing their game of tag, dashing between and around the vehicles, sometimes almost bumping into the adults on their forays. When the pontoon was halfway across, Narina and Moses disengaged from the front group. They threaded themselves between the vehicles and people, to stand at the edge of the stern-side ramp, behind the peacock's forlorn feathers. Here they were partially obscured from her father's view. There, she quickly tilted her head up and shyly and lightly kissed Moses on his cheek. Then touching the tips of their fingers, they looked at the wake of the raft stretching back across the river.

One of the children scampered out from between the two front vehicles, around the dusty scratchy pickup, and dodged between the adults as he looked back to check for his tagging pursuer. The boy pulled up sharply, realizing he was about to bump into the back of a woman. It was too late. His momentum barely nudged her back. Despite the flailing of her arms, she toppled forward into the water.

Gideon once watched a soldier drown on the Kavango River. Drowning is a quiet affair. Lungs are filled with water, not air to shout with. It was the cries of the men trying to reach out to grab her which drew everyone's attention. Everybody rushed to the back of the raft. Mustafa screamed frantically for someone to pull his daughter out of the water. With horror-filled eyes, Gideon saw Narina struggling to stay afloat. She had the strap of a bag over her shoulder. It weighed her down, as did the bangles on her ankles, and the shoes, and the clothes, and the wet hat drooping like a wilted flower on her head. Her struggles were barely enough to stay afloat; not enough to make any progress back towards the raft against the current, which was winning the battle. Slowly the distance between her bobbing head and the raft increased. Suddenly there was a splash.

Moses had stripped-down to his shorts and dived in after her. He was swimming powerfully out into the middle of the river. The pontoon came to a stop, but being tethered in place, it was helpless to follow the current down to pick her up. Its occupants were shouting, gesticulating and waving.

As they saw the figure swimming strongly out towards the girl, everyone fell silent. They were pointing, as if to give Moses some aid in his rapid, steady strokes towards her. Raising his binoculars, Gideon quickly scanned along the bank line. He couldn't see anything. Moving the glasses back to the action, to his relief he saw Moses reach the struggling girl.

With their old training, he knew he could do it. Moses turned on his back, grasping Narina under her chin, then with one hand and using the other and his legs, he began backstroking towards the bank.

Gideon shouted to the operators to start moving. "Quickly! Quickly! Get to the bank."

The engines coughed black smoke and clattered like a pair of castanets. Gradually, Moses dragged the pair of them across the current towards safety. The pontoon had not yet ground its snout into the gravel when Gideon leapt ashore and hurtled along the riverbank, oblivious to the thorn shrubs tearing and ripping at his clothing and skin.

He was meters away, almost able to grasp Moses's hand, when Moses screamed as never before. It was deep, desperate, from the heart of Africa. Like Precious's scream at the crocodile man.

"*YANGA! YANGA FUMAPAPO!* Go! Get away from here!"

Behind them, the sinister, elongated snout of a huge crocodile broke the surface of the water. For a moment, suspended above the water, was an arm decorated with the loveliest of tattoos, a floral filigree etched onto the amber of sun burnished skin. Its pattern brushed behind a flailing elbow, then delicately reappeared as the fronds teased to the edges of a slender wrist. With a flicking tug from Moses's desperate grip, and with a swirl of water, an African Eden was stripped of its innocence.

Old Africa claimed its sacrifice.

41

Postscript

A few of the old timers of Lusaka tell of the days when they were young, back in the fifties and sixties, when on a long weekend they would cut away early on a Friday afternoon from their jobs serving Her Majesty's colonial bureaucracy, to leave the Jacaranda shaded suburbs of the city by two o'clock.

Heading out towards Angola, they would deviate to the Northwest at Mumbwa, the shabby disheveled little town which did, and still does, serve as an administrative center in the western province. If they drove at elevated speeds, as young men are want to do when spurred on by alcohol and a sparse and sympathetic police presence, some hours later, soon after dark, they would be at the Lubungu pontoon, the gateway to some favorite fishing spots.

On the flat open ground, with beers already at hand, they would set up camp for the night in the light cast by the headlights of the vehicles until the kerosene Primus lamps could be lit.

The next morning, waking to the clink of the kettle set on the wood fire by the servant invariably in attendance, they would slowly extricate themselves from their blankets. Dressed in their khaki shorts and with their cut-sleeved bush shirts ruffled by slumber, they would nurse their hangovers. Then, as slowly, they would lace up their leather veldskoen shoes and saunter over to warm themselves with hands spread towards the heat of the fire.

In the pre-dawn gloom and with their coffee mugs clasped in their palms as a substitute for the warmth of the flames, they could wander over to check out the focus of their visit. There before them, spreading northeast and southwest, with broad lazy twists and loops, like the long swaddling sashes used by the African women to strap their babies to their backs, they could see how the Kafue River wended its wide way, tucked broadly into the lush opulence of its banks.

Soon their hangovers would be assuaged by the hot coffee, into which they dunked their big rusk biscuits. When the dregs had been flicked onto the dry grass, and the mugs given to the servant to clean, they would call to the pontoon crew.

After some haggling with the ferry foreman as to the 'incentive' price needed for an early start, six local men would saunter over to join them from their nearby huts. As this crew spread themselves out evenly along the up-stream edge of the pontoon's platform, they would be hugging themselves and rubbing the bareness of their forearms to ward off the air's chill as it seeped down to cover the river with a cloak of early stillness. Then with the pressure on their mallets gripping the cable, in chanted unison, their heaves would edge the floating hulk like a prehistoric beast over the broad surface of the river.

Once the visitors and their vehicles were ferried across the river, and with the unfurling rays of the sun prying apart the cloak of mist on the water, they could head a tad further, as the road drifted northwards. They could cut back to meet the river further upstream, or simply camp on the far side where they would launch their boats using the pontoon beach head for a ramp.

David Maritz

Either way, here on the river's clear and eddying currents, the young men would spend the next few days, largely unaware of the hindsight that would in six decades, allow them to realize that they had been in a Garden of Eden. By then the youth and vigor of those young men would have been blown away by the wings of time.

Strangely, it was at a wedding on the other side of the world where, like an ancient mariner, one of them, recognizing my accent, had tugged at my sleeve. He would not let go until he had finished his tankard and told me of those halcyon days when as a young man, he sojourned in paradise.

I wondered if I should tell him that despite everything, the political upheavals, the population explosion spilling out hungry people to swarm over wild areas, not all of his utopia is lost.

Much as they were confined within the sprawl of his mind, the streets of his memories are still adorned with the leafy crowns of the gracious Jacarandas. Some of those same trees, with six more decades of growth, arch across the roads like the buttressed ceilings of a cathedral. Should I have told him that only a few months before, I had camped for the night on the banks of the river, where awakening while still sheltered from the chill air in my sleeping bag, I had lain listening to the clink of the kettle? In the brief dimness that precedes an African dawn, I had been an audience to nature's symphony, unspoiled by man, the grunt of a hippo, the bark of a baboon, the wild bray of a Hadeda ibis taking flight. And the most beautiful of them all, the Heuglin's robin, in the same thicket as that of the old man's memory, with its call rising to crest in a crescendo as climatic as any passion lost amongst the decades of his exile.

Surely that song must still linger in his nostalgia, as must the rusted hulk of the pontoon. Should I relate that it is the same hulk, unchanged except for a pair of crank-start panting engines, and that it still plies its slow deliberate way, back and forth across the river?

But then, I realized that the old man wasn't alone in his estrangement. I had recently commenced my own, and who would be around in future decades to listen to my stories of a rusted hulk plying across a river, and a bird singing in the thickets of my own mind?

Hence, dear reader, before my memories fall away like the discarded flutterings of the Jacarandas, I have attempted to record this narrative of halcyon days spent in an African Eden.

- Gideon (Bwana Penga)

David Maritz

Printed in Great Britain
by Amazon

40466473R00218